Also Available From Mitch Davies

Stolen Breeze

The Inn of Fallen Leaves

Undertow of Loyalty

This novel is a work of fiction. The characters and events are creations of the author's imagination. Any similarities between the fictitious characters and events to persons living or dead and events past, present or future are purely coincidental.

A Wind In Montana

By

Mitch Davies

Chapter 1

Rory Coleman stood looking down at the pink guidance counselor's appointment slip that his homeroom teacher had handed him. "Why," he thought, "am I getting one of these this late in the year?" He hadn't had a guidance appointment since the first month of school and that was the obligatory I'm-your-guidance-counselor-this-year meeting. "What the hell does he want? I don't need to talk with him about anything."

It had bothered him through his whole first period. When he notified his second-period teacher of his appointment, the teacher looked at him skeptically and asked to see the slip. Rory strained, trying to make sense of the mumbling he heard while Mr. Dorval talked on the phone with the counselor's office. When Mr. Dorval returned, he handed the appointment slip back to Rory and said, "Surprising, but it's legit."

"Why is it surprising?" Rory asked.

"This time of year, the guidance guys are busy with juniors trying to figure out what classes they need in order to graduate, and seniors trying to figure out how to fill out a university application form. Sophomores only get appointment slips when they've done something wrong, or when they've forged one. Yours appears to be genuine. So what kind of trouble are you in?" the teacher asked, ribbing Rory.

Rory smiled half-heartedly and forced out a chuckle. He was pretty sure he hadn't done anything wrong. But still the impending appointment had just become less welcome.

At his appointed time he waited in the guidance counselor's outer office, reading job descriptions displayed to help the students consider their futures.

It was too early for sophomores like Rory to be evaluating these jobs seriously, but he decided that reading was better than worrying about the reason he was there. He scanned the poorly copied pink, yellow, and blue sheets of paper stapled to a large corkboard. Plenty of take-away copies were provided in plexiglass bins hanging on the wall below the board. He picked out the ones with the highest starting salaries.

With colored sheets in hand, he sat in a wooden desk-chair that had a small banjo-shaped tabletop attached to one side. The chair's chipped and peeling Formica top had a number of profane messages inked onto its surface by previous occupants. "Some of them would be funny, if I felt like laughing" he thought. "Why am I here?"

His chest constricted as he tried to figure out, again, why he had received the unsolicited counselor's appointment; maybe it had something to do with his scholarship application. Rory had a knack for chemistry. For some reason, the information he gained in chemistry class and in the Chemistry Club made more sense to him than any other subject—and Rory's marks in his other classes were great. His chemistry teacher, Mr. Duggin, had told him about the scholarship and encouraged him to send in an application.

He had already submitted his course requests for his junior year, courses that would be beneficial for working toward the scholarship.

Then he wondered if the appointment was related to something outside of school. He didn't know what that could be, because he never did anything outside of school. Whatever the reason turned out to be, he wanted to get into the counselor's office and get the worrying over with.

A class bell rang, startling him. His counselor peered out of his office and discovered Rory sitting at the desk. "Okay, you're here. I'll call Mr. Keltch."

His mind raced with the news that the band teacher was somehow involved in the appointment. "Not him, not now!" he thought.

"Rory, come in and sit down. I want to have a word with you before Mr. Keltch gets here."

The office closed in on Rory with its too-warm air. He could detect the salty smell he remembered from previous visits. Mr. Shelton wore multiple hats as the guidance counselor, the varsity basketball coach, and a physical-education teacher. There were times when he had to go directly from the gym to a student's appointment while still wearing his sweat-soaked gym clothes. Students cringed when this happened, because when it did, they had to experience the smell and spectacle of Mr. Shelton as he sat drying across the desk from them.

"So what are you going to be doing for conditioning this summer, Rory?" he asked.

Physical conditioning held a low ranking in his plans for the summer. He had casually considered getting a job, but what he really wanted to do was hang out with Alyse. They were starting to get adventuresome when they were making out, progressing at a speed that had him a little scared. He wondered if they were getting to a point where he would have to be the one to slow things down.

"I might play some golf, but that's about it," Rory replied.

"Golf?" Mr. Shelton said, squinting at Rory, "Golf doesn't get you in any kind of shape for basketball. You'll probably be on the varsity team this year, so you need to work a little harder during the off season. If you're planning on playing basketball again, you have to do some serious conditioning."

Rory hadn't been expecting to confront the varsity coach with his decision to quit basketball until the beginning of the next school year. But now he was going to have to have it out with him. "To tell you the truth, I'm leaning towards not playing."

"Not playing?" Mr. Shelton held his hands out with his long fingers spread wide. "Why are you leaning that way?"

Rory knew he wasn't going to be getting much playing time with the varsity team. He'd been a backup player on the junior varsity for the past two years, and he got very little playing time at that level. Once, this past season, with a little over a minute left in a game, he was sent into the action. The other team was behind by a large margin, but still had their starters on the court to try to pull out a victory. Rory had a chance to show his defensive ability against the other team's best players. He'd intended to play his man tight, making sure his opponent didn't score.

Instead, he fouled out in fifty-four seconds. He mistimed his swipes at the ball and hit his man on the wrist. He created moving blocks and got called for it. He made hard contact with his man when his man had the ball, and each time received a foul. The result was his man shot ten free throws, making eight of them. Even though Rory's team won the game, he felt like an idiot and didn't see any game action again for the rest of the season.

Sitting on the bench and serving as a practice dummy for the varsity starters didn't appeal to him. Simulating the other team's offense for his team's defensive practice was fun for a while, but it wasn't leading anywhere. He knew he couldn't really improve if the coach only wanted him to mimic the opponent's offensive patterns.

"I'm not very good. And I don't think I'll ever get good enough to play in any games," he told Mr. Shelton.

"You won't improve if you don't stay in shape and practice. You've been playing since you were what, eight years old?"

"Twelve."

"Well even so, you don't want to blow away that kind of time investment. Besides, we need players like you on the team."

"Well, I said I was *leaning* toward not playing. Who knows? Maybe I will play," he lied.

The doorway darkened as Mr. Keltch arrived to join their meeting. Mr. Keltch stepped into the room, looked down at Rory, and gave him a slight nod. He turned the chair next to him ninety degrees so that when he sat down, he faced Rory in profile.

Rory admired Mr. Keltch's clean-cut look. How his clothes never seemed wrinkled. How the shirts tapered sharply to his waist, his tie always dead center in his collar. When Mr. Keltch moved his hand across his forehead to brush at his hair, Rory noticed that a section had sagged slightly. It held in his normal crisp, solid sweep of bangs for an instant, then sagged again. The band teacher leaned forward in his chair resting his elbows on his knees, clasping his hands between them. With his head tilted down, the renegade swatch of hair dangled between his eyes, eyes he had rolled up in their sockets so the pupils sat directly below his thick eyebrows and stared intently at Rory.

"Mr. Shelton, did you tell Rory why I asked you to call him here today?" Mr. Keltch asked, without taking his eyes off Rory.

"No, I was leaving that for you."

"Okay," he paused, "Rory, a few days ago I looked at the enrollments for this summer's band camp. You weren't on the list. When I noticed this, I made a mental note to talk to you about it before school ended. Then yesterday, the class lists for next year arrived on my desk. I didn't find your name in any of my classes. I went to the office and looked up your class request sheet to see if by accident you had been left off. After seeing your class requests, I was very surprised. It looks like you didn't request band next year. So, I figured I had better have a talk with you right away. Would you mind telling me what you plan to do about band next year?"

Rory had not planned on confronting Mr. Keltch about his decision to quit band until the next school year, either. He looked at Mr. Shelton apologetically. His guidance councilor was about to hear a story about band similar to the one he had heard a moment earlier regarding basketball.

"I'm leaning toward not playing in the band next year."

"Leaning? You didn't enroll. How is that leaning?"

"Okay, I've dropped out of band. I decided I could make better use of a study period next year." Rory spoke quickly to get it out fast. He felt lightheaded but sounded confident. Rory held Mr. Keltch's stare for what seemed like an hour of silence, intensified by the blunt reality of Rory's ending his involvement in the band program.

"Very disappointing, Rory," Mr. Keltch finally said. "You've put in a lot of time with the band. You've been able to fit your studies in with band in previous years. What makes you think you can't do it any longer?"

Rory was getting tired of early mornings; band members had to be at school an hour earlier than other students, to allow time for extra practice. When he added in the miles and miles of carrying a tuba around on the football field, his decision had almost been made. Although he could carry a tuba while marching without much of a struggle, it was still a chore. With those two negative aspects of the band, he still needed one more to push him over the top. And that occurred when he admitted how little he enjoyed the actual playing of the music.

Just as Rory knew he was not a great basketball player, he knew he was merely adequate when it came to playing the tuba.

The excuse of the extra study hall period had occurred to him the split second before he said it. Even as the words came out of his mouth, he knew he spoke a truth. He would be able to spend more time on his homework, or in the lab. What teacher was going to argue against him wanting more time to do homework?

Certainly not his chemistry teacher. Mr. Duggin had recognized Rory's talent and enthusiasm for chemistry during Rory's freshman year. It was Mr. Duggin who had informed Rory about the chemistry scholarship awarded to a junior student every year. Since he had applied for the scholarship, chemistry had taken on a higher priority for Rory scholastically.

"I probably could do it again, Mr. Keltch, but I don't want to. Besides, you have plenty of tuba players and all of them play better than me," Rory replied.

"That's not true. You are a fine tuba player, and the band needs all of the tubas we have right now. In fact, we probably need more. All bands need more tubas. And you know there's a high probability for tuba players to get a scholarship. You could get your schooling paid for," Mr. Keltch said.

He stopped and waited for Rory's reaction.

Rory felt it wouldn't be right to receive a scholarship by staying in the band. He didn't want to benefit from something he didn't do well, or because there was a shortage of tuba players.

"I know, Mr. Keltch, but I don't want to be a musician. And in all honesty, do you think I have enough talent to deserve a scholarship?"

Mr. Keltch had not taken his eyes off Rory since the discussion had started, but when he was asked this question, he looked at the opposite wall in silence for a few seconds before he answered. "If you stay in the band and you practice really hard, who knows what could happen? If you really want it and work hard, it is possible," Mr. Keltch said. He smiled at Rory and held his arms out with balled fists that he jerked slightly.

"But that's the thing... I don't really want it."

Mr. Keltch leaned back in his chair for the first time. Rory watched him while he seemed to wonder what argument he should use next. Rory felt the increasing warmth of the room close in on him. He nervously rubbed his upper lip and noticed the sweat for the first time. He could feel his pulse thump in his wrist, neck and chest. He knew if he spoke, his chin would quiver and his voice would break. He was glad he had been direct and honest, but he wondered what Mr. Keltch would think of him now. He had cut off all argument by stating he didn't want music in his life any longer. Maybe he had been too direct. Mr. Keltch was one of the cool teachers, and they had always gotten along well. It seemed to take Mr. Keltch forever to respond. During the silence, his posture became more upright and he rose in his chair. His eyes squinted and his jaw muscles bulged as he tried to keep himself from exploding.

Finally, he looked into Rory's eyes. His hair had slipped a little farther down his forehead; his eyes seemed bruised and his skin a little redder.

In a staccato voice he said, "We will miss you, Rory. It sounds like there's nothing I can say now to make you change your mind. But I need to point out that if you don't go to the camp this summer and you do change your mind about staying in the band program, you will be at a disadvantage to the others."

He looked at Rory with a tight-lipped smile. He stood up, looked at Mr. Shelton, raised his eyebrows and walked out of the room.

Rory watched the empty doorframe. His stomach felt nauseous over making his teacher unhappy, and churned with worry for their injured friendship. His first instinct was to backtrack and give in, but he realized giving in wouldn't really make him feel any better. He spoke honestly when he said he didn't want to be a musician. Music had never been part of his long-term plan.

"You've quit band for sure, and you're leaning toward quitting basketball. What's with all the quitting, Rory?" Mr. Shelton said. "Is something going on?"

Rory turned back from the doorway to Mr. Shelton. He felt he had to make changes that were best for him. The reasons for quitting the two programs met his requirements, even if they didn't satisfy anyone else's. He said, "Nothing's going on. I just think I can make better use of my time. Can I go now?"

"I want to talk to you a little more about basketball."

"I haven't decided," Rory said slowly. "I'll let you know. I have to go. Okay?"

The councilor took a read on Rory for a second or two, then said, "Go."

Rory raced out the office door and through the waiting room, thinking, "It's my time, it's my school year, and it's my plan. What do they care if I play basketball or tuba? It won't make one bit of difference to them next year whether I'm in the band or not."

He hadn't noticed Mr. Keltch walking some distance ahead. The band teacher suddenly stopped, turned and began walking back toward him. When he did notice, it was obvious that Mr. Keltch wanted a few more words with him. Walking quickly toward Rory, Mr. Keltch had the exploding look he had been able to control in Mr. Shelton's office; but now, the controls weren't working.

"I think it's because you have a girlfriend now. You can't go changing everything you do because of your love life, Rory. You get a new girlfriend, you start to get some new physical experiences; and for that, you're willing to throw away the things you've been working so hard for. Is it worth it?" he said, his voice getting faster.

"What are you talking about? She has nothing to do with this and it's—"

"She's changed you," Mr. Keltch interrupted. "She's changed you a lot. Think about it. You let me down. I expected more from you. I expected you would have come to me and let me know what you planned to do next year, but instead I find out through paperwork. Who else are you going to let down? You know who you're hurting the most with this, don't you? You're hurting yourself. Oh yeah, and another thing... The reference letter I wrote for you for your scholarship application, well, the kid I wrote about wouldn't have let me and the band down. That kid is not the kid you are now. I will be rescinding my letter of recommendation, Rory. I hope you haven't quit on any of the other teachers who wrote for you." He finished the last sentence, talking over his shoulder as he walked away.

Rory, with his face reddening, couldn't find the words he needed to come back at his band teacher. Mr. Keltch is wrong. I am the same kid. I knew I had to drop out of music even before I was seeing Alyse. Why should I have to check with him and let him know what my plans are? He would have just tried to talk me into staying in the band. He would have liked that, but he could care less about what I want. He doesn't know about my ability in chemistry, or what this scholarship means to me.

Chapter 2

The students considered Mr. Duggin the new chemistry teacher. The old one, Mr. Butcher, was so old that some students figured he'd invented the periodic table in the first place. When the current school year finished, it would be Mr. Butcher's forty-second at Big Sky.

The new chemistry teacher had graduated from Oregon State University two years previously with a degree in science and education. He migrated to Montana, because four years of the Oregon rain had depressed him to the point that escape from the cold damp coast became a necessity. Now, the moist air from the ocean rose quickly up the mountains, dropping all of its precipitation on the western slopes, making Mr. Duggin happy in his new warm, dry home.

The old chemistry teacher, Mr. Butcher, had graduated from a teacher's school in Wyoming, and then moved to Montana to teach in a small schoolhouse where he could handle more than one subject. Time passed. As he changed schools during his early career, he became more specialized in the subjects he taught, and ended up becoming a chemistry teacher.

The old and the new reflected different styles of teaching.

The young Mr. Duggin required plenty of lab time from his students. He presented them with problems and theories, then turned them loose to find out for themselves how chemistry worked. The experiments were practical. He designed them so they applied to things the students were exposed to every day. Sitting back in the lab, and watching the effect of discovery on his students, provided his daily joy.

By contrast, the old Mr. Butcher assigned homework at the end of his lectures and looked forward to the quiz he would administer during the next class. He drew enjoyment from seeing the measurable results of his students listening, taking notes, and studying. But his style didn't transfer the least hint of enthusiasm for chemistry to any of them.

When Mr. Duggin arrived at Big Sky, the Chemistry Club had been extinct for over fifteen years. It had taken a considerable amount of convincing and cajoling on his part to get Mr. Butcher to restart the club. Once it did get going, Mr. Butcher was at all of the club meetings, enjoying the interaction with the students. The recent batch of kids had more energy for science than previous generations, or so he thought. It was great to see them doing extra chemistry for the fun of it.

When the amount of additional time he spent at the school began to grind Mr. Butcher down, he suggested that he and Mr. Duggin alternate attending the meetings. Mr. Duggin agreed. Then he found he couldn't get enough of the club, and he ended up attending all of the meetings anyway. When Mr. Butcher saw the students turning to Mr. Duggin for guidance more often than they turned to him, he stopped going to the club meetings altogether.

Under the sole guidance of Mr. Duggin, the Chemistry Club grew to twelve students in two years. Most were sophomores from his regular classes. However, there were a few juniors and seniors who had heard he made chemistry fun, by letting the students self-direct the area of chemistry they wanted to explore. Once they tried it, they liked it.

A group of students always waited to see him after his classes, and the club meetings. He knew their names, he knew their areas of interest, and he knew them as individuals. Having them waiting outside the classroom with questions related to chemistry, and even to other non-school subjects, showed him they took an interest in their schooling as well as what happened in the world around them. He wanted to encourage them to maintain and expand their interest in all things. If they found the learning enjoyable, then he found it enjoyable too.

Final exams were approaching. To help the students do a little extra preparation, Mr. Duggin administered a simulated chemistry exam. All students, not just the Chemistry Club, had been invited to attend. A swollen number of twenty-seven had written the mock exam the previous week. The actual final exams from the previous year were used to make the simulation as real as possible. At this week's chemistry meeting they were getting their test results back, so all twenty-seven students were crammed into a lab designed to accommodate only ten.

Every chair was occupied. Some students sat on the stainless steel countertops, while others stood leaning against the walls.

Once Mr. Duggin had passed out the exam results, he returned to the front of the room. "I'm going to make a few observations about your tests in a moment. First, I have a question for Harry Beninger. Harry, are you not a junior?"

Harry looked down at the floor, then up again. He lifted his eyebrows and scanned the room by shifting his eyes while keeping his head still. Then he stared up at Mr. Duggin and responded that he was, for sure, in the eleventh grade.

"Which would mean you wrote the tenth-grade chemistry final exam last year?"

"Yeah, I guess so," Harry said, cocking his head a little to one side.

"Didn't you notice the exam you wrote last week was the exact same exam?"

Harry appeared frozen in thought for a few seconds. "It was as tough as last year's final."

"It should have been easier, since you had some experience with it. You were supposed to write the eleventh-grade exam, not the tenth." Mr. Duggin said.

Harry turned red, as the other students chided him for not realizing he had written the same exam.

"Déjà vu can be boring after you've done it a few times, Harry," one of the students joked.

"If it feels good, do it… again and again and again. Right, Harry?" a second student jibed.

Harry shook his head and groaned, "Oh, man!"

"In all fairness, the error is partly my fault, since I must have handed you the wrong exam. So I feel a bit foolish myself, Harry. The good news is, you did score higher this year than you did last year," Mr. Duggin said sympathetically. "In general, everyone did pretty good on their exam. Everyone should review the questions they got wrong and study the relevant areas a little more intently before the actual final.

"There were no perfect scores, but there were two students with only one wrong answer. Good work, Victoria Beach and Rory Coleman." He turned toward Victoria, who hadn't looked up, then said, "Victoria, have you ever considered joining the Chemistry Club?"

"Not really," she answered, flashing her eyes up from the desktop to make eye contact with Mr. Duggin for a brief, uncomfortable instant.

"Which question did you get wrong, Victoria?" Rory asked.

Victoria hadn't opened her exam, but now she flipped through the pages until she saw the question with the X beside it and said, "Nineteen."

Rory flipped to question nineteen. "Ah, balancing equations. I blew it on fifteen. Can you believe I missed an atomic weight question? Man!" Rory shook his head, then turned suddenly and addressed Mr. Duggin, "Mr. Duggin, do you have the tenth-grade final exam from two years ago?"

"I'm sure I can get it. Why?"

"I want to challenge Victoria to another chemistry exam, if she's willing."

The group turned as one to look at Victoria, who sat staring at the floor in front of her desk, showing no reaction to the challenge.

"Victoria, what do you say? Do you want to write another chemistry final?" Mr. Duggin asked.

Victoria continued to stare blankly. She remained perfectly still while all of the other students waited silently for her answer.

Finally, she turned and looked directly at Rory. "Sure, but what's the point?"

"A tie is like kissing your sister," Rory replied. "There has to be a winner."

"You have to have a winner? You have to beat someone?" Victoria asked, drawing some chatter from the group.

"You don't have to write again, if you don't think you can win," Rory responded. This caused an increase in the background chatter.

"So now you're going to try to taunt me into a competition?" she held Rory's stare for a second, then continued, "The point isn't whether or not I think I can win, it's that I don't *care* if I win. Do you want to write another exam knowing your *competition* is indifferent about the results? That even if you get a better score, I could care less?"

The students hooted loudly at the escalating clash between the chemistry combatants. Rory continued to lock eyes with Victoria, then nodded. "Mr. Duggin, when can we write?"

"I can probably find the exam and be ready in a couple of days, but..." He raised his voice to address the whole group. "This isn't a competition between Rory and Victoria. Therefore, the exam will be open to everyone interested in additional practice."

Mr. Duggin turned to Harry. "Harry, you come, too. This time you can write the correct exam."

Harry slumped and said, "Oh, man!"

Victoria was the first person out the door when the meeting ended. When Rory made it from the far side of the crowded lab to exit the room, she was already out of sight. He made his way down the hall to the first set of stairs, then up to the second floor and on to his locker. Turning down the next hallway toward the new school wing, he saw Victoria at her locker.

Rory didn't want Victoria to think he was a win-at-any-cost jerk, which is what he felt she had implied with her comments in the lab.

When he walked up beside her, she had just completed entering her combination. She pulled open the lock.

"Well, Miss Vicster," Rory opened in a friendly tone, "I hope you realize I'm only trying to make some fun out of the chemistry exam. I don't really want to beat you at chemistry."

Victoria turned to him. With her head slightly tilted and a smile on her rounded lips she asked, "Rory, isn't it?"

"Yeah," he said.

"I'm Victoria. We haven't met before, have we?"

"Gee." He furrowed his eyebrows and frowned at the formality of the introduction. "I don't know about that, but I know who you are; we've been going to the same school for two years."

"Yes, and we've even had some classes together. However, we've never had a reason to talk. Kind of odd. But maybe not." She stopped and stood smiling for a moment. "'A tie is like kissing your sister.' Pretty good use of a cliché, Rory. I'm surprised that when you said, 'Somebody's got to win,' you didn't somehow add a reference to the *Gipper*." She took a deep breath of air and swallowed nervously. She looked up at the ceiling tiles. When she turned her gaze back to Rory, she clenched her fingers to make her hands stop fluttering, then continued, "Do you really need more chemistry practice? It seems to me that you have a pretty good knowledge of the subject. I will admit I enjoy studying for exams and getting the work right, but I have no desire to make it any more *fun* than it already is.

"You're not like the rest of the jocks, but I still think you're a little too competitive. In any case, I am going to take the second practice exam, not to compete with you, but to see how I do. If you take the exam as well, then I hope you have *fun*. I will even let you know what my mark is, so you can chalk up another one in the won or lost column. Hmm, did that sound like another cliché?

"And another thing, I do think you want to beat me at chemistry. But I'm not taking it personally. I think you would have challenged anyone who had tied or beat you in the exam. We all know you've applied for the Mortenson Scholarship. Now it seems like you're trying to prove you're a chemistry superstar. Good luck." She turned her attention to the inside of her locker.

Rory shook his head as if waking up. "Wow! Am I sorry? I didn't mean to get you all hot and bothered with my little challenge. Man, I only wanted to make things a bit more interesting by having a little friendly competition. And you say we've never talked to each other in two years?" Rory asked, shaking his head and scrunching his eyebrows. "That can't be right."

"I think I would know," she stated, while shuffling items in her locker.

"Maybe, but you might have forgotten."

Victoria stopped abruptly. She turned to glare at Rory with dark brown eyes that he noticed required no adornment from makeup. He saw that her eyebrows were thick and dark, but not what would be called bushy. Her black hair hung straight in a simple cut. She was a pretty girl, though not in a classical fine-boned way. He liked the aspects of her features that were outside the norm. Her lips a bit large, her nose a bit broad. Rory realized that her shapely, yet non-athletic, physique appealed to him.

"I know I wouldn't forget," she said.

"Okay," Rory smiled sheepishly, "I guess the competition is off. And for your information, I'm not trying to be a chemistry superstar. I like chemistry and I thought maybe you enjoyed it as much as I do. You know, like you always give it a hundred and ten percent, or you felt like when the chemistry gets tough, the tough get chemistry. Oops, I forgot; you don't like sports clichés. I'll see you later."

Rory turned and walked back toward his locker. Victoria watched him until he turned the corner and was gone.

———

Although it was evening when Rory left the school, the late spring sun continued to shine as the Montana days lengthened. An Air Force jet sneaked up from behind and screamed overhead, banking above the hill and away from the city.

He felt good about his exam results. This feeling added to the excitement of going to his daily after-school meeting with Alyse. He normally stopped every day to check out her homework assignments and confirm what they would review later over the phone. At her house they would go down into the basement where Alyse had a desk set up in the family room.

There, he would grab her and pull her to him while attempting to kiss her. She slapped his hands away, yet made sure to stay within reach and keep him grabbing. Eventually, he would get a good enough grip to pull her close and wrap his other arm around her. She would fight to prevent him from kissing her for a suitable period of time, before they embraced and began a series of soft kisses. They didn't embrace with a hunger, only with a desire to feel the other's lips, cheeks and eyes with their own lips. They wanted intimate touching. The kisses stayed soft but they grew longer. They periodically broke for a few seconds to look into each other's eyes.

Rory would pull his hand down her back onto her hip, then bring it around her waist and up her stomach, until the back of his hand rubbed against the bottom of Alyse's breast. She would press into his hand, encouraging him. Then he would slide the back of his hand up over her breast to see if she was wearing a bra. Most often she wasn't, so Rory would slowly twist his hand to place his palm fully over her breast. He would caress the breast slowly until he felt her nipple harden. His own hardening was apparent to them both as he held her close, putting pressure on his groin.

She would let him touch and rub while she arched and moaned. Their body heat created moisture on their foreheads, while the pace and depth of their breathing increased.

It was at this point that Rory didn't know what to do next, so one day to advance their touching game a little he pulled his hand down to her waist and slipped it under her shirt. He moved it up the skin of her stomach, skin more silken than anything he had ever touched. Then, when he touched her bare breast, an excited pleasure rippled through his groin and chest up to his ears, which burned with a rush of heat. She enjoyed this new touching and allowed it to go on. Then she broke their long kiss to look him in the eye, apologetically suggesting they had better stop. He withdrew his hand immediately, then kissed her softly and thanked her. He left in a trance shortly afterward, feeling joy for the wonderful experience of touching Alyse's soft, smooth flesh. But with this pleasure he also felt dread; he worried that he might have offended her by touching her when she really didn't want to be touched. She acted like she enjoyed it, yet maybe she had been afraid to stop him, thinking he would tell everyone that she was a prude.

After the first episode of skin-to-skin contact with Alyse's breast, he didn't try anything for another week. Confusion reined as he tried to determine whether or not Alyse had really welcomed his advance. Eventually his desire to feel the sensation of her skin again made him summon the courage to try once more. He succeeded, and the second occurrence was equally wonderful. Alyse seemed to take more enjoyment this time, allowing the play to go on a while longer. When he left her house that day, he was so worked up his own sexual state was on the verge of release.

But this night, after the chemistry exam results, he tried to talk with her about the exam. The conversational beginning to their meeting ended when she coldly rebuked him for violating their after-school protocol. To recover from the bad start, he reached for her; and their game proceeded in the normal manner. When he reached the point of sliding his hand up inside her shirt, instead he moved it along her waist to her belt buckle. He gripped it tight, with his fingers down inside the waistline of her jeans, and pulled her close. He broke their kiss and looked into her eyes, wondering at her reaction. She looked at him for a few seconds, then looked down. His hand was frozen. When he allowed himself to appreciate the sensations originating inside of Alyse's jeans, he realized he was feeling pubic hair. It quickly dawned on him that, as he gripped her buckle, his hand not only went inside her jeans, it also went inside her panties.

"Maybe we better cool it," he said. Without looking her in the eyes, he released his hand from her buckle and withdrew it. "I'm really sorry, Alyse."

"We can't do this sort of stuff while my parents are home. We're going to have to wait," she said.

"You're right. I'm sorry. You make me crazy."

She wrapped her arms around his chest and hugged him tighter and tighter. "You make me crazy, too."

Chapter 3

Mr. Keltch held one-on-one final exams for his band classes, which meant they had to be spread out over a number of days. The three or four students scheduled for this day waited in the orchestra room for their turn to go into Mr. Keltch's office, while those not being tested enjoyed time in the study hall. Rory sat in the orchestra room with his friend Gary Milton, reading over his music one last time before his exam. Periodically they looked at each other as they waited. Rory wanted to get the exam behind him.

The large room had multiple levels curved around a central conductor's platform. Acoustical tiles protruded from the walls on snake-like fixtures that could be moved and tilted so the acoustics could be adjusted. From the high ceiling hung additional tiles that gave the room a more three-dimensional feel. Large, open storage shelves for the bigger instruments lined the perimeter of the room. In one corner, randomly placed music stands waited for their eventual move to the auditorium for use in the final assembly concert of the year.

One of the trumpet players had been first to go during this class period. Sounds of her examination filtered out from the office where Rory feared to go, now that he was on Mr. Keltch's list of people who were of no use to him. First the trumpet player had played scales, then she played a section of the music the band had played during the year. Finally, she played new music neither Rory nor Gary had heard before.

"I hope I'm next," Gary said, "I sure as hell don't want to be with Keltch after he gets through with you."

"Yeah, it could be bad," replied Rory.

"He's going to nail you, man. You dumped him."

"I'll talk to him and we'll see. It's not like he can do a whole lot of harm. Besides, maybe if he nails me with the exam he won't nail me with the scholarship."

"Sure, dream on."

Gary held a saxophone reed in his mouth to keep it moist and ready for his exam. Each time he talked to Rory, he pulled the reed out.

"It's kind of obvious you're on the outs with Keltch. He made like you weren't even in the class this week, and he used to treat you so special," Gary said. He replaced the reed in his mouth.

"Will you shut up? I have to concentrate on this music. And I think *you're* really his pet, the way he goes to bat for you all the time."

"So he saved my ass from being kicked out a couple of times. He did it because he needs a good sax player."

Gary had real talent with his saxophone. He never practiced the music played in class; in fact he only played the band music during class, at rehearsals or during the concerts. Reading music came easily to him. He intuitively knew the right way to play any piece he read. Mr. Keltch had seen Gary struggle with his other subjects and knew his best chance to make something of himself would come from music. But he had to graduate first. He had a difficult time convincing Gary that he had to get passing grades in his other subjects in order to do that. To help Gary, Mr. Keltch had arranged for special tutoring in some of Gary's classes. Rory had been one of Gary's tutors, and they had become friends.

Gary sucked on his reed for a few seconds, but he didn't like to sit in silence. "Rory, you getting any trim from Alyse?"

"Am I getting any what?" Rory asked.

"Trim, you know." Gary made a piston movement with his fist.

"Trim...trim means sex?"

"Yeah."

"Trim is a word for sex?" Rory asked, without expecting an answer. "Who's in charge of making up the words you use to mean sex, and how do they come up with something like trim? I mean, balling I can see, getting your oil changed I can kind of see. But, what the hell does 'trim' have to do with sex?"

Gary took the reed out of his mouth. "Who cares who makes up the words or whether or not they have anything to do with sex? Let me make it easier for you, is Alyse changing your oil?"

"Man, I'm not going to tell you that."

"Why?"

"It's none of your business, that's why."

"Hey, I'm the guy who told you to go talk to her in the first place, so I have an interest in what you two are up to. You owe me, for making you build up the courage to go and meet the best chick you ever met. And you may owe me even bigger, if you are getting your oil change. So, do you owe me big or bigger?"

"Go suck your reed, I don't owe you nothing. And stop talking, I have to concentrate on the music."

Gary put the reed back in his mouth, but he wasn't finished with the subject. Twice, when he pulled the reed out to say something, Rory held up his hand and tilted his head away from Gary, so the reed ended up back in his mouth. After a short time, though, the silence became unbearable for him. He pulled out the reed again and when Rory's hand went up, Gary talked right over it. "I always tell you about the girls I'm making it with. So what's the big deal?"

Rory sighed and looked over at Gary. "You mean you tell me about the girls you are trimming. See, *making it* sounds like sex but *trimming*? I don't think so. Besides, I don't believe a word you tell me about those girls, so I don't think you've told me anything."

"You're starting to bug me, Rory. Guys tell guys about this kind of stuff. It's like the code of the west, man. Everybody is always talking about who they did and what the chick looks like naked. You talk about the kind of sounds they make when you're banging away, plus all the goofy love things they say after you're done. Telling the other guys about it is one of the best parts of sex. The only guys not talking about it are the guys who aren't getting any." Gary's eyes opened wide and a leering smile appeared on his face. "Wait a minute, that's it! Isn't it? You're not getting any, are you? You won't fess up because there's nothing to fess up to. Right? And everybody thinks you're getting it big time."

"You want to know the truth?"

"Yeah."

"It's none of your business. Now shut up."

"Up yours," Gary said, then began sulking.

Soon after, the trumpet in Mr. Keltch's office stopped playing. Rory and Gary listened to Mr. Keltch's muffled voice, trying to hear what he had to say to the student inside. Soon their efforts ended when the door opened to let the student out, and Mr. Keltch appeared in the doorway. He stood looking back and forth between Rory and Gary, until his gaze stopped on Rory. He held it there then said, "Gary, you're next."

"Shit. Oops! Sorry, Mr. Keltch, I forgot to put my reed back in my mouth and it's dried out." Gary turned to pick up his saxophone and muttered to Rory, "See what you made me do, you prick?"

"Good luck, asshole," Rory whispered supportively.

Gary walked across the orchestra room, past Mr. Keltch and into the office. Mr. Keltch smirked at Rory, then turned, went inside, and closed the door. Rory watched the other student pack up her trumpet and leave. Alone and no longer interrupted by Gary, he wondered how tough Mr. Keltch would make his exam. This would be their first meeting since they had met in the counselor's office.

He had thought about what he would say to Mr. Keltch, but hadn't been satisfied with any of the approaches he had developed.

The musical exam was a lame duck as far as he was concerned, but he wanted Mr. Keltch to think he took it seriously. In preparation, he had practiced his scales and music more diligently than he had practiced the whole time he had been playing the tuba. He had even come up with a great solo piece for the optional music portion of the exam. If he did well in the exam, it would show he still respected music and its importance to others, even though the importance to him had dwindled. If Mr. Keltch saw this respect and if he hadn't already sent the letter, maybe he would be willing to discuss Rory's reason for dropping out of the band. Once he understood Rory's intentions toward chemistry, maybe he wouldn't feel the necessity to send the letter after all.

"But how do I get the discussion rolling after the exam? Do I just come out and ask him?" he thought.

He stood up and walked to the corner to grab a music stand, and brought it back to his chair. He placed his sheet music on its ledge. His tuba sat on its bell beside him. He grabbed the mouthpiece, put it to his mouth and started to warm up by blowing scales. The raspberry, quacking noises he produced made him laugh and embarrassed him a little. Once he had the mouthpiece warmed up, he picked up his tuba, inserted the mouthpiece, and played a few scales. After the scales, he turned to his sheet music and began to play his solo.

The jazz solo, written in a humorous style, had been a lucky find. Rory had gone into a number of music stores looking for something different, and had finally found this piece which featured the tuba. He hoped it would be a pleasant surprise for Mr. Keltch and would put him in a good mood.

Rory worked his way through the piece, playing it better than he had during any of his previous practice sessions. He had a good tempo. He added emphasis to certain passages, to bring out the swing of the music. He slowed some parts down and picked up the tempo in others. He would play some parts quietly, then gradually build a crescendo. He felt he had penetrated deep into the music and was playing on a new level, when he heard the door to the office open. He stopped playing, mid-note. *That* was quick; Gary shouldn't be finished yet. He looked over at the office door where Mr. Keltch stood with pursed lips. "Rory, do you mind? Can you give a little consideration to someone else while they have their exam?" said Mr. Keltch.

"Sorry," Rory replied. He pulled his neck into his shoulders. "I was just trying to get a little extra practice in."

"Then use one of the practice rooms."

The door shut and Rory heard muffled voices behind the door before Gary began to play again. Rory's heart was pounding. He knew if he stood to go to a practice room his knees would be weak and wobbly. He also knew he wouldn't be able to concentrate on practicing after screwing himself in deeper with Mr. Keltch.

He sat and he waited. Finally the music inside the office stopped. A few seconds later Gary walked through the door toward Rory, and when he got close he said, "Nice going, dickhead. You made it bad enough for me, but now he's going to kill you."

Rory looked at Mr. Keltch, who stood impatiently in the doorway nodding his head.

"Yes, it's your long-awaited turn. Make sure you put the music stand back in the corner," he said to Rory, then disappeared.

"Any last requests?" Gary asked.

"Yeah, if I don't make it back alive, take this music stand and trim him with it."

In the scales portion of the exam, Mr. Keltch requested some of the most obscure and difficult scales Rory had ever attempted. In some cases, Rory didn't even know which note to begin with. In the band music section, Rory played well because of his familiarity with the music. The new music section of the exam tested the student's ability to read music he'd never seen. For this, Mr. Keltch had found a piece of music written in three-eighths time in a key Rory had never played before. Three-eighths time often required the musician to move a lot of air through the instrument, while executing some pretty quick tonguing action to produce the short notes. It also meant taking very quick breaths to maintain an even tempo. The piece Mr. Keltch inflicted on Rory started out with quick notes and kept them coming. Rory fumbled wildly. Mr. Keltch stopped him many times to make him start over. Then he would give up on a section and skip ahead to a different place in the piece to let Rory fumble around for a few bars before skipping ahead again. It was a disaster.

Finally, Rory got to play the jazz solo. He explained how he had found it and what he knew about the music. Mr. Keltch seemed impressed as he looked over the music before Rory played.

He played the solo with only one or two mix-ups. Technically he played the piece fairly well, but the first three dismal sections of the exam had sucked all the feeling out of him.

"You played the solo better when you were interrupting Gary's exam," commented Mr. Keltch. He focused on the notes he had been taking, before looking up at Rory. "You were riding a C up until now, but I don't know if you will maintain it after this exam."

"It was pretty tough, and I pretty much blew it."

"Uh-huh. You chose a pretty good piece of music for your solo, though. I might give it to some of the other tuba players to work on for next year," He paused for a few seconds, then said, "Well, the final marks will be posted by the end of next week. And don't forget the extra rehearsals for the final concert. Unless there's anything else, you can go now."

"There is something else. I want to talk to you about me dropping out of band and all," Rory said. He felt he had sounded weak so he sat up straight in his chair to confront Mr. Keltch with a little more spine.

"Go ahead," Mr. Keltch invited. "But what is there left to say?"

"I wanted to know if you've actually sent another letter to the scholarship people about taking back your recommendation."

"I have it right here," Mr. Keltch said while picking up the lone sheet of paper sitting in his out basket.

"I guess I would like to ask you not to send it. I honestly believe I'm doing the right thing for me. I do really well in chemistry, and I've discovered I enjoy it a lot. I feel there's a lot I can discover if I concentrate on it. It's as if for once in my life, I know what I want to do and I actually have the ability to pursue it successfully.

"As far as letting you and the band down, I don't think I am letting anyone down. The band is just as strong without me. I'm only trying to do what's best for my future and my chance of getting the scholarship. I don't know if you know, but the scholarship is awarded based on the student's work in chemistry during the first half of their junior year. Because it starts in the junior year, I needed to make my decision now. I need the extra study period to do extra work in chemistry. First to get the scholarship, then to keep it. That's what I wanted to tell you."

Mr. Keltch sat silently, making Rory fidget in his seat.

"I realize the benefit of having the extra study time. But as I mentioned in our last meeting, you've been able to do both chemistry and band in the past. For this reason I think you're probably good enough at chemistry to continue to do both for another two years. You don't know for sure if you're going to get the scholarship, so what happens if you don't? You've blown away band for nothing and you won't need the extra study time. Will you?"

He paused to give Rory a chance to think about life without the scholarship.

"You should have come and talked to me about it, Rory. We could have figured out a schedule to get you extra time for chemistry and still play in the band. We could have covered all of the bases for you so even if the scholarship didn't happen, you wouldn't have risked your future with the band. Now, you've committed to the scholarship alone. But I'm not surprised. You used to come and talk with me about school all the time. Now, you don't have the time because you spend it all with your girlfriend. I asked Mr. Duggin if he had noticed this about you as well, and he confirmed my thoughts. He said you still get to all of the chemistry club meetings and you still talk a lot about chemistry, but not much else.

"You have to be careful how you spend your time, Rory. If you really want the scholarship and you really think you need to drop out of band to have the extra time for chemistry, then you better be sure you spend the extra time the way you intended."

Rory didn't appreciate the lecture, but he wasn't going to say anything to anger Mr. Keltch. "I'll think about it. Are you still going to send the letter?"

"Well, let's see. I still want you to go to band camp and I still want to work out a schedule designed to keep you in the band. You may have to give up some of the time you had planned to spend elsewhere. If you can do those two things, I don't have to send the letter."

Rory drew back in his chair, not believing what he had just heard. After learning the level of importance Rory placed on the scholarship, and hearing Rory describe the pressure he would experience to keep the scholarship, Mr. Keltch ignored everything. He brought it all back around to what was best for himself and the band. All the effort and extra practice to try and please Mr. Keltch had gained him nothing.

Rory gripped the hand rest of his tuba until his knuckles hurt and turned white. He needed to control his own explosion of anger this time. How could Mr. Keltch not understand what he had just heard? How could he be so stubborn?

Rory stared at the music stand, waiting before saying something he might regret later. Words that if spoken now would relieve the building fury, but probably accomplish nothing else. He could go off, venting his frustrations, but that wouldn't affect Mr. Keltch in the least. Losing his temper would only let his teacher know that Rory understood how his own stature had been diminished in Mr. Keltch's eyes.

"I'll tell you what... I can't do those two things. I'm asking you not to send the letter because it would be better for me if you didn't." Rory spoke calmly and intended to leave it at that; but he heard his voice continue saying, "But I can see you don't care what's best for anyone except you."

Rory stood and walked out. Halfway across the orchestra room he heard Mr. Keltch speaking from the door with a raised voice, "The letter is on its way, Rory. I'm sending it in your *best interest* because I'm going to teach you a lesson." The door slammed shut.

Rory knew he could expect a D in music and his grade point average would suffer for it, but the letter being sent to the Mortenson Board hurt the most. He knew his efforts to prevent it from happening had accomplished nothing.

Chapter 4

Mr. Duggin's crowded, noisy lab had the sweet and heady smells of students performing a series of experiments on ethers. The various lab teams created pleasant artificial scents by mixing and heating a variety of compounds. With each successful creation, a group would shout with enthusiasm, then take the scent they had created around the lab and let everyone guess what they had made. So far they had produced the scent of apples, apricots, bananas and vanilla.

Mr. Duggin watched and waited for the inevitable. Ethers, once the air became heavily laden with their molecules, began to combine. When they did they created a cloud of rotten-egg stench.

He remembered his own high school chemistry teacher standing and waiting for the conversion from sweet smells to foul odor. Now he waited for the same chemical punch line.

"Whoa! Who made that one?" one of the students asked.

Mr. Duggin knew what would happen next. The class started looking around the lab at each other, then re-smelling the scents they had just made. The students were all waving their hands and scrunching their noses while backing away from their putrid-smelling experiments. The room filled with the groans and noises of disgust.

"Somebody must have used the wrong stuff. It reeks in here. Open the windows," one student pleaded.

"Yeah, why doesn't someone do that. And then I want you all to extinguish your burners. I'll turn on the fans," said Mr. Duggin. "When you've cleaned up your lab areas, I'll explain what happened."

Mr. Duggin described the combining of the molecules, and then led a discussion regarding contamination of experimental results and why some kinds of experiments required isolated environments. He went on to ask the students about what kinds of companies would utilize these types of experiments with ethers. The first response, perfume companies, came easy; but then the student's suggestions dried up.

"You can't think of anything else? Come on, what about you, Larry? How about you, Denise? Think about things that have a nice smell."

"How about after-shave lotion?" offered Larry.

"No, that's the same as perfume." Mr. Duggin replied, and then scanned the students again. "Okay then, how about air fresheners? They have pine-scented and flower-scented varieties. How about fabric softeners to make your clothes smell like rain? How about candy made from sugar alone, but

35

smelling like fruit so that you think it tastes like fruit? Then there are shampoos and hair creams with their own 'natural' smell. I think you get the idea. All kinds of companies employ chemists to improve or embellish their products.

"Now, your homework. In addition to writing up your experiments, I want you to come up with a list of five things in your homes that you think may have artificial scents added to them. And you can't list family members or pets.

"I also want you to write a poem about ethers."

Upon hearing about the poem assignment, the class started to grumble and complain.

"You sure we have to write a poem? We hate poems." someone said.

"Yes, I said a poem. It has to be at least five lines, but it can be more. It can be any form of poem you like, so if you want to write a sonnet, feel free."

The bell rang and everyone left, grumbling about writing the poem. Mr. Duggin hoped they would hate the poem-writing exercise more than they hated writing up the experiment, and would do anything, like writing up the experiment, to put off writing the poem.

Rory waited to talk to Mr. Duggin. When all the students had left, he walked up to the front of the lab. Mr. Duggin was stuffing papers back into a folder on the bench table at the front of the room.

"Hi, Rory, what's up?"

Rory looked straight ahead and recited:

"There once was a chemist who dabbled,
 With ethers he made smell like apples.
 When he mixed up a bunch,
 The molecules crunched.
 And the results of his work smelled like crapple."

"Pretty good, but too easy. Your reward is, you get to write another poem, and the second one can't be a limerick."

Mr. Duggin smiled at Rory, then said, "So, you were pretty quiet today. Something bugging you?"

"I just had my band final and it didn't go so good. But really I wanted to ask you if you found the other chemistry final, and to see if you're still going to let us write again."

"Yes, I did find it. Funny, Victoria stopped by to ask me the same question. You know, I don't want the two of you turning this into some kind of sport. The more I think about it, the more I think I should give you the exams to take home— and not mark them. That way you can't really compare the results."

"No, don't do that. I told her I wasn't trying to challenge her, I was only trying to make it a little more fun. I don't care about beating her at chemistry exams."

"Good. I told Victoria we would do it at Tuesday's club meeting, anyway," Mr. Duggin said. "I haven't made up my mind about making it a take-home." He changed the subject. "What happened in your band final?"

Rory quietly stared at the folder Mr. Duggin had lying on the table. His failure at trying to smooth things over with Mr. Keltch had bothered him all day. He wanted to figure out some other way to prevent him from sending the second letter.

"Rory, did you hear me?" asked Mr. Duggin.

Rory looked up. "Yeah, sorry. I really prepared for the exam, but he was gunning for me. He made it really tough. I'm going to get a D in band this year, and everybody's going to think I'm a quitter. That's going to look bad when I send in my marks to the Mortenson Scholarship Board.

"I tried to explain to him why I dropped out of band, but he wouldn't listen. I did find out he hasn't sent his second letter to Mortenson. But he's going to send it now."

"What second letter?"

"He didn't tell you about the second letter? When he found out I dropped band, he said he'd be writing a letter to the

Mortenson Board, telling them I wasn't the kid he thought I was and taking back his recommendation."

"No, he didn't say anything about a letter." The teacher paused, then said, "This is serious, Rory. I would really like to see you get the scholarship. This is going to hurt you. We're going to have to do something about it. He is such a..." Mr. Duggin stopped himself, then began slowly shaking his head.

At first Rory felt the chances of winning the scholarship would be weakened by Mr. Keltch's letter. Now he felt they were wobbling and about to collapse. "I thought he had talked to you. I thought he would've told you what he intended to do. He said I've changed since I started hanging out with girls, that I wasn't the same guy I used to be, and that you had said the same thing."

Mr. Duggin had been listening while looking out the window. Now he turned to focus on Rory. "We weren't talking about you, specifically, but he did ask me if you still hung around to talk with me like you used to. I don't recall saying you had changed."

"That's okay; I'm not too worried about it. What do you think I should do about the application?"

"I don't know, but let's not worry about it too much yet. A guy your age is supposed to change, Rory. You're growing up, and you need to start making some choices for yourself. You should also realize that with each of your choices comes a consequence. I don't know why Mr. Keltch would want to make the consequence this severe."

With classes over for the day, Rory walked back to his locker. The halls were empty, which suited him fine since his mood had been a little off-key after the botched music exam. He had tried to avoid everyone all day, preferring to be alone. He didn't notice Victoria as he walked past her locker. "Hey, Rory," she called out to him. "Tuesday night, right?"

Rory looked back at her with no comprehension. "What?"

"Tuesday night, the chemistry practice exam. You're still going, aren't you?"

"Right, I'm still going." Then he turned and walked away.

Victoria watched him go, and muttered, "What's with him?"

When Rory arrived at his locker, he found Alyse waiting for him. He looked up and down the hallway in both directions, and when he saw no teachers nearby, he put his free arm around her and they kissed. He took slow steps moving her backwards until he pressed her up against his locker and he held the kiss for a long time. He pulled his face a short distance from hers, told her how good she tasted, then kissed her again.

When they heard people talking somewhere down the hall, they separated. Rory gently pushed Alyse a little to the left so he could open his locker.

"Gary told me you had your band exam with Keltch today. How'd it go?" she asked, while he dialed in his combination.

He didn't want to think about the exam any longer; he commented, "Tougher than it should have."

"Did you talk to him about dropping out? And about the letter?"

"He hadn't sent it, but he's going to. I couldn't convince him otherwise. He still wanted me to go to band camp. Do you believe that?" Rory opened his locker door, slamming it back against the adjacent locker. Alyse jumped at the unexpected bang.

"Sorry," he said, feeling his face get a little flushed.

"Take it easy, Rory. So he sends the letter. By the time they award the scholarship, they'll probably forget about the letter. So no big deal."

He slowly turned his head to look at her. He said nothing; his expression made her fidget. He turned back to his locker to put away his books. He wanted to tell her that this really *is* a big deal. It's something that he wants more than anything he's ever wanted. He knew he could do so much more than stay in Great Falls and work at some job that serviced the Air Force base. Unable to afford a good college without help, he realized his only chance came with this scholarship. It's not just a big deal, it's the biggest deal. And it's the only deal.

"You want to study at the library tonight?" Alyse asked, trying to change the subject.

The school library was open evenings for a few weeks leading up to final exams. Normally Rory and Alyse didn't see each other on school nights, except for the short time he spent with her when he stopped by her house on his way home from school. They tried studying together at Alyse's house—with no success, because they spent more time trying to make out than studying. With her parents at home in the evenings, they had to be on the alert for her mother sneaking down the stairs to check on them, so they didn't get much making out done either.

Due to the inefficient attempts at studying, they decided they would be more productive if they discussed their homework on the phone.

With the library open they could get together, away from her watchful parents. Then they usually left the library a little early, to enjoy some kissing. They had found a recessed doorway on one side of the school building. There was a high wall a few feet away from the doorway, so they felt comfortably isolated.

Once inside the doorway, they would start to kiss each other and then their hands would start to roam over each other's bodies, softly caressing and feeling the other through their clothing. They both wanted to go further than the doorway would allow, and felt frustrated by the lack of a private location in which to extend their intimate journey. Rory was always looking for an opportunity for isolation and a chance to hold and feel Alyse's body. It excited him to think she searched for the same thing.

Alyse's parents didn't always let her go to study at the school library, but whenever she suggested the idea to Rory, he urgently hoped she would be allowed out that night. The thought of getting together in the doorway warmed and excited him.

Rory left Alyse at her gate with a kiss, and said he would call her as soon as he got home. His bus arrived after a short wait and he rode quietly in the back seat for the twenty minutes it took the bus to get to the end of the loop. He was always the last passenger. The bus driver usually took his break at the last stop, pouring himself a cup of coffee while waiting to start his next run.

"I'll probably be heading back in about an hour. See you then," Rory said as he climbed down the bus's steps.

"Yeah, I'll be back about then."

Rory had to walk another mile from the bus stop to his home. He knew that by now Alyse would have talked to her parents and would know if she could go to the library. If she could, he would have to do a quick turnaround. Knowing he might be in a hurry, he hoped his mother had made dinner early so that it would be ready to eat, and he could head back for the bus fairly quickly. But, with the daylight lasting as long as it did this time of year, she usually didn't realize how late it had become and ended up making the meal later. He would have to grab a sandwich or hope for some of last night's leftovers. Leftovers that might still be in the fridge, but only if he arrived home before his brother.

It was still warm out. He could see gophers scampering about in the empty lots. The new housing developments were moving closer and closer to his old house out in the boonies.

Mitch Davies

He kept walking with a hollow feeling in his chest, the feeling of something left unresolved.

Chapter 5

Victoria walked along the street to her home, feeling a little perplexed by Rory Coleman. Although she had only talked to him twice before, and in both cases felt she had been a bit too aggressive, she believed they could develop a friendship. She decided the next time she had an opportunity to speak with him, she would try to be a little more personable. Tonight, in the school hallway during their brief conversation, he had completely shut her down. She wondered if her attitude in their previous encounters had created the distance.

She had a few other friends, but a friendship with Rory seemed like it could be different. She decided that she wanted to find out what this difference might be.

Rory counted all of the school athletes among his friends. As a member of the junior varsity basketball squad, he was comfortable being around them in any social setting. He also had a good relationship with some of her friends, the intellectuals of the school.

Through his interactions with her friends, she had noticed Rory more often over the past months. She'd noticed him in the halls, in the classrooms, and even at the mall. And all of these observances had taken place before he had talked with her after the mock chemistry exam. For the past two years, she had known of Rory, but hadn't had any occasion to actually meet him. They were in the band together, they had been in the same freshman math class, yet never had they crossed paths to the point of even a casual greeting.

From the age of six, Victoria had been playing the oboe. Her well-honed music skills ranked her as the best musician in the school. Her father, a music teacher, had instilled in her the important and inspiring role that music can play in a person's life. He had coached her on a path leading her toward a career in professional music. His desire for his daughter to play in a famous orchestra consumed him. He wanted her to play in one of the best philharmonics in North America or Europe. Giving music lessons or doing pit work at summer ballet camps would never be good enough for his daughter. Victoria genuinely liked to play music, and she also liked being involved in the music world. It made her father happy that she shared his love of music. Her high level of skill, and the fact that she played a double-reed instrument, assured her of numerous scholarship offers. To help generate these offers, she had played in a series of highly visible recitals. This grueling course of action had resulted in an invitation to attend an elite summer music camp; the camp exposed her to a number of people in the international music community, people who could take notice of her ability.

Victoria excelled at everything in which she had an interest. She outperformed most of her fellow students in the arts, the sciences, and the humanities. But the skills she possessed in mathematics made her confess to herself that she enjoyed math the most. She recognized the relationship between math and music, feeling no surprise that she took to both of them so easily.

The house where she grew up provided a very musical environment. Victoria's younger brother and sister both played musical instruments. Her mother taught piano lessons at a local music academy, and teaching usually had her out of the house during the early part of the evening. The family owned a television set, but very seldom turned it on; other than music practice, the kids spent most of their time doing homework and reading for pleasure.

Mr. Beach also gave music lessons. That, or rehearsing with the Air Force band, the lodge band or any one of the swing bands he couldn't say no to, made his absence from home a common occurrence.

Most days Victoria would arrive home from school and look for the note her mother had left. It usually pointed out the existence of a casserole in the oven, stated the time she would be home, and confirmed that she loved them.

Her brother and sister, always arriving home before her, would keep themselves busy with homework to kill time until all three could sit and eat together. When she did arrive home and had gone to her room to change, they each retrieved their own plate and utensils, placing them on the table in front of their designated chairs. Victoria, being the oldest, would retrieve the casserole from the oven and place it on the hot mat their mother had left in the center of the table. The three of them would talk and tease and laugh about the events of their day.

Halfway through their meal that night, her brother informed her that a boy had called for her and wanted her to return his call. With this announcement, they tried to tease her about having a boyfriend, but Victoria never let her siblings get under her skin. She stared at them with a bland expression. After allowing them to tease her to their hearts' content, she asked if they had taken down his phone number. They tried to tease her again with some 'Wouldn't you like to know?' and 'Let me see, where did I write that down?' type responses, but none of them worked. They couldn't get even the slightest rise out of her. Eventually they gave up and pointed to the phone number of a boy named Rory written on the chalkboard.

Good, maybe Rory and I can have a normal conversation, she thought.

They finished their meal and Victoria placed the casserole back in the oven for her parents to eat later. She played scales on her oboe, then returned Rory's call. The person who answered the phone said he had seen Rory earlier but couldn't recall if Rory had left again. He yelled Rory's name then put the phone down. Victoria listened to a few minutes of a television squawking in the background. Then the same voice that had answered came back on the line and said that he guessed Rory had gone out and to try again later.

Victoria hung up a little disappointed, then carried on with her normal evening activities. In bed that night she lay awake later than usual, rehearsing the conversation she hoped would happen the next day with Rory. She intended to be more personable, more friendly and resolved to conduct the conversation in a casual manner. She looked forward to talking with him and considered it a challenge to make a new friend.

———

The school cafeteria had long rows of tables and chairs, enough to provide seating for about four hundred students. At one end of the large hall, students crowded the food serving area, waiting to be served. The room sounded of cutlery clanging on dishes, chairs being scraped across the tile flooring, and students blowing off steam before heading off to a variety of noon-hour activities.

Ellis McCormick, one of Rory's friends from the chemistry club, stepped into the cafeteria from the central stairway. He and another member of the club, Gill Berry, surveyed the lunchroom activities. They looked the entire room over, starting at the end farthest from the food services area. They spotted the off-duty teachers eating their lunches. The low number of four bolstered their spirits. They scanned back across the students to get a general feel for the numbers in the room. Then their eyes moved over to an opening at the back of the room where the cashiers took the money and made change. Students poured out past the cashiers to a large condiment table that held bins of knives and forks, plus bowls of sauces for the students to spread over their hot dogs and hamburgers. At this point, Ellis and Gill exchanged glances and nods, acknowledging their satisfaction with the setup. They looked down a row of tables to a spot near the condiment area, where they spied the two on-duty teachers who sat eating while monitoring the students.

"Oh man, it's Shelton and Vanier. They'll kill us," Gill said in a low voice that only Ellis could hear.

"Only if they see us, and I'll make sure they don't," Ellis replied.

"Look, there's Rory," Gill said.

When Ellis and Gill joined the chemistry club in their freshman year, it hadn't taken them very long to recognize Rory as the star of the club. They had looked up to him from that point forward. Now the two boys slipped over to where

Rory sat eating his lunch and talking with Alyse and Gary. When they got close, Ellis bent down close to Rory's ear and spoke without looking at Rory. "Keep your eyes on the table with the mustard," he said.

By the time Rory registered the words and looked up, he saw Ellis walking away.

He watched until Ellis disappeared into the throng of students coming out of the food serving area, then returned to his conversation with his friends.

Ellis and Gill moved against the flow of the other students. They took positions against two large concrete pillars at the end of a row of tables situated immediately across from the condiment table. Gill could see Mr. Shelton and Mrs. Vanier as they sat watching over the students, but the pillar Ellis stood beside blocked his view of the teachers. Students eating their lunches at the adjacent tables paid them no attention.

Gill signaled Ellis. They both slipped down slowly to a squatting position. They reached into their jacket pockets and pulled out small bundles and cigarette lighters. Ellis also pulled out a single gelcap that had a fuse protruding from one end. He signaled Gill again. Gill nodded back. They were ready.

Ellis flicked his lighter and touched the flame to the fuse of the homemade firecracker, then sent it rolling along the floor in the direction of the two teachers. He threw it with enough force to make sure it skidded past them. It flashed unnoticed across the floor then; still moving, it went off with a loud rich bang. Everyone stopped talking and looked in the direction of the noise.

Upon hearing the firecracker's explosion, Rory looked in that direction and then remembered Ellis' advice to watch the table with the mustard. He turned to look toward the condiment area where the big bowls of mustard, relish and ketchup sat on the long table. Motionless students, wide-eyed with puzzled expressions, stood near the table, staring at the smoke hanging in the air where the firecracker had gone off. Rory picked out Ellis and Gill as they lobbed something through the air toward the table, then disappeared.

In the next instant, two larger noises sounded in color. One created a large spray of yellow, the other an even larger splash of chunky green. All eyes spun toward the new disturbance. Students near the table screamed. They backed away, covered with mustard and relish. Those that had been seated near the mustard table stood looking down at their splattered clothes.

Ellis and Gill scampered under the tables. With all students standing, the space under the tables provided the two boys with a clear passage to take them away from the current center of commotion. When they came to a break in the tables, they popped up and looked back at their demolition work. No one noticed them except Rory, who watched them as they looked on, pretending to be stunned and confused like everyone else. They joined in with the crowd, calling out and asking what had happened. At one point they looked at each other, acknowledging their successful mission with the slightest of grins.

Mr. Shelton and Mrs. Vanier moved to the mustard table, took a quick look, saw chaos beginning to erupt. They held up their arms and began to yell for everyone to stay calm. The students covered with condiments grumbled and complained, while those further away from the action lost interest and resumed their lunch as the teachers managed to get everyone settled down.

Ellis and Gill made their way back to Rory. Ellis, in search of eyewitness reports, asked eagerly, "Hey, Rory, we didn't see what happened. Did you see anything?"

"Yeah, mushroom clouds of mustard and relish went up and sent debris all over the place."

"Did you see who did it?" Gill asked, a little apprehensively.

"No, but I'm sure they'll be caught and punished. Whoever did this will have to pay it back somehow, don't you think?"

"Pay what back?" they asked simultaneously.

"I don't know, maybe the mustard, maybe the dry cleaning. Of course, they need to be caught first."

"Yeah, right. Well, see ya round." The two of them hurried away up the stairs that had brought them to their mission.

After the last class of the day, Rory walked toward the band room in the new wing of the school. His route took him past Victoria's locker. As he had hoped, she stood before it, looking at the contents inside the open door. From a distance, he watched her casually flip the book she held toward the opening. It impacted with the side of the locker and fell to the floor, where she stared for a second or two before kicking it violently, sending it flying down the hall.

"Miss Vicster—," he said, starting to greet her in a friendly tone, but stopping when she turned toward him. "Oh! You're one of the victims of the mustard bomber."

"Yes I am, thank you very much. Those bastards!" she said, then worked the muscles in her jaw. She had worn a pair of her favorite slacks, ones she felt flattered her slender body. Their dark purple color matched nicely with the tapered, light purple blouse she wore. The outfit accented the slimness of her hips and the fullness of her chest. Yellowish stains spotted her everywhere. She had tried to wash some of the splotches out of the blouse, but they had only run deeper into the material. "I hope they get caught and get their asses kicked for this. And

I'd like to do the kicking. Look at my clothes. They're done in, they're garbage, they're shit, all because some jerk thought he was being funny."

"Gee, I'm sorry you got hit." Rory paused, not knowing what to say next. He knew who had caused this damage to her clothing, and that he could provide the target asses she wanted to slam with her foot. But knew he wouldn't. "Maybe I better get going," he said. "I'm going to see your father."

She continued to look down at her stained garments, taking deep, noisy breaths through her nose, until Rory's words penetrated her anger. She looked up and asked, "My father? What do you mean?"

"I'm going to my music lesson," he said, thinking it would make things clear. But she continued to stare with no hint of understanding. "Your dad gives me tuba lessons. Didn't you know that?"

She lifted her head and it bobbed a little. Her anger wound up a little tighter. "Why would I know that? He doesn't tell me who his students are. Do you think because he's teaching *Rory Coleman*, he should go running around telling everyone?"

"No, I don't think that." Now Rory's temper rose. Once again she implied he thought too much of himself. "Your father's been giving me lessons for four years. For some reason, I thought maybe you knew. I guess not. How stupid of me! I better go."

Rory turned and left.

Victoria leaned back and chastised herself. For the third time she stood alone at her locker, watching Rory Coleman walk away.

Rory turned into the stairway at the end of the hall to go down to the band room. "What's with her?" he thought. "She's not very easy to talk to."

He entered the band room and hauled his tuba into one of the lesson rooms. He then took his mouthpiece across the hall to the boys' washroom, where he held it under hot water to warm it up before playing. Back in the lesson room, he set up his music and played scales until Mr. Beach arrived.

Mr. Beach was a stocky man of normal height, with a short military haircut misted with gray. From their first lesson together he had been very formal, wearing a suit with a white shirt and tie. The jacket, always buttoned, had no spare room inside.

Mr. Beach opened the satchel he carried, and selected his tuba mouthpiece from the many stored inside. He indicated for Rory to continue with the scales while he blew into his own mouthpiece to warm it up. He asked Rory to recite the music he was going to play at the next band performance. Periodically, as he listened to Rory play, he would interrupt by extending his arms to indicate he wanted the tuba. Rory removed his mouthpiece and handed him the instrument. Mr. Beach inserted his mouthpiece in place of Rory's, demonstrated the way the music should be played, and discussed tonguing techniques that would help Rory play better. This happened a number of times during each lesson.

Having Mr. Beach play his tuba, and swapping mouthpieces, had always bothered Rory. He didn't touch Mr. Beach's mouthpiece with his own lips, but he knew that the act of blowing into the instrument transferred moisture. When he had to release the spit valve to eliminate the bubbling, he would be releasing the accumulated saliva from both himself and his teacher. Whenever he did this, he made sure to hold the tuba as far away from his body as possible. When Rory received the tuba back and held it to play, it felt warm against his chest and hot on the hand rest where Mr. Beach had been holding it. Rory didn't consider Mr. Beach a creepy guy, he just didn't want to feel the man's body warmth on something he himself held close to his own body and put his mouth on.

He wasn't going to miss these lessons at all.

"Well, you played that piece pretty good. We'll go over it again next week," Mr. Beach said, bringing the lesson to a close.

"Okay. But Mr. Beach, I need to tell you that I quit the band. I'm not going to play the tuba anymore," Rory said. Mr. Beach hunkered down and leaned forward slightly. Rory felt his heart beating faster. Had he angered Mr. Beach the way he had angered Mr. Keltch? "So, I still want to do the lesson next week, to prepare for the concert, but it will be the last one."

"I see. That's too bad. You're still improving, and I think you will find something missing in your life when you no longer play music. Why are you stopping after all these years?" he asked.

"I want to do something else," Rory said, hoping to avoid explaining his reasons for leaving the band.

"Hmm. As I said, that's too bad," he paused for a few seconds, then asked, "Did you remember to bring the check?"

"Oh Jesus, sorry... I mean my language. Ah, I forgot to ask my mother again. I'll make sure and bring it next week." Rory felt like an idiot and a welcher, every time he forgot the monthly lesson check.

"Well, be sure to bring it next week, since it looks as if it will be your last."

Both of them remained silent while Rory packed his music and Mr. Beach packed his mouthpiece back into his carrying case. They left the room together, only exchanging goodbyes as Rory turned to put his tuba back on the shelf.

Chapter   6

Rory found Mr. Duggin in his classroom looking at experiment reports. When Rory walked into the room the teacher put down the paper he had been marking.

Rory asked if Mr. Duggin had any news regarding Mr. Ketlch's second letter, and Mr. Duggin began to update him on the situation.

"First, we need to be certain about whether or not he actually mailed it. I know he told you he intended to, but we aren't really sure. I wouldn't want to approach the Mortenson Board to try and fix something that doesn't need fixing.

"When I talked with Keltch, ah, *Mister* Keltch, to find out if the letter had been sent, he wouldn't say either way. He seemed uninterested in the matter. When I tried to explain what I believe your intentions are for pursuing a career in chemistry, he didn't react at all. So we still don't know what you might be up against, and we still need to find out if the letter is on its way. Until we know, there's nothing we can do.

"So after talking with Mr. Keltch, I talked with Mr. Butcher, which brought up another slight problem. He got a little miffed at me for letting him learn this late in the process, that you had applied for the scholarship. Since he's the head of the chemistry department, I should have informed him of your application long ago. But, that's my fault and now he knows. He thinks we should call up the Board and tell them what happened. He said if they know you are intent on pursuing a career in chemistry to the point of trimming your normal activities and making more time for chemistry, then your actions would be viewed in a positive light.

"He could be right, and he made me re-think your situation. I still think it's bad, but he gave us a card to play. I don't want to create an opportunity for them to question your character if we can avoid it. What do you think?"

Rory brushed his eyebrows with his index finger and thumb from the middle outward a few times, then said, "I don't know. I guess I'll try and talk with Mr. Keltch again to see if he's sent the letter."

"Yeah, and maybe you should talk with Mr. Butcher. I made an error, not keeping him in the loop about your application. Since he knows now, we should keep him informed of the whole situation."

"Yeah, okay. Next subject: How many people signed up to write the practice exams again?" he asked.

"Only about six. I guess chemistry exams haven't caught on as the latest after-school recreational activity around here yet. But I'm working on it."

"Did Ellis and Gill sign up?"

"No. Had they planned on writing?"

"Oh yeah, they're definitely writing the exam. Count them in."

———

The old, one-level ranch house out in the boonies, as Rory liked to describe where he lived, had asphalt shingles and white paint turned gray from the wind blasting it with grit. A collection of what appeared to be refuse cluttered the sparsely graveled driveway and the thinly grassed grounds nearby. Broken down lawn equipment, old saddles on tilted saw-horses, rusted bicycles, stacks of moving blankets (collected from who knows where, since they had never moved), a trampoline with shredded fabric, a non-working truck, a non-working car, his mother's car, his brother's car and his father's truck. Atop the house stood a television antenna. It bent at funny angles and resembled a broken clothes rack intertwined with a divining rod. Behind the house a thick twisted black wire served as the electric umbilical cord between the house and the unpainted barn where his father kept his horse, stacked some hay, and tinkered endlessly in his workshop.

Right of the barn at the base of the hill stood a small shed of faded gray wood. A window without glass sat in the middle of the wall. Chunks of cracked white putty barely hung on in the corners. The sides lacked a complete set of boards; the structure's doorway, beside the window, had rusted hinges but no door. The shed held an old dirt bike, a collection of retired sporting goods, and a few ropes his father used on cattle.

The trio of buildings sat in a coulee entered by a dirt-and-gravel road, a road that began at the end of a newly paved street in the latest phase of a newly built housing development.

A car drove up slowly and started a wide curve as if to pull a U-turn, then stopped in front of the house. The driver sat looking at the house, trying to decide if he had found the right place. Inside, Rory and his brother Pat watched the car, wondering if yet another motorist had turned down the wrong road.

After a minute or two the driver shut off the engine and got out of his car. Rory, recognizing him, said, "Shit, it's my music teacher. What the hell does he want?" He opened the door before the visitor knocked. "Hi Mr. Beach. What brings you out here?"

"Oh good, I found the right house," Mr. Beach said with relief. "Hi, Rory, I just wanted to drop in. How are you this evening?"

"I'm good. Come on in."

Rory led his guest into the family room where Mr. Beach asked if he could talk with his parents. Rory went to get his mother. He told her of their visitor's arrival and his request to talk with her, but he had no idea what the man wanted to talk about. She sighed, put down the newspaper, took a sip of her drink, and went out to meet Mr. Beach. Rory followed, then stood quietly listening.

"Hello, Mr. Beach," said Rory's mother. "It's been a long time. What can I do for you?"

"Well, I wanted to talk to you about Rory dropping out of music. I feel it would be a mistake for him to abandon something he's worked at for so many years. And I hoped I could convince you and your husband to talk Rory into continuing with his lessons and staying in the band."

"Yes. Well, Rory told us about quitting the band, and I guess if he doesn't want to do it any longer, why force him to do it? I mean, if he doesn't want to do it, he won't do a very good job at it, right?"

Mr. Beach smiled for a few seconds. He had hoped that Rory's parents hadn't been informed of Rory's decision to quit the band, so they would be shocked when they found out. He wanted them to be his allies in his effort to convince Rory to stay in music. He planned to explain to them how music becomes an important element in people's lives, that it opens up a whole new set of experiences for a person to enjoy. It provides a chance for a person to exercise their creativity and adds a new dimension in their life. The possibility that Rory's parents accepted his decision to drop out hadn't entered Mr. Beach's mind.

"Yes, well, what I wanted to say is, Rory is a good tuba player and the tuba is an important member of the band. The band is always weaker when it loses a tuba. I hope you will all reconsider."

"If he wants to reconsider it, okay. But, like I said, I'm not going to make him do something if his heart's not in it," his mother said dryly.

Mr. Beach stammered slightly when he added, "I...I just wanted you to know I think he is making a mistake and...and so does his band teacher. I feel like I would be, ah, avoiding a responsibility if I didn't let you know, ah, how I felt about a student dropping out of the band."

"Fine, thank you." Mrs. Coleman smiled politely and remained silent.

Mr. Beach cleared his throat and said in an overly friendly voice, "There is one last thing then; Rory forgot to bring the check for this month's lessons the other day. I figured I could pick it up while I was here. Next week is the last lesson so he won't have another opportunity to deliver the check if he forgets it again. Is that all right?"

"Sure," Mrs. Coleman said. She then went to write the check in the kitchen. Rory put his hands in his pockets and felt around trying to identify their contents. He pulled out a handful of coins and counted them before putting them back in his pocket to start his search again. This time he seemed to feel more coins so he pulled them out again, counted them once more and arrived at the same total. Back in the pocket. As his hand massaged the coins again, he could feel eyes watching his redundant search, eyes belonging to another music teacher who had come to spoil his plan for his future. Why won't these guys leave it alone? I don't want to play music any longer; why do they want to force me? Rory wanted Mr. Beach to leave, to get out of his house and to stop interfering with his life. He had no desire to make conversation with him. The overly long zone of uncomfortable silence ended when Mrs. Coleman called from the kitchen, "It's thirty-two dollars for four lessons, right?"

"That is correct," Mr. Beach called back in the direction of the kitchen.

"Wait, Mom. Just make it for three lessons." Rory looked Mr. Beach square in the eyes. "I don't think I'll go next week."

Mr. Beach frowned with his eyebrows but said nothing. They held a stare; then Mr. Beach turned away, shaking his head.

As Mrs. Coleman handed over the check, Rory's father came into the family room. He saw his wife passing a check to a stranger. With an inquisitive smile, he looked from the stranger to his wife, then back to the stranger before finally saying hello.

"This is Rory's music teacher." Mrs. Coleman explained. "He stopped by to pick up his check for the lessons he gave Rory."

"I thought Rory quit music."

"He did."

"So why are we paying him?"

"It's for the last three lessons. Rory forgot to ask me for a check."

"Gotcha," he said, then thanked Mr. Beach for all his help with Rory's lessons. He turned to Rory and said, "Tell me again why you're quitting the band."

"Dad, I've already told you. You said it was okay."

"Maybe I did, but I don't remember *why* it was okay. So tell me again why you're quitting the band."

Rory didn't miss the edge in his father's voice, but felt this topic had been discussed and settled between them long ago. Discussing it again, in front of a stranger whose arguments were opposed to his own, embarrassed him. And it could potentially reverse his father's thinking.

Mrs. Coleman slipped away to avoid involvement in the upcoming argument.

"Dad, I told you I wanted to drop out so I would have more time to study and work on my chemistry class. I've applied for a scholarship and I need to do extra work in chemistry to get it. And you said it was okay."

"Oh yeah, now I'm remembering. But not quite the way you said. I figured you were just trying to find a way to spend more time with what's her name. I still don't recall if you ever convinced me otherwise."

"You agreed, Dad. I told you I could do better in chemistry. I told you band had nothing more to offer me and you agreed," Rory stated heatedly. He stood straight and pulled his shoulders back while he took a half step forward.

"Yeah, but before, you used to say you could get a scholarship playing the tuba, and now you're saying you can't go anywhere in the band. What's the real story, Rory?" He turned to Mr. Beach. "You're his teacher; can he get a scholarship playing the tuba?"

"It's very likely. There are plenty—," Mr. Beach started to say, but was cut off.

"See, Rory, you could still get a scholarship with the band," Mr. Coleman threw back at Rory.

"Dad, I don't want to go through college playing the tuba, and you already agreed I could drop band. Don't you remember? Are you going back on your word?" Rory began to raise his voice.

"If I gave my word, I don't remember it. And I don't want you missing an opportunity to go to college. Seems like the tuba may be the best way to do it, is all." He turned back to Mr. Beach. "He's determined to drop the band... but I still think he needs to stay in."

Mr. Beach nodded in agreement and then confirmed it by saying, "I think it would be the best thing for everyone."

"I agree. Rory, I think you should plan on staying in the band."

"But Dad, we've already been through it, and you said—"

"I don't think I agreed, Rory. I don't think I said you could quit," he finished in a discussion-ending voice.

Mr. Beach thanked him for the check and quickly said goodbye.

Rory's father watched from the family room window as the car disappeared around the hill that blocked their view of the city.

"Is he some kind of a mistrusting tightwad that has to drive all the way out here to get his money?" asked Rory's father.

But, Rory didn't answer. He had already left the room.

———

With only eight students writing the second practice chemistry exam, the exercise took place in Mr. Duggin's classroom. Mr. Duggin sorted the test papers as he leaned against the front of his desk. "Before I hand out the exams, I need to ask for your help. Since next week is the last week of school, I will be doing an inventory of the lab equipment. And I'm authorized to pay two students, ten dollars each, for assisting me. I hope I can find a couple of volunteers in this group of obvious chemistry devotees, to help me for a couple of days after school. Any takers?"

The students all lowered their eyes or looked sideways at each other so they wouldn't be asked silently by Mr. Duggin's direct look of inquiry.

"Come on, you all. It's an easy ten bucks."

Rory looked over his left shoulder at Ellis, who hunched and looked down to avoid Rory's gaze. Rory cleared his throat, bringing Ellis' focus off of the desktop and over to him. He raised his eyebrows as if to say,"'Well?" causing Ellis to volunteer both his and Gill's services for the inventory.

"Great, I really appreciate the help. And to top it off, I'll order in pizza and sodas," Mr. Duggin said.

"Now, let's get to the matter at hand. Harry," he said, as he walked to Harry's desk and handed him an exam, "Do you agree with me, that what you hold in your hands is the chemistry exam for students in the eleventh grade?"

Harry looked it over, then looked up at Mr. Duggin and nodded.

"Good. I think you will find it a little more challenging than the last one you wrote. Good luck."

Harry shook his head. Mr. Duggin passed out the rest of the papers.

Victoria was first to finish the exam. She didn't go back over any of the sections. She packed up her books, handed in her test and left.

After Rory finished, he sat quietly at his desk. When Ellis was done, they both got up to hand in their papers. They left the classroom together and waited outside for Gill.

"Dirty trick, Rory. You've just committed blackmail, you know."

"It's not blackmail, it's punishment. Besides, you're getting paid and it gives you a chance to suck up to Mr. Duggin."

"Yeah, right," Ellis said without much enthusiasm. "What do you do in an inventory?"

"I did it last year. When we first started, we counted the test tubes and equipment he had on this big list of stuff that is supposed to be in the lab. After a while he noticed most of the stuff had spots and grunge on it, so we ended up cleaning it while we counted. Gruesome work, if I ever saw it."

"On the behalf of Gill and myself, may I take this opportunity to thank you again."

"Sure... but remember: It's the least, not the last, I could do."

The door to the classroom opened and out walked Harry.

"How did it go, Harry?" Ellis asked.

Harry stopped and looked at the freshman. He hadn't spoken to one for the entire year and he wasn't going to start now. He turned to Rory and said, "I'm screwed."

―――――

Two days later, Rory leaned against the trophy case in the hallway near the main entrance doors when Victoria approached him.

"Hi, Rory. I picked up your chemistry exam for you. I didn't find you at your locker, so I was taking it back to the classroom. But here you are," she said in a friendly manner.

"Oh, now wait a minute here," he said with mock suspicion, "You've got my paper, so you've seen my score and you've come to gloat because you beat me and you wanted to see my reaction when you kicked my ass, right?"

"Wrong. I asked Mr. Duggin to fold the top page so I couldn't see your score. So, after you've looked at yours, I'll tell you my score and you can announce the winner. Happy?"

"You said you could care less who won. What happened?"

She smiled at him and raised her eyebrows. He turned his back and hunched over his paper, exaggerating his attempt to prevent her from seeing his score. Before he unfolded the top page, he looked back at Victoria, faking concern that she might look over his shoulder to try and get a glimpse. He then quickly flipped the page open to see the score and just as quickly folded it back again.

He turned to her with his chin high in the air to look down his nose at her. His right eyebrow cocked as he said, "Okay, what did you get?"

"Eighty-eight."

He lost all of his phony airs when he heard the score. "You got three wrong? How did you manage to get three wrong?"

"I guess I hurried too much. What did you get? Did you beat me?"

He smiled sheepishly and nodded.

"Good for you. Did you get a hundred? Acing a final exam would really be something."

She displayed no disappointment at being out-scored. When he first indicated he had a higher score, he had expected her to jump all over him about notching up another victory. But, instead of ranting about being too competitive, she actually acted quite pleasant.

"No, not a hundred." He said. "I still have a little studying to do. I got ninety-six."

They flipped through the exams looking at their errors. Victoria had gotten the right answer to the question Rory had wrong, so they could determine the correct answers to all of the questions as they went over them together.

When they had accomplished this task, they stood silently, both searching for something to talk about. He found himself staring into her eyes and noticing how clear they looked and how the dark brown pupils made the whites look whiter. Then he noticed her smiling at him as if to say, Go ahead, enjoy looking at my eyes.

He looked away.

"Oh, I'm not taking music lessons from your father any more." He paused. "I thought I'd let you know. You know, 'cause last time I assumed you knew I took lessons from your dad and you kind of got mad at me."

"Yeah I know. I shouldn't have. The mustard thing got to me. It really bummed me out."

"Well, I don't blame you. But, mustard thing aside, the last time I passed you at your locker, I acted kind of short with you. I was mad about Mr. Keltch." Rory felt his face heat up and he knew it would turn red. The thought of Mr. Keltch made his ears swollen and hot. "Anyway, I phoned you to apologize."

"I phoned you back, you know, but you had gone out. I knew I could catch up with you the next day and talk to you. But then the mustard hit the fan. Anyway, so what's up with you and Mr. Keltch?"

"He's mad at me for quitting the band."

"You quit band? I didn't know. Why did you quit band, especially when juniors get to go on the band trip?"

"Oh, I hadn't thought about the trip. Damn! The trip would have been fun. But, anyway, I got tired of the early morning thing and I wasn't getting much out of the music anymore, so I figured I could use the extra period for study hall or to take an extra math class. I explained this to Keltch, but he only got pissed. I didn't expect him to be happy about it but I think he's gone a little bit overboard."

"You'd think he'd realize you're better at chemistry than you are at music, so you're better off doing more in chemistry," she said sympathetically.

"Right. But not him. At first I felt bad, you know, guilty. I always liked him but now I think he only cares about himself and his shortage of tubas. My god, what is his band going to sound like when it's missing a tuba player?" He gave Victoria a look of shock, then continued, "So now I don't feel guilty at all. He's not concerned about my best interests; therefore I'm not concerned about his. Anyway, I phoned you that night, to apologize for being so short with you. I thought I acted like a jerk."

"Me too," she looked up, agitated. "Whoa, not you acting like a jerk, I mean I acted like a jerk too, a couple of times."

"Yeah, it's okay. Oh, here comes Alyse." He looked at Victoria's brown eyes and got stuck again; a deep black dot centered in a dark brown pupil surrounded by solid bright white. Under the point of her right eye he spotted a tiny freckle. He checked for Victoria's smile and happily saw its approval once more. "I better go. Good luck in the finals next week."

"You too. See ya."

———

On the last day of the school year, Victoria had no classes and no exams. She had come to the school to attend the final assembly. When it ended, she went to her locker to get some of the things she would need over the summer.

When she opened her locker, a small envelope dropped out onto the floor. In a poor imitation of a ransom note, the printing on the front had been deliberately garbled. It said, "From the Mustard Guys."

Inside the envelope was twenty dollars.

Chapter 7

      Every morning before sunrise, Rory caught a ride with his brother, who had a summer job as the morning man at the SuperFast gas station just off of the interstate.

      Pat would drop him off at the municipal golf course where Rory would play the back nine for fifty cents, then walk or take the bus to the school to wait for Alyse. She was re-taking the math class she had failed during the spring semester. Rory sat and read in a small compound on the west side of the school while waiting for Alyse. He usually had an hour of reading time to kill before her class finished. When it did, she left the school from the front exit and start walking home. Rory walked around the school to meet her and sometimes, when he managed to keep track of the time, he would wait out front so they could walk together. Most times he didn't pay attention to his watch, and kept on reading. On those occasions, he would catch up to her somewhere along the way, or if he read way too long, he went to her house where she waited inside. She had never been aware that he read on the other side of the school while waiting for her, and never wondered why sometimes he walked her home and other times he arrived later.

Alyse's father worked during the day and her mother tended duties with the local cattlemen's association each afternoon until two o'clock. This meant Rory and Alyse had the house to themselves for a few hours.

Her parents, of course, had laid down the rules:

Alyse couldn't leave the house until she completed her homework and reviewed the math covered in the morning's class. After that, her girlfriends could come over or she could go out. But Rory could never enter the house, under any circumstances, until after her mother had come home. This complicated how they would go about violating this rule.

To avoid being seen entering the house together, a block away from Alyse's home Rory would split off, leaving Alyse to follow her regular route and go into the house alone. Rory would go around the block and come back down the alley from the opposite end, then enter the yard of the working couple who lived next door. He would hop the fence between the two houses into Alyse's yard. Lifting his golf bag over the fence proved to be difficult, due to the extra care he had to take to insure it didn't drop and create a lot of clatter as the steel shafts banged against each other and the sidewalk. He left the bag between the houses until his departure, when he would heave it over the fence again on the way out.

In the yard, he crouched and ran to stand beside the garage before making his way to the back door. This limited the risk of being seen by the nosey neighbors from across the alley.

Alyse watched his covert maneuvers from inside the house. First, from a window on the side of the house, where she could see him hop the fence, then from a window at the back to watch him scamper across the backyard to the door. When he finally arrived inside, she would make fun of the effort he put forth so they could break the rules and have some time alone.

Once inside the house, he grabbed her and she didn't resist. They held onto each other while they kissed until Rory's hands started to explore. Then she would push him away and ask him to help her with her math. They wrestled a little, but eventually opened the books and got to work. After all, when the math ended, they could do whatever they wanted. He always wanted to feel her naked skin, and since she had a willingness to satisfy his wants, he complied eagerly with her request for math help in order to get the homework over with.

Alyse's schooling would eat the first six weeks of the summer and when it finished her family vacation would consume the remainder. When she asked Rory about his family vacation, he laughed and said they all took separate vacations; his started every day when he left the house.

During the math homework, she always received a number of phone calls from her girlfriends, which involved planning the afternoon's and evening's activities. Rory would sit trying not to listen, so Alyse tested him by joking with her girlfriends about the things she and Rory were doing and calling them math exercises. Rory always blushed at her innuendoes, and became aroused by the thought of what she implied. He silently urged her to get off the phone so they could get the math work over with and start some real exercising. By the time they completed the math, they usually had less than an hour before her mother got home.

Most days the telephone interruptions resulted in arrangements for her to meet her girlfriends at the mall. On those days, after some long kisses and some touching under her shirt, a disappointed Rory would head back out through the neighbor's yard and meet Alyse a block or so down the street. At the mall he would hang around with her and her friends for only a short period of time. Dragging a set of golf clubs around the mall proved cumbersome, and Alyse seemed more interested in talking with her girlfriends than paying attention to him. So eventually he would leave her with her friends and go to find out what Gary and Harry had planned.

Some days Rory's father disrupted this routine when he needed an extra hand on one of the ranches where he did some cowboy work. He would enlist Rory's services and provide him with a day's hard work. Rory always complained, but when his father told him the work had its rewards-- meaning he got paid--the complaining stopped. He hated the work, but of all the methods available for him to make some cash, this one had the fewest drawbacks.

Manual labor didn't make the list of Rory's favorite things. He loved to work hard with his mind, on subjects and activities that really interested him. Things of no interest, he considered tedious, time-consuming delays that prevented him from getting on with the rest of his life. The days working with his father felt like the longest days of the summer, especially when he thought about what he would have been doing with Alyse. His father, with one or two other men, would work a ranch performing tasks on the rancher's cows. Sometimes they branded, other times they nutted the young bulls. On the days the work involved handling calves, they always tried to get Rory's help. Rory was big enough to lift and throw one, and strong enough to flatass it if he had to handle its rear end. Usually in the summer the calves required some kind of inoculation, so they used a team of four men plus his father's working dogs.

The dogs would hold the calves in one corner of a corral, until the ropers called them off so a calf could be cut loose from the herd. The ropers snagged the calf at both ends and, with the bellowing animal wide-eyed and drooling on the ground, a third man would give the calf an injection. Afterwards, Rory cleaned the needle in a bucket of disinfectant and refilled the syringe with the correct amount of medicine. By the time he finished, the next head had been stretched out on the ground and the man would reach back to receive the needle again. Repetitive, monotonous work. At least he didn't have to lift and throw the beast, or hold down the shitty end while they castrated the bewildered animal. For this he got about four bucks an hour; but he only received pay for the time actually working the animals. The often long travel time, plus loading and unloading the horses, didn't count. He did these long days about once a week to keep himself in spending money, always glad to have done it but never wanting to do it again.

On the days when Rory worked with his father, Alyse would walk home alone, expecting Rory to show up at any minute. She would look out the side window and wait for him to show up in the neighbor's yard. When he didn't, she would remember he had told her about working that day. She would look at her books on the table, then go into her room and lie on the bed until one of her girlfriends called. She would take the calls in the kitchen and do her work while talking on the phone. She made numerous errors and took more time to get the work done. When she did finally finish, she usually had to rush to the mall to meet the girls, because of the extra time it had taken to do the homework. She missed Rory on these days, preferring the days when she felt his touch on her skin and his body's warmth along the length of her as they lay on the floor.

On the days after Rory's absence, Alyse usually kept the phone calls brief, and concentrated on the homework in order to finish as fast as possible. When they finished early, they had more time for each other and they would get more intimate. On one of those days when they had finished her homework early, she closed the books and stood up from her chair, swinging her leg over Rory so she sat straddling him. She looked him in the eye and then kissed him long and soft. She broke the kiss, then sat straight upright, smiling at him while she crossed her arms and grabbed the bottom of her shirt in both hands, then raised and uncrossed them to remove her shirt.

Rory stared open-mouthed at the seam of her cleavage showing above her bra. His hands moved up the smooth bare skin of her sides, while his chest pounded, fluttered and heaved. He slipped his right hand around her back and under her bra strap, then slowly brought it forward to cup her breast. It was uncomfortable. The tightness of the bra forced him to hold his wrist bent backwards, restricting the movement of his hand and preventing his full enjoyment of her wonderful skin. His left hand reached around her back to release the bra. But the clasp's workings totally mystified him. He twisted and pressed and squeezed, trying to get some pressure going in opposite directions so the damn thing would open. He experienced difficulty concentrating on this frustrating task while simultaneously trying to enjoy the soft, warm breast he held in his other hand.

Alyse reached back and flipped the clasp open, instantly releasing the pressure from his wrist. "She must think I'm totally inexperienced with women and bras" he thought. A wave of embarrassment washed over him, but it passed quickly when he breathed in the slightly musky smell of her warm skin and focused on the sensations he gained from the touch of her naked breasts.

His left hand had moved around to her front. Now he held both of the world's most perfect breasts, and felt their weight in his palms. He looked up at her with a smile and saw her smiling back. She bent down and kissed him as he softly kneaded her flesh. They kissed for a long time until he broke to push her upright again. He stared into her eyes, then lifted his hands and her loosely hanging bra so he could view her dark nipples and see the complete mounds for the first time. Alyse held the back of his head in her hands, her fingers laced and woven into his dark brown hair. Looking up at her, he suddenly felt a deep, stirring urge in his groin and he wondered if she would satisfy this heat. He turned his eyes down and away, slightly embarrassed yet anxiously hopeful, wondering if she noticed his hardened state. Days later he still wondered if she too had an urge like the one he had felt.

As the summer moved on, they proceeded further with their intimacies and allowed their desire for each other to reign a little more freely. He often removed her bra, making her naked above the waist. Then one day he removed his own shirt so they could embrace skin against skin, and she responded with heightened urgency to his touch and the new form of contact. Cool at first, then with their combined warmth, melting together. Pressing against each other hard, they yearned for deeper contact. One day Rory ventured tentatively to undo the button and zipper of her blue jeans. She held her breath. Her eyes popped back and forth from her waistline to his eyes as his hand slid inside her panties. His hand roamed over her soft pubic hair for a moment then moved further down. His groin pulsed. He could feel it drawing blood and energy from his entire torso. When he noticed her lying rigid, without reaction, he removed his hand, kissing her, slowing things down.

When he left that day, he felt the same guilt he always felt after she allowed his hands and eyes to caress her naked skin. He took pleasure from her, but after seeing her rigid daze, he wondered if she took any pleasure from him. She moved and responded to his touch as if she enjoyed their play, but she almost never initiated any advancement of their actions or expressed a preference in their bodily contact. Did she really want to do these things with him? He knew he wanted to do them with her, but did he want it all with Alyse?

For a week or so after that session, there seemed a distance between them. He still wondered if she enjoyed their explorations, or if she merely endured him and his enjoyment. Then he felt guilty, because only now did he start thinking about her expectations, when the explorations had been going on for a number of weeks. Was he so caught up in his own pleasure that maybe everything he did, he did wrong? He'd never experienced any of these things before, so how would he know? Maybe she became detached from their activities because he didn't know what he was doing.

At this point, he had tied himself into such an emotional knot that he avoided starting anything physical. One day when they had plenty of time for naked exploration, instead of getting amorous, he asked if she wanted to play golf.

"Golf?" she said, "That's not what we do now." And she proceeded to unbutton his shirt while pulling him over to the sofa. They kissed for a long time. Finally she asked him why he seemed less interested. He felt his face flush when he asked her if he did things the right way. She said she didn't know. She had never done any of these things before, but she liked them. He smiled at hearing what he needed to hear. A warm sensation grew inside him again. It spread hot from his groin and made him heady with thoughts of sexual athleticism, until she frowned and told him that sometimes while they rubbed each other, she felt guilty. She wondered what her mother would say if she knew what her daughter did, alone in the house with a boy. When these feelings of guilt overcame her, she didn't know if she wanted to keep playing or stop their touching forever.

The rapid extinguishing of the hot sensation culminated with Rory apologizing for creating these feelings of guilt. He told her he didn't want her to do anything she didn't want to do. She smiled and kissed him. While they kissed, her hand reached down and began to press and squeeze his erection through his jeans. The hot sensation rose in him again as she undid his button and zipper. He didn't stop her. He soon achieved his first sexual release produced by a companion.

When Rory's time to hop over the fence on his way out arrived, the golf bag seemed lighter, his frustration level lower; he existed in a relaxed state of bliss. He now considered himself to be experiencing sex.

From that point onward, they ended their play each day with her hands setting him free.

Alyse and her family were leaving for their vacation soon, so she and Rory wouldn't see each other for the last two weeks of the summer. He yearned for the sexual encounters they would miss and the yearning made him much more eager for the sessions to come before their separation.

Alyse finished school on the Thursday of the last week of class. The next morning had all the makings of a good one. No waiting at the school, and no homework, meant bonus time. Excited about spending their last day together before her vacation, Rory came up with a pretty good excuse to get out of working with his father. Free for the day, he still accepted a ride from his brother, and because his brother left so early, Rory still played the back nine at the golf course. But that morning his game resembled pedestrian polo more than golf. He got his round out of the way, and then did a speed walk to Alyse's house. Bounding over the neighbor's fence with extra spring in his legs, he flew high and landed soft before doing the crouch-run to the back door. Alyse let him in and they went into her living room. They sat looking at each other, occasionally kissing between snippets of small talk, while Rory waited for an opportunity to start something a little more undressed.

"We have some time today. What would you like to do?" Rory asked.

"Since we aren't going to see each other for a long time, I thought we could do something special," she said, with a smile that rang chimes in Rory's groin.

He took a deep breath. When he exhaled, the air stuttered out of his lungs. "Like what?"

"Let's go in my room, draw the curtains, make it dark and romantic, then get completely naked. We've never felt each other completely naked."

"Okay, sounds good. Yeah, good! Okay, let's," Rory babbled.

As he stood to walk to her room, his legs weakened and he felt conspicuous as they walked. He had been in her bedroom before, but those times he had only hoped something good would happen. This invitation to get naked with her left no doubt of whether or not he would see her body and touch her skin as completely as he wanted to.

They entered her room and closed the door. He stood like a zombie, watching her close the curtains. Then she shocked him by pulling down the covers of the bed to expose the sheets. It hit him; they were going to bed together! She walked over to him and put her arms around him so she could hold him for a minute. She stepped back and they stood smiling at each other, until she raised her eyebrows and started to remove her clothes. It hadn't occurred to them that the act of undressing each other could heighten their pleasure, so they stood facing each other, removing their clothes as if undressing in a locker room. They both hesitated when they began to remove their jeans. Even though they had been inside each other's jeans with their hands, they hadn't removed their below-the-waist clothing before. They remained shy about revealing their anatomy's most personal points of interest. They turned away out of modesty and removed the garments, then with shy smiles turned back to face each other's nudity.

Observations registered as they stood in a state of frozen amazement. Their eyes bounced from place to place over each other's body, a real body fully nude, seen in person for the first time.

Alyse stepped to the bed and climbed in. She lay on her side and let Rory continue to observe her soft shape for a while longer. Finally, with a knowing smile, she made him come join her on the bed. He lay on top of her, looked into her eyes and took deep breaths, appreciating the situation and searching for a clue as to what to do next.

"You can't go inside, Rory. Promise me you won't go inside."

He continued to stare into her eyes and said, "I won't." And he made a silent promise to himself to get some condoms soon.

They touched each other; they kissed each other; they drew back to look again at each other's body. They spent a long time on slow caresses, while contemplating what the summer had meant to them. They exchanged the pleasure they had each built up for each other over the past six weeks. They didn't think of this moment as their last fling of summer. They thought of it as the beginning of a new part of their lives, to be directed by their desires.

Later, when Rory left her house, he had help when he jumped the fence. Help partly from his good mood, and help because he wasn't carrying his golf bag. It lay forgotten on the sidewalk at the side of the house.

That night, he and Alyse went to a movie as a last date before she went away. When he met her at her house and they first saw each other, they smiled meaningful smiles to each other. But the remainder of the evening seemed a little odd to Rory. They talked small talk without any real conversation. He noticed after a while she would no longer look him in the eye. "Maybe she's a little embarrassed," he thought. He felt a little embarrassed as well, still wondering if she had enjoyed their afternoon and if the things he had done for her had made her happy. When he left her at her house, he left by the front door. So he didn't discover his forgotten golf bag.

The next morning, as Alyse's family packed and loaded their car, her father found the set of golf clubs. He casually mentioned them to Alyse and his wife, but both expressed no idea as to how they came to rest beside the house. Her father pressed the issue a little, and her mother looked at her suspiciously before asking Alyse if anyone had been at the house the day before.

Alyse hesitated briefly before she answered, "Yes. A couple of my girlfriends stopped by and on the way over here they ran into Rory."

"I told you he couldn't come in the house during the day. Don't you listen?" her mother asked angrily.

"He only stopped by with the girls. He didn't come in, he just wanted to make sure about going to a movie and then he left. I guess he left his golf clubs behind."

"If I find out you let him in this house, you're in big trouble, little girl. I shouldn't allow you to hang out with boys anyway."

With this bit of suspicion in the air, the family left on their two weeks of fun and relaxation. Alyse spent the whole vacation dodging her mother's attempts to trip her up and find out what had been going on in the house all summer. She also had to listen to a non-stop lecture on the behavior of young ladies.

Her mother was relentless.

Chapter 8

Victoria found the high humidity of Florida's gulf coast claustrophobic and uncomfortable. The only thing she found good about the humidity was that her oboe reeds didn't dry out as quickly as they did back home. She appreciated the reduced need to continually moisten them during her rests.

She had enjoyed renewing her friendships with the students she had met in previous years and meeting new students to start new friendships.

The students had to live with a grueling music schedule packed with rehearsals, tutorials, and more rehearsals. Somehow the administration found time for two breaks each day to allow students to relax and enjoy their surroundings.

Rehearsals for the entire orchestra included a long session in the morning and a shorter one in the early evening. The afternoon consisted of a sectional breakout session with, in Victoria's case, a group of five other oboists, practicing and exchanging techniques.

During the afternoon session, a German tutor put them through their paces. Werner Brock was a graduate student from the University of Berlin. He had been a student at the camp a number of years earlier, before Victoria had ever attended. He was young and slender; his long blonde hair swept across his forehead and flipped slightly at the ends of his bangs. His eyes were blue, his cheekbones high, his nose pointed and a little thin for his face. He wanted to make his tutorship at the camp an annual event, so he worked his group very hard while also trying to make it fun. His group's evaluation of his tutoring was an important factor in determining whether he would be invited back next year, so he paid close attention to creating a good relationship with each of the group members. He tried to talk and joke with his students in a peer-to-peer manner, even though light banter, especially in English, didn't come easy for him. To show he cared for his group, he would even sit in with his oboists during the full rehearsal to provide additional tutoring. Victoria and two other girls in her afternoon session agreed that Werner was cute.

Since the three girls had last been together, there had been some additions to their interests in life. In the past they had talked about the music they performed, the music they listened to, movies, movie stars, school, and their plans for their musical future. This year, they added the topic of boys and discovered the returning girls in the other woodwind groups also had a deep interest in talking about boys. At first these discussions revolved around the 'boys back home', but after the girls realized the 'boys in camp' were noticing the girls of the woodwind sections, all boy talk revolved around the males in the near vicinity.

Between the morning rehearsal and the afternoon breakout sessions, the attendees took a long lunch break, which included a little time to enjoy some of the Florida beach scene. Many of the female students would skip lunch to work on their tans, either by the pool or on the beach, while the boys would goof off with some diving or try a little body surfing. What the boys ended up doing depended on where the girls decided to work on their tans, and then both groups spent the entire break within fifty feet of each other. Despite this proximity, the two sexes had very little interaction and those were limited to short snippets of conversation.

"You girls should quit laying around and try some bodysurfing," said a boy.

"You guys should stay under water longer; it's so much more peaceful when you do," replied a girl.

"Hey, you want me to spread lotion on your back for you?" asked another boy.

"Sure, some time when I'm hard up," replied another girl.

After each of these interactions, the boy walked away shaking his head and the girls conducted a long discussion regarding the worthiness of the boy who had attempted to engage them in a conversation. The discussion involved some teasing and interrogating, as each girl tried to find out if any of the others found the boy attractive.

Victoria participated, offering nothing positive to say regarding any of the boys. She found them all rather plain, uninteresting, and not much to look at. Despite her continuous negative input, the other girls always wanted her opinion. They enjoyed Victoria's biting satire as she ridiculed the finer points of the poor fellow who wandered into their sights.

After a few weeks of the camp, one of the girls had asked Victoria if she found any of the boys even halfway worth looking at. When she said no, they asked her what a boy had to look like in order to get her attention. She said she didn't know; she never really thought about it. But the question disquieted her, and became one she asked herself often for the remainder of the summer. To answer the question, images of young television or movie stars popped into her head and she chopped them up, taking parts of each to build the perfect boy. She did this to keep her mind off the track she knew she would eventually follow.

After a week or two of fighting the idea, she started to let the boy she was building become Rory. When she finally did admit to herself that Rory interested her, she pulled her finger out of the dike, allowed the dam to break, and thought of him every night. About how she had wanted him for a friend and realized she also wanted more. Why did she want more, and when had she started wanting it? She avoided thinking about how much time Rory and his girlfriend spent together back in Montana. Her reluctance to concede that it might be a lot, and her embarrassment at hoping it would be only a little, made her chuckle at herself.

She discovered she wanted the summer to end so she could go back to school. She also realized that when she did go back, seeing Rory with his girlfriend would present some difficulties. This thought saddened her. She had to keep telling herself to snap out of it and not get herself too worked up. He had a girlfriend; he had never showed the slightest hint of interest in her except when he had looked in her eyes that day. She fell into the funk of losing at love before she'd had love to lose.

One day, with three weeks of camp remaining, the girls lay tanning on deck chairs, half-snoozing in the warm humid air. One of the girls asked Victoria, "What's going on with you and Werner?"

"Me and Werner? What do you mean?" Victoria asked back in a drowsy voice. She left her head on the pillow she had fashioned from a towel.

"I think he has the hots for you. Haven't you noticed how he watches you almost all of the time? And how he asks you to play solo more often than he does the rest of us?"

"He does not," she said, in an awakened staccato voice.

"Oh, yes he does. He's trying to get your attention and you just play your music and go about your business. It's probably driving him nuts the way you seem so uninterested."

"I don't think so. Besides, he's old. Why would he be interested in a sixteen-year-old girl?" Victoria said. She rose onto her elbows.

"He's not old, probably twenty or so. You watch him today, you'll see. He's trying to redefine the tutor-student relationship. Plus, he's been here a long time so he's probably getting horny."

"Thanks... a guy has to have four weeks of horniness behind him in order to take an interest in me."

"Every guy here has four weeks of horny going for him. We should all be really popular."

During the afternoon's session, Victoria paid closer attention to the tutor's actions. She casually observed him out of the corner of her eye. It did seem as though he faced her direction most of the time. When she risked a direct glance at him, she found his eyes already locked onto hers. When he stopped the group's playing, and the group instinctively looked up at the tutor, he always gave Victoria a slight nod before he addressed the group.

Victoria's friend kept an eye on the interaction between Victoria and Werner. Whenever Victoria noticed Werner's attention, she looked away from him and over to her friend, who raised her eyebrows and silently mouthed, "See?"

At the end of the group session, Werner informed the students he planned to join them again during the evening's full rehearsal. He informed them of the envy he felt every evening when he sat and listened to them play. How it reminded him of the enjoyment he had felt during the rehearsals when he had attended the camp as a student. He was happy that the conductor allowed him to play along with his students.

The other girls teased Victoria throughout dinner. They reminded her of the way Werner kept his eyes on her during the afternoon sessions, and said he probably joined the orchestra in the evening so he could be close to her and impress her with his own musical ability. In her normal, calm manner, she had allowed them to go on without giving them any reaction for their efforts. Inside she churned with dread and excitement. What if they were right?

When the rehearsal began, Werner sat in the chair beside Victoria and shared her music stand. In his previous appearances, he had always sat in a chair behind her. Victoria felt an elbow nudge her in the ribs. When she turned, her friend smiled and again silently mouthed, "See?"

Victoria and Werner played side by side, reading the same sheet music. She noticed he played extremely well and that, acting gentlemanly, he took over the page-turning duties on the stand. A few times during rests, he would quietly make technical comments to her about the music, usually regarding the composer's markings and the way the conductor ignored them deliberately.

When the rehearsal ended, she turned to leave but stopped when she heard her name. She turned back toward Werner.

"You played very well tonight," he said. "I enjoyed playing along beside you."

"Thank you. I... I enjoyed it too, I guess." She smiled and turned to leave again.

"I would be very interested in talking with you about what your plans are with your music. Why don't you come to the afternoon session a little early tomorrow, so we can talk?"

She stopped with her back toward him and hesitated before turning to face him. He stood with his head slightly tilted and his neck craning forward to punctuate his question.

"I usually hang out at the beach during the break. You know, try to enjoy a little of the Florida sunshine."

"Yes, of course. Well, I'm always in the room early if you would like to stop by. And don't worry, I don't bite," he said with an easy smile.

Victoria laughed a nervous laugh, then turned and walked away.

During the noon-hour break the next day, Werner's hypnotic, trance-like obsession with Victoria topped all subjects of the girls' discussion, and became the subject of most of their jokes. Victoria confessed that she didn't know what she should do. She didn't really want to talk to him about her plans for a career in music, and she didn't want to talk to him for the sake of conversation. At the same time, she didn't want to be rude and completely ignore him, either.

The other girls had plenty of suggestions regarding how she should address the situation. One suggested she go and throw herself at him, to call his bluff. Another came up with the idea of going in early, but not too early. Then, with limited time, he couldn't try anything funny—unless she wanted him to try something funny, in which case she should go in real early. A third plan involved going early but not showering after sweating on the beach; then he wouldn't try anything because she would be a smelly turnoff.

In the end, she decided to extend him the courtesy of conversation. She would go a little early and she would indeed shower. The others called her a hussy and a gold-digger trying to set a trap for the poor old man in order to bilk him out of his musical secrets. She accepted their ribbing and went off to what they referred to as her torrid rendezvous.

She found Werner alone in the group room. When she entered the room, he stood smiling broadly, as if he hadn't expected her. They sat and talked about music, education paths, and careers. When Victoria's friends arrived earlier than they normally did, he said he had enjoyed their talk and to please come again the next day.

She did.

For the remainder of the camp she would go once or twice a week to talk with Werner. They gradually moved away from music and began to talk about more personal subjects, like where they lived. He had heard of Montana, and he enjoyed her stories of life in the west. She found it incredible that he lived in a split city surrounded by a communist country.

At night she thought about him and what would happen if a relationship developed between them. He, an older man; she, an underage but mature teenager. They could probably make it work age-wise. But what about the distance between where they lived? Her parents would never let her go to a city surrounded by an unfriendly nation to visit with an older man. Certainly not while she was still a minor. And he couldn't come to live in Montana without being arrested just for thinking about being with her! At this point in her nightly imaginations, she chastised herself for foolish fantasies.

Even though she knew she had the freedom to start a romantic relationship with anyone she wished, she knew it would never happen with Werner. He really hadn't done or said anything to indicate a desire for anything beyond friendship.

She remained perplexed. Every night she allowed these ponderings to distract her. But eventually her thoughts would turn to Rory, where she felt ease, comfort and fulfillment. A boy she liked, and one who lived where she lived. Along with the feeling of comfort, she ached with a premonition of the void she would soon be forced to live with; the void of being near to him, but not near enough.

During the last week of camp, and two days before the final concert that six weeks of rehearsing had been preparing them for, Victoria sat with Werner in the group session room. They talked about the camp, and how each felt about going home. They knew that soon they had to say goodbye, and they both tried to keep the conversation on other topics in order to delay their farewells. Finally, during a brief silence, Werner stood and walked to Victoria, offering a piece of paper to her.

"This is my mailing address. I hope perhaps we could write to each other. You know, keep in touch." He stopped to see her reaction, then asked, "Do you think you would write to me?"

She thought about this, then said, "Yeah, sure. I could do that."

"It would require that you provide me with your address, so I could write back, you know. Would that be okay?"

"Yes."

"Okay, great." He stood beside her, smiling. It made her feel a little uncomfortable. Then he said, "Victoria, I have enjoyed your company very much this summer. The time went by too fast, I think."

He stepped a little closer to her and lifted his hand to lightly run the back of his first two fingers down her cheek and around to the front of her chin. He tilted her face slightly upward. She saw him begin to bend down as if to kiss her. She looked down and away, slipping her chin off his fingers, leaving his hand suspended in air. He dropped it to his side.

"I would have liked to have seen you more often, Victoria. But listen to me. I find the voice I wished to speak with, too late." He paused and then let out a sigh. "I would like to find a way to see you again, before we return to the camp next year. But I can't think of one. I have become rather stricken with you, in case you haven't noticed. I want you to know I will look forward to seeing you again. Do you think you will be back next year?"

Victoria kept her eyes on the floor, trying with difficulty to take in his words. *This really is more than being friendly. He wants this to be more.*

"If they invite me back, I guess I will. My father would have a fit if I didn't come to camp. He is so gung-ho about me and my music," she said, not wanting to directly address the topic of seeing him again. "If you lend me your pen and a piece of paper, I'll write down my address for you."

Werner retrieved a pen from his music stand and handed her a writing pad on which she scribbled down her address. He stood silently watching her.

"There. Well, I guess the others will arrive soon. Are we going over the concert material again?" she said.

The next day she stayed on the beach for the entire break. Lying in bed after the evening rehearsal, she thought about Werner for a long time. She felt like she should have acknowledged the special feelings he had revealed and she felt guilty for leaving him without doing so. At the same time, she felt flattered. An older man had expressed a desire for her! She again entertained thoughts of letting some type of relationship grow out of this encounter. It had to be desire on his part; after all, he touched her cheek and leaned down to kiss her. Then she felt embarrassed about not knowing how to react when he tried to let her know about his feelings for her.

She would see him again at the final concert and she would say goodbye to him then. Should she let him know she was aware he tried to tell her something? But, what if he wasn't? After considerable thought, and many changes in her approach to saying goodbye, she decided she would thank him for his great tutoring and for taking the time to talk with her. Then she would promise to write and to let him know how her school band progressed over the coming year. She rehearsed her lines, intending to keep things light and charming.

At the end of the concert, she delivered her lines as she had planned. When she had said her piece, she offered him her hand in friendship. A short, awkward silence commenced.

Werner took her hand and pressed it firmly between his. "You are a wonderful player, Victoria. Come to Berlin if you get a chance. You will be welcome."

"Thanks. Maybe we'll see each other here next year."

"I will surely look forward to that."

She smiled, then turned and walked away, relieved he had not said anything more about what she now thought of as their relationship. She wondered, as undeveloped as the relationship was, was it over? Had she let an opportunity slip by? Did she want it to be over before it had even started? Then within a few steps, she realized she needed no answer. She was going home.

Chapter 9

On Rory's sixteenth birthday, he met his brother Pat at the gas station at the end of Pat's shift so they could go to the DMV for Rory to take his driver's test. He breezed through it, since he had been driving with his father from the age of thirteen. Not just driving truck on the farm, either; his father would often put him behind the wheel on the highway so he could take a nap.

Now that he had his license, he got up early every morning and drove Pat to work so he could keep the car for the rest of the day. Then he tried diligently to avoid getting stuck working for his father, but usually gave in to the lure of money. On the few days he succeeded to get out of work, with a set of wheels at his disposal, he traveled to more distant golf courses and played a full eighteen holes.

When he had remembered to retrieve his golf bag from Alyse's house, he found it beside the garage instead of beside the house where he had left it. This caused him some concern. He hoped Alyse, and not one of her parents, had moved it.

He enjoyed the early morning golf, and being the first one out on the course most of the time. He preferred to play his round alone and usually finished in less than three hours. Playing fast was the way he liked it. Playing with others irritated him, especially when they constantly complained about the slow speed of the foursome ahead. In contrast to his own desire for faster play, he wondered why the others would want to play in a hurry. If you like golf and the game takes a long time, then don't you get to enjoy it longer?

Playing alone in the early morning had become his favorite way to start a summer day. That way he didn't have to worry about any other players and what happened in their games. He had enough trouble worrying about his own.

As he walked in the rough looking for his ball, thoughts of Alyse began to form. First, he conjured up the physical pleasure he enjoyed with her, making him ache for her touch, to feel her body warmth, to smell her smell and to taste her kisses. Then the thoughts drifted to the times when it seemed she had an out-of-body experience, letting him have his fun but not wanting any herself. She had said she felt guilty during their touching while her mother's image occupied her mind. Boy, what a way to shut down the engine.

Then sometimes, like the last day they spent together, she would block out everything else and become exclusively involved in what her body wanted for its own pleasure. He worried about what would happen to the Alyse that felt guilty, when the Alyse that felt pleasure went too far. Did the responsibility for controlling their sexual progress fall on him? If it did, could he stop when they needed to stop?

Then he would begin to think about other things he and Alyse did together. So far, they had gone to movies, they had gone to the mall, and they had done homework. What else could they do together? There had to be more. She seemed interested in talking with her girl friends, but he didn't follow what they talked about half the time; so he usually tuned out when they got together with her friends. Even still, with not much in common, they had a lot of fun together.

Rory liked sports and wanted Alyse to enjoy them with him. She seemed bored when he tried to get her to watch a game, so he tried to get her interested in a different way. Thinking she might enjoy sports more by doing rather than watching, he took her to a driving range to hit golf balls. She swung at the ball like it was high and outside. Obviously, she would never get to the point of actually playing something resembling golf. She laughed every time she swung and missed, she didn't get mad, she didn't try harder, and she made no adjustments; she just swung again and laughed harder.

Her abilities as a student were similar to her golf swing. She could cram when she needed to in order to scrape out a passing mark, and that's what she did for every exam in every class. She saw no benefit in doing the work; getting the learning over with seemed to be her goal. He enjoyed helping her with her homework because it reinforced his own understanding of the subjects. However, the extra work he forecasted for himself over the next two years would limit the time he had to provide this assistance. She never spoke of her feelings related to learning; she had no idea what she wanted to do beyond high school. When she got frustrated at the number of homework assignments she had, she often expressed her desire to graduate and put an end to her school days. Then she would pout because her parents would probably expect her to go to college anyway, and then she would have even more homework.

His morning meditation on Alyse always finished by returning to the physical relationship and the vivid memories of her body, of her pretty face, of how he felt when their skin touched. The part of the summer he spent with her had been exhilarating. Sneaking into the house so they could each gain intimate knowledge of the other's body, couldn't be topped as the highlight of the summer!

In two years, he would go away to school. He wondered if their relationship would last, or if he would be saying goodbye to Alyse forever.

After golf, he would drive to Gary's house to see what plans Gary had for the day. Barely awake but mobile enough, Gary would join Rory in a drive to the convenience store for cola and a muffin. Once the sugar and caffeine started to work, Gary would scheme up some type of adventure for the day. Most days he came up with a long drive to somewhere, requiring plenty of gas money and more time than they had available before Rory had to pick up his brother at the end of his shift. As a result, most trips got postponed. After the postponement, they would end up dropping in on one of their friends who had a job. There they would hang out until they became a detriment to commerce, and the friend indicated they had worn out their welcome. Sometimes the boss kicked them out of the place, but being sent on their way didn't bother them. They didn't care what they did to kill time until after the lunch hour rush ended so they could go hang out in the restaurant where Harry worked. They had large burger-and-fries appetites, and always took their patronage to their friend's restaurant. They would buy a glass of chocolate milk, a plate of french fries and a burger, with the intention of making them last for the rest of the afternoon. The lunch patrons were mostly gone, so the owner didn't hassle them about how long it took them to consume their meal. Harry bussed the tables, washed dishes, mopped the floor, and helped get things ready for the dinner crowd. Sometimes, if needed, he would stay to work through the dinner rush. He liked the extra shift because the evening business generated a bigger tip pool.

He worked pretty hard at his job. His boss didn't mind if he sat in the booth with Rory and Gary when he took a break. He even chose not to notice when Harry refilled his friends' milk glasses and brought them another heaping plate of fries.

"How's it going today, Harry? You getting any from these waitresses yet?" Gary asked. He couldn't get enough of what interested him most, sex and who got it from whom.

"Going about the same. These girls here are pretty frigid. I've asked every one of them out on a date. No takers. I think they're all afraid I might be the key to cracking open their locked-up boxes and showing them what there is about a man that makes life worth living."

"Yeah, you'd show them, all right. Where would you take them to do this unlocking? Do you think you could sneak them past your mother?" Gary teased him.

"Wouldn't you like to know where I go?"

Gary then bolted up in his seat as if the solution to a long outstanding puzzle he had toiled over unveiled itself in a burst of the obvious. "Hey, Rory... you're not getting any right now, are you?" Gary started, then turned to Harry to inject, "...and Harry, I'm generously implying you *were* getting some but you're currently in a bit of a drought, even though I know you never get any. ...Anyway." He turned back to Rory. "How long has your muff been gone?" Gary stared at Rory, slack-jawed, his head bobbing.

"Muff?"

"Oh Jesus, I forgot you don't like code words. Alyse, how long has she been gone?"

"A week."

"Man, all the lovin' you two must have been making over at her house while her parents worked, and now nothing for a week. You must be ready to burst." Gary leered.

"Shut up, Gary."

"Okay, but then I won't tell you what I was thinking."

"Which will likely benefit us all," Rory said.

"Well, I'm going to tell you anyway. Here's what we're going to do tonight. We're going out to the whorehouse in Shelby. Harry can finally get his gun off. And you look like you need some relief. What do you say?"

"The whorehouse in Shelby doesn't exist. Everybody says they've been there or knows somebody who's been there, but it's never been confirmed."

Harry sank down lower, hunching his shoulders and looking up at Rory and Gary with a serious conspiratorial expression. "When my cousin came to town he went up there, and he said they deliver whatever you order, and whatever you order is on the menu."

"You see, another secondhand story. Did he say where you find this place in Shelby?" Rory asked skeptically.

"No, but he said you can't miss it," Harry said.

"I don't think so. Anyway, how would we get there and what makes you think they let high school kids into their whorehouse?"

Gary looked at Rory and shook his head, "Let's see now, you dumbass, how would we get there? Man, you're driving a car right now. I know this because it got us here and it's sitting out in the parking lot. Maybe we should use the very same car that got us here, to get us there."

"My brother's not going to let us take his car up to Shelby."

"I already thought of that, so here's what we do; We all chip in a little gas money and when you pick him up from work, you give it to him, then you ask him if he wants to go get laid. Who would say no to that? And just to make sure he gets the full picture, I'll go with you when you pick him up."

At first Rory thought another one of Gary's grand schemes had been hatched, all bravado and going nowhere, but now he worried about Gary getting his brother involved. If Pat heard the scheme, it wouldn't be long before the car headed down the road to Shelby. He still didn't think the whorehouse existed. But if it did, his brother would find it and either put the myth to bed or discover, firsthand, what they had to offer. He cringed at the thought of going to a whorehouse and knew that even if they found it, he wasn't going in. He searched for a reason to extinguish the whole idea and not go at all. "Even if we find it, we won't get in," he said.

"They want the money, Rory; we'll get in."

"That's another thing. How much money will it take and who has enough money to go spending it on whores?"

"I heard it only cost five bucks for a regular. And a little more, if you want a little something more. Harry makes enough in tip money every day for what we need; he can lend it to us, right Harry?" Gary had all the answers.

"Yeah, I guess. What the hell, let's do it." Harry conceded.

"You're crazy. I'm not going, and I won't go in the place even it does exist. We'll never get in. So why waste gas and time?" Rory said.

"Rory, you know you're going. Even if it's just to keep your wild-ass brother out of trouble, you know you're going," Gary said.

Rory knew Gary could convince his brother to make the trip and if Pat took the trip, then Rory had to go too. Not only to keep him out of trouble, but also because he didn't want his brother to think he was afraid to let off a little steam.

When they gave Rory's brother the gas money and laid out their plan for him, he stood smiling, his thoughts turned inward for a few seconds. Then he said to no one in particular, "Madame Belinda's."

"What?" Rory asked.

Pat came back to the real world and looked at Rory. "The whorehouse. It's called Madame Belinda's."

"It exists? Bullshit. You mean there really is one?" Rory asked in shock, not believing his own brother could dispel the Shelby Whorehouse myth so easily. They hadn't even had to use their wits to dupe some Shelby local into revealing the whorehouse's existence or location.

"You high school dorks don't know shit," his brother said, "What time you want to leave?"

On the road, Pat reached into his jacket pocket and pulled out a paper bag full of condoms. He passed them over to Rory. "Any of you dipsticks know what these are for? If you do, take some. If you don't, then don't bother."

Rory took several, without saying a word, and passed the bag into the backseat.

The four of them arrived in Shelby a little before sunset. Pat pointed out that the daylight worked to their advantage, since he doubted he could find Madame Belinda's in the dark. Even with the light they still had to drive up and down a number of streets, some of them twice, before Pat spotted the house. They pulled into the driveway of a large, sprawling single-level building sitting up against a steep hill. The driveway took them along the side and behind the house. Its sides had dark brown wooden siding with white trim at the edges and on the windowsills. Behind the building a gravel parking lot had spots for about six vehicles. Two of the spaces were occupied. The cars couldn't be seen from the street, and the steep hill prevented them from being viewed from behind.

Rory questioned whether or not they had pulled into the right place, but Pat insisted his friend had described this exact house in detail. A long porch with tables and chairs ran along the back of the house. In the middle of the back wall, a sliding galley-style window provided service to the outside deck.

They parked and got out of the car, then stood waiting to see who would make the first move to go inside.

Rory spoke. "Guys, let's come to our senses here. I saw a diner down by the tracks on the way in. Why not go get something to eat and head back?"

"I came here to get laid and I'm a going to get laid," Harry committed.

"Well, I'm not going in and I'm not paying money for sex," Rory said, stubbornly.

"Better to have loved for cash, than never to have loved at all. Right, Harry?" Gary said, then turned to Rory. "I guess you're going to have to grab yourself a seat on the porch and wait while we have a little fun with the rubber maids. You can figure out that code, can't you?"

"Shut up, Gary."

Gary led the way across the porch. He opened the big white door. A small chime rang inside, causing him to stop before pushing the door open any farther. He stuck his head inside for a look around. What he saw met with his approval, so he pushed the door open wide. They all, except Rory, disappeared inside, leaving the door slightly open.

Rory stood looking at the partially opened door, listening to the faint sound of music, then walked across the porch and sat down. He heard his brother's laughter, followed by the laughter of the entire group. This piqued his curiosity, but nothing was going to get him inside the house. After a short while that seemed like forever, Gary, holding a can of beer, stuck his head out the door. "Come on in and have a beer, man. You can at least do that?"

"I'm not going in there," Rory replied stubbornly.

Gary shook his head and withdrew slowly, as if swallowed by a large reptile.

As more customers arrived at the house, they glanced at Rory and contemplated his reason for remaining out on the porch. Some tried to guess and he suffered a number of teasing inquiries.

"It's a bitch when you finish first and have to wait for you friends outside." Chided one customer.

"I remember my dad used to make me wait outside too, when I was a kid." said another.

"Are you the DV? Designated Virgin," said a third.

But a female voice came to his defense. "No he has to wait out here. He's not allowed in because Belinda doesn't allow one man gang-bangs."

Turning in the direction of the voice, he saw a woman in a tight skirt with a top made of very sheer cloth, so light that the breeze caused by her forward movement kept the material pressed against her chest. She walked toward him carrying a can of beer. His eyes bore in on the raised nubs pressing outward against the flimsy gauze of her top. She placed the beer on the table in front of him, then stood with one hand on her hip while the other held her chin. Her eyes focused in the distance as if watching phantoms enacting pleasant dreams of her past or ones yet to come. Rory's eyes leveled at her hardened nipples and he watched them with unflinching concentration. He didn't think his voice would come out right, so he remained silent. Here he sat, on the porch of the mythical Shelby Whorehouse, a real lady of pleasure standing before him, practically revealing her bare breasts for his enjoyment. A woman he presumed had performed any number of different sex acts with any number of different men.

"Your friend sent you the beer. I don't know which one," she said as she turned away, breaking her thoughtful pose.

"Thanks." Rory managed to croak with more air than voice.

"They said you're not coming in because you're in love. I told them you must be a sweet boy," she said, then grinned. "I'm real naughty to sweet boys."

Rory's mouth hung open as she turned and walked back into the house.

Inside, Harry, Pat and Gary sat drinking beer, watching the activities going on in the room. Four ladies mingled with the patrons, talking to the various men but keeping their distance from the boys, waiting to see if one of them would build up the nerve to make an approach. The waitress checked on them frequently; and when she found out they had a friend outside who wouldn't come in, she had suggested they send him a beer and she would make sure it got delivered in style.

When the woman came back from delivering the beer, she looked over at the three boys and commented, "It won't be long now." The three of them laughed and hooted at what Rory's face must have looked like while he talked to a lady of the flesh. He had resisted the trip so much that they were convinced his terror of doing something illegal, with a woman, for money, had consumed him.

The allure of a woman wearing a tight navy mini-skirt, and a tight white top with a hole in the chest displaying her deeply tanned cleavage, pushed Harry's courage to the sticking point; he offered to buy her a drink. She joined them at their table, at which point Harry became tongue-tied and Gary had to keep the chat going to avoid sitting in a clumsy silence. Pat, trying to make like a man of the world, acted as if he hadn't noticed the arrival of a female. Once one of the women had sat at the table, another walked over with a box of cigars and offered them to the boys. The women loved to watch the young boys turn green after lighting up a cigar. Gary and Harry gawked at each other to see if the other was going to buy, but then looked at the cigar woman and declined. Pat decided he would smoke, so he took a cigar and a box of wooden matches.

Pat made a deliberate show of his knowledge of lighting cigars. First he rubbed it under his nose to smell the fresh aroma, something he had seen in a movie. Then he checked the end to see if it needed trimming; but he could tell it was a quality cigar, because the hole was already there. Next he stuck it deep into his mouth, moistening one end, then turned it around to moisten the other. Gary watched this display of cigar expertise in wonder, while Harry and his companion stood to leave the table.

Harry didn't know the protocol for escorting a hooker to one of the rooms in back. He started on her left side and held her elbow as if to guide her, then two-step side-shuffled behind to her right side to offer her his arm and almost walked into a barstool.

Pat, with his cigar expertly prepared, watched Harry's gallant efforts, then prepared to light up. He picked up the small box of matches, selected one, then closed the box and struck the match head along the gritty side of the box.

As the tip of the match head began to ignite, a small chunk of the combustible material shot off of the stick, bright and hot and straight into the corner of Pat's right eye.

Pat jumped up screaming, knocking over the table, spilling the beer and dropping the cigar from his mouth. He reached for his burning eye socket.

Gary stood in shock, yelling, "What? What?"

Harry turned and froze, looking at the now bent-over Pat, who was clawing at his face and howling in pain. Harry hadn't seen the accident, so he wondered from which direction Pat had been attacked. He began to back up toward the open door when something hit him from behind, knocking him to the floor.

Rory, after hearing Pat scream, had rushed into the room, anticipating a fight with his brother's attacker. He had collided with Harry's shoulder on his way to thrash at the assailant. He saw a stranger standing, looking on while Pat screamed the screams of the tortured and kicked about on the floor.

Rory jumped on the stranger's back and wrapped his arms around a pair of huge iron-hard shoulders. When the man realized he was being attacked, he twisted and shrugged, sending Rory sprawling on the gritty floor. Rory scrambled to his feet in a rage and charged at the man again. The stranger saw the crazed look on Rory's face as Rory came at him. Rory ducked to tackle the man at his waist but the man sidestepped and gave him a push on the backside as he rushed by. Rory staggered with the added speed and landed on the floor again. He shoulder-rolled and quickly popped back up on his feet. He turned, stared and snorted as he prepared for a third attack.

"You come at me again, kid, and I'm going to deck you," the man said, causing Rory to charge. Gary caught Rory from behind, wrapping his arms around Rory's mid-section and turning him away from the larger man.

Gary looked into Rory's wild eyes and yelled, "Rory, nobody hit Pat, he did it to himself."

"What? What the hell are you talking about?"

"I think the match got him. He was lighting a cigar and it looked like the match shot some of the hot shit into his eye."

The rest of the people in the room stood watching the dramatics, wondering what had happened. Rory scanned the room then relaxed and dropped to the floor to steady his brother. He got Pat's hands away from his face and looked at the eye. A web of red veins covered the white, and blood pooled up in the corner of the eye under the surface. No blood ran out because the little ball of molten sulfur had cauterized the wound as it penetrated his eye. Rory couldn't see much, due to the frequency of Pat's involuntary blinking. Harry crawled over from where he had landed on the floor during

Rory's entrance. "Jesus, that's gruesome," he said, looking at Pat's eye.

The others in the room started to gather around Pat and Rory. From over his shoulder, Rory heard the voice of the woman from the porch. "Sweet Boy? You better get your friend's eye looked at."

Rory stood, ordering Gary to grab Pat's other arm. They lifted him to his feet and walked him out the door.

On the drive home, Gary, Harry and Rory sat in the front seat while Pat lay moaning in the back. Periodically Rory would look over at the silent and down-trodden pair beside him to blast them with a fiery gaze, but they wouldn't take their eyes off of the road.

Chapter 10

Alyse and her family returned home from their vacation a day earlier than they had planned. They decided they could use an extra day at home to decompress from their trip and perform the annual back-to-school activities with a little less rush.

Alyse unpacked and did her laundry, then sat around and worried. She declined to go shopping with her mother, deciding instead to steep in her sad funk of wondering what to do about Rory. When it began to get dark, she called and chatted with some of her friends, planning what they would do on the first day of school. She thought many times about calling Rory, but she couldn't make herself dial his number. He didn't expect her to return for another day, so she decided to wait until he called.

When the call did come through the following afternoon, Alyse's mother answered. She had been fastest to the phone all day.

"Hello," she said into the receiver, then waited, hoping the caller was Rory.

"Hi, Mrs. Bellyard. It's Rory. Is Alyse home?"

"Oh. Hello, Rory." Her voice slow and deep. "I see that you picked up your golf clubs."

"Ah, yes, I did. Thanks for moving them beside the garage." Shit, they know I was at the house.

"How did they get in the yard in the first place, Rory?" she asked.

Oh boy, what do I say now? "I know I'm not supposed to go to your house when you're not there, Mrs. Bellyard, but I only stopped by on my way home from golf and I guess I left them behind."

"Were you by yourself when you stopped by?"

Rory paused for a second, then said, "No."

"Were there boys or girls with you?" She wasn't going to let him off the hook.

"A girl."

"Hmm. Well, Alyse isn't home right now."

"Oh, okay. Could you tell her I called?" he said, as the air escaped from his sails of eager anticipation.

"I will. Goodbye."

Rory waited at home for the rest of the afternoon and didn't go out that evening, even though his friends had tried to get him to hang out on the last night of summer vacation. He had turned them down in hopes of getting together with Alyse, but by mid-evening he knew his chances of seeing her had vanished. Alyse hadn't returned his call by nine o'clock, and he wondered if he should try calling her again. Worried that Mrs.

Bellyard would answer the phone, he chickened out. He didn't want her mother thinking he didn't trust her to deliver the message. In reality, he feared that the message had been delivered and ignored. Their thrilling experience that last day together followed by two weeks of waiting to see her again made the hours of anticipation a painful test of his patience.

He finally went to bed and lay on his back, staring into the darkness. He could see nothing from any light visible to his eyes, though clear and dreadful visions emanated from his imagination.

He didn't want to give her up. He'd felt all along they would eventually separate, but he didn't want it to happen now, not after they had given each other the pleasure and the trust of each other's bodies. To him, that exchange started a new type of commitment, a new type of relationship.

He enjoyed the pleasures he and Alyse had shared, but tonight his imagination only showed her face as it looked when she distanced herself from their acts of touching. The confused, pre-occupied look she displayed when she had let him continue for his own satisfaction, not caring for her own.

He didn't think he was in love with Alyse. But if not, then what feeling did they share? He considered their relationship the best experience of his life, and now he felt it being torn away from him because he had acted selfishly, allowing their sexual activities to go too far.

He didn't know if he slept. When he got out of bed to prepare for school, he felt he had been conscious the entire night. He hadn't toss, and turn, but lay still as if in a deep coma.

His mood turned foul when he realized that, even though he had a driver's license, he still had to ride the bus like some fifteen-year old kid.

Thinking about seeing Alyse again cost him his appetite. He didn't eat breakfast and now, while he rode the bus, his stomach growled.

If she thought he hadn't called her, then she would think he didn't want to see her. If she had chosen not to call him, then he concluded she didn't want to see him. Had the golf bag created trouble? These questions tugged, poked and prodded at the turmoil he wished would go away.

Once he arrived at the school, he discovered tables set up along the main hallway, each with a range of the alphabet printed on a sheet of paper taped to the front. A swarm of eight hundred students tried to pick up their first-day information packets, packets that held their class schedules and homeroom assignments. The high noise level distracted Rory as he searched the newly clothed students for Alyse. He waited at the A-through-D table where he had picked up his own packet, in case she showed up. She didn't. When a warning bell rang, he went to his homeroom without making contact with her.

He hoped that he and Alyse would get the same homeroom, but when he arrived at the one assigned, she wasn't there. Gloom set in as he listened to a number of announcements before setting out to do a trial run of his schedule.

During the trial run, he moved through all areas of the school as he went from class to class. During one of the changes, he passed by the band room. Mr. Keltch spotted him, and smiled as he yelled out across the tide of students moving through the halls, "Hey, Rory, welcome back. I'm glad you reconsidered."

Rory furrowed his brow and called back, "Reconsidered what?"

When Mr. Keltch heard Rory's question, he lost his smile, "Your tuba instructor said you were staying in the band. Is that not true?"

"No, it's not," Rory replied. He kept moving; soon he was too far down the hallway for the discussion to continue.

In every class on his schedule, he hoped to see Alyse sitting in the room. He knew the chances of that were slim for his regular classes, but his hope paid off in the study hall. He spotted her talking and laughing with one of her friends. When she noticed him, she briefly lost her smile then forced a false one across her lips.

"Hi. How was your trip?" he asked. He took a quick and sheepish glance at the other girl, hoping she didn't gather from his question that he and Alyse had not seen each other since her return and therefore something had gone wrong between them.

"Good, I guess."

He wanted to kiss her but saw no hint of invitation.

"Can I sit here?" He gestured at a seat near her.

"Yeah, sure."

She continued to talk with her friend without paying any attention to Rory, who sat looking down at his schedule, fighting the urge to interrupt her. The bell rang, starting the five minutes they had before moving off to the next class. The teacher spouted out the study hall rules.

The fact that she wouldn't talk to him ate at him slowly, especially when he felt such a strong need to talk. When the teacher stopped making announcements, Rory turned to Alyse immediately to get her attention before she could start talking with her friend. "Alyse, it's good to see you. When can we get together? I need to talk to you." He hoped it didn't sound like a plea.

"It's good to see you too." She met Rory's eyes briefly; then turned away, looked down at the tabletop, and said, "Meet me at the main entrance when the morning ends."

"Okay, I'll see you there." He felt some relief and ventured to broach the touchy subject that had bothered him since the day before. "I talked with your mother yesterday."

"I know." She continued to look downward as she spoke these words in a vague and absent manner.

Rory detected hurt in her voice. Dumbstruck, he didn't know how to respond.

The bell rang, startling them both. All of the students rose, pushing back their chairs, which made scraping noises on the newly polished floors.

He turned to her and started to bend down to kiss her but stopped to see her reaction. She showed none. With his intentions clear, he continued and very briefly placed his lips on hers. He felt she had firmed her lips to kiss him back, and his waves of worry ebbed slightly.

They walked out of the study hall. When they split to go in different directions, he confirmed he would see her later, at the main entrance.

During the remainder of the dry run, he sat through his classes but paid little attention to what the teachers said. His mind churned in an endless loop, reviewing what had happened with Alyse. After he made the short stop in his last class, he had to return to his homeroom where more announcements took up more time. When they finished he left in a hurry, thankful for the shortened first day of school. Now he had to find out how Alyse's summer vacation had gone. He arrived at the main entrance before Alyse. After a few minutes he began to panic. What if she didn't show up? His increasing gloom slackened somewhat when he saw her approaching. She let him kiss her again and the gloom subsided further. When he asked if she wanted to go for a soda she said, "No, but you can walk me part-way home."

He had no interest in polite chatter to get the conversation rolling. He asked right off what her mother had said to her about his call the day before.

She told him about the conversation. "After she talked to you, she got really mad. Somehow she figured out we were alone at the house that last day." His heart plummeted over a cliff.

Alyse continued, "She knew before we left on vacation that you'd been there, because you left your golf bag. At first, I thought I had convinced her that we weren't alone. But her suspicion never died, and she lectured me about a lot of stuff.

"She thinks I'm too young to date and she doesn't care if the other girls do, because she thinks they're too young, too." She stopped and looked at Rory. "I never did let her know what we did, Rory. I would never tell her any of that. But she kept going on and on about how we had plenty of chances to do things we shouldn't do. And if she found out we'd done any of them, I'd be in big trouble. She kept warning me about it the whole trip.

"Then after she talked to you yesterday, she said she was afraid we had been alone doing the bad things she had warned me about."

Rory felt stunned. His palms got moist. He felt his sex life was on display for the whole world to criticize, that it wasn't his private life any longer.

"Oh, man," he said. He felt empty; his heart had already dropped and now his knees grew weak.

"She says I can't see you anymore, Rory."

When he heard those words, he lifted his head to look at her. She met his eyes without fear, embarrassment or emotion.

"So, what's going to happen? What are we going to do?" he asked. The look she had on her face caused the harsh edge of fear to begin slicing him from inside.

The answer did not come immediately. When she spoke, the fear had carved its way out and he could tell what she would say next.

"I think she's right; we shouldn't see each other."

He waited to let the sentence sink in, then he waited some more to let the first wave of despair subside. His hand rose and covered his mouth. He took a long deep breath, then exhaled very slowly before speaking.

"Why should we not see each other? To make your mother happy? If we stop seeing each other it's like admitting we've done something wrong and we're willing to accept our punishment. If we stay together, we're saying we did nothing wrong and we're not ashamed of anything we did in private."

Alyse took a number of shallow breaths before she spoke. "I don't know if I feel that way. Sometimes when I thought about what we did, I didn't feel right about it. Even while we did it, I didn't feel right about it. I felt guilty, almost every time I let you under my clothes. I know I started it sometimes, and I know sometimes it made me feel good, it made me feel crazy. But now I know I shouldn't have done it. We shouldn't have done those things, Rory. We shouldn't have done any of them."

"Why didn't you say something? Why didn't you tell me to slow down? I would have done anything you asked." He could hear the desperation creeping into his voice. "We can start over. We'll stop with the under-the-clothes stuff, until you feel like you want to do it again, and then we'll do what you want at your pace."

She shook her head, then said, "No. I think my mom is right. I think we had better not see each other anymore."

He could feel the strength of her commitment to her mother's decision, and decided not to attempt talking her out of the breakup. If she wanted to let their relationship end, then he couldn't prevent it. He wanted to show his willingness to do things the way she wanted. After some time away from each other, maybe she would come around to his way of thinking and then they could get back together. That's what he would hope for. You can't make someone stay with you for your sake; they have to decide it's for their own sake.

Accepting her decision, he calmly said, "I thought a lot about the things we did. I've been thinking about them since you went on vacation. I worried that you didn't enjoy it as much as I did, that you did those things for me, not for you.

"Alyse, I want you to know I really enjoyed what we did and I don't think we did anything wrong. I thought we did what we both wanted and you wanted me to touch you as much as I wanted you to touch me. If that isn't the case, then I'm truly sorry. I hope you enjoyed at least some of what we shared. We can't undo it and it wasn't wrong, so please, don't think we did bad things. We did these things in private and I believe that makes it ours to say whether or not it was bad. We gave something to each other. I'm glad it happened. We did nothing wrong."

Alyse looked down at the sidewalk for a few seconds. Her breathing deepened, her lips pressed tight together. "I'll see you at school, Rory." She turned and walked away.

Rory watched her walk for a short time, then turned and walked back to school. He passed in front of the main entrance on his way to the bus stop. But when he got to the stop, he kept on going until he had walked all the way home.

Chapter 11

Rory had a quiet week the first week back at school, as he tried to stay away from all of his friends. He arrived at school barely before the first bell, and when the school day ended he went straight home after his last class. He hadn't even talked with Mr. Duggin after chemistry class, choosing instead to get to his next class as quickly as possible, find his desk, and then sit and stare at the back of the desk in front of him.

During his study hall he sat in a back corner of the room, as far away from Alyse as he could get. She never looked back at Rory and he tried not to look at her. In order to keep his mind off of her, he cracked his chemistry books. His goal was first to get ahead of the regular course work; then he could branch out into his specialized area of study.

As part of his application for the Mortenson Chemistry Scholarship, Rory had to establish a curriculum outside the normal class material. His customized curriculum needed to be documented and submitted to the Mortenson Board as the second phase of the application. The document had to outline two projects, and list a set of challenging but realistic goals he hoped to achieve. If the proposed projects were too ambitious, the Board might remove the student's name from consideration. If this occurred they would write indicating that he should not continue with the application.

All of the approved applicants then had to complete their first project and provide documentation relative to its completion. This included write-ups of experiments, and affidavits from supervising teachers. Submissions for the first project's results had to arrive at the Board before the end of January. Based on the input submitted, the Board would announce the scholarship designate by the end of March. The designated student then had to complete the second project of the curriculum, documenting it the same manner and again submitting the documentation to the Board.

At the end of the junior year, one of the Board members would interview the student as part of the process to determine if the student should continue as the scholarship designate in their senior year. If the student retained the status, they had to again develop and complete a customized curriculum. If the student did not retain the status, the scholarship for that year would not be awarded.

Rory worried about where he would find the time to do the extra work to prepare for the scholarship. Even though he would no longer spend time with Alyse, he foresaw a tight schedule for himself. He had been lonely throughout the first week and had found doing extra schoolwork made the time go by a little faster. By week's end, the void of not seeing Alyse had shrunk to a minor abscess in his stomach.

A few times during the first weekend after the breakup, he did stop and wonder about Alyse. When he did, he would let himself sink a short distance into loneliness—then realize the pointlessness of staying there. By the time Monday rolled around again, he had reestablished his sense of direction, that being to do whatever it takes to get the scholarship. Now that he had his head on straight to start his school year, he wasn't going to let anything disrupt him.

He still had to ride the bus to school, a fact which annoyed him. He made a mental note to talk to his father about his mother's old broken-down car sitting out by the shed. Its brown paint had turned to powder; the grass underneath grew up into the engine compartment where some of the blades escaped through the windshield-wiper openings on a search for the sun. Once, when his father's truck had broken down, Rory had heard him say he needed to get that old piece of crap going again. His father had a way of keeping old things running.

He felt more like himself again the second week of school. After his last class on Monday, he waited to confirm with Mr. Duggin that the Chemistry Club was going to start its regular meetings the next day. He also wanted to make an appointment to talk with him after the meeting. Mr. Duggin agreed, and Rory left to take care of some business in the band room.

Mr. Keltch stood leaning on the conductor's podium talking with Gary, who held his saxophone while sucking on the reed. When they noticed Rory, both Gary and Mr. Keltch stopped their conversation. Rory nodded to them.

"Hey, Rory! How's Long John Silver?" Gary asked, after pulling the reed out of his mouth.

"Who?"

"Your brother. Is he still wearing the eye patch?"

"Oh, yeah. I think he gets it off next week, or maybe it's off already; I haven't noticed," Rory said with a touch of impatience, then turned to Mr. Keltch, "Can I talk to you for a minute, Mr. Keltch?"

"Sure. Let's go into my office."

"I thought you were coming back to band, Rory. What happened?" Gary asked as Rory entered the office.

"That's what I'm here to talk to Mr. Keltch about. I'll talk to you later." He smiled, then closed the door.

Mr. Keltch walked behind his desk, he sat down, and crossed his arms over his chest. He tilted his head to the side and wore a blank expression on his face. After Rory sat down Mr. Keltch made a closed-mouth smile, took a deep breath, exhaled a sigh through his nostrils, and spoke. "Mr. Beach told me you planned to return to the band. He said he had convinced your father that you should stay in, and your father actually told you to do so.

"I was glad to hear the news; but when I saw you in the hall and you said it wasn't true, I became very disappointed again. So why don't you tell me what *is* true?"

Rory calmly addressed Mr. Keltch. "Mr. Beach was at my house, he did talk with my father, and my father did agree with him; but he never said I had to stay in the band."

"Mr. Beach made it up, did he?"

"No, he just doesn't know my father. You see, my father likes to tell people what they want to hear, so he kind of agreed with Mr. Beach."

"Kind of?"

"Yeah. My father said I should stay in the band, he didn't say I had to. And even if he tried to force me back in, I knew I could eventually talk him out of it." He stopped to allow Mr. Keltch a chance to comment. Mr. Keltch just stared at him silently, so Rory continued. "I came to say I'm sorry, again. You thought I was coming back, and I'm here telling you I'm not. Like I told you last year, I need the extra time to work on my scholarship application and do the extra work required to keep it. Chemistry is what I want to do, so I'm finished with the band; and anyone who tells you I'm not, is wrong."

Mr. Keltch sat looking disappointed, but cocked his head as if he accepted Rory's decision. Rory felt a little more at ease; he had prepared for more of an argument. Mr. Keltch looked down at his hands and scraped something invisible off one of his fingernails. After clearing the non-existent substance, he looked at Rory with a dark and somber expression.

"I guess I will be talking to your father about this. I'm going to tell him how you're letting me, the other members of the band and yourself down.

"I will also tell him what I really think about you and your scholarship. That I don't think you're as committed to this chemistry thing as you would like us to believe. I think you're using it for the purpose of getting out of band and basketball. Sure, it sounds pretty noble to want more time to study. But you're not fooling anyone. You want more time to hang out with your friends. It's not cool to be in the band, so you're going to get out.

"You'll make a bit of an effort for a while, an attempt to show everyone that you really mean to follow your chemistry pipe dream, but pretty soon you'll give it up too. Then it's too late for band, too late for basketball, and too late for Rory Coleman.

"You make it sound as if my telling all this to your father, won't have any effect on him. But I think he needs to know what you're up to and what kind of person you're turning into. So, I accept the fact you're definitely not coming back, but I'm not going to make quitting easy on you. You have to pay some kind of a price."

Rory sat listening and wondering why Mr. Keltch wouldn't let it go. Why, after learning of Rory's keen interest in chemistry, should he still try to tear him down? Did he want Rory to give up something that motivated him, in order to participate in something that didn't? Did he want Rory to toil and endure activities so he didn't let others down, at the cost of letting himself down? Did it disappoint or offend him to see a student make a decision regarding his own future, a decision that flew in the face of what Mr. Keltch thought the student should do?

Rory knew there was no more he could explain to Mr. Keltch, and no more he himself could listen to either. He realized he had made a mistake in judgment. He saw that Mr. Keltch couldn't be reasoned with when you didn't do what he wanted. The friendship they once had no longer existed, and now Rory knew Mr. Keltch wasn't the kind of person he would want as a friend in the future.

————

The next day after school, Rory attended the year's first meeting of the Chemistry Club. More students attended this meeting than there had been at any meeting the previous year, but the regulars knew that a few pseudo-enthusiasts usually showed up at the start of each new school year. Ellis and Gill sat at the back lab table where they had been a fixture all of the previous year. Rory saw that two freshmen sat at his own usual table. He went to roust them away. But before he got to them he noticed Victoria sitting alone at the lab table on the far wall.

"Well, the Vicster decided to check out the chemistry geeks." He walked over and sat at the table with Victoria.

"Hi, Rory, how are you?"

"Some people say I'm a nine out of ten, but I have a higher opinion of myself," he said, smiling. "So, did you have a good summer? What did you get up to?"

"Band camp," she answered.

"Not that march-until-you-drop thing in Helena that Keltch wanted me to go to?"

"Oh no, I went to something a little more exotic. The International Musical Youth Camp in St. Petersburg Beach."

"Get stabbed. No way," he said, somewhat envious. "You went to a music camp in Florida?"

"Yeah, my third one. But it's not always in St. Petersburg. I went to Maine once and Montreal last year. It's pretty cool to see those places."

"I guess," he said enthusiastically. Then he lowered his tone. "I went to the exotic town of Shelby."

"I heard."

Rory threw his head back. "What do you mean, you heard?"

"People say you, Gary, and Harry, went up to Shelby to find some dates. Did you?"

"Well, not really. What else did they say?"

"I don't know. I didn't pay much attention."

"Good. Waste of time anyway," he said. "What made you decide to come to the chemistry club?"

"Mr. Duggin suggested it last year, and when I saw him in class he asked me again about joining. So here I am, willing to give it a try."

"Good. I like it in here. You get to do a lot more than in class. Everyone here wants to do chemistry, not like class where most of the students put in time to fill a science requirement. I'm kinda glad to see you here."

She smiled at him. He noticed the curved lines of her lips. When Mr. Duggin called the meeting to order, Rory turned and started to move to his regular lab table, the table where he felt most comfortable, but he stopped partway off of the stool. Stuck between standing and sitting, he turned back to look at Victoria. He interpreted her expression as saying, "Yes,

I want you to sit with me," so he sat back down, with the realization that his own expression had asked if he could stay.

Some organizational comments occurred at the beginning, which turned into discussions regarding each student's expectations from the club. Mr. Duggin then outlined what the club expected from the students. He told them if they wanted a place to goof around while hanging out, then they should go somewhere else. The club required each person to participate in experiments and to learn from the results they produced.

The students asked a few extra questions to get Mr. Duggin's attention; then the meeting ended and the kids trickled out. Victoria waited to leave with Rory; since he made no move to get off of his stool, she asked him which way he was headed.

"Oh, I'm staying. I'm meeting with Mr. Duggin about the scholarship. I'm a chemistry superstar, you know."

"Right, I forgot. Okay then, I'll see you around. Maybe you could tell me more about the scholarship sometime?"

"Okay. I'll hunt you down tomorrow."

After Victoria left, Mr. Duggin asked, "What was up with you last week? I didn't see you around much, and when I did, you didn't seem your normal self."

"I know. I had a pretty bad week, but I think I'm over it." Rory sat contemplating whether or not to believe what he had said. He seemed willing to sit and think about it forever.

"Hmm. Anything I can help you with?" Mr. Duggin asked, breaking in on Rory's silence.

"Naw," he said. After a short pause, he went on. "I broke up with Alyse. Or I guess she broke up with me. I don't know. We broke up, and last week couldn't have been worse."

"Oh, I'm sorry. That's too bad. I know it's pretty tough when something like this happens. And it's even tougher to listen to someone who's trying to comfort you. You know what

I mean; they want what's best for you, they think they're helping; but nothing anyone can say can make you feel right. They try to tell you it may be the best thing that could happen to you. But deep inside, you know you would do anything to have things back the way they were.

"I wish you didn't have to feel this way, Rory. It's not easy to go through, but you have to go on."

Rory nodded. He had a lingering sense of failure, that made him want to go back and turn the situation into a success. But then maybe the breakup was the best thing that could have happened at this time; after all, it would allow him to concentrate on his schoolwork.

They reviewed chapters of the chemistry text. Mr. Duggin offered a few more ideas related to some collateral studies. Then, because the textbooks didn't provide enough detail for Rory's needs, Mr. Duggin supplied him with a list of additional texts to use for research.

With the direction established for his curriculum, Rory wanted to discuss the letter Mr. Keltch had said he intended to send to the Mortenson Board. Neither had any additional information on whether or not it had been sent, so Rory proceeded to tell Mr. Duggin about his latest meeting with Mr. Keltch and the misunderstanding about Rory returning to the band.

After listening silently to Rory's narrative, Mr. Duggin said, "Sounds like you made him angry again. He thought he had won a victory by getting you back in the band, and you snatched it away from him when you set him straight. If he hadn't sent the letter before the summer, he will surely send it now. Did you ever go and talk to Mr. Butcher about the letter and the scholarship?"

"Not yet. I guess I better go see him."

"Yes, you better. He's pretty good at evaluating a situation. Also, while you're there, ask him about ideas for special projects. He does an awful lot of reading related to what he teaches. He may come up with some pretty interesting topics for you to chase down."

"Okay, I'll make sure and see him this week," Rory said. "I better get going. Thanks for your help. You know... on everything."

Mr. Duggin smiled and nodded, then said, "No problem. See ya later."

When Rory arrived home in the early evening, his family had eaten but his mother had left him a plate warming in the oven. He set himself up at the table and ate his meal alone, happy to sit quietly. At sixteen, having recently been dumped by his girlfriend, still riding a bus to school, and with teachers accusing him of being a quitter, he felt no peace in his world; so he accept this temporary quiet.

"Rory, is that you?" his mother's voice called from her room.

It entered his mind to stay perfectly still. Maybe she would leave him alone so he could prolong his quiet time. But he knew he had to answer.

"Yeah, it's me," he called back.

"There's some supper in the oven for you."

"Thanks, I found it."

"Okay. When you're done, your father wants to see you. He's out in the barn."

Rory took his time. He finished his meal and washed it down with another glass of milk. He rinsed his dishes and went out to the barn. He knew his father would be there; his mother didn't have to tell him that.

When Rory walked into the barn, his father's horse lifted its head above the stable to see who had arrived. It stared at Rory for a brief time, then lowered its head and snorted. The barn smelled of fresh hay, and hay that had recently been digested. Two stables made up the left side of the barn, a walkway ran down the middle, and on the right wall an open door led into his father's workshop. There, his father worked untwisting a rope he had recently used during one of his jobs. The shop consumed most of his father's time, and he tinkered endlessly in the clutter of small fix-its. A snapped trailer-hitch chain lay along the wall waiting to be welded, branding irons waited for straightening, and a saddle waited for leather work on a separated stirrup. He always had a million things in line for repair; and he believed handling cows for a living didn't just require full-time attention, it required all-time attention. He had heard the barn door open and seen his horse look up, so he anticipated Rory's arrival and watched his son turn into the open doorway.

"Say, Rory, what's going on?" he asked, then looked down at the rope.

"Not much. Mom said you wanted to see me, and there's something I want to ask you about after."

"Okay. Well, I wanted to talk to you about your music teacher. He called a little earlier and said you're not in the band anymore. I remember we talked about it when he came out here and we decided for you to stay in the band. So. What's going on?"

"I think we're talking about a different music teacher, Dad. The one who called you today is from the school, he's not the one who gave me tuba lessons."

"Okay. Whoever he is doesn't change the fact you're supposed to stay in the band," Mr. Coleman said as his tone got a little angrier.

"I know you said I should. But we talked about this last year and I told you band didn't interest me any more, so I thought I'd quit. You didn't seem to care about it back then, so at the end of the year, I quit. Now, you seem to want to make a big deal out of it." Rory sounded frustrated.

"I'm not the one making a big deal out of it, it's your band teacher who's doin' it. He says he's afraid you're going to start dropping out of everything. I don't want you to be a quitter, Rory. That's why I said you should stay in the band."

"Dad, here's what's going on. I don't want to be in the band. I decided I could make better use of my time by quitting band. And by the way, I'm quitting basketball too. I'm in for a lot of work over the next two yeas, and band doesn't fit in with my plans. I could sit through another year of music classes; but why waste the time doing a bad job at band, when I could use it to do a good job in my other classes? It's time for me to start getting serious about my school. I'm serious about chemistry, so I took the step of quitting the band. Why don't we agree once and for all, I'm done with the band and it's a waste of time for people to try and keep me in it?"

"So, you've quit basketball too? I guess this music teacher's right, you're starting to quit on things. You going to be a quitter, Rory?" His father's voice strengthened.

Rory raised his to match. "I'm going to quit every waste-of-my-time activity I'm involved with. I'm not going to go through the motions to make everybody else happy."

"How you going to spend your extra time, huh? Hanging out with your girlfriend and your buddies? Is that making better use of your time?"

"No. I don't have a girlfriend anymore. I've applied for a scholarship so I need to do tons of additional homework. Did Mr. Keltch tell you about that?"

"Yes, he did. He said in time you'd probably quit on it as well."

What right did Mr. Keltch have, trying to get his father to start doubting him? He was about to accuse his father of taking the side of a stranger against him—but then a sudden sense of calm settled over him. Convincing his father of Mr. Keltch's intent to ruin his chances of receiving the scholarship seemed pointless; he knew his father felt intimidated by people in authority and would yield to their side of the story over his. Rory couldn't figure out why Mr. Keltch continued making these attempts. And now he knew it didn't matter, like he knew it didn't matter if his father believed he would turn into a quitter. Following his own agenda is what really mattered. Taking the path of doing things for himself is what he needed to do.

"Keltch is wrong, Dad. I've decided what I'm going to do and how I'm going to do it. I'm not asking for anyone's help, I'm only asking for people to stay out of my way," Rory said.

"So you're saying I'm getting in your way?"

"No, I'm saying Mr. Keltch is getting in my way. And he's trying to get you to help him. He doesn't want me to leave his band because then he thinks it makes him look bad. I used to spend a lot of time talking things over with him. Then I make one decision on my own and he's pissed at me to the point of trying to get you pissed at me too. I'm asking you to not let him do it.

"You've always trusted me to make my own decisions about school. Band has no future for me, so I quit. There's a lot of promise for me in chemistry, so I'm going to concentrate on it from now on."

Mr. Coleman squinted at Rory. "Well, we'll see, won't we? What did you want to talk to me about?"

Rory asked his father about fixing up the old car parked by the storage shed, knowing his father was finished with the subject of band for good.

Chapter 12

Rory sat in the back of the study hall, reading one of the chemistry texts Mr. Butcher had recommended. Alyse approached and sat down at his table. He greeted her, noticing a peculiar expression on her face. She attempted to speak, then stopped, searching for the right words. She would make brief eye contact with Rory, then look away; each time she did her demeanor changed, from sadness to dejection and finally to anger. To his eye, she now appeared ready to cry.

"Alyse, what's wrong?" he asked, leaning toward her.

Alyse sat upright and away from him.

"Did you go to the whorehouse in Shelby while I was away?" she asked in an accusing tone.

"Who told you about—," Rory started to say, but stopped. "Yes, but I didn't go in until Pat got hurt."

"But you went to a whorehouse? You went to a whorehouse before we broke up! I leave town, and you go to a whorehouse." Her words got quieter instead of angrier as she let the meaning of her statements fill in her own understanding of what she said. She had physically withdrawn from him while speaking, acknowledging the truth. She looked down at her fidgeting hands.

"Alyse, I went. But I didn't go there to get sex. I wouldn't do that."

She looked up at him, then asked, "Why else would you go there?"

"I had to go. I wanted to make sure Pat didn't get into any trouble. But did you hear what I said before? I didn't go inside until Pat got hurt, and I— "

"You expect me to believe that?" she interrupted. "You expect me to believe you went on a joyride to a whorehouse and you didn't go there for sex? You asshole!" Now her anger showed.

"Alyse, will you just listen for a minute? Will you let me explain?"

"No! My mother is right. Boys only want sex. I didn't give it to you, so you..." She took a breath. "So you went to get it somewhere else. You wanted sex from me, that's all."

He tried to calm her down. He still cared about what she thought about him.

"That's not true, Alyse. I wanted the things you and I did. I didn't go to Shelby to get sex."

"You're a liar. A bastard and a liar. How do you think it makes me feel, when my friends hear my boyfriend made a trip to a whorehouse?" She got up from the chair, turned, and walked away. Rory watched her for a moment, then looked down at his books without seeing the pages. Maybe I'm a bastard for going on the joyride. But I'm not a liar.

————

For the next four months, Rory concentrated on his chemistry studies. He had decided to stay completely away from girls. Alyse wouldn't talk to him at all, so he still felt unsettled about her. He hoped at some point an opportunity to set things straight between them would present itself.

Thanks to Mr. Butcher, he had been guided to a study on enzymes as his first project in his scholarship application. The subject piqued his interest because it combined biochemistry with chemistry, and he had seen commercials on television for new detergents that used enzymes to "get the stains out". Mr. Butcher had also pointed out medical uses such as a new treatment for back ailments in which the injection of enzymes from papaya juice into a herniated disc caused it to dry out and shrink. This often led to the relief of pressure on the nerves being pinched by the disc as it bulged into the joint of the spinal column. The release of pressure produced relief from back pain and stabilized the afflicted region of the back as effectively as a bone fusion, without the need for major surgery. Mr. Butcher had explained this to Rory as an example of how chemistry could change the face of something as complicated as medicine, making it safer for thousands of people and eliminating the need for some major surgeries.

Rory found the study interesting and saw a wide range of practical applications for enzymes.

After the long, dreary holiday break, Rory had to perform and document an experiment as part of his first project. This required spending extra time in the lab, setting up his experiment with Mr. Duggin.

The members of the chemistry club had vacated the front corner on the wall opposite the door, so Rory had a lab area for himself. Victoria still sat at this table at the beginning and end of the club meetings, but when the other club members dispersed to work in their groups, she left him alone at the table. Before leaving, she would rib him about being shuffled off to a different lab table because of his VIP status.

If she noticed changes in Rory's experiment, she would stay awhile to get an update on how his study had progressed. Then after cleaning up her work area at the end of the meeting, she would return to talk a little longer about his work before leaving him alone to work with Mr. Duggin.

During the final week in January, he put the finishing touches on the results of his enzyme study, before passing them on to Mr. Duggin and Mr. Butcher. As part of Rory's submission to the Board, both teachers would write evaluations of Rory's work. These evaluations covered the academic progress he made in his regular classes, as well as the experiment he had performed for his first project.

Once Mr. Duggin completed his review and evaluation, he forwarded the documents to Mr. Butcher for his final contribution. Then the whole package got bundled together and shipped to the Board.

The beginning of February started a full month of waiting for the announcement of the scholarship designate. Although the month could supply Rory with a little downtime, he realized he couldn't completely relax. Start dates for other projects loomed just around the corner. He planned to continue with his special curriculum as if he had already been awarded the scholarship, so he wouldn't lose the head of steam he had built up with regard to his work habits. But he also thought it would be a good time to catch up on everything going on around him.

His father had been successful in his efforts to revive the old car, so Rory had a method of transportation. So far he had only used it to drive back and forth to school; what else would he use it for? Even with a car and the desire to do something different, he didn't know what to do with his spare time since he hadn't had any for so long.

At the first chemistry club meeting after he had finished his scholarship submission, he had nothing to work on when the other students broke into their groups. He wandered among them, peering over their shoulders, trying to find out what type of experiments they performed. He found it all interesting, and the other students enjoyed describing their projects to him. However, none invited him to join their group. He understood their reluctance to engage his assistance; they knew the danger that they would end up letting him do the work and not learn on their own.

When he got to the table where Ellis and Gill had set up shop, he approached them with suspicion.

"What are you guys cooking up, more explosives?" He chided the two.

"Ha ha ha, verrry funny," Ellis said dryly, "Explosives are kid stuff. We're working on big-boy stuff now, like what happens to shaving cream as it expands while coming out of the can."

"Good idea. I guess some day you two might need to shave. Until then, it doesn't hurt to become familiar with the tools required for the task. I don't think I want to be in the cafeteria when you start blowing up cans of shaving cream."

"Shh, not so loud. Anyway, this will be way better."

"I know nothhhing," Rory said.

After visiting all the groups, he went back to his table and waited for Mr. Duggin.

"Kind of bored, are you?" Mr. Duggin asked, when he had some time to join Rory.

"A little. The first week of waiting has been tough; I don't know if I can take it for another three."

"You'll make it, but you should do something different than hanging out here. Why don't you read a novel or go hang around the gym for a change? You need to think about something other than chemistry while you have the chance."

"I don't think Mr. Shelton will let me hang around the gym. But a book isn't a bad idea, even though I spend a lot of time in the library anyway. Hanging here isn't bad; at least on Tuesdays I have something scheduled. All the other days, I don't have a clue what to do."

"Did you decide on how you're going to approach your next project?" Mr. Duggin asked.

"Not quite. I've been reading as much as I can about batteries. I can find quite a bit of material related to the traditional kind, but rechargeable ones are still so new and secret. It's hard to find out anything about them. The companies who make them won't send me any information about what they're doing. I don't know what the big deal is; I'm only trying to make a project out of it."

"Well, think about how many batteries are sold each year. Maybe the companies that make the normal ones don't want rechargeable batteries to come to market, so they won't send you what they know about them. And maybe the ones that do make the rechargeable batteries don't want anybody to know about their products because they want to control the market. I'm sure they have their reasons for not sending their information out to anyone that asks."

"I guess so," Rory said a little dejectedly, "I guess I'll read up a little more and see if there's enough material to make a project out of it."

"I wouldn't give up on the idea because you don't find enough information. You could treat this as an opportunity to generate your own information."

Mr. Duggin left Rory alone at his table to get back to the other club members' labs. Rory thought about what Mr. Duggin had said, and began to feel excited about setting up a more research-oriented project. For the next few days, he studied up on the process of research itself, rather than reading about batteries.

When the club time ended, Rory packed up his books and prepared to leave with the other students because, for a change, he had no reason to stick around this week. Victoria came back to his table to pack up her books, get her coat and prepare to go out into the sub-zero night. He noticed she put on a number of heavy items of winter clothing.

"You're wearing a lot of sweaters, jackets, scarves and hats there, Vicster. How much of the frozen landscape do you plan on hiking across?" Rory asked.

"Not much; but once I get cold, I stay cold. This is all preventative."

"I know what you mean. I used to freeze my ass off waiting at the bus stop," he said and then realized he could help her stay out of the cold. "Say, you want a ride home? I have a car now."

"No, that's okay, I can walk."

"No, no, no... I can drive you home. It's not out of my way." He insisted.

"Well, if it's no trouble."

"It's no trouble at all, but you may want to put all your stuff on anyway. The heater in the car works, but it takes a while before it blows warm air. And the car needs to warm up for a while before taking off, or it will stall."

"Anything sounds better than freezing in the wind."

The car doors groaned as they opened, then banged hard against the frozen latches as they closed. When they sat in the bucket seats, the fabric stretched fine but the vinyl portions squeaked under their weight. Victoria sat with hunched shoulders while Rory started the car, and their breath instantly fogged up the windshield. Rory turned on the defrost fan, bouncing cold air off of the inside of the windshield and providing an additional chill against their faces. Victoria sat rigidly while Rory got out and scraped ice off the windows. She could hear his shoes crunching in the recently fallen snow; it reminded her that she would be much colder if her shoes were making the crunching sound on her walk home.

Rory re-entered the car, letting in a new blast of cold air, which made Victoria shiver. He adjusted the radio dial so the music could be heard above the static that was rasping out from the frozen speakers.

"Okay, let's see if this thing will roll," he said as he slipped the transmission into reverse. The fan belt screeched and the tires crunched as he backed out and turned the wheels. They pulled away slowly. The thump of the tire's flat spot gave Rory another short-lived anxiety attack, as once again it fooled him into thinking the tire was out of air. He drove out of the parking lot and cruised in front of the school. He checked in the rear view mirror for traffic, scraped frost from the inside of the windshield, then placed the back of his hand against the glass to feel the air blowing out of the defroster. He confirmed he was in drive, not low, and then tried tuning the radio again to see if he could clear up the sound a bit more. After all of his fidgeting and about two blocks further on, he said, "So, I'm going to need directions; I don't know where you live."

"All right, it's back the other way."

"Well, we better turn around then."

Shortly they pulled up in front of Victoria's house just as warm air began to clear holes in the windshield frost, holes big enough for Rory to see the road without hunching down over the steering wheel. Victoria could see her brother and sister looking out of the picture window. Their heads bobbed up from the steam they had blown on the glass, so they could get a clearer look at their sister and the other person in the car.

Victoria looked back at Rory, smiling. He sat with a slight grin on his face, with nothing to say and seemingly nowhere to go. His eyes moved from her eyes to her nose to her cheeks and to her chin, then finally rested on her mouth, her lips.

"Thanks for the ride, Rory," she said. "I really appreciate it."

"Oh, no problem." He smiled. "Victoria, you want to go get a soda or something?"

"Oooh!" she let out, while a shudder rippled softly over the skin of her back. "The thought of a cold soda makes me shiver even more."

"Right. Well, how 'bout a cup of coffee?"

"Thanks, maybe another time." She tilted her head toward the house and her brother and sister. "They always wait for me so we can eat dinner together. They're both probably bursting with curiosity to find out who gave me a ride home."

Rory looked up and saw the two figures for the first time, then looked back at Victoria and said, "Okay then, I guess I'll see you around."

"Yes, you will. Thanks again." She smiled, then turned and left the car. Rory looked up and saw her brother and sister bolt away from the window. Before Victoria made it halfway up the sidewalk to the door, it sprung open and the two smaller figures began firing questions at her.

———

The next week after chemistry club, Victoria asked Rory if another offer of a ride home would come her way, and if so would his offer to go for a soda come with it. He replied it was a standing offer. After the meeting they got in his car and drove to the restaurant where Harry worked the evening shift. The dinner rush had died down. They took a booth along a frost-framed window, looking out onto the lighted street.

"So, will your little brother and sister starve to death waiting for you?" Rory asked.

"No, I told them this morning I'd be late and they should eat without me. They're old enough to feed themselves. I had to get my own supper when I was younger than they are now, and I had to do it alone."

"Why were you alone?"

"My parents were always giving music lessons. They either had students in our living room on our piano, or went out to one of the students' homes. I was an only child until I was six years old."

"So, you and your parents have always been heavy into music?"

"All... my... life," Victoria responded, sounding somewhat resentful.

"What, you don't like the music? Everybody thinks you live for music. Everybody knows you're smart at all the other subjects, but they also know the other subjects take a back seat to your music."

Victoria had never before considered how others viewed her, and she didn't know if she now liked the outside view. Did she present an image of total commitment to music? she wondered. Up until this year, when she joined the chemistry club, she had participated only in music at school. She was realizing that she didn't do anything but music outside of school, either.

She remembered receiving her first plastic recorder and her first music lesson from her father, at the same moment. She couldn't remember her exact age at the time, nor could she remember anything else related to the event that would establish a time frame. She remembered her father smiled at the way she played. When they finished the lesson, she had put the recorder in its red felt bag and gone to play with her other toys.

The next thing she remembered about her early music was her father always asking her if she had practiced with her recorder. Most times she answered no, because she hadn't wanted to play the instrument. That response would produce a dejected look on her father's face, but he never raised a fuss. When she told him she had practiced, he would smile broadly and praise her for practicing, then ask her to play for him. Gradually she began to practice regularly, and the more she played the more she enjoyed it. Within a year, she had realized the limits of the recorder; on her next birthday, her father gave her an oboe.

With a real instrument in her possession, Victoria was hurled into a new set of music lessons, also provided by her father. She accepted the challenge of the oboe, and in no time, asking her to practice wasn't necessary. The sound of the oboe saturated the eardrums of those within the Beach's house. Her mastery of the instrument required a huge amount of work, which she discovered she truly enjoyed. She felt pride in what she accomplished, playing in the school band and in the extracurricular musical ensembles her father lined up for her. People began to see that she could do more with music than the local music scene offered her and they recommended that she perform at recitals in order to display her talents for a more critical audience. An intense year of travel with her father followed. Every weekend they attended a recital in a different city, some at considerable distances from Great Falls.

Near the end of that year, she became exhausted from the amount of effort she had put into her music. But when she saw how much effort and energy her father put in, and saw his more enthusiastic response each step of the way, she wouldn't allow herself to let up for even a moment. Finally, at the age of twelve, she received a letter inviting her to the International Musical Youth Camp. Someone at one of the early recitals had written to the organization to tell them about Victoria. This caused them to solicit information from her band instructors and to inquire about her future recital schedule. Somewhere along the way, a respected member of the musical community attended one of Victoria's recitals and reported back to the organization, saying Victoria had the type of talent that belonged at their camp.

When the invitation came, Victoria suggested they could now reduce their recital schedule, since they had achieved what they had set out to do. But her father wanted to continue with the recitals because, he said, it never hurt a musician to play another recital. Victoria's mother finally convinced her father they should both stay at home for a while so Victoria could begin to prepare for her first camp.

For the next month, Victoria played her oboe only during school-related activities. Her father asked her every day if she had practiced, and again produced his look of dejection each time she answered no. Victoria was willing to put up with the look for the entire month just so she could take a breather.

Victoria finished telling her musical history to Rory, and sighed. "I still don't work at it the way I used to, except at the camp. Then it's kind of a challenge again, and I always want to work harder than the others."

"No wonder your dad used to look like he'd blow a gasket every week when I told him I hadn't practiced." Rory commented. "He must have been really pissed when I quit, music being such a big thing with him. That's probably why he decided to go and talk with my dad."

"Yeah," said Victoria. Then she looked down at her hands for a moment. When she looked, up Rory saw a look of concern on her face. "So, you said everyone thinks I'm only about music. Who says that?"

"Everybody. When people mention your name, they say something like, 'Victoria Beach, you know, the musician,' that's all."

"Hmm. I guess I've got to get out more often."

"Yeah, it's good you joined the chemistry club. You should try some other things too."

Victoria smiled as she looked at Rory's face; thick eyebrows over dark brown eyes, high cheekbones centered by an almost straight nose with not much flesh at its end, lips with sharp edges meeting in very sharp points and a straight jaw that formed a square chin.

Rory watched her eyes as they softly brushed across his features, fully aware she was looking at him with a relaxed and possessive gaze. He held still to allow her to complete her taking of his face.

Chapter 13

During the last week of February, Victoria received a letter from Germany. Werner Brock wrote to tell her he would arrive in the United States earlier than planned. His summer schedule had him teaching a workshop at the end of the spring semester on the campus of the University in Seattle, then proceeding to the International Musical Youth Camp in San Diego. In his letter he asked Victoria how long it would take to drive from Great Falls to Seattle, and if she could manage it, did she think she could come to visit him during his teaching assignment. He also informed her of his free time between the end of his class and the beginning of the music camp, stating he would love to spend some of it visiting her in Great Falls.

Victoria was excited to receive the letter; seeing Werner and visiting him in Seattle sounded great. But before she replied to his letter, she had to work out a few details with her parents. She could never visit him in Seattle without one of her parents along, and she didn't know if she could extend an offer for him to stay with the family if he visited their home.

When her parents returned from their evening lessons, Victoria told them about the letter. They both reacted in an unenthusiastic manner to this older German man corresponding with their daughter.

"How old did you say this Werner is?" her father asked.

"Around twenty, I guess. I never asked him."

"Well, I don't know. I don't think I want you traveling around to visit older men even if I go with you, and it's going to cost a lot of money for a hotel in Seattle," Mr. Beach commented. "Those hotel people in that town like to get all the money they can from you. Remember when we went for the recital? They wanted what I consider a major investment for a room with twin beds, a chair and a color television. Ridiculous."

"Werner said he could arrange for us to stay in the student dorm. Most of the students have gone home, so they let people stay in the dorm rooms for next to nothing. Besides, we don't have to stay very long, maybe a day or two," Victoria responded.

"Why can't we wait and meet him when he comes here? It will save us a long drive."

"I thought it would be polite for us to go meet him. He's traveled a long way and won't be going home for a long time." She saw this approach made no headway toward gaining her father's approval, so she tried the crowbar she needed to pry open his interest. "Also, we'd show him we are willing to travel to meet him, since he wants to talk to you about an appointment for me to a music conservatory in Berlin."

"What?" he asked, raising a single eyebrow.

"Werner said an old professor of his has recently been made the director of music at the Von Goss Conservatory in Berlin. He said I should consider applying to go there after I finish school. He wanted to make us aware of the conservatory, so we could check out what they had to offer."

"The Von Goss Conservatory? I've never heard of it," Mr. Beach said with a contemplative look on his face.

"So don't you think we should go and find out a little more about it from Werner?" Victoria asked.

"We'll see. We could talk to him when he comes to visit; we don't have to go to Seattle."

"Right, but if we do go to Seattle, he'll see we're really interested and might put in a good word with his old professor."

"We haven't talked about any of the options available to you once you finish school. Going to a conservatory in Europe sounds attractive. But who knows if it's the best alternative?"

"Well, I think we should go and check it out," Victoria said sternly.

"We'll see."

Victoria went to her room where she flopped down backward onto her bed and lay staring at the ceiling. The thought of going away to live in Germany put her into a daydream state. Getting out of Great Falls to live in a different place, in a new life style, seemed exciting. She would be in control of everything she did. She wouldn't have to listen to her father telling her *exactly* what he deemed to be in her own best interest. Moving away would signal the start of the real life she wanted to live.

Within her daydream state of mind, a hidden anchor pulled her to the ground, the pull of a new weight that had entered her mind only once before. Recently she wondered if she really wanted to dedicate her life to music. Music had always been her main focus, but she hadn't tried anything else to see if something more enjoyable or more exciting existed. How would she know if making music her life's work would be the right decision; how could she find out if something better awaited her? At play in her mind, and conflicting with her desire to try something new, she knew music could easily help her attain her one major goal—to get away from the life she would live if she stayed in Great Falls. Could she get away if she decided to concentrate on one of her academic subjects, like math, instead of music?

She saw what music had done to her parents. They earned a living; but did they enjoy life? She realized neither of her parents had been given opportunities like those being presented to her. She would most likely become a performer, not a teacher as her parents had settled for. But did she want to be a performer? Tainting her options was the fact that if she didn't pursue music, she would disappoint her mother and shatter her father's heart and dreams.

Rory had said the other students viewed her as being a musician. Which she interpreted to mean, a musician and nothing more. But she knew she was more.

———

Rory sat on a concrete stairway at the back of the school overlooking the parking lot. The sun reflected off of the rapidly melting snow, forcing Rory to squint when he looked up at Gary leaning against the brick wall. The sky was the deep, rich source of everything blue on earth. A warm chinook wind blew strongly, raising the temperature by thirty degrees since early this morning, breaking the students' lunch-hour cabin fever of the past few weeks.

"Do you know how often you mention her name or talk about something she said?" Gary asked Rory.

"What are you talking about?" Rory asked back.

"Man, you just said you're going out for coffee with Victoria again tonight. What and who do you think I'm talking about? You ought to nail her and get over it."

They looked at each other in silence, Rory slightly disgusted. Gary held the look, then finally said, "Nail?"

"Yes, asshole, I know what 'nail her' means," Rory said.

Rory had noticed how often he mentioned Victoria in his conversations. But if others were taking note of his frequent references to her, then in some peculiar way she had invaded his mind. He had been enjoying the time he spent with her, but he didn't know if he really looked forward to the next time he would see her, or if it was just okay if he saw her again. He explained away his casual attitude toward Victoria by blaming it on his idle mind. He told himself that once he found out about the Mortenson decision, his work would not allow him to give any of his time to anything other than chemistry.

With the ringing of the afternoon bell, Rory stood and both boys made their way back into the school. Gary turned to go to the band room, leaving Rory to walk to his locker alone. His path took him by the gym. As he passed, Mr. Shelton approached to inform him that Mr. Duggin had come looking for him and needed to see him as soon as possible.

Rory arrived at Mr. Duggin's classroom after classes had started, but he caught Mr. Duggin's eye through the small wire-reinforced window. Mr. Duggin raised his index finger, signaling for him to wait a moment. After assigning his class some reading, he came out and led Rory off in a hurry.

"It's someone from the Mortenson Board, Rory," he said as they walked down the hallway. "He wants you to call him; he wants to ask you a few questions."

Rory followed behind. "What about?"

"He didn't say. But there isn't an interview scheduled at this stage of the selection. I think it's about Mr. Keltch's letter."

"Oh shit!" Rory let out.

"Hey." Mr. Duggin stopped and scowled at Rory.

"Sorry."

The teacher turned and started walking again. "Mr. Butcher said to use his office to make the call. I'll get you connected to the guy, then I'll have to leave you alone. Come back to my classroom at the end of the period." They walked into Mr. Butcher's office.

Mr. Butcher rose from his desk and advised Rory to answer every question honestly during the interview. Mr. Duggin agreed, and added that Rory should try to relax and just be himself. Then he dialed the phone. He greeted the person at the other end of the line by indicating he had found Rory, then turned and with his hand over the mouthpiece said, "This is Dr. Carl Stapleton. Come see me later."

The next thing Rory knew, he was sitting alone in Mr. Butcher's office, holding the telephone, about to talk to a complete stranger. A stranger who had the power to affect his future. He had no idea of the tone or direction the conversation would take.

"Hello," Rory said.

Fifteen minutes later, Dr. Stapleton thanked Rory for answering his questions and said goodbye. Rory had been nervous the whole time, but felt some relief when he cradled the handset. Dr. Stapleton had asked his questions and listened to the answers, giving no indication as to whether or not he found the answers acceptable. The questions, as Mr. Duggin had guessed, were related to Mr. Keltch's letter, although Dr. Stapleton had not referenced the letter specifically. He asked questions regarding the priority of his studies. He asked questions about Rory's certainty toward pursuing a career in chemistry. He asked about the work schedule Rory had maintained since the beginning of the school year and he asked Rory if he remained committed to becoming the Mortenson Scholar.

Rory had responded honestly to everything asked. When he answered Dr. Stapleton's final question, regarding what he would do in the event he didn't get the scholarship, Rory replied he would still work on his special projects because he had already finished with the regular course material in chemistry. Then, for his senior year, he would approach Mr. Duggin for permission to continue performing additional projects outside of the regular chemistry curriculum.

He went on to say he would take chemistry at a university or community college regardless of what happened with the scholarship, even though it would require financial aid from other sources.

Mr. Duggin listened to Rory's description of the interview without asking any questions. When Rory finished, Mr. Duggin nodded with a vacant stare.

"So, what do you think?" Rory asked.

"Hmm, sounds okay. We'll know next week. I guess our only choice is to wait and see."

Rory could do nothing except continue to plan for his next project. It hadn't occurred to him that if the award went to another student, he would face a void of activities related to chemistry. With his regular chemistry class material already completed, and no reason to perform the work related to the scholarship, he could coast through the remainder of the year. But he didn't intend to coast. During his interview with Dr. Stapleton, he realized he couldn't avoid working in the field of chemistry. Rory Coleman was already a chemist. People who knew him and watched how hard he worked at what he loved, told him he needed to slow down. Rory discovered he didn't enjoy the idle time; his busy pace of work suited him just fine.

He didn't feel like he missed out on other things when he studied chemistry, he felt like he missed out on chemistry when he did other things.

Chapter 14

Rory's research into rechargeable batteries had confirmed Mr. Duggin's idea that the new project required a more experimental approach than his first one. He decided which track he wanted to explore, and put together the list of materials he would require for his research. Then he set about the task of determining how he would source the materials the school lab couldn't provide. He had been interacting quite often with Mr. Duggin over these matters, so when he received a request to meet Mr. Duggin at his office during the lunch hour, he didn't regard it as anything special. However, his attention awakened when he showed up to meet Mr. Duggin, and a state of confusion broke out as his teacher ushered him briskly to Mr. Butcher's office.

Mr. Butcher wasted no time. "Rory, you did it! You've been designated as the recipient of the Mortenson Scholarship. Congratulations! You did fine work on this, son, and you deserve it." Mr. Butcher spoke these words to Rory with the pride of someone who had helped and guided, but who also recognized where the real credit for the success belonged.

"I don't believe it! I got it?" Rory said, turning to Mr. Duggin.

"You got it, Rory. Congratulations!" Mr. Duggin shook Rory's hand with both of his and Mr. Butcher came around his desk to slap Rory on the back.

"Keltch's letter surely caused some problems, but you did a good job to overcome them, young man," Mr. Butcher said.

"I think you had a lot to do with overcoming that letter, Mr. Butcher. Thank you for your help. And Mr. Duggin," Rory turned again to the younger teacher, "This wouldn't have happened without you prodding me along. Thank you, I still can't believe it!"

"Believe it, Rory. You're in the Mortenson hot seat now, you're going to believe it more than you imagined from this point on," Mr. Duggin said with a huge smile.

Rory felt elated as he left Mr. Butcher's office. He stepped outside into the hallway, not knowing which way to turn or where to go. But it didn't matter because he felt so good! He looked one way down the hall and saw nothing, even though students crowded the hall. To him they appeared to progress in a freeze-frame motion as they moved past him in both directions. After a brief, inattentive scan, he picked out Victoria's face from the herky-jerky crowd moving through the hallway. Victoria stood still, leaning against the far wall of dark green lockers and looking him straight in the eye. He made his way to her.

"Victoria, do you think you would go out with me sometime?" he asked.

"You mean on a date?" she asked back.

"Yeah, on a date."

"Okay," she said.

"Good. I'll meet you at your locker after school. Maybe we can figure out what we're going to do."

"Okay."

"Okay, great. Guess what? I got it. I've been designated for the scholarship!" He beamed at Victoria, making her smile back at him; then he turned and left.

His afternoon was a waste of time, academically. He couldn't concentrate in any of his classes. His mind bounced back and forth between his two strokes of good fortune and the conflict they represented. Achieving his goal of being named the scholarship designate thrilled him. He knew now he could work hard at something he enjoyed and his hard work would help him accomplish his next set of goals. The recent phone interview had caused him to wonder about things like the Mortenson Scholarship and the unknown elements that could affect his application, elements he had no control over. His hard work could have been rendered futile by the presumed bitterness of Mr. Keltch's letter, or by an attitude Dr. Stapleton might have developed during the phone interview, or by some minor aspect of another applicant the Board found more favorable. Any of these elements could have changed his future forever, but remained unknown to him.

Setting up a date with Victoria also thrilled him. It hadn't been in his plan and he hadn't seen it coming, but when he saw her across the hallway, he felt they should do something together, something with more meaning than a ride home or a trip to the coffee shop. Gary had teased him about Victoria. He figured if Gary saw something different, then a more stirring element existed in their relationship. It wasn't a sense of relief he felt, a relief from pressure or hopeless desire, but a sense of newness and accomplishment. He felt like he had started something good. Intelligent and attractive, Victoria stimulated him on both of these levels.

For the moment, he enjoyed the thrill; yet he couldn't let himself bask in his good fortune for long. He wondered if starting a relationship with Victoria, despite how good it felt, would be a good idea. He knew without question he would perform the work his studies demanded, and he knew he wouldn't compromise his efforts toward success by reducing the time he spent at his work. He also knew he wanted to have a relationship with Victoria. Being with her made him feel different than he had felt with Alyse. He couldn't describe it any better than to say he felt more comfortable with Victoria, less tense, less anxious, because they had started as friends and were evolving into something more. With Alyse, it had been more of a physical attraction at first. When friends discovered the attraction existed, they pressured him into asking her out. Then he got to know and appreciate her. With Victoria, Gary had made his typical lewd suggestions, but Rory discounted them immediately. Asking Victoria out on a date for the purpose of trying to develop a relationship was his own doing, and that added to his level of comfort.

At the end of the day, as Rory approached Victoria's locker, he didn't feel the nervous embarrassment one might feel when meeting a prospective date for the first time after the initial request for the date. He felt an eagerness to discuss what they would do next to develop this new level of their relationship.

"Hi, Miss Vicster, how was your afternoon?" Rory asked as he reached up and gripped the top of her open locker door.

Mitch Davies

"Good, and yours?" she responded with a smile.

"I don't really know; I don't remember a thing I did."

"That's understandable, considering you had such good news. Congratulations on the scholarship. You left so quickly I didn't get a chance to say it then. What exciting news! You're going to go to a great school when you get out of here. Are you excited?" Victoria beamed at him.

"It's pretty great, all right. It's one of the steps I had to achieve to do what I really want. It's a relief to have accomplished that step. Now, I have to make sure I keep it."

"You will."

"I'm sure going to try. So, I'm also pretty excited about doing something with you, too."

Victoria smiled, then blushed. Without quite realizing it, she looked down at her feet.

Rory continued, "We've talked about a lot of stuff. Well, maybe not a lot of stuff. But I've never really asked you about what kind of things you do. You know, for fun. So like, what would you like to do?"

Victoria hesitated, then said, "Anything, I guess. Whatever you want to do."

"Man, I haven't done anything for so long, I don't really know what there is to do. I haven't had any fun time lately and don't know how much time I'm going to have from now on. What about you, what kind of stuff have you been doing lately?"

Victoria looked up at Rory. It took her a few seconds to answer. "You know, Rory, I don't do much outside of school other than music. Weeknights, I practice and do homework, on weekends I play in a community band with my father or I babysit my brother and sister while my parents are doing their thing. I guess like you, I haven't had any time to do anything, so I don't know what to do either."

152

There followed a moment of silence for the two dull lives they had been living and hoped to change.

"Well, we could go to a movie, find a party, or go to a game. What do you think?" Rory suggested.

"Sure, whatever you like."

"I guess we don't have to figure it out right now, we just have to figure something out by..." Rory paused and looked at Victoria, "Friday or Saturday?"

Victoria nodded and said, "Okay, either one. I don't think my parents have me tied up at all this weekend."

"I tell you what, what time do you get to school in the morning? Are you up early?"

"Pretty early, why?"

"Well, let's think about what we would like to do overnight, then let's meet here early in the morning. I'll bring doughnuts. Six-thirty okay?"

"Sure."

"Okay, I'll meet you here at six-thirty. You want a ride home?"

"No, you don't have to, it's warmed up a lot. I can walk."

"I know, but I want to give you a ride."

"Okay then, but my brother and sister are going to go nuts when they see me riding home with you and it's not after chemistry club."

When Rory dropped Victoria off, he asked if he could call her later that evening. She blushed again when she said he could.

Chapter 15

Victoria's brother and sister noticed an absence of conversation during their meal that evening. They had picked up on a disturbance in their older sister's mood. She had spoken to them in short sentences, giving them sharp little commands, as if directing them how to perform their tasks for the first time. As they ate, they shared inquisitive glances with each other, while Victoria stared at some vacant spot in front of her face. They tried asking each other questions intended to draw comments from their older sister, but she didn't pay them any attention.

With less than half of the food on her plate eaten, Victoria stood, said she wasn't hungry, and left them. Once she was gone from the kitchen, the two looked at each other, shrugged, then finished the rest of their meal in silence.

In her room, Victoria sat at her desk for a few minutes trying to remember what homework she had due the next day. Impatiently she swiveled in her chair, then began to unpack and assemble her oboe. She slid the cork-lined joints of the instrument together, prepared the reed assembly, and then laid the whole thing back down across the blue, velvet-lined case. She placed the double reed in her mouth and lay on her bed while it moistened.

I can't believe I blushed. I acted like some nerd girl who's never been around boys before. Rory must think I'm socially backward. He was so casual about meeting again, and it didn't even bother him when he suggested a few things to do and I said 'sure' like a go-along idiot. Then, I couldn't think on my own of anything we could do. And why couldn't I? Because I'm clueless and I have no social life. So, instead of making the impression that I've been around a bit, I prove without a doubt that I haven't. He must wonder what he's gotten himself into.

Victoria went on beating herself up for the remainder of the evening.

———

In complete darkness, Rory pulled up at his home. The chinook still blew with force from the coulee behind the house. The warm wind had made its changes to the land the house stood on. The snow had melted. Rory walked through water mixed with dry grass floating on soil that would soon soften into mud. If the wind kept blowing, he would drive out on a slippery quagmire in the morning; if it didn't, he would drive out on ice.

He entered the house through the garage so he could leave his running shoes in the mudroom. He saw no other shoes

155

in the room, though Pat's car sat parked out front; it hadn't clicked with Pat to enter from the garage. When Rory entered the kitchen, his father stood over the stove preparing the family meal. Pots steamed and meat sizzled as he entered. His father stopped his cooking activities to take in the apparition walking silently through the door.

"What the hell?" his father exclaimed.

Rory smiled but said nothing. Pat called in from the other room, "What is it?"

"It's not a what, it's your brother. I guess he found out I'm the cook tonight and wants to get it while it's hot."

"That's right," Rory said.

"What happened, fire at the school?" his father joked.

"No, I have some news I want to tell everybody. We going to eat at the table?"

"I suppose we could. Your mother's got one of her chinook headaches, but I'm sure she can sit at the table for a few minutes. Supper's ready in about fifteen, go tell your mom."

Rory went into the living room and flopped down at one end of the sofa. Pat sat in the recliner watching television with a beer in hand. He continued to watch his show for a few minutes without acknowledging Rory, then without taking his eyes of the screen he asked, "What are you doing here so early?"

"I missed you," Rory replied.

"Shithead."

"Mom's got the headache again?"

"Yup."

"She complaining about the ions?"

"Yup."

"I better go tell her about supper."

"She's not going to eat anything. You know how she gets with those headaches."

Rory rose and walked slowly to his mother's room. He tapped quietly on the door, then entered. She said nothing, probably sleeping. He stayed with her until he heard his father calling them to eat, at which point he left his mother's room, closing the door as quietly as possible. When he got to the kitchen table, he told his father she wouldn't be coming out.

"I figured she wouldn't," he said, "It's not just the headache either; she can't stand my cooking."

Rory smiled and looked down at the food on his plate. "It looks good," he said.

"It's lucky you came home at mealtime, Rory. I probably would've forgotten to make enough for you to eat later if you hadn't."

"Even if you had, Pat would eat it before I got to it."

"Damn right," Pat said.

They started their meal in silence, putting butter, salt and pepper on their boiled potatoes, then spooning a little honey over their peas. They tore off chunks of the thick slices of bread and dipped them into the brown gravy smothering the fried hamburger patties. After a period of satisfying his initial hunger pangs, Rory's father asked, "So, what's this big news you want to tell us?"

Rory swallowed his food and cleared his throat before answering. He could feel his heart rate increase as he searched for the right words to break his news.

"Do you remember the scholarship I applied for? Well, I got it."

"Wow! Good goin', Rory," his father said with a smile. "And yes, I do remember you talking about the scholarship. Didn't I get into a fight with your music teacher over it?"

Rory considered agreeing with his father to make things easier, but decided on answering with the truth.

"Well, actually you got into a fight with me. You and the music teacher sided together until I told you that the chemistry scholarship was more important than music."

"Yeah, right, now I remember. You ended up doing what you wanted, like you always do. So what does the scholarship mean?"

"It means I get to go to a good school."

"Jesus, I'll bet this will cost me a pretty penny. We can't afford to send you to an expensive school, Rory, even with a scholarship. Why can't you use the scholarship at the State University?"

"It's a pretty big scholarship, Dad, and Missoula isn't on the list of schools they say I can pick from. Besides, the scholarship covers living expenses. You won't need to pay for anything, unless you want to buy me a better car."

"Your car runs pretty good," his father responded. Then he looked down at his plate and began to prepare another forkful of food. Before he got it into his mouth he stopped and looked at Rory with the most important question on his mind, "How much is pretty big?"

"Up to forty thousand dollars a year, depending on the school and the materials I'll need in the lab. It covers everything."

Pat stopped eating. Mr. Coleman sat up straight and began leaning back in his chair. They looked at each other, then sat looking at Rory until Pat said, "Bullshit."

Rory tilted his head and shook it while grinning at his brother, then returned to his meal.

Mr. Coleman leaned forward and rested his chin in his left hand, turning to the right and looking down at the floor. He took a deep breath, then let out a sigh. "People will think I'm rich, sending my son off to an expensive college. Wait, no they're won't; they're going to think it's a good thing Rory got somebody else to pay for his schooling, because his father sure as hell couldn't afford it. Shit," Mr. Coleman looked at Rory with a perplexed expression.

"Dad, even rich people try to get scholarships for their kids. It's like a status symbol. You know 'I raised a smart kid, so smart I don't have to pay for his schooling.'"

"Yeah, people I know aren't too likely to think Toby Coleman figured out a rich man's trick. What did your mom say?"

"She said it was good." He knew his father had little tolerance for his mother's headaches.

"It is good, Rory. So when do you move out and where will you live?"

"Not for another year and a half. There's still some work to do; I only get the scholarship if I complete high school and do some extra projects. As far as where will I go, I don't need to pick a school until next year."

Pat, still mesmerized, had stopped eating and sat staring at Rory, nodding his head from time to time.

"Forty grand a year to go to school. When I go to junior college next year, it's going to cost three hundred and eighteen dollars per semester, and I'm working my ass off in a gas station to save up. You waltz in here and throw out forty grand a year," Pat said in disbelief.

"Some people got it," Rory said, rubbing it in.

"Prick," Pat shot back, then returned to his food.

"All right," their father interjected, "So Rory works hard at his school and he gets himself a great scholarship. Your mom and I are proud of you."

When the meal was over and the dishes stacked in the sink, Rory went to his room and sat at his desk in the dark. He heard Pat leave. A light outside his window told him his father had gone out to work in the barn. His mother still rested. The house became quiet.

———

The warm wind had blown all night. The snow was gone and mud had taken its place. With the warmth, the water in the windshield-washer fluid tank had melted, so Rory could spray the glass and keep it clean. With the melt that had occurred overnight, he would use it frequently.

His telephone conversation with Victoria the night before had seemed short. She had been quiet, like she didn't want to talk, so they only confirmed their meeting in the morning. Driving to school, he concerned himself with her quiet mood on the phone, wondering if she had second thoughts about their date. In their previous conversations they had talked with ease, so last night's conversation stood out as being odd. When he arrived at the school, he put his coat into his locker, then grabbed his bag of coffee and doughnuts and started walking to meet Victoria. When he turned the corner to enter the hallway where her locker was located, he saw her solitary figure walking toward him. They both smiled as they approached each other. When they met they continued to smile. Neither one spoke until Rory finally said, "Hi."

"Hi." Victoria returned.

Rory stepped a little closer and bent down to her, placing his lips gently over hers. He pressed his lips against her a little more firmly, then he moved them, again a little more firmly. As he did, he felt her moving her lips against his. He broke the kiss and pulled back, but stopped, still very close to her. Her lips then came forward and pressed his for an instant and they both pulled back to look at each other.

"Thanks," Rory said.

"For what?"

"I wanted to kiss you, and you let me. Thanks."

"I wanted to kiss you, too."

"Good. Come on, I brought you a doughnut."

Rory turned, indicating the direction he wanted to go, and waited for Victoria to start walking. He paced along beside her as they walked toward the gym. They went inside, then walked up the stairway at the side of the stage to get behind the curtain. In the darkness backstage, they took another stairway which led down under the stage. Rory turned on a light to reveal a large area with a low ceiling. The school athletes used the area as a training room. They walked down the long room to the far end, where they found a small room without a door. The athletes came to this room to get their ankles taped before games and practices. Inside, shelves stacked with athletic tape, rolls of pink foam, brown bottles of tincture of benzoin, and gauze lined the room. A small padded table sat in the middle and the scent of Tiger Balm made the room feel fresh.

"This is the only place I could think of where we could sit without being interrupted. The jocks don't use this place in the morning." Rory said.

"Is it okay for us to be in here?"

"I doubt it. But nobody's out there looking for people using this place without permission. Wait here for a second. I want to go turn the main light off."

While Rory ran his errand, Victoria did a slow spin to take in the room. She found herself in a place she hadn't known existed and would never have visited if she did.

Rory returned and offered to fix her coffee. They each took a doughnut. Rory asked her, "You do drink coffee, don't you?"

"Well, we've been out for coffee before. Why do you ask?"

"Because we *have* been out for coffee before and it seems every time you have a cup of coffee, you fix it differently. Once black, once with sugar, once with cream and sugar; and today you took it with cream only. It's like you aren't sure how you want your coffee. I don't think you ever drank more than half a cup anytime we went to Harry's."

"You're right, I never had coffee before we went to the restaurant the first time. I've only had coffee with you and I don't think I like it. So I've tried it different ways to see if it ever gets any better. Sorry."

"No reason to be sorry. How do you like it with just cream? Any better?"

She shook her head no.

"Do you like tea?"

"I've had tea and I liked it, but usually I drink orange juice at breakfast."

"I'll bring you OJ next time." Rory held her gaze for a few seconds, then said, "Why didn't you tell me you didn't like coffee?"

"I didn't know I didn't like it. You liked it, so I wanted to try it for myself to see if I liked it. Maybe I'll try tea next time."

"Okay. Victoria, I want you to tell me if you don't like something. I don't want you to do anything you don't want to do."

Victoria sat frozen by the look of seriousness on his face. She nodded quick little nods. Rory smiled, suddenly realizing how somber he must look.

"I like doughnuts," Victoria said, taking a bite out of her chocolate-glazed treat. She opened her eyes wide and nodded while she chewed, to exaggerate letting him know what she liked. "But not too many of them."

"Okay, okay. Say, Gary's having a party on Saturday. Would you like to go?"

"Gary Milton? The sax player? Isn't he a druggy?"

"Gary? Hell no. At least, I've never heard him talk about it. So, then you don't want to go?"

"No, I only asked out of curiosity. I heard somewhere that Mr. Keltch had to get him straight once. That's all."

"I know Mr. Keltch helped him deal with low grades a few times, but nothing more. So you'll go? If you don't like it there we can take off and do something else."

"Okay, let's go and see what it's like."

Rory sipped his coffee. He looked over the rim of the cup at Victoria and found her looking down at her hands as she rubbed her palms together. He placed his cup on the padded training table, then touched her hand as he hunched down to look at her face.

"What's wrong?" he asked in a whispered voice.

"Rory, there's something I want to ask you."

He sat up straight. "Go ahead."

"Tell me if it's none of my business. It's about you and Alyse," she paused.

"What about us? Hmm, that's weird, I haven't thought about her and I as an 'us' for a long time."

"I think you just answered my question," she said with a sound of relief in her voice. "You see, I knew you and Alyse broke up, and since then you haven't dated anyone else. I also noticed that the two of you don't even talk to each other. So, I wondered if you still thought something might happen between you and Alyse."

"No, I don't think anything will happen. It took a while, and without going into any details, it seems like she was right to split us up." Rory pursed his lips and looked away. "Do you know why she won't talk to me now?"

"Yes, you went to a whorehouse."

Victoria's statement caused him to breathe deep and hold the air in his lungs.

"I knew that story got around to everyone. You brought it up to me first. Do you remember that?" Victoria nodded in answer. "Well, everybody seems to forget one little aspect of the story. I didn't go there for sex and I didn't go in until my brother got hurt. Alyse doesn't believe that; she thinks I cheated on her with a hooker."

"Everybody knows that's why she won't talk to you, but I know you didn't cheat on her."

Rory looked at Victoria with a furrowed brow.

"How would you know that?"

"Harry told me about it in the cafeteria one day. We had been out for coffee a couple of times and he said it looked like you, in his words, 'had the hots for me,' so I'd better know the truth about your trip to Shelby. He told me how you sat outside waiting and you only went inside when, like you said, your brother needed help. He said he's told that part of the story before but he wanted to make sure that I heard it from someone who was there. I asked him why he didn't tell that part of the story to Alyse, and he said he did but she didn't believe him. He said she accused you of making it up for him to tell her."

"You say you believe it?"

"Yes." Victoria looked Rory straight in the eyes.

"Good," Rory replied, happy with her directness. "We better get going."

Rory packed up the litter and they stepped out of the trainer's room. He stopped to flip off the light in the small room. Victoria stood a few steps away. With the switch turned off, they found themselves in a black void. At the far end of the room a strip of light seeped in from under the landing door, but the darkness absorbed it before it could reflect off any surface to provide them with some visibility.

"Victoria?" Rory called out for her.

"I'm here," she said, her voice coming from closer than where she had been when the light went out. He reached out, making contact with her upper arm; at the same time he felt her palm press against his chest. His hand moved up her arm to find her face, so he could guide himself to her mouth. He bent down to kiss her and her hand moved around behind his back to pull him toward her. They pressed together kissing, their mouths opened, their kisses strong. The bell rang and they separated their kiss, but continued to hold each other. They stood with Victoria pressing her cheek against his shoulder, while Rory held his cheek against her head. He enjoyed the scent, the warmth of her body and the feeling of comfort.

They made their way through the dark, to the light from below the door. When they reached it, Rory took her in his arms again and kissed her once more before they stepped out into the light of the hallway. Together they walked back to Victoria's homeroom where he left her, to go make attendance at his own.

Chapter 16

Mr. Keltch had asked Victoria to return to the band room at the end of the day, saying he needed to discuss something with her. She had agreed, and then gone about the rest of her day without giving the meeting another thought. She had planned on meeting Rory after class, but she knew she could meet up with him later in the evening. For the past two months they had seen each other often, early in the mornings, to spend an hour together under the stage or after school when he gave her a ride home. They spent their evenings studying. Occasionally they would get together at the school library, but for the majority of the school nights, they kept in contact by telephone.

Rory had given her a concerned look when she told him about the meeting with Mr. Keltch. She thought about that, then decided his concern originated from the memory of his own discomfort during his meetings with the band teacher.

When she arrived at the band room after class, Mr. Keltch was occupied with another student. She waited in the main band room until the student left, then went in and sat down. He seemed relaxed, smiling across his desk at her. His hair looked as fresh and in place as it had at the start of his day, not as if it had endured a busy day conducting students who probably wanted to be doing something else. His shirt was clean, white and crisp and his tie was still in a tight knot. But his jacket was off. As he smiled at Victoria, he made a small performance out of undoing the buttons of his shirt cuffs and rolling them up to the middle of his forearms. Victoria viewed this act as unusual; for him to stray from his very formal style was rare. His neat glass-top desk had nothing on the shining, dustless surface but a pencil holder and a gold-plated conductor's baton. Four frames mounted on the wall behind him displayed the artwork of the program covers for the annual band concerts. They represented the four years Mr. Keltch had been at the school. To the left of his desk, a large area contained two chairs facing a conductor's podium, behind which sat an over-height chair. On the podium lay the scores of the music the band currently rehearsed. Mr. Keltch read and reviewed the scores here, using the podium as his work area more often than he used his desk.

Victoria had been in this office on other occasions and it had always looked as it did this time, with the exception of Mr. Keltch himself, not wearing his jacket.

"You said you wanted to talk to me about something," Victoria said.

"Yes, a number of things actually," he said, then paused and smiled for a second or two. "We don't get to see you in the band room very often any more, so I wanted to talk a bit."

"Sure," Victoria said as she fidgeted in her chair.

"You know, you used to hang around after school to do a little practice here in the band room. Now, you do your classes and you come to rehearsals, but as soon as they're over, you clear out pretty fast. So I wonder, what makes you leave in such a hurry, and what you do with the time you're not spending in the band room?"

"Well, I guess I'm getting involved with some other activities around the school, but I hadn't really thought of them as taking me away from band. This year I joined the chemistry club and had some fun in there, plus I've checked out the math club, too. You know, stuff like that. And I've been doing a lot of homework."

"Yes, I know about those things. Mr. Duggin mentioned your attendance at the chemistry club a number of times. These are all good things to be involved with. You should try them to see if you like them. I guess I want to know how much you like them. I want to talk with you about these new activities of yours, to see what you think of them, and provide you with someone you can talk to about these matters. You know, kind of like a guidance counselor, only one with a little more understanding of how to put things into a perspective more in line with your interests."

Victoria shifted in her chair, then asked, "What do you mean?"

"You *are* a musician, Victoria. I don't want you to forget that. You are, first and foremost, a musician. These other things you are getting involved in can certainly help you as a person. The better the person you become, the better the musician you will be, and the more you will bring to your musical career. I want to make sure you realize that the benefits you receive from these other activities should be regarded as support for your main focus. Do you understand what I mean?"

"In a way I do, but the reason I'm involved in these other activities is because I want to try something other than music. It occurred to me that the only thing I've ever done is play the oboe, and I decided I had better try something else. I want to find out if I've already chosen what I really want to do, or if it is still out there somewhere. So, I don't know what my main focus is right now, and I'm enjoying all the new activities I'm doing."

"Good, you should enjoy it. But please remember that what you've done with the oboe is pretty good, too." Mr. Keltch said, full of enthusiasm. "You and your father spent a lot of time together developing your oboe skills, so I don't want you to lose sight of all your accomplishments. The recitals you attended and the invitations to the Musical Youth Camp, those things didn't happen merely because you had the will to work hard, they happened because you also enjoy what you do. I can't imagine you would work as hard as you do, if you didn't enjoy the work.

"You know how wonderful it is to have music as a part of your life. With your ability to play an instrument as well as you play, you must feel some joy in what you do; to achieve what you have achieved, the joy shines through so much that others see and hear it as you play. I don't want you to lose sight of the joy you feel when you play."

"Fine. Do you think I've lost the joy? Do you think that my playing has gone downhill or something?" Victoria asked.

"No, not at all, and I want to make sure it doesn't. You are still the best musician in the school."

"Then there really isn't any cause for concern, is there?"

"Sure there is, and I wanted to make you fully aware of that concern. Now I've done that. The other thing I want to talk to you about is the camp this year. Are you looking forward to it? It's your last, unless you return as an instructor." Mr. Keltch leaned forward in his chair. His elbows rested on the desktop and he laced his fingers together.

"Yes, I'm really looking forward to going to San Diego. I always look forward to getting together with the other girls, and this year I'm looking forward to seeing the oboe tutorial instructor again. I told you about him last year. This year he's coming to Great Falls before the camp starts. You should meet him, Mr. Keltch, he's really into music. He wants to talk to my father about me going to a music conservatory in Berlin next year," Victoria said.

"Sounds great. I would very much like to meet this instructor. Maybe we could get him to address the class."

"I'll ask him. We're going to see him in Seattle before he comes to Great Falls."

"Great," Mr. Keltch said, still smiling, "I hoped you were looking forward to attending."

"Why wouldn't I?"

"Well, you appear to have more of a social life these days. I understand you are seeing a lot of Rory Coleman." Mr. Keltch continued to lean forward, watching her closely.

"Yes, I am, but what does that have to do with anything?"

"I like Rory. You know Rory and I used to get along pretty well together, before he let me and the rest of the band down." He stopped to see her reaction.

Victoria displayed no reaction, so Mr. Keltch went on. "I think when he left the band program, he acted very selfishly by quitting to chase after his own agenda; he gave no consideration to the commitment he had made to all of us. He's pretty sore at me now. I hope he feels guilty about what he's done. I wanted you to know what kind of person he is, and warn you that he's going to do whatever best serves his own purpose with no consideration for others. I don't want to see you get hurt by him, and I also don't want to see you become influenced by him."

Victoria felt blindsided and she knew her face was flushed.

"Mr. Keltch," she started, then paused briefly to settle herself down, "It seems a lot of people are trying to influence me right now. As far as getting hurt by Rory, that risk is mine to take. I don't know if Rory feels guilty about leaving the band or not, but he wanted to pursue chemistry. The scholarship offered him a great chance to do that. He took the chance, earned the scholarship, and moved on with his choice."

Mr. Keltch saw Victoria's anger rising, so he changed the subject back to her music. They talked about the camp and the conservatory. Victoria didn't know how long they talked. She sat and appeared to listen but no longer registered the words he spoke. Mr. Keltch continued to emphasize how much fun the camp had been for Victoria and how much music can improve a person's life. He also pointed out the certainty of her receiving a scholarship to one of the best musical schools in the country. The current opportunity with the conservatory in Berlin proved that her talent had been noticed.

Finally, he couldn't resist returning to the topic of her other activities. He concluded by saying she should try to experience a variety of activities. And that she should always view them in the context of what they could mean to her musical life, the life that had provided her with so much. He told her of his concern for her level of awareness of how her choices at this time in her life could affect her future.

———

In the early evening while Victoria gathered her books to go with Rory to the library, she failed to hear her father's arrival. When she had her things together and went to the living room to wait, she was surprised to see him.

"Hello, Victoria. Did you practice today?" He asked his usual question in his usual mocked-ominous voice.

"Only during class," she told him.

"You should always do a little extra on your own."

"Yes, I know. Today I didn't have time and I'm going to the library tonight."

He looked at her with his saddened look of disappointment. She moved over and sat on the sofa by the window to watch for Rory. Lately, her father had been more diligent in stressing the importance of her practice habits and she had been very short, but adamant, in her explanations of why they had changed. She could feel him staring at her back as she watched out the window.

"Did you make a decision on which weekend we should go to Seattle?" he asked her.

"No, not yet."

"Why not?"

Victoria turned to look at her father. She waited a few seconds before she exhaled through her nose and said, "Dad, you don't even want to do this trip, so why do you keep asking me when we're going to go?"

"Because when you first asked me to go you were so excited about it. You convinced me that we should take advantage of a good opportunity and go. Now, it's like you can't be bothered with it. What happened to make you change your mind?"

"Nothing. I haven't changed my mind. I still want to go. How about this weekend?" she asked in a challenging voice.

"That's not enough notice."

"Then next weekend. How's that?"

"It should be okay. Will you contact Mr. Brock, to make the arrangements at his end?"

"Yes," she answered, then turned to look out the window again.

"Victoria, are you mad at me?"

"No," she said, still watching for her ride.

"Victoria, your sister tells me you have a boyfriend. Is this why you've lost interest in the trip to visit Mr. Brock, and why you don't practice anymore?"

"No, it isn't," she answered curtly, without turning. Her father had hit very close to the mark; but it wasn't all Rory. Her interest in other subjects took her away from the music, as well. When they went out together they studied those other subjects; they didn't go out and goof off.

"Okay, then why aren't you practicing as much as you used to, who is this boyfriend, and do you plan on letting us meet him?"

This caused her to turn. With a curious expression on her face, she said, "Other school work is what is taking up all of my time. I've been concentrating on my math and science a lot more. And you've already met my boyfriend; you used to give him music lessons."

"Really. Who is he?" Now Mr. Beach had a curious look on his face.

"Rory Coleman; he played the tuba."

Mr. Beach said the name to himself a couple of times.

"Yes, I remember him. An okay tuba player."

"That's partly why he quit, he was just okay."

"He should have stuck with it."

"He had more important things to do, and it looks like he made the right decision. He's received a scholarship in chemistry."

"Hmm. Well, good for him. Your mother and I still want to meet him."

"I'm sure you will. I got to go," she said as she stood up. She had spotted Rory's car as it came around the corner.

"Victoria, what time are you coming home?" Mr. Beach asked as she opened the front door.

"Shortly after the library closes, about nine-thirty." She closed the door.

Mr. Beach stood and walked over to the window and watched Victoria get into the car and drive away.

At the library, Rory and Victoria walked toward the entrance. Before going in, Rory stopped to kiss her. Her lips were warm but barely accommodating.

"What's eating you?" he asked as he pulled away from her.

His question hit her the wrong way.

"I guess absolutely everything is eating at me, at least that's what everybody seems to think. Keltch, my Dad, and now you trying to find out what's bugging me... Nothing... is bugging me. Why does everybody think I'm being bugged by something?"

Rory stood looking at her, then shrugged. "I guess for me, it's because you didn't say a word in the car. Then, when I asked you what you planned to work on tonight, you answered 'stuff.' And, when I kissed you, it felt like I'd just received a left jab, instead of the knee-wobbling, knockout punch that I normally feel. I add it all up and it makes me think something is a little out of sorts. Me being a nice guy, I wanted to offer you a chance to let it all out on a set of sympathetic ears, but I have to tell you I'm currently rethinking my offer."

"Forget it. I'm not talking because I don't want to talk."

Rory's lighthearted approach had not softened Victoria's mood to any visible degree. "Suit yourself," he said.

Inside, they sat in the area adjacent to the stacks that held the science and technology resources. Victoria usually worked from her own class textbooks rather than the library's texts. Tonight she opened each of her books and started to work on some of the exercises, but quickly got bored and moved on to the next text. Rory had difficulty concentrating on his own research because of the commotion Victoria created at her end of the table. After making her way through the texts she had brought along with her, she got up from the table and disappeared down one of the rows of books. When she came back a few minutes later, she placed the four new volumes she had picked out onto the table and attempted to read them, but again failed.

Rory looked at her. When he caught her eye, he placed his hands behind his ears, slightly cupped with their palms forward and mouthed to her, "I'm all ears."

Victoria smiled with obvious venom and went to pick out a few more books. When she returned, she set the books on the table but didn't touch them. Rory watched as she sat thinking. She turned and looked at him again. This time he mouthed, "I really like you."

Victoria smiled sadly then spoke, "I—" out loud, disrupting the other students. When she realized she had actually spoken, she covered her mouth, stared wide-eyed at Rory and began to laugh quietly into her hand. After she regained control of her laughing, she mouthed to Rory, "I really like you, too. How long do you want to study? Can we go out for some tea?"

Rory mouthed back, "About ten minutes. That should give you enough time to speed read another dozen books." But Victoria didn't pick up all of the words in the last sentence and looking a little confused said, "What?" out loud again, only louder than before, and had to cover her mouth as she snorted with laughter. Rory began packing up his books immediately.

In the car Rory asked her again what was eating her. She started to tell him about her meeting with Mr. Keltch. She had barely started her story when they arrived at the restaurant, and two cups of tea later she told him about her discussion with her father.

"It bugs me how they're trying to force me to concentrate on just music. I keep telling them I want to check out other things, but they don't want to hear it."

"Did you actually tell your dad you wanted to check out things other than music?" Rory asked in amazement.

"No, I said that other homework was taking up my time. I don't want to get him too upset about it yet. I shocked my mother when I told her, so I can imagine how my father's going to take it."

"You can't blame them, really. They don't want to see all of your work go to waste, and that's what they think will happen if you decide you want to do something different."

"I know. My dad will be so disappointed."

"Sure he will. But you haven't really found anything interesting enough to make you want to quit music, have you?"

"No."

"So they should know that. They should know it would take an awful lot to make you want to switch."

"Right, but they should also know if I do find something, then it's up to me to decide on whether or not I want to switch."

"You're right. They may know it but they won't accept it."

"How did you get your parents to accept your decision to drop band and basketball?"

"There's a little difference in our situations. My parents are never involved in what I do, not even close to the way your father is involved with what you do. My parents couldn't give a rip what I decided. They had no idea I had applied for the scholarship, they don't know what I did to receive it, and they don't know what it takes to keep it. But you know what? It's simpler that way."

"Simpler, but isolated. It's nice to share things with family. You want them to be proud of you, don't you?"

"I'm proud of me, Victoria. That's what I think is important. I'm sure my parents are interested in what I do, only not enough to get involved. So I keep them informed and that's about it." Rory's speech sounded matter-of-fact.

"I don't want to upset my dad."

"Maybe you won't. You just need to make sure your biggest priority is not upsetting yourself. You want to make yourself happy, Vicster. Your parents aren't going to perform any solos for you, they aren't going to write any math exams for you, and they aren't going to win any scholarships for you. You're the one who's going to do all of that stuff, so you better do it in order to get something you want. Don't get caught living the life they wanted but couldn't achieve. You can easily achieve musical success, but you may find you can also achieve something better."

Victoria arrived home later than she had predicted. When she entered through the front door, her father was sitting in his chair reading. This was not normal. He always went to bed by ten o'clock. She prepared herself for a barrage of questions he would fire at her, questions designed to make her feel guilty.

Her father looked up from his reading and said, "Hello. Did you have a nice evening?"

"Yes, it was okay," she replied, still standing by the door.

"Good, I'm glad," Mr. Beach said, then looked back at his book.

"How come you're still up?"

"Reading... This is a good book."

Victoria walked across the living room to go to her bedroom, but stopped as she entered the hallway.

"Sorry I'm late," she said, then stood waiting for her father's response. She didn't want him to think she ignored her late arrival in order to avoid having to give him an explanation.

Her father looked up again. "That's okay. It is a little late for a school night. I wouldn't want you to do it too often."

They both smiled. Victoria didn't want to say it wouldn't happen again, so she turned and went to her room.

Chapter 17

Rory had been spending most of his time researching rechargeable batteries. It had been difficult to find a thread to follow; but as in most research projects, once you found one, it led to a patch of material where many threads offered a diverse group of options to chase. The one he chose required that he get his hands dirty. He dismantled both traditional and rechargeable batteries in order to compare the internal structures and their chemical compounds. This analysis led him to study the chemistry of nickel and cadmium blends. From this point he had to turn to his knowledge of physics, since he had to introduce the recharging process to the batteries. This meant an outside agent, electricity, was applied to the compounds; and this outside agent would have a physical effect on the structure of the chemicals inside the battery. The physical effect created a chemical change, which led to a whole new round of analysis.

He found the work invigorating. The threads he followed wove a net of knowledge he knew he wanted to support him for the rest of his life. He enjoyed the process of developing data that he would later analyze and turn into information. He knew, with each new fact and each new inference, that his capacity to learn had increased. There was no room for doubt regarding his decision to follow a life devoted to chemistry, and his work on his two projects thus far confirmed that he had made the correct choice. He didn't miss music and he didn't miss basketball. It had become a waste of his time to think back on those activities.

His work in chemistry reaped benefits in his other subjects as well. Every class he took seemed easier; his enjoyment of learning in chemistry generated more enjoyment in his math, physics, English and Spanish classes. Math and physics would obviously aid his logical approach to chemistry, as the sciences built upon each other; but he began to see also how the study of literature and language opened his mind to more creative ways to view problems. His preference for work on his chemistry research caused a small but continuing problem with his other subjects; the potential to forget about them existed. To make sure he didn't forget them, he had to make a conscious effort to stay on top of the homework in his other classes.

So he developed a routine to follow consisting mainly of checkpoints. Several times each day, he reviewed a list of reminders that he kept in the front of his school binder. A checkpoint occurred when he had a definite change in activities. Leaving the school at the end of each day was defined as a checkpoint. When he got to the door leading to the parking lot, he would stop and look at his list to make sure he didn't have any activities requiring material that wasn't in his binder. When he finished his evening meal at home, he checked the list to review each of his subjects and remind himself of any tasks related to a specific class that required his attention. Everytime he reached a checkpoint, he checked his list. To make sure he addressed all of his homework, he had to make sure he added tasks to his checklist throughout the day. The main school subjects held the top spots on the list, so he had to think of them first every time he checked. But if something special came up, like picking out a new novel for an English assignment, he had to put it on the list as a specific reminder.

One of the checkpoints that occurred every night was his phone call to Victoria. Even when they met to go to the library, he called just to maintain the discipline of the checkpoint. Only a brief call, but it meant he had to check his list. If they hadn't planned on meeting, they would talk for a longer period about more personal topics. Then at the end of the call, he checked his list. If he got carried away with some research or some other homework and forgot to call, Victoria would call him and the checkpoint discipline would be maintained.

At sixteen and a half years of age, Rory had distilled his life down to two interests. One, academic work; the other, Victoria.

Both interests overlapped during the time they spent together in the library. But away from the library, they did a variety of other normal teenage activities, and Rory enjoyed these activities to the point of forgetting about school completely. He had discovered, over the past few months, that being with Victoria had this effect on him.

One Friday when he arrived home from school, he found a letter from the Mortenson Scholarship Board waiting for him on the kitchen table. Inside the envelope he found a request for permission to release his name to the schools on the Mortenson Scholar eligible list, so those schools could send him recruitment information. These forms required the signature of his parents. His mother could sign right away, but when he went out to the barn to see his father, the truck, trailer and horse were gone.

He found out from his brother Pat that his father had left to do some work down in Helena.

"You think he's going to Ogden's?" Rory asked.

"That's the only place down there I know he does any work, so I'd bet he's at Ogden's."

"Do you think my car will make it to Helena and back?"

"You out of your mind? I can't believe you made it home from school in that piece of shit. Every night, I wait for the call where you ask me to come and pick you up because your car has up and croaked."

"I guess I have been defying the laws of probability. How about you lend me your car tomorrow?" Rory said, in a tone implying his brother had a generous soul.

Pat stood silently and stared at Rory before saying, "There must be a hole in the gas tank of your car; I think you're high on fumes."

"Well, then you better expect the come-and-get-me call later."

Early the next morning, Rory and Victoria set out on the highway to Helena. The road passed through, fields and rolling hills of blended green and brown grass shoots as the new spring hay began to replace the dry husks of last year's crop. The wind gusts bent the blades of grass, sending shiny ripples across the surface and occasionally pushing the car to the shoulder of the interstate. The climb from the changing hills into the evergreen mountains worked relentlessly against the little car. The tiny aluminum engine pinged melodically up the steady grade. Rory stayed in the right lane, watching as every vehicle on the road passed him by.

The concern he felt about over-stressing the engine dissipated when they crested the first pass and started on the downhill curves into Wolf Creek. He pulled off at the exit, turned under the highway and crossed the tracks to the small town's main street. He wanted to check out the car, let it rest for a while, and have some breakfast. He pulled off the main road, the shoulders of which turned into a sparsely graveled parking lot in front of a small coffee shop. The shop used the bark-covered castoffs of a nearby mill as siding, and had a wooden sidewalk running in front of the building. The one four-pane window had a cardboard sign leaning on the inside ledge. The faded, black, felt-penned word 'Open' invited them in. The heavy wooden door pulled against Rory as he opened it for Victoria, and once inside he had difficulty closing it against the force of the steady wind.

The only customers were a group of three older men who stood eerily still in front of a Keno machine. Shortly, they flailed their arms and yelled curses at the numbers the blinking machine had chosen to display. After presumably releasing all of their bad luck in this manner, they changed positions and one of the other men tried his luck by dropping in coins and keying in a selection of numbers. A waitress, enjoying a cigarette in the booth adjacent to the machine, looked up and told Rory and Victoria to seat themselves, then, while stubbing out the cigarette, asked them if they both wanted coffee.

The smell of potatoes fried in bacon grease filled the room, letting Rory know nothing had changed.

"My dad and I stopped here every time we came down to work for Ogden. Both on the way here and on the way back. I'll bet he had breakfast here yesterday," Rory said. "I don't remember the Keno machine, but I see it's the same waitress."

"Do you think she'll remember you?" Victoria asked, while looking around to see what the old building had to offer.

"Doubt it: I've changed a lot since I was eleven."

The waitress arrived with coffee mugs, menus and a pot of coffee. She kept her eyes on Rory for a few seconds as she filled his cup, then left.

"I think toast and grapefruit," Victoria stated, without looking at the menu.

"You'd be making a big mistake if you only ordered toast and grapefruit. They make the best fried potatoes in the world in this place. You should have a big breakfast: it's the specialty here." Rory said. He nodded his head to confirm the truth he told her. "Watch the waitress when I order. I'm going to order exactly like my dad orders his breakfast, and we'll see if she remembers."

The waitress returned and asked Victoria for her order, and Victoria told her to double whatever Rory had. The waitress gave her a look, then turned to Rory and stood poised to write down the order.

"Bacon... crisp, toast... buttered to the edges, eggs... over easy and keep them loose, potatoes... slightly burnt." He spoke with a definite pause after each item before he stated how he wanted the item prepared.

The waitress looked up from her book and cocked her head to the right. Her expression showed she was working up a question, but she needed to lean toward Rory and scrutinize his face more closely to formulate it.

"Are you Toby Coleman's kid?"

"Yep."

"Jesus. The little one that used to come through here with him all the time?"

"That's me."

She paused to remember him from the past. "I guess you don't want chocolate milk any more, huh?"

"I still like chocolate milk, but not this time."

"You know your dad came through here yesterday?"

"I kinda thought he would. Did he say where he was headed?"

"No, I don't recall he did. Let me go get your order in."

They ate their breakfast while chit-chatting with the waitress. She asked Rory questions about what he had been doing while growing up; and commented on how big he had grown, and about how much of a trouble maker he used to be when he came into the restaurant.

When they finished, Rory paid the bill, leaving a tip larger than he had planned, a tip that cut into his gas money. They drove across the street to the filling station and checked the tires and the coolant before heading back out onto the interstate.

"My father likes to stop at the chains," Victoria said from the passenger seat. "He likes to know the food he's getting will be the same no matter where he goes." She looked toward Rory with her head resting on the window.

"My dad's kind of like that," Rory said, "but he knows the food will be the same because he always goes to the same places. I don't even know if they have any other restaurants back in there in Wolf Creek. If they do, he never took me to any of them."

From time to time Rory would take his eyes off the road and look over at Victoria. Having her along on the quest made it more enjoyable, even though the quest was minor. Each time he turned to look at her, he saw something different on her face; and each time, he confirmed the feature held its own beauty. He grew more and more light-headed and content each time they were together.

The car's engine sang loudly as they climbed out of Helena, made it up the grade, and turned off onto the two-lane road to Winston. After a few more miles, they turned onto the unmarked Bentley Road. The Bentley ranch had been the first ranch in the area; Mr. Bentley created the access road so he could get to his home, which he built as far from the main road as possible. The ranchers who arrived after the Bentleys benefited from buying other parcels of land along the road; they thanked Mr. Bentley for arriving first, saving them the trouble of creating an access road themselves.

The Ogden family had purchased their ranch some years after the Bentleys, but they had been ranching on it for a long time. The current Mr. Ogden had continued to work the ranch when his brothers and sister left to enjoy the city life a long time ago. In his sixties, with no family of his own, he still ran enough cows to need help at certain times during the year. He had one full-time hand about his age to keep him company; but those times when he needed extra help, Rory and his father used to stay and work for a few days. It had been five years since Rory had been to Ogden's, but his father still came when needed.

Rory slowed as he passed the entrance of each ranch, not quite sure which one led to the Ogden's. Then he recognized the arch made of sun-bleached, barkless poles hung over the dirt road to the ranch house. The Ogden house was not old by the area's standards, but only because it was the second ranch house built on the property. The current Mr. Ogden had built it about twenty years earlier, when he realized the original house would soon fall apart. The new split-level log home with a shake roof stood three steps off the ground. As an afterthought a small deck had been appended to the steps leading up to the door. The creosote-soaked logs and roof had lost their smell long ago.

The original Ogden house sat back about a hundred yards from the new one. It had a swayback roofline, and the whole building leaned a bit in the direction the wind always blew. The top of the chimney had fallen, and lay in a heap at the end of the house outside the kitchen.

In past visits Rory's father had always told him to stay away from the old house. When they got out of the truck and greeted Mr. Ogden, Mr. Ogden would repeat his father's instruction to stay away from the old house. Bill, the hired hand, warned him the third time, by reminding him that he himself had been walking by the old house when the chimney had fallen, and how it had barely missed crushing him to death.

Working in one of the outer buildings, Mr. Ogden saw Rory's car arrive. While he walked over to greet the visitors, Rory parked in front of the new house. He and Victoria got out and stood on either side of the car looking at the house. Mr. Ogden called out, "Can I help you?"

Rory turned to the familiar voice. "Hi, Mr. Ogden!" As he walked toward the rancher he said, "It's me, Rory Coleman."

They continued walking until they stood face to face. "Rory, I'll be damned. Oops! Pardon my sorry mouth," he said, looking over at Victoria. He reached out and grabbed Rory by his shoulders. He shook Rory slightly and Rory could feel the strong grip tighten and relax as he measured Rory's muscles. The hard nub of what remained of Mr. Ogden's right thumb pressed deep into Rory's left shoulder. Then Mr. Ogden stepped back and stuck out his hand, "Rory, how you been? Boy, have you grown up."

"I guess. Is my dad here?" Rory asked, as Mr. Ogden pumped his arm with his strong rough hand.

"No. Is he supposed to be?"

"Pat told me Dad intended to come down this way and I figured he would come here. So, you haven't seen him? Shit."

"All grown up, and you've got a sorry mouth, too." With the last word he turned again to look at Victoria, "Looks like you got a girlfriend, Rory. Are you going to introduce us?"

Rory made the introductions. Mr. Ogden invited them into the house. As they walked to the steps, he stopped and turned back toward the outbuilding and yelled, "Bill, drop what you're doing and come make coffee." Then he turned and they went into the house.

Once Bill joined the group, they went through another round of 'how big Rory had grown' then the two old ranchers began to tell stories about Rory's past visits. They made Victoria laugh a number of times, and they made Rory blush even more.

"He never did do much work when he came," Mr. Ogden said. "He was too little. But we used to pay him a quarter for keeping the cats busy."

Bill added, "He made more work for us because we had to check out what kind of trouble he always got into. One of us would have to leave the cows, or whatever, to go make sure he wasn't all horse stomped in the barn, or crushed under the chimney that fell off the old house."

"The chimney had already fallen, Bill, it wasn't going to fall again," Rory said.

"I know it, but you were a crazy little kid. I'm sure you could have found some way to get under them bricks."

Mr. Ogden went on, "Rory always had an interest in the mess these animals made. The first thing he told me, the very first time he came to work here, was how big a turd his father's horse had made in the trailer. From then on, if he wasn't running around looking for the cats, and did end up watching us work, he always ran over to where some cow pumped a fresh pie, or some horse poured a leak, to check it out."

"And," Bill contributed, "yelled about how bad it stunk."

"I don't remember any of this. I think you're making it up," Rory responded.

"I think Bill may be frying some baloney, but everything I've said has been the truth," Mr. Ogden defended himself.

Bill said, "We all thought if you went into ranching, you'd only have animals so you could harvest the cow shit— Well, God damn me all to hell, if I don't watch out for my God damn, foul-mouthed cursing." Bill stated, angry with himself for swearing in front of Victoria.

"I think you two are generating the bull shit," Rory laughed.

"Listen, will ya? He grew up a cheeky smartass," said Mr. Ogden.

Rory smiled at his two old friends. "Well, I think we better get going. I want to show Victoria around a little. Is that okay?"

"Go ahead. Come back in before you leave, though."

"And Rory," Bill pointed his bumpy finger at him, "keep Victoria away from the old house. And Victoria, if he takes you into the barn and gets himself stomped by a horse, come and get us."

"I will," she replied smiling.

When the tour ended they went back to the house to say goodbye. Bill worked away at something in the kitchen, while Mr. Ogden sat outside in a chair on the deck.

"Good of you to stop by and visit, Rory, particularly when you bring a pretty girl along. Bill and I together couldn't convince a pretty girl to look at either of us cross-eyed, let alone set foot on this place. Tell your dad to come visit too, we haven't seen him for a long time," Mr. Ogden said from his chair.

"You haven't?" Rory asked curiously.

"No, maybe two years since he come here."

"I thought he still worked the branding with you."

"Not lately."

"Humph," Rory grunted. "Well, I'll tell him."

Mr. Ogden turned his head sideways without taking his eyes off of Rory and yelled, "Bill, drop what you're doing and come say goodbye."

Seconds later Bill came out of the door and they all walked to the car. Bill grinned large while he shook their hands once more. Mr. Ogden grabbed Rory at arm's length by the shoulders again and squeezed him. He nodded his goodbye to Rory and turned and thanked Victoria for coming to visit.

When Rory started the engine, Mr. Ogden could hear the pings and rattles coming out from under the hood, "Rory, you make sure you're careful on the way back. That sewing machine with tires you're driving is depending on you to get all three of ya back home in one piece."

Rory smiled and pulled away, turning back toward the arch. When he turned on the access road to get back to the highway, he waved his arm out the window and spotted the two old ranchers standing where they had been when the car pulled away, waving back.

"Well, this has been a waste of time. Sorry I got you to ride all this way for nothing," Rory said.

"It's okay. I liked meeting those old guys and hearing about what you did as a kid. You're pretty cute when you blush. Plus, you made me realize something."

"What's that?"

"I don't want to drive to Seattle with my father next weekend. I realized how much I don't miss driving on these highways. Don't get me wrong, I liked driving with you, because there's you; but driving with my dad, no thanks."

"Okay."

"I can't imagine being on a long drive with him again. Eleven hours in a car with somebody you don't want to kiss the whole time." Victoria leaned over the stick shift and kissed Rory on the edge of his lips.

"What had you going to Seattle?"

Victoria told Rory about Werner Brock, the Von Goss Music Conservatory in Berlin and about Werner's visit to Great Falls prior to her going to the music camp.

Rory listened quietly without looking at her, which made her feel a little uncomfortable.

"My father's going to have a fit when I tell him I, for sure, don't want to go to Seattle now." She stopped and looked at Rory. "Rory, you're being pretty quiet over there."

Rory continued to stare out at the road for a while longer before saying, "Yeah, well, I just realized you're leaving for six weeks this summer. I hadn't really thought about it before." The truth had hit home: They would be separated while she attended the music camp. He felt the same vacant-chest, aching emptiness for Victoria that he had felt when Alyse had gone on vacation. Only this time he knew what to expect; he knew the longer period of her absence would be more difficult, since he cared more deeply for Victoria than he had for Alyse. The longing for Alyse had been the worst feeling he had ever experienced, and he began to fear an even more agonizing hurt when Victoria went away. Then his mind conjured up a dreadful memory. When Alyse had returned, he lost her. He lost her due to things going on during the absence. The thought of losing Victoria while she attended the camp sprouted a tiny root in his phsyche.

"If we head straight home we'll be a little early for Gary's set. Do you want to do a little sightseeing?" he asked, intending to get his mind off of what the summer would bring.

"Sure. Where are you taking me?"

"To see the dam and the lake it created. It's up one of the state roads ahead."

"Is the car going to make it?"

"You've hit on the one item of concern I have about the whole plan. But I'm willing to risk a few extra miles if you are."

"Okay then. Let's go check it out."

The state road turned out to be in better condition than he expected. They parked at a small campground on the lake side of the dam, then walked along a path worn into the brush close to the lake and a few yards away from the line of tall evergreens. The lake cooled the air, but their walking kept them warm and the trees kept them out of the wind. In the early spring at the lake's high altitude, the possibility of a snowstorm blowing in on them still existed. They would sweat when the sun hit them, and when a cloud or trees placed them in shadows their moisture chilled their skin. A chill crawling inside their clothing, not just on the exposed flesh. The calm, beautiful area made them want to go on but the sun had lowered below the tops of the trees and created constant shade. They decided to turn back before the cold became really uncomfortable.

Rory put the keys into the ignition but didn't start the car. He turned to Victoria, then leaned over and kissed her. First soft and gentle while his hand held her chin, then longer and pressing his lips more firmly against hers. Finally, he opened his mouth and pressed his tongue inside to meet hers. They held the kiss for a long time, until Rory pulled away and looked in her eyes and said, "I've been wanting to kiss you all day."

Victoria smiled at him, proud to make him want to kiss her. Their mouths found each other again and the eagerness of their movements built up a strong desire in them both. Rory's hand moved down her side and then inside her jacket. He left it resting slightly above her hip, where he could feel the heat of her body through her shirt and sweater. Her hip moved slightly when his hand increased and released its pressure as he tried to feel more of her through the clothing. He resisted moving his hand higher, afraid to advance their relationship too quickly. Up to this point their physical contact had been limited to holding each other and kissing; there had been no touching in the most intimate areas. Before he could stop, he placed his hand fully over her right breast and pressed it to her body, joyously feeling its warmth and firmness in the palm of his hand.

As quickly as he had made the contact, he pulled back.

He pulled away and sat upright in his seat, watching Victoria to see her reaction.

"I'm sorry. I shouldn't have done that." He sat still, watching Victoria, who had not moved. "Actually, I've wanted to do that for a long time and—"

"I've wanted you to do it for a long time," she interrupted.

They stared into each other's eyes and read that they both wanted to move their relationship to a more sexual level. Victoria lifted slightly away from the car door, removed her shirttails from her jeans, then moved her arms behind her back. She reached up under her shirt and released the clasp of her bra. She unbuttoned her sweater and the bottom three buttons of her shirt, then lay back against the door. Rory watched all of this silently, while inside his chest, his blood pounded against his breast and upward to his throat. He placed his hand inside her unbuttoned shirt and leaned forward to kiss her again. While their lips moved and explored, Rory's hand rose and enveloped her breast. He felt a tremor run through his torso as the meaning of her smooth warm skin with its hardened nipple made itself clear. Victoria arched her back, enjoying the pressure of his hand, telling him his touch provided enjoyment for her as well.

His hand moved from one breast to the other as their mouths continued with their strong and wanting kisses. He pulled away to look at her face while he held her breasts. He wanted to see the approval he felt in the way her body pressed back and the way her kisses answered his urgent request for more.

Neither of them noticed when it started to rain.

Chapter 18

After their stop at the lake, Rory and Victoria still had plenty of time to make it back to Great Falls before going to see Gary's set at the club downtown. The two-lane road back to the freeway had become slippery; knowing his tires had little tread, Rory kept his speed down. By the time they reached the freeway again, the worst of the storm had passed, leaving the road covered with wet, half-melted snow. Turning north, he drove in the tracks a large truck had recently cleared so his laboring car didn't have to plow so much slush. The temperature hadn't dropped below freezing, so there was no chance of ice underneath the slush and little worry regarding traction. When they reached the other side of Helena, there was no sign of the spring storm.

They drove nonstop to Great Falls. The car came close to overheating once as they made the climb north out of Wolf Creek, but it cooled off on the downward side when Rory put the transmission in neutral and coasted to the bottom of the hill.

When they arrived in town starving, Victoria stated her need for food, so they went to Harry's restaurant for a quick bite. In the parking lot, Rory stopped the car and walked around to Victoria's side, meeting her as she got out. Standing inside the jaw of the open door, he put his arms around her waist and pulled her close to him. He looked at her face and saw nothing but beauty. "You're really something special...You know that?"

Victoria smiled and stared intently into his eyes as he bent down and placed his mouth over hers for a long kiss.

They had a quick sandwich in the restaurant, then hurried out to go to see Gary. When they tried the car, it wouldn't start. Rory turned the key a few times; with each attempt, the engine would grind and whir, but it wouldn't turn over. Although disappointed with the car, he couldn't let himself get angry at the lifeless, metal carcass. He stood looking at it from behind, then turned to Victoria and said, "I'd kick it, except it may have given up its life for us today."

"What will you do for a car, if it did?"

"I guess I'm going to do what I did before, ride the bus. Hopefully, my dad can get it going again."

Victoria grabbed on to Rory's elbow and they walked the few blocks to the Grange Hotel. The four-story brick building had seen better days in decades past, when Great Falls bustled like a growing city.

Rory's father had often talked about how in earlier times, on Friday and Saturday nights Main Street had non-stop traffic. People cruised in both directions, looking to be seen while gawking at the other cruisers. New dance clubs and showrooms had opened their doors to showcase the top bands and a few Las Vegas headliners. The Grange, because of its Main Street location, did a good business back then. It had a transient, but regular, clientele that would come to town to take in some of the big-name entertainment.

After a few years, things slowed down for the town. And for the Grange as well. The old Greek who purchased it oversaw its transition to a long-term resident hotel and realized it no longer required the normal amenities offered by most hotels. He sold off the bar, restaurant and shops located on the main floor thus recovering the majority of the money he had used to buy the hotel. He then moved into the main suite on the second floor and turned one of the regular rooms into a laundry with coin-operated machines. From the living room of his suite, he sold laundry supplies, soft drinks and candy bars to provide his tenants with a small amount of convenience and to generate a little additional income. Time passed. The downtown neighborhood became considerably run down. A large population of homeless people moved in and began to cruise the alleys. Main Street became deserted.

Later, a revitalization effort changed the downtown area by closing Main Street to vehicle traffic and making an open-air mall. It took a while for the foot traffic to build but eventually the Main Street Mall became a trendy place to go on the weekends. Tourists, locals, and the homeless mingled peacefully in the center of town.

The former restaurant and bar of the Grange Hotel had been changed into a small jazz club called *Home On the Grange*. When the city converted Main Street into a mall, the owner took out a few of the tables, to put up a small plywood stage, and began offering live music on weekends. It became a place where local jazz musicians had an opportunity to play in public and earn a few dollars. Some nights the bands would really let loose; when they did, the owner and residents of the hotel, all older people who appreciated their quiet, placed threatening phone calls.

Rory and Victoria arrived at the entrance as a squabble started.

"I call cops you don't keep the noise down, you hear?" the old Greek yelled into the doorway while shaking his finger at someone inside.

"The band hasn't even started yet; what the hell are you getting so excited about?" came back out the door.

"I jus' warn you. I call cops. My customers want no noise from you tonight."

"Tell them to take a pill."

"You take some pill. You make noise, I call cops." He looked at Rory and Victoria then added, "I tell them you got minors in bar."

"I'll tell them you have hookers in your rooms."

The old Greek turned red and shot a searing gaze at the voice from inside the bar, then spoke in his native tongue. After a long sentence in which words emphasized with force and flying saliva had been shouted, he shook his fist at the person inside, then turned and walked away.

Rory and Victoria entered the doorway where a large scowling man, in a small brown leather jacket, sat on a chrome-legged stool. Beside him stood a small stand with a cash box on top; adjacent to the stand a red velvet rope hung suspended between two portable posts, barring the actual entrance to the bar.

"Did you get all that?" Rory asked the large man, trying to lighten him up a bit.

"Yeah, I think he questioned the validity of my parents' marriage license. What can I do for you?" The large man's voice carried tones of dismay, left over from his previous conversation.

"We're friends of one of the guys in the band; we came to hear them play," Rory answered.

"Did you hear the old guy say he would call the cops and tell them we let minors in the bar?"

"Yeah."

"You look like a minor. I can't let you in."

"We don't want you to serve us drinks or anything, we just want to listen to the band."

"Normally, I would; but since Zorba there says he's going to call the cops, then he's going to call the cops. You and your girlfriend can't be inside when they come. Sorry."

Rory almost pointed out Gary's age of sixteen, but cut off the words and asked instead, "Do you leave the door open while they play?"

"Sometimes."

"Can we hang around out here for a while?"

"Suit yourself," he said, while taking in Victoria from the ground up.

They turned and went back out on the sidewalk to mull over their next move.

"What a screwed-up day. Nothing, not one god damn thing, worked out." Rory's anger built as he spoke.

"We could try the alley and see if there's a back door," Victoria suggested.

Rory took a deep breath and looked at Victoria. He could feel himself settling down, so he nodded in agreement and they set off toward the end of the street.

At the opening to the alley, they stood and looked into the darkness of the dingy lane. They had second and third thoughts about approaching the dim yellow light illuminating a small patch of gravel down where they expected the back door of the bar to be. They looked at each other, each hoping the other would suggest turning back, but then they both took a stride toward the dim light. The buildings seemed higher in the alley than they did on the street. They walked at a quick pace down the close, dark canyon of grungy brick, lined on both sides with metal garbage bins near the double doorways of the buildings. Some of these had loading docks; others had recessed entries potentially hiding bloodthirsty attackers within their darkened spaces. They heard something scrape, then rustle, as they passed one of the loading docks. The noise caused Victoria to move closer to Rory; they both increased the length of their strides. As they drew closer to the lighted door, they could hear the sounds of dishes clanging together and cutlery being thrown into a metal sink.

They approached the door; inside they saw people rushing about in steaming work areas with various sizes of pots and pans hung from hooks. Rory managed to catch the eye of one of the workers, and asked if the kitchen belonged to the Grange and if the band had arrived. The worker told them the next doorway down led into the bar. They stepped back out to the edge of the kitchen light and stood still, not wanting to continue any further down the alley. It was darker than they remembered it just seconds before. They proceeded anyway. After about twenty feet, the wall receded to another dark place where weak ambient light reflected off of the outline of a car. Beyond the car they could see the glow of a cigarette. They stopped and asked if they had found the back door of the Grange.

"Yeah," a voice from the dark said, then the glow brightened for a second.

"Are you in the band?" Rory asked the glow.

"Nope," the voice said.

"Do you know if the band is here? We're friends of one of the guys in the band."

"Which one?"

"Uh, Gary Milton."

"The young guy. Wait here."

They saw the glow moving, then heard a door open and watched the glow disappear. They stood for what seemed like a very long time in the pitch-black alley, staring at the point in the dark recess where the glow had been. Rory gripped Victoria's arm and pulled her close. Finally, they heard a click and the rattle of the door handle. But still no light.

"Who's there?" said Gary's shaky voice.

"Gary, is that you? It's me, Rory." Rory said with obvious relief.

"Rory, what the hell are you doing back here?"

"The guy wouldn't let us in the front door, so we came back here. Victoria's with me."

"Christ, you take her for a walk down the alley behind a bar? Nice guy!"

"Shutup, Gary!" Rory said.

"Hello, Gary." Victoria said.

"Hi, well, come on, get in here."

They walked cautiously toward his voice. When Victoria's foot hit the chair in which the glowing voice had been sitting, she screamed, causing tingles to run up all three spines. The crash and clatter of the collapsing chair caused them to scurry into the building.

Gary took them to a vacated table and told them to sit tight. Then he went and joined the band, whose members were preparing for the set by slowly moving music stands, hooking up straps, adjusting instruments and scooting chairs. They seemed in no hurry to get started and moved with the lethargy of people performing an onerous task, one they had performed many times before but never once enjoyed.

Gary sat on the plywood stage sucking his reed while waiting for the rest of the ensemble to finish their preparations. Rory and Victoria kept their eyes on the stage, so they didn't notice the man approaching them.

"What do you two think you're doing in here?"

Rory and Victoria turned to see the figure now sitting at the table with them, and said at the same time, "Mr. Keltch?"

In the dim light of the room they could barely make out his features, but they could tell by his formal teacher's posture that he wasn't happy to see them.

"You're both under age. You shouldn't be here. Rory, I can imagine you sneaking into a bar but, Victoria, this is way out of line."

Victoria looked at Rory while trying to think of something to say. Finally she turned aggressively to Mr. Keltch, "This is the only place I could come to hear Gary play, so I guess I had to sneak in. I had no choice."

"You certainly did have a choice. Both of you leave right now."

"Are you going to make Gary leave? He's under age too." Rory queried with challenge in his voice.

Mr. Keltch stared at Rory for several seconds, then said, "No, he's playing."

"He's still under age. Being in the band doesn't mean he's allowed into the bar. Did you come to hear him play or did you come to make sure he wasn't breaking the law? If you came to hear him play, then I'd say you have no problem with minors being in a bar. If that's not the case, then I guess you better go tell Gary to pack up and leave too."

Mr. Keltch sat stoically, then slowly said, "I want you two out of here."

Rory stared at Mr. Keltch as Victoria sat watching the standoff.

"We'll leave when Gary leaves." Rory could feel his heart racing, and his adrenaline release made him lightheaded.

Before Mr. Keltch could respond, the man in the small brown leather jacket from the front entrance placed both hands on the table in front of Rory and bent down, placing his head right in front of Rory's face, eyeball to eyeball.

"I don't know how you got in here, kid, but I know you're not staying. I told you, you couldn't come in, so let's go. You too, sweetheart."

Rory didn't take his eyes off Mr. Keltch as he stood, then he and Victoria left the bar. They found themselves on the front sidewalk where they had been a few minutes earlier.

Rory, still angry, said, "Keltch is such a potlicker."

"What do you think he'll do?"

"Who knows with him? I guess we're forced to listen from outside, anyway." They turned and saw the doors close; the sound of music could not escape.

"Come on, I'll walk you home," Rory said with resignation.

They had anticipated the close of their evening would arrive much later, but thanks to the abrupt end of their concert experience, they found themselves heading home early. Victoria invited Rory in for tea, but Rory didn't want to meet her father yet in his new role as her boyfriend. They went to the side of the house where they said goodbye for a long time. They kissed and held each other, feeling the welcome body warmth of a person they desired to touch. When they parted, Rory waited to make sure Victoria made it safely into the house, then walked back to get his car. When he arrived, he tried the ignition again, but the vehicle remained lifeless. He went inside the restaurant to see Harry and use the phone.

"Pat, my car's dead! Come and get me!" He started the conversation trying to impart a sense of urgency.

"I knew it. Where'd it happen?"

"A few miles west of Whitefish."

"What! Whitefish? For Christ sake, what happened, you get lost?"

"No, I missed my exit."

"It's the first exit. How could you miss the first exit?" Pat admonished his younger brother. "Well, I ain't coming; it's too far on real ugly roads."

"Pat, come on, I'm stranded out here. Victoria's crying her eyes out, and she's freezing, man!"

"Shit. If you take your girlfriend out on the highway in that crap can you call a car, then you got what you deserved. Now Victoria is another story; it's not fair to her, you stunned prick. It's going to take three hours to get there; can you both stay warm enough?"

"We'll stay warm. I'll tell you what, though, make sure you bring the towing cables, and then, take the short cut past Harry's restaurant. If you see a dead car in front looking a lot like mine, then I managed to nurse it back that far in record time."

Rory hung up.

Pat stood looking at the telephone. "Asshole."

The next morning Rory got up early to make breakfast for his brother. He felt guilty about having to enlist Pat into towing his car, and also for pulling his leg about breaking down a long way from home. Pat had consented to make the long drive, so Rory decided his brother deserved more than a simple thank-you; but Pat didn't get out of bed in time for breakfast and had to enjoy the pancakes cold.

After cooking Pat breakfast, Rory spent the rest of the morning reading. He had planned on doing something with Victoria later in the afternoon, but without his car he figured they wouldn't see each other. When they talked on the phone, Victoria had said she was in her father's doghouse because of the cancelled trip to Seattle, so she planned to practice her oboe for a good chunk of the afternoon. It turned out just as well that they couldn't see each other.

After talking with Victoria, Rory went back to his reading. The next thing that distracted him was the smell of food, along with the sound of someone setting the table. When the meal ended, Rory stood drying the last of the supper dishes; he saw his father's truck and trailer rig pull up and maneuver into its usual resting spot. He heard the boom of hoofs stomping on the plywood floor of the trailer, and knew his father would be in after he dumped some oats into the horse's bucket and threw some fresh hay into the stall.

"Hey Rory, how ya' doin'?" his father asked in a cheerful voice.

"Good."

"Say, Janice said you'd been in for breakfast. She said she couldn't believe how big you got. What were you doing down in Wolf Creek?"

"Looking for you."

"I know you were looking for me. What for?" Mr. Coleman realized Rory wasn't too receptive to his friendly tone of voice, so he dropped it.

"I need you to sign some papers for me. They're for the scholarship."

"Sure. They got to be there tomorrow or something? It couldn't wait till I got back?"

"It's no big deal. Getting you to sign them was a good excuse to go for a drive. There's no hurry."

"Okay. Well, go get 'em and I'll sign 'em."

"It's okay, you can sign them later," Rory said, then tried to leave the kitchen.

"Wait, Rory. Why are you acting like you're mad at me?"

Rory stopped with his back to his father. He stood for a minute, then asked, "Where were you? I went to Ogden's and you weren't there, so where were you?"

His father hesitated, then said, "I went to another ranch. I don't go to Ogden's any more."

"Well, Mr. Ogden asked you to stop by sometime. He asked me to tell you." Rory left the kitchen.

———

Victoria sat in her room preparing to place a phone call to Werner Brock. She waited to give herself time to gain control of her anger, anger aimed at her father. Earlier, when she told him they should cancel the trip to Seattle, he had started to yell at her about losing focus on her future and thinking about nobody but herself. Had she forgotten he had rearranged his schedule so that they could make the trip? Had she forgotten her own words about Werner wanting to help her education, for no gain of his own?

She had responded by reminding him of his reluctance to make the long drive in the first place. It was, therefore, considerate of her to not waste his time going to discuss something they could discuss in June when Werner came to visit. Mr. Beach then launched into a lecture on commitment and how she had changed now that she had a boyfriend. A boyfriend who felt that music had no importance in a person's life. He had already swept his own interest in music out like some unwanted inconvenience, and now he influenced her to sweep away the most important part of her life. His comments stunned Victoria. She pointed out that Rory had not tried to influence her away from music at all. He had indicated she should try other areas of interest only to see if she missed the music; but the decision to actually try these activities, she had made on her own.

Mr. Beach became very aggravated by this statement. He told her the plans for Seattle stood, and they would be driving west the following weekend. Victoria's temper did not provide an option for being told what to do at that moment, so she stood and told him to consider her part of the plan undone. And if he chose to drive to Seattle, he would be driving alone.

Sitting in her room, she could feel heat radiate from her face. Her hands still shook, just as they had the first two times she had lifted the telephone receiver to dial Werner. She had never spoken to her father in the manner she had just used with him. Normally she tried to appease him, and in the past she'd had no reason to object to whatever plans he made regarding her pursuit of a musical career. This time she saw little benefit to making the trip, and the little she saw, she felt she could forego. When she had first planned the trip, she did so primarily due to being flattered that Werner wanted to see her. She had used the conservatory to gain her father's interest and to commit him to the trip, but now she didn't want to waste the time and money.

She picked up the receiver again and this time she felt she could talk in a normal tone. Werner answered the phone and she could hear delight in his voice. He listened quietly as she explained to him how she had been on the highway the previous day and realized how long it would take to drive to Seattle. She explained she and her father would need to drive all night on Friday in order to spend Saturday with him. They would arrive very tired and probably be very poor company. Then, they would have to leave sometime Sunday morning in order to get back to Great Falls at a reasonable hour to prepare for school the next day. "So, Werner, I think it best to wait until you come to Great Falls. Spending a weekend driving for such a short visit isn't very fair to any of us. I hope you don't mind, and I hope this doesn't cause you any trouble," she concluded.

Werner remained silent at his end of the line. She listened, waiting to gauge his response. Finally he said, "I see. I understand, it is just that I was so looking forward to seeing you again."

"And I look forward to seeing you again too, but—"

"Do you?" he asked, interrupting her.

The interruption caused her to lose her train of thought and she stammered for a second, "Well, ah... yeah so, ah... when you come to Great Falls, we can have a better visit." She wondered what he meant by his question; why wouldn't she want to see him again?

"Hmm," came back through the speaker, "I hope so Victoria, because I don't want to inconvenience you."

"Oh no, Werner, you won't. You're more than welcome to come. My whole family wants to meet you."

"You are sure?"

"Yes."

"Okay. I will wait to see you then. I still wish you were coming this weekend, but I will see you soon."

"Yes. Sorry about the confusion, and I'm sure we will talk again before you come to visit."

They said goodbye and Victoria felt better now that the trip was definitely off.

Chapter 19

Rory's research had bogged down. With only four weeks to go before he had to submit his results, he was stuck treading water and flailing wildly. The results of his experiment differed every time he performed a certain step, and when he analyzed his procedures to find his error, he always confirmed they had been performed correctly. Believing he always did things the right way had blinded him.

Out of desperation, he reviewed his readings on the process of research and came across a section suggesting he take a step back to get a fresh view of the problem. The readings recommended trying to find another reason for solving the problem. The example given in his readings asked if you need a ladder to reach something suspended high from the ceiling in the middle of a room versus something suspended high up on a wall, what kind of ladder would you design? For the object on the wall you need a single straight ladder that leans against the wall. But for the object in the middle of the room, a ladder with two sides that could stand alone would be required. By slightly changing the problem to solve, you may find a new approach to developing a solution.

The thought of potentially starting over—with only four weeks to go—frustrated him. Final exams approached and the workload of his other classes became more intense. Despite the difficult situation, he still enjoyed every frustrating minute of his work.

His frustrations intensified because his dates with Victoria had become less frequent due to his chronic shortage of time. They still talked every day at school and on the phone each night. They still went to the library together, but because of the final exams, they riveted themselves to their studies and deemed their time together in the library a coincidence. To put in extra work on their studies, they sacrificed the time they had reserved for each other.

This last sacrifice went almost unnoticed. Rory hardly noticed it because of the urgency of his project work; Victoria, because she had a visitor.

Werner Brock had finished his teaching assignment in Seattle and had started on a driving journey of the western United States. He arrived in Great Falls, planning on spending a few days before continuing his tour southward to San Diego. Mr. Beach had been very impressed by Werner and his musical credentials. Having grown up in Berlin, Werner had been exposed to the musical history of the Berlin Philharmonic. Any music student in the divided city couldn't help but have numerous first-hand experiences with the members of the orchestra. It thrilled Mr. Beach to talk to someone with these experiences.

Discussions related to the Von Goss Conservatory also produced a favorable reaction in Mr. Beach. Werner had explained the history of the conservatory and how his former professor became the current headmaster. He explained his former instructor's intention to dedicate the conservatory to the enrichment of students who had dedicated themselves to music.

At this point Werner began to talk about Victoria's ability to play the oboe, and the enthusiasm she displayed while performing. He said the conservatory looked for students of her ability, and he had presented Victoria's virtues to the headmaster.

The Von Goss Conservatory offered a lifetime commitment to the student. Residency was required during the first three years, and then the student could leave to start a career or continue on at the conservatory for an unlimited time. If they did leave, they could return at any time, either in residence or for periodic attendance. Both choices, staying on after the first three years or leaving and then returning, came with some financial implications.

For the first three years of residency, limited grants and scholarships were available from sources known to the conservatory, but students could acquire sufficient additional scholarship funding from other, more public sources based on their appointment at Von Goss. Beyond the first three years, the grants provided by the conservatory would no longer be available, so the students needed to make up the difference from other sources or pay the difference themselves.

The Conservatory opportunity impressed Mr. Beach very favorably. He wished he had been able to attend a musical institution like the Von Goss in his youth and now, through his and Victoria's hard work, his daughter could receive a chance for a tremendous musical education and career.

Victoria listened to Werner, as he outlined the opportunity to her father, with a feeling of remote involvement. Werner occasionally looked in her direction while he explained how the conservatory worked, described its location, and provided a description of the daily life of the students. But, when he talked of the benefits and prestige of the institute, he looked at Mr. Beach, who never took his eyes off of Werner and never checked with Victoria about her feelings regarding the conservatory. It all sounded great to her, but it represented only one option to consider when she thought about her future.

Werner only talked about her attending the Von Goss in her father's presence. With her mother, he would talk about Montana and the United States. He asked a lot of questions and appeared genuinely interested in this place where they lived. When just Victoria and Werner talked, he asked her questions about herself, the things she liked to do, her friends, and about school. She had told him in her letters about her boyfriend, but he had never asked about Rory, either in the subsequent letters or here in person. When she mentioned Rory during their conversations, Werner would smile and move on to another subject.

She had noticed that when they talked with her father, Werner seemed to pay all his attention to Mr. Beach. Without her father present, she noticed he never took his eyes off of her; he would occasionally turn and look at others involved in the conversation, but not for long.

Rory had not been aware of Werner's arrival until a few days later when he called to talk with Victoria and was told she had gone out to get ice cream with her visitor. Rory remembered having heard about the visitor in earlier conversations with Victoria, but the visitor hadn't entered his mind since. He did remember about the visitor being a music teacher she had met at the music camp. A picture of an older man with wild, gray hair and rumpled clothes had come into his mind when Victoria had first mentioned him, and the image returned now.

The call to Victoria triggered his impulse to look over his checklist. He discovered he had a reading assignment due for his English class, so he picked up the book and immersed himself in reading. It surprised him how much time had passed when Victoria returned his call.

"How was your ice cream?" he asked, after they had said hello.

"Okay. I wish you could have come."

"I need an invitation first." He teased. "Maybe next time. I didn't realize your guest had arrived. How's the visit been so far?"

"Okay, I guess. I think my dad really enjoys having the guy around. All they do is talk about music. He's really working on my dad about this music conservatory in Berlin."

"What, he wants your dad to go over and teach in Germany?" Rory asked.

"No, he wants me to go to the conservatory after high school. I told you this a long time ago. Don't you remember?" She said in mock anger.

"Not even a wisp. What's it all about?"

Victoria told him about the conservatory and the structure of the program. Rory listened quietly as she told him about the three years of residency and the lifetime acceptance. Then she told him about Werner's connection to the conservatory and how it might help her get accepted. When she finished he said, "Sounds great. It would be kind of cool to go live in Germany." He hoped his enthusiasm sounded somewhat genuine.

"Yeah, it does sound pretty good. My dad thinks it's a great opportunity and I kind of agree. Werner is pushing the idea pretty hard."

For the first time, Rory thought about the end of their senior year when they would most likely separate. The separation while she attended the music camp this summer would hurt, but he knew when the six weeks ended everything would be back to normal. Separating at the end of school made him think their relationship would end permanently, that they would be breaking up when they really wanted to stay together. There would be no getting back to normal then.

He knew the paths their lives currently followed would pull them away from each other, and he knew he could do nothing about it. He would never stop pursuing his chemistry career, and he could never ask Victoria to stop pursuing her music. If she chose that path. She could probably find a good music program somewhere close to his school, but maybe it wouldn't be the best program available to her, and he knew he had no right to limit her opportunities for his own sake. He knew if she chose to attend the conservatory, their parting could not be avoided. The idea that steeped in his head indicated separate journeys in order for each to fulfill their potential. He wanted the best for Victoria; he wanted her to achieve everything she had the ability to achieve. He wanted the same for himself. But his desire to be with Victoria began to outgrow these wants.

———

Rory pulled away from his house the next morning and started along his regular route to pick up Victoria; but half way to her home, he remembered she had made other arrangements to get to school. The visiting music teacher would participate in all of the day's band classes, so she would be riding to school with him.

Mr. Keltch had been infected with enthusiasm by the idea of having a visiting musician attend his classes. He had asked for Werner to spend the day providing demonstrations and pep talks to his students. When they met, the effect on the schoolteacher changed. Mr. Keltch saw the youthful Mr. Brock, and how the students might identify closely with him. He could see that Werner communicated comfortably with young students, by the easy dialog he engaged in with Victoria.

He also noticed that Werner constantly watched Victoria. Once she had left to go to her classes, he observed Werner looking toward the door every time it opened, and he wondered if Werner watched in hopes of seeing Victoria returning to the room.

In each of the classes, Werner talked briefly about his schooling and the musical opportunities in Europe. Then he would play a section of music on his oboe. Finally he would yield the class back to Mr. Keltch by asking if he could sit in with the orchestra while he, Mr. Keltch, conducted. Werner loved to play, and it showed. Mr. Keltch loved to have this obvious zeal for music displayed to his class. When he conducted, he began to feel less threatened, more supported by Werner's presence.

He stopped each class a few minutes early and brought Werner back to the podium so the students could ask him questions. The majority of them raised their hands to take advantage of the opportunity and when Werner responded, they all listened with great interest.

When the junior band class period rolled around late in the morning, Mr. Keltch saw Werner react with extreme happiness to see Victoria again. Then, during the session when Werner played for the class, he asked her to join him and they played a duet, one they had been practicing in the evenings since his arrival. Mr. Keltch again watched the interaction between Werner and Victoria, noting how they seemed to isolate themselves as if they were alone in the room. Then, when Werner joined in with the band's practice, he sat with Victoria, sharing her music stand.

At the end of the junior class, Mr. Keltch, who earlier had arranged to take Werner to lunch, asked Victoria to join them. When they left the band room, they found Rory talking with Gary while waiting for Victoria. Mr. Keltch stood and watched as Victoria introduced Werner to Rory. He noted the politeness of the exchange, but also that Rory seemed a little shocked by the visitor, who in turn seemed a little distant and uninterested in Rory. After a couple of Werner's short answers to Rory's bland, 'How are you enjoying your visit?' and 'What do you think of Montana?' questions, Victoria indicated they had better get going and said she would talk to Rory later. Mr. Keltch hadn't acknowledged Rory but had observed him closely, taking some pleasure in seeing him treated indifferently by Werner. He did wonder why Rory was the object of this indifference: In the classroom, Werner had been friendly with every student he talked to and more than willing to engage in conversation regarding his impressions of America. To Rory he had offered no opportunity for conversation. And where the other students were keen to engage Werner in a dialogue, Rory seemed to want to escape.

Gary and Rory set out for the cafeteria after the others left for their luncheon. Rory couldn't quite put his finger on why he felt a little low.

"Man, that was cold," Gary commented. "That guy seemed like a decent guy in the classroom, but he sure didn't have much time for you."

"No kidding. I didn't know what to say to him."

"And you should have seen him in class, man. He wouldn't take his eyes off of Victoria. I think he's after your girl, my friend."

Rory stopped abruptly and stared at Gary. He tilted his head to one side and mulled over Gary's words.

"How old do you think he is?" he asked Gary.

"I think he said twenty-one."

"Hmm. I had this image of an older guy until just now. Even so, he's too old for Victoria. Victoria would have been in the sixth grade when he was a junior. Could you imagine being interested in a sixth-grader right now?"

"Don't be perverted, Rory. But you do realize a girl is a lot more of a girl when she's a junior, than when she's in the sixth grade. Werner sees a real girl, not a sixth-grader."

"I know, but can you imagine being interested in a girl five years younger than you?"

"Not at the age I'm at now. But when I'm twenty-one and I see a girl like Victoria, I think I might forget about the age thing."

"Nah. There's no way at his age he's interested in Victoria."

"Well, it's time to put out for her twice as much as you normally do, to make sure she doesn't get interested in him."

"Shut up, Gary."

"Come on Rory, tell me you're getting it from Victoria, you've been going out with her for three months. And so you don't think I'm trying to get away with any code words, *getting it* means *having sex.*"

"I know that, you nimrod," Rory said while shaking his head, "And it's none of your business what I get."

"Okay, okay. I don't want to put more wood on the fire, but I noticed Mr. Keltch seemed a bit jealous of that Werner guy when he saw them play together. It's like all of a sudden, everybody's interested in Victoria."

"Thanks for those comforting words."

———

At the end of that school day, as at its beginning, Rory didn't see Victoria. Under normal circumstances they would meet at Victoria's locker to chat for a few minutes before Rory went to the lab to work on his project; but today, Victoria had left early because of Werner. Rory's uneasy mood had stayed with him for the entire afternoon; and although he was reluctant to admit why the mood had persisted, he began to understand. He couldn't be with Victoria because someone else was.

He went to the lab. When he arrived, Mr. Duggin seemed relieved to see him.

"Rory, what are you planning on doing this summer?" Mr. Duggin asked.

Rory felt agitated by the question. He remembered being asked this question before the previous school year ended, and the turmoil he had created with his response to Mr. Shelton. "I hadn't really thought about it, but I guess I'll end up doing the same as last summer. Except I wanted to talk to you about my project. Is it possible for you to give me access to the lab, or can I take some equipment home? You see, I don't think I can finish the project in time for the Mortenson submission date, so I want to keep working on it over the summer."

"Oh, really. That is a bit of a concern." Mr. Duggin had a worried look on his face, which made Rory uncomfortable. "I'm sure we can work something out to get you access to the lab or allow you to take the equipment home, that's no problem; but missing the submission date could be a serious problem. I could tell you'd been struggling a bit with the project, but I didn't bring it up because I wanted to let you try and work it out on your own. You still have at least three weeks to go. Why do you think you won't make it?"

"Well, you already know I had to start over. With the new approach I'm taking, I think it's going to take more time to get the results to support my hypothesis."

"I don't think you can ask for an extension, but I'll check to see if they provide some kind of grace period for submissions. Remember when we first talked about how they look at the projects you submit to make sure they are achievable? Well, you could be in trouble if you don't complete what you said you would."

"I know, and I intend to complete it. If I have to send in partial results to make the date I will, but I'm still going to keep working on the project."

"Okay, good. Let's think about this for a few days and I'll talk to Mr. Butcher." Mr. Duggin went on, "I asked you about your plans for the summer because I think I found a pretty interesting job for you. It's working in the lab at Copper-Glen Mines. I think you should see what it's like in a real lab, doing real work. What do you think? Interested?"

"Man. Sounds great. It beats getting stuck at the shit end of a calf by a mile. Oops, sorry," Rory apologized when he saw Mr. Duggin's brow constrict. "How did you hear about it?"

"They called and said they wanted to hire a student for the summer. They want the student to interview with one of the chemists out at their site one day after school, but they seemed to indicate they would hire whoever I recommended."

"Wow! That would be cool. That would be real cool."

"It requires driving to their site every day. You do have a car, don't you?"

"Yeah, if I can keep it running, I do. I'm sure I can make it out there; how far is it?"

"About twenty miles."

"I can get there." After writing down the directions for getting to the interview, he went to start working on his project.

"Do you want to know how much they're going to pay you?"

"Oh, yeah, I guess so."

Mr. Duggin shook his head and smiled. "Minimum wage. You still interested?"

"Minimum wage is still better than the shit end of a calf-- Oh, sorry."

––––––

The darkening blue sky to the west began to make its way toward red as Rory stopped his car. The sunlight peered from under the roiling dark clouds climbing high over the hill behind the barn; the wind lifted the loose straw, sending the blond spears flying across the yard. Rory squinted as he walked into the wind toward the house.

Over the Salisbury steak his father had cooked, he told his family about the job he would like to take for the summer and asked his father how long the car would last. His family seemed barely interested in his good fortune. Pat and his mother said it sounded good, and his father continued to eat without speaking. Pat ate fast because he had somewhere else to go; his mother ate very little, so she finished quickly and returned to her room. Rory and his father finished their meal together. Their knives and forks worked efficiently enough to keep their mouths full, so conversation didn't exist. When their crumpled paper napkins had replaced the food on their plates, they looked at each other across the table.

"So, I guess I'm going to lose my best flatasser," Mr. Coleman stated.

"Sorry, Dad. I just can't pass up a good chance to work in a lab with real chemists. That's why I want to do it."

"I know. I looked forward to having you work with us again, is all. I thought I'd have you helping me for at least another summer. I knew for sure next year you'd be gone."

"Well, the job's not mine yet. But I sure would like to get it." Rory's gloom returned when he saw his father's disappointment in knowing they would never work together again.

Rory couldn't remember much of his life from before he started to go to the Ogden ranch with his father. Since then, he couldn't remember a summer when he hadn't worked at least a few days as a cowhand. In the earlier summers it had been like Mr. Ogden and Bill had said. Rory was a tagalong kid getting in everybody's way and he created more work than he produced. Then as he got older, he could do any task his father assigned him. Like any teenager, he grumbled about performing the manual labor; but in the end he enjoyed what he had accomplished. His father had never been mean or demanding; Rory knew that whatever his father asked him to do, his father had probably done at an earlier age. He also knew he would only be asked to do what he was capable of and at the end of every summer, Rory knew he had developed into a better cowhand.

"I know we're going to miss you out there, Rory, and now sooner than I expected."

"I can probably put in a few days, Dad, and like I said, this job's not a sure thing."

"You'll get it, Rory."

Both of them knew this summer would be different from all of their other summers. At this moment, they both knew Rory was moving on.

Chapter 20

       Sitting in the athletic trainer's room under the stage, Rory and Victoria shared orange juice and poppy seed muffins. It was their first non-study date in two weeks, and the first time they had been alone since Werner Brock had come and gone. When they arrived in their hideaway, they left the lights out and ignored their food and drink while they embraced each other, holding on for a long time. They removed their jackets and held each other close while exchanging long, soft kisses. They refreshed their memory of each other's taste and feel and scent. As they renewed their physical connection, they agonized over the unexpected separation they had just endured. They realized what they had missed by not having the touch of each other for so long, and they both felt growing pangs of despair over the separation to come this summer.

Rory broke the silence by asking Victoria if the recent visit had been very much of a problem.

"Not really," she replied, still in his arms with her head against his chest. "Werner's heart is in the right place, and he really wants to help me. But he did change our family's routine while he stayed here. Everyone in the house had to check to see what Werner had planned, to make sure he wasn't bored. I'll tell you one thing, though, I'm sure glad my dad liked him. He took Werner out to a lot of places, which meant I didn't have to, so I could stay on top of my schoolwork. The only problem with them spending so much time together was they always talked about my future, and I don't know what they committed me to."

"As long as you know what you've committed yourself to, then there's nothing to worry about. I wouldn't let them provide anything, other than suggestions, related to what you decide to do after high school. You don't want them to ramrod you into something they choose," Rory said in a stern voice. He turned on the light so they could share their juice and muffins.

"I don't think they will. I'm sure that without each other to scheme with, they'll both forget about any commitments they had about my future. The only way I end up doing what they want, is if I decide I want the same thing."

"Good. That's the way it should be."

"I agree. Don't think I can't control what I'm going to do." Victoria's voice became heated. "I'm not some lost soul with no interest in my own future. Don't you take a tone as if I need to have my eyes opened. I don't need you or anybody else looking out for me. I can look out for myself."

"Sorry! I'm just telling you what I think. I didn't mean to say you couldn't control it yourself."

"Well, I can," she said with finality. "So, what's the latest with your project?"

"My project... Yeah well, it's got a bit of a sweet and sour aspect to it right now. I've written my final draft and given it to Mr. Duggin and Mr. Butcher, but I'm not finished with the experiment. It got more complicated than I had expected, and we're trying to figure out how it's going to affect my status. I'm meeting with them after lunch."

Rory provided her with a little more detail regarding his project, but right now he didn't want to spend too much time talking about schoolwork. Class time was approaching. He wanted to turn the lights out so they could renew their physical bonding. When he stood and moved toward the light switch, Victoria smiled at him while she undid the buttons on her blouse.

———

At noon, Rory talked with Victoria before she went into her rehearsal; the delay caused him to arrive at the cafeteria later than usual. As he turned into the stairway that led to the main eating hall, he spotted Ellis and Gill, his fellow chemistry club members, sitting in the far corner of the landing. They looked too casual as they sat, seemingly waiting for something to happen.

"What are you two urinal mints up to?" Rory asked.

"The usual," Ellis said, "Taking it easy, hanging around, checking things out, shooting the shit."

Rory nodded, then continued on down the stairs.

Once Rory left, Ellis turned to Gill and said in a leering conspiratorial voice, "I think we're about ready to take the lid off and let the jam out of the jar, Gill. Should we synchronize our watches like they do on TV?"

"What are you talking about?" Gill responded, not picking up on the satire in Ellis' question.

Frustrated, Ellis went on, "You're going to the other exit and I'm staying here, so we better have a countdown to make sure we go off at the same time. What time have you got?"

"Twelve-twenty-seven."

"I've got twelve-thirty-four, so change your watch." Ellis ordered.

"No, it's too hard. I can never remember how many times to click the stem to get it into change mode. You change yours."

Ellis looked at Gill and sighed. "Okay, let's do this; I'll give you four minutes to get to the other exit. Once you're there, I figure it's going to take you another four minutes to tape everything together and then move out to the stomping ground. So when your watch says twelve-thirty-five, you step on it. Got it?"

"Got it," Gill said, then set out to take his position.

Inside the cafeteria, Rory could see students still making their way past the cashiers; but when he got into the food line, he was alone. He grabbed one of the few remaining sandwiches, paid for it, and went out into the crowded, noisy room to look for Harry. He soon found him at a table near the stairway entrance.

Ellis, now alone on the landing at the top of the stairs, uncovered three soft, square plastic bottles all taped together. One bottle was filled with a liquid of highly concentrated soda, another filled with vinegar, and the third with liquid dish soap. He removed the caps from all three and proceeded to tape a short length of rubber hose to the top of each bottle; then he taped the ends of the three hoses together. Finally he taped a mesh basket over the end of the hoses so that when the liquids came out, they would mix in the basket and exit through the mesh.

He and Gill had calculated the minimum amount of each liquid they would need for their special purposes and then built in a three-hundred-percent margin of error.

Gill performed the same procedures as Ellis in a small isolated hallway close to the other exit of the cafeteria.

Ellis looked at his watch, which read 12:41. He had a minute to wait, but his patience ran out and he moved down to the bottom of the stairs.

No one inside the cafeteria noticed that the doors at both exits had been closed.

After closing the door, Ellis got into position about six feet away from the door, then placed the three bottles on their sides and stacked on top of each other. Ellis lifted his leg high above the three bottles, took a deep breath, and stomped down on the top bottle with all his weight. The pressure of his foot crushing down on the soft-sided bottles forced their contents out at high speed into the mesh basket. Froth began to churn in the mesh while a strong hissing noise emanated from the basket. When he heard the hissing, he turned and ran as fast as he could up the stairs two at a time, and out the main entrance door. Once outside of the school, he turned and walked to the far end of the building to wait for Gill.

Rory ate his lunch and Harry stayed to keep him company. The noise level in the room hung at its normal high level until a sudden loud, shrill scream sounded above the din. Every head in the room turned to look toward the exit at the far end where the scream had originated. When they did, they saw students clamoring backwards, away from the door, being pursued by a huge wall of foamy white suds. In a matter of seconds, the wall had moved about ten feet into the room and begun to spread out. Another scream broke out when someone opened the door at the exit nearer to where Rory sat, and a second white wall of foam cascaded into the room, chasing the students back from the door.

Everyone now stood and looked from one door to the other. Some began to back away from the fast-approaching foam. The large room got smaller and more crowded with each second, as the foam ate up all of the available floor space around the two exits. The smell of vinegar mixed with lemon began to fill the air. The supervising teachers waved their arms to get everyone to move away from the foam. In a short time, the students calmed down from the initial confusion and started to laugh at the sight. One or two of the boys started to wade into the foam toward the door, while the teachers yelled at them to leave the foam at once. Upon hearing this order, one of the boys ducked into the wall of foam and disappeared. He reappeared a few seconds later, coughing and wildly trying to wipe the foam away from his face. After a few swipes he yelled that he couldn't breathe.

Others grabbed him and started slapping his back, trying to help him get air into his lungs.

Rory looked at Harry with a concerned look on his face.

"I guess you can't breathe if you go into that stuff," Rory stated.

"Shit. How are we going to get out of here?"

"I don't know; let's go talk to Lendorf."

They approached Mr. Lendorf, who watched over the boy choking on the foam. When they tried to talk to him, he only yelled for everyone to stay back; he didn't acknowledge Rory and Harry.

"Let's go into the kitchen and see if there's another door," Rory said.

The other supervising teacher had moved into the kitchen and phoned the main office to let them know the cafeteria was sealed off with foam. When the principal heard the news, he charged out of his office and down the hall toward the stairway. Foam began to flow upward from the doorway at the top of the landing into the main hallway. He waded into the foam, which now filled the entire stairwell, and heard a strange hissing noise rising from somewhere down the stairs. The foam kept building; and from where he stood, a few steps above the top of the suds, he could see the doors of the school's main entrance.

The principal plowed through the chin-high foam down to the landing and opened one of the doors. Foam poured in massive folds, out onto the exterior concrete steps. He then opened more doors so the foam had more outlets. Once he had finished, he went back inside where the foam had already lowered to the height of his waist. He could still hear the hissing and decided to go down to locate the source. He took a deep breath and, with his hand on the railing, made his way down the steps. The hissing became louder. He bent down to feel around for whatever made the noise. He had no luck. But he hadn't felt any heat, and he felt relieved because it meant the hissing probably wasn't from steam. His lungs pulled hard to open up his throat and suck in air, so he retraced his steps upward, still holding onto the handrail. He broke through the top of the foam, but he couldn't see. When he opened his mouth to take a breath, he tasted soap, and stopped inhaling in time to prevent any from entering his throat. Once he cleared his mouth and nose, he drew in great long breaths of air.

The hissing persisted as the foam continued to lower due to the flow outdoors.

The principal took another lungful of air and dropped into the foam again. At the bottom of the stairs, he held the very end of the handrail and felt for the hissing object by extending his leg. He made contact as his lungs pulled hard for air again, but he waited a little longer and managed to hook the object with his foot, pulling it against the bottom stair so he would know where to find it on his next dive. At the top of the stairs he cleared his face of the foam and inhaled. He looked back; this time the foam had dropped low enough so he could see the top of the doorway. He plunged back into the foam. At the bottom of the stairs he found the hissing object immediately. It wasn't hot but it did vibrate, so he carefully felt around on the device until he managed a firm grip. With the device in hand, he returned to the top of the stairs, dragged the contraption outside and tossed it off the steps.

When he returned inside to the top of the stairs, he could see an opening in the cafeteria doorway where Mr. Lendorf stood, peering out over the foam.

Rory and Harry returned to the main cafeteria after finding a delivery door leading up another stairway to the parking lot. They told a number of students about the exit, and a steady flow of students began to make their way out. When they explained their findings to Mr. Lendorf, he thanked them, then told them the foam had stopped growing, so they needed to move it out of the way and clear the exits. He asked them to find something they could use to start clearing the foam.

The principal made his way down the stairs and into the cafeteria to check out the situation inside. He heard the hissing noise at the far exit and made his way in that direction to dispose of the second foam generator.

Rory and Harry returned with cookie sheets and cake pans and began to shovel the foam. Within a few minutes, they had cleared a path to the top of the stairs and started clearing one from the landing upward to the main hall. They finished as the bell rang for the students to go to their afternoon classes. The students who had remained down in the cafeteria now made their way out to go about their normal activity. Upstairs in the main hallway, a crowd of students craned their necks to watch the proceedings. They stood and watched the recently released students parade through the door, celebrating like returning heroes.

Rory and Harry then returned the cookie sheets to the kitchen. As they left to go to their classes, they saw the principal and Mr. Lendorf having a discussion. They didn't want to get any more involved, so they slipped by them and went to class.

At the beginning of the second period, the classroom phone rang and summoned Rory to the principal's office. When he arrived, he had to wait for a few minutes before being ushered into the inner office. He knew the principal would try to find the person responsible for creating the foam, but he didn't think they would want to talk with him this quickly.

Mr. Ware, the principal, and Mr. Lendorf sat waiting as Rory entered. They smiled politely as Rory took his seat. Mr. Ware began their discussion. "Thanks for your help in the cafeteria today, Rory; we sure needed your assistance. Did you get a chance to see anything down there before the foam started to pour into the room?"

"No, I turned from eating my lunch when I heard a scream."

"Any idea what made the foam?"

"Not really, but it's fairly easy to do," Rory said, shaking his head.

"Any guess at who did this stunt?" Mr. Lendorf asked.

"No."

"None at all, not even a clue?" Rory noticed a sudden change in Mr. Lendorf's tone.

"Well, it could be anybody in any chemistry class, but somebody who knows a little about that kind of stuff."

"Don't you think it very likely, that a fairly *good* chemistry student did this, a student who could whip something like this together with very little difficulty?" Mr. Lendorf persisted while Mr. Ware observed Rory's reaction.

Rory moved his eyes back and forth from the two men, trying to get a reading of what they were after, then said, "I guess. That would leave the top chemistry students, mostly the ones in Chem Club."

"If you took a wild guess, who do you think would be most likely to do this type of thing?" Mr. Ware asked.

Rory thought, They should know the top chemistry students without asking me. He answered, "I wouldn't know."

"Were you and Harry in the lunchroom the whole time the foam poured in?"

"Yes. I'd come in a little later than usual; that's why I was still eating. Harry hung out to keep me company. Do you think we did it?"

"We have to ask everyone in the Chemistry Club about this, Rory. We aren't accusing anyone. You and Harry knew about the back door, and you seemed calmer than everyone else in the room, so we wanted to talk with you two first. You're also pretty good in the chemistry department," said Mr. Ware, "If you didn't do it, we thought you might suggest who else could. That's all."

"So you do think I did it? Thanks."

"No, Rory, we're checking every possibility. We asked Mr. Duggin for a list of the students in the club, and as I said, because you saw the whole incident, we're checking with you first."

"Well, I didn't do it and I don't know who did."

"How many members of the club would know how to mix those particular chemicals together in the manner used? Any idea?" Mr. Ware tried using a different approach.

"I don't know how you mean."

"The way the chemicals were delivered to the mixing area."

"I don't know what you're talking about."

"Rory, you've been designated as the Mortenson Scholar and as such you're representing your high school, the city of Great Falls and the state of Montana. I can't let you represent all those things if there are any suspicions regarding your involvement in a dangerous prank. If we find out you had any involvement, I will contact the Mortenson Board to report what you've done. Now, that said, I ask again. Do you know who pulled this stunt?"

Rory glared at Mr. Ware and said, "No, I don't. And I may be representing the school, the city and the state, but I'm also representing myself. You don't have a clue how important this scholarship is to me, or you'd know I wouldn't risk losing it to get some cheap thrills from a practical joke. You finished?"

Mr. Ware leaned his long thin frame back in his chair, laced his fingers together in his lap and nodded his head.

———

Mr. Duggin and Mr. Butcher listened to Rory's description of what had happened in the cafeteria. They asked a few questions, but otherwise showed little interest in the event until Rory mentioned Mr. Ware's comments regarding the scholarship.

"Don't worry Rory. If they think you're the culprit, then why did they ask for a list of all of the Chemistry Club members? Though a list of the experiments the students had worked on would prove a lot more interesting," Mr. Duggin commented.

"Why is that?" Mr. Butcher asked.

"It would allow them to set some priorities regarding who to talk to first. That is, if they understood what the experiments involved."

"Do you think you know who did this?" asked Mr. Butcher.

Mr. Duggin said, "I know who I would consider my primary suspects, and I suppose I'm obligated to reveal my suspicion to Mr. Ware sooner or later."

"I think you better. The intentions of the prankster may have been innocent. But when it scares people and causes someone to panic, we need to let the students know that this application of chemistry is unacceptable. We also have to remove Rory's name from the list of suspects; after the music teacher's attempt to ruin Rory, we don't need the principle raising any concerns with the Mortenson people." Mr. Butcher turned to Rory and said, "Now Rory, your project submission. I like the way you justified your failure to complete your project; but nonetheless, it is a failure. You sure you want to submit it this way?"

"It says what I did. I started with a theory I believed I could prove in the time I had, but I took the wrong approach. I don't think there's any choice except to explain what happened and what I learned from my effort, regardless of the result," Rory answered.

"We could ask for an extension."

"Mr. Duggin didn't think they would allow one."

"I agree." Mr. Butcher sighed, then sat staring at the top of his desk for a moment before continuing. "If this is the way you want to submit your results, then I will support you. Leave it with us to complete our observations."

Chapter 21

After the final band concert, the final awards assembly and the distribution of the final report cards, the final day of school ended. While Victoria attended a final party for the senior band members who had played their last concert, Rory waited in Mr. Duggin's office.

Mr. Duggin had tidied up his room and had placed a box of books and papers by the door to take home for the summer. For a change, Rory didn't need to move a sloppy stack of papers off one of the tattered and peeling vinyl chairs to sit down.

"Who's helping you do the lab inventory this year?" Rory began their conversation.

"Two, shall we say, volunteers made themselves available, once I explained to them that I had managed to wrestle the responsibility for their punishment away from Principal Ware."

"Was Mr. Ware ready to kill them?"

"He was ready to kill you. He accused me of trying to protect you when I told him I knew who set off the foam. I asked if I could punish the pranksters, and hoped he'd go along without making me reveal their names but he said no dice. I had to tell him in order to prove you had nothing to do with it."

"I don't get it. Why did he think I did it? I got stuck in the lunch room like everybody else."

"Mr. Lendorf suggested you set off the foam at the doors, then went around to the parking lot and came in from the kitchen entrance that, in his words, 'you had prior knowledge of.' He said sneaking back in to become a victim would remove suspicion and provide a great place for you to view the results of the prank."

"He's crazy. Thanks for setting them straight I appreciate it," Rory said.

"Well, I think they accepted my explanation. It's kind of obvious who did it."

Rory had come to visit Mr. Duggin to discuss his project submission to the Mortenson Board, so he asked, "Did you get my package off?"

"Yes, it's gone. You're back to the waiting game, only this time I think it's a little more complicated."

"Why more complicated?"

"Last time you completed your project, this time you didn't. Last time you only had to wait for word from the Board while this time you do an interview with a Board member before they renew your status."

"I forgot about the interview. It happens toward the end of August, right?"

Mr. Duggin nodded.

"Something else to help me through the summer," Rory said with a sad grin on his face.

———

To get to the Copper-Glen mine, Rory had to drive about forty minutes east of the city. The hills were low and rolling, and the rivers he crossed were high and racing hard. The lush green grass of spring hinted at its parched-straw dullness of summer. Rory wound down the access road to the bottom of a coulee where a large flat area had been created to accommodate the offices of the mine.

He parked in the gravel parking lot. Before going into the building, he stopped to look at the two-story set of rectangular boxes painted white and spotted with aluminum doors and windows. A small sign on the grass in front announced the company name. The single-storied right end of the building stretched out three times the length of the double-storied portion. Angle-parked golf carts formed a line in front of the sliding garage doors which made up the far end of the low side of the building.

A stand of cottonwood trees, split down the middle by a gravel path, grew near the edge of the compound. Behind the building, Rory could see the eroded wall of the coulee. The fast-flowing water undercut its foundation as it crashed down from a small set of falls; the wall echoed the sounds of splashing, rippling water to wash over the building. The river curved past the base of the coulee wall, to settle smoothly and run babbling over a wide bed of flat rocks, slowing the water for the run downstream.

Rory reported for work, and after performing a number of new-hire functions, was led to the laboratory where he would spend his summer. The person from Human Resources introduced him to the lab technician who would be his supervisor, and left him in the technician's care.

Randolph Morgan was in his early twenties. Taller than most men, he had a slender—but not skinny—build. He had black hair with long curving locks hanging in front of his ears, like sideburns, but without the undergrowth of facial hair. His pale skin tone displayed blue veins resting just under the surface near his temples. Thin black eyebrows swept around his eye sockets, swinging down low to the points of his eyes.

At their introduction, Randolph rigidly shook Rory's hand, pumping it three times. When Rory called him Randy, he was corrected and asked to use the more formal *Randolph*.

Randolph wore a white lab coat on which he had clasped a plastic laminated security tag prominently displaying his picture, name and title.

"I suggest we take a tour of the laboratory first, then go outside to take a look around the tanks. When we finish, we'll come back inside and I'll explain what you're going to do here this summer. Sound okay?"

"Sounds okay to me, Randolph." Rory wanted to make sure to demonstrate that he understood he wasn't dealing with a Randy.

The lab's many work areas, each with so much apparatus available, impressed Rory. Their orderly cupboards and shelves held many instruments, scales, and glass vessels, the likes of which Rory had never seen before. At the end of the lab stood a glassed-in area with a sliding glass window and a counter full of pens and small pads of paper. Randolph explained to Rory that he would be using this chemical dispensary often, and that he would receive a half-day training session on the order control system for requisitioning chemicals.

When they finished in the lab, they went out and jumped into one of the golf carts. Randolph backed the cart out then turned onto the gravel path leading into the cottonwoods Rory had seen when he first arrived. Once in the woods, the path bent out away from the river to a clearing, then curved back through another opening in the trees leading to a large uncovered cement holding tank full of water. One end of the tank consisted of a large wheel and a series of valves. Along the side of the tank was a small parking area with a single step up to a white concrete deck running around the tank. Stretched across the tank, at ten-foot intervals, were a series of bridges, barely six inches above the surface of the water.

"These are the holding tanks where this mine used to store the contaminated water. There are four of them," Randolph said as they drove by the tank and into another gap in the trees. This gap led to three additional tanks. When they arrived at the fourth tank, Randolph stopped the cart and they got out.

"These tanks are filled with river water. We don't mine anything in this area any longer, so we don't contaminate the water here. We keep the water moving through these tanks so the walls don't collapse, and to take benchmark measurements of the river in its natural state. One of your tasks is to come down here periodically and dip samples, so I wanted to show them to you."

"Okay."

"Good. Let's go back to the lab."

Back inside the lab, Randolph explained the job, outlining the various procedures he would perform. He also provided Rory with the schedule and timings for each of the steps. By the time the orientation concluded, the morning had gone by.

Rory went to the cafeteria, which had been pointed out to him earlier. Randolph had said to grab a table and he would follow him after he went to get his lunch. Rory felt out of place as the stranger sitting by himself. Randolph arrived.

"You're not eating?" he asked.

"Well, yeah, I was just holding the table."

"You could have gone for food and then grabbed the table."

"Yeah, I guess."

"Go ahead. I'll be here."

Embarrassed, for what he didn't know he went and purchased the lunch special. The conversation with Randolph took the rest of the hour.

The afternoon was taken up entirely by his chemical dispensary training session. Day One of Rory's laboratory life seemed to end before it had started. He couldn't wait to come back the next day to get started with his assigned work.

The sun remained high as he drove westward. His car ran smoother than he could ever remember; it displayed pep never before evident, as it swung smoothly around the curves of the winding road.

He arrived home and found a big pot of chili simmering on the stove. He pulled a bowl from the cupboard and helped himself. At times he had to remind himself to eat. His thoughts drifted toward the dispensary procedures he had learned during his training, then on to the settling tanks. How many were there again? Then he caught his head bobbing and he felt sleep would be nice.

But he had things to do. He called Victoria then ran out the door to pick her up. They had a date to go downtown and hang around on the Main Street Mall. With only two weeks to go before she left for the music camp, they planned on spending every evening together. Sleep could come later.

Victoria finished brushing her hair, then went to wait for Rory. She sat in the sofa by the window looking down the street, watching for his car. Her father, whose student for that evening's session was away on vacation, sat in his big chair on the other side of the room. He asked, "You going out with Rory again?"

She turned and nodded at her father, then answered, "Yeah, we're going to go hang out at the mall."

"You always go to the mall now. Always with Rory."

"We're going to see each other every night until I go away. Boy is that going to be hard! I almost don't want to go this year."

"What do you mean, you don't want to go!" Mr. Beach's voice got deeper and his expression turned dark.

"I would like to spend more time with Rory. I'm going to hate it when I leave."

"So now you're going to hate going to the camp. You've gone to this camp for the past three years, and it's this last one when you have to make your best impression. If you go into this camp with less than full commitment, you won't get recruited. You have to really perform this year."

"I know, Daddy. You've only told me a thousand times. I'm still going to go, and once I get there I'll be fully committed to the camp. But I wish I had more time with Rory. Time when we aren't at school working like crazy, time to just hang out."

"I'm beginning to worry about you, Victoria."

She spun around quickly to face her father and said, "Well don't; there's nothing to worry about."

Mr. Beach felt a rush of warmth rise up through his face. "I don't think I like what's going on here. You start seeing a boy, you begin to hate music and now you sass your father," he said with a rising voice.

"Daddy, I'm not sassing you. I'm telling you there's nothing to worry about. I'll do fine at the camp. Right now I'm enjoying other things. But when it comes time to perform at camp, I will perform. I don't need you and Werner and Mr. Keltch reminding me of what I've been doing my entire life. And stop telling me that my other interests are risking everything I've accomplished. I know what I've accomplished and what I'm risking.

"Right now, and until I go to the camp, I'm going to enjoy doing those other things. So please, stop trying to make me feel guilty, because I don't feel any guilt at all."

"No one is trying to make you feel guilty," Mr. Beach said sternly while rising from his chair. "We only want to be sure you do the right thing. We know what you're capable of, we know a great future stands waiting for you, and we all care for you. It would be a shame if you didn't complete what you set out to do. It would be a bigger shame, if those of us who love you didn't point out the concern we hold for the way you're playing with your future."

Victoria sat motionless, staring at her father. At first she felt anger building due to how little respect he showed her, implying she had no concern for herself and her future. Without saying a word, she let the anger peak and let her heart stop thumping in her chest. She maintained her control and realized he was right about her tone; she had never spoken this way to her father, and she had never spoken to him with intent opposite to his. She had hurt him by not seeing things his way, and by letting him know she was taking over responsibility for her future. He could worry if he wanted; but she would make her choices. When she understood the step she had taken, her anger dwindled. Her father was trying to hold on to the responsibility a father feels for his daughter, and she had let him know she had taken it away.

"I know you care for me and my future, Dad, and it means a lot to me that you do. But my future means just as much to me. So I have to make the choices I think are best for my future. You're always so certain of what my choice should be, but it's not clear to me at all.

"You don't know how much I've prepared for the camp because you aren't here all day. You only see me when I'm going to go out with Rory. You don't see me practice everyday. I'm still going to the camp with the intent of doing my best and making the most of my last camp. It's possible this camp will prove beyond any doubt that music is my future. But it may prove music has run its course for me, and that I should move on to something else."

Mr. Beach stood for a long time without speaking. She didn't know what to expect from him, now that he had heard her view of the future.

"I don't know what to say, Victoria. I guess it's good to hear you haven't shut the door on music, but it's very disappointing to hear there is a possibility you will. I don't understand why you are changing."

"I'm older and I'm trying to be more normal," she said to her father in a calm voice. She was aware of Rory parked outside; she turned and looked out at his car to make sure her father was also aware, then indicated she had better go.

When she climbed into the car she said a brief hello then sat silently looking out through the windshield.

Rory asked if she was okay.

Victoria nodded. Rory could see her thoughts needed mulling. He pulled away without expecting her to answer his question.

"My dad and I had a little discussion before you arrived. It wasn't an argument; at least I don't think so," she said, breaking her silence as they sat on a bench on Main Street, sipping frozen colas.

The sun had lowered over the western hills, its light dimming slowly. They were in the brief time before the street lamps came on, when the natural light made objects nearby eerily crisp and those in the distance strangely fuzzy. When the street lamps did come on, the natural and artificial light fought for domination. During the transition neither could claim the right to illuminate completely; and in the iridescent confusion, visibility both near and far became hampered. No breeze blew to take away the evening mosquitoes, so Victoria had punctuated her statement with a series of slaps to her arms and ankles. It had been a warm day, but with the changing light they felt the evening cool.

"So, he's mad at you?"

"No, it's the same old 'I'm disappointed you aren't totally dedicated to music' pressure he's been pulling off. Tonight I kind of told him he should stop worrying about my future, that it's up to me, not him."

"What did he say?"

"Nothing really. He said he wanted me to pay more attention to my music. I wish he would see I haven't abandoned music, and leave me alone."

"At least he's interested in what you're doing. My parents would never try to tell me what I should do because they don't care. They raise a little hell and they act interested if someone from the school asks any questions but as soon as things get back to normal, their interest level goes back to zero.

"In a way, it's kind of nice your dad is still after you about the music. And it sounds like you're letting him know that you're making your own decisions. He'll get used to it."

Rory was sitting with his jacket lying across his knee. Victoria started to shiver; she pointed at the garment and asked, "You going to wear your jacket?"

Rory smiled and lifted it, shaking it to spread it out. "No, I brought it for you," he said, and placed it around her shoulders. As he stretched his arm behind her back, he could smell her hair. The scent made him lean in closer; he kissed her cheek, causing her to turn toward him, so he softly kissed her lips.

She tilted her head to one side, looked into his eyes and smiled. "How was your first day of work?" she asked.

"Wow, it was cool! It's a bit of a long drive, but it was cool." Rory visualized his entire day all over again. He told Victoria about the building and about the laboratory with all the instruments and he told her about the chemical dispensary. He told her about the training session and he made her laugh when he told her about how Randolph wasn't a Randy, but a Randolph. Then he told her about the water tanks and how they didn't really use them any longer but he would still take samples from them for comparisons.

"If you don't do anything with the water in the tanks, why do you need to sample them?" she asked inquisitively.

"I help test samples coming in from the settling tanks at the operational mines, and eventually I get to kill fish with them. You see, every day we get containers with water samples from the mines. We measure the contaminants in the water and calculate how much of the neutralizing chemicals we need to add each day. Once we make our calculations, someone phones in the prescribed amount of chemicals to add to the tank. Then we wait for the next sample and do it again."

"But what's this about killing fish?" she asked with even more of a question in her voice.

"Well, once the contaminants in the sample get to a low enough level, we dump the sample into a tank with some small goldfish. If they survive for three days, the water is safe enough to release back into the river. Randolph said most times the fish die, so we put more neutralizers in the tanks."

"I guess that sounds like fun," she said, while the thought of the cold river water started a slight shiver in her neck. The small tremor quickly grew to a quake that rocked its way down her spine.

They wanted to stay on the bench a while longer; but after drinking the frozen sodas, creating an internal chill which received support from the cooling night air, they could stay outdoors no longer. Rory stood and beckoned Victoria out of her seat. He placed his arm around her and began to lead her down the mall to a record store where they could go inside and browse for a while. Without a jacket, he started to think the warmth inside the store would feel pretty good.

They made their way into a few of the stores on the mall; together they looked at the items for sale, knowing they wouldn't buy. After a while they went for coffee at Harry's restaurant where they sat and talked. With Rory now a working man facing a long commute each morning, he couldn't stay out as late as he would like. As much as he looked forward to his job, he couldn't wait for the weekend so he could spend two full days with Victoria.

Chapter 22

Rory was shown the daily tasks he would perform and then given his own lab coat. At first he thought he would look stupid with the coat on. He had never worn one in the lab at school, why wear one here? Then he noticed he felt better wearing the coat; he looked more like the others and it made him feel like he fit in. When he spotted his reflection in a pane of glass, he also thought he looked pretty good wearing it.

His day started when samples of water arrived from the mines. He logged them in the receipt book, then distributed them to the appropriate work areas. Next he took samples of river water from the large holding tanks and filled the fish tanks in the lab. Then he measured the contaminates in both the mine samples and the tank samples. By the last day of the week, he was working independently and it seemed that five o'clock arrived too soon. He would arrive at work, get involved in a procedure, and the next thing he knew lunch break had arrived. Then, after a quick peanut butter sandwich, one he made before he flew out the door each morning, he would get back to his lab work. In what seemed like no time at all, Randolph stood over his bench and told him to start cleaning up. He enjoyed every fast minute of every fast day, and when he took a minute to think about what he had done, he found he had accomplished many things. It gradually dawned on him how similar his job was to the work he did in the lab at school, but the results of his work in the lab had real and immediate uses. This is what excited him the most. It wasn't experimentation he performed, it was the practical use of chemistry and a chance for him to apply his knowledge. He understood everything he measured, and the purpose for the measurement. He didn't blindly perform the tasks assigned to him by some expert scientist, he performed functions that had their foundations in science he already knew.

If this is what he would build his career toward, then he knew he had made the right choice. He loved working in the lab.

Driving home at night, he couldn't believe how fast the days vanished. If he had been working with his father, he knew he would be counting cows to see how many they had left to process before his day would end. Then the long drive home, from whatever faraway ranch they worked on, would take forever. His body, exhausted from the physical labor, would stiffen in the bench seat of his father's truck as he tried to catch some sleep. He also remembered that, with the sun staying out so long in the summer, the days working for his father would have been longer than the eight hours he spent in the lab, and therefore he would get home later at night. The late arrival and his exhaustion would compromise the little time he had to spend with Victoria.

"Thank you, Mr. Duggin!" he said out loud as he steered toward Victoria.

They had gone to the Main Street Mall every night. Some nights they walked through the stores, others they stayed on the street and talked. They always ended their evening with a trip to visit Harry in the restaurant and enjoy a late dessert. Rory always wanted to take Victoria home after dark so they could sit in the car around the corner from Victoria's house and embrace. At this point in their relationship, exploring each other's flesh came without any feeling of embarrassment. They touched and felt each other until they overcharged the car with sexual energy-- heightened by the dread of Victoria's departure.

The late sunlight worked against them. They had to stay late in the restaurant, waiting for sundown. As a result, they stayed longer in the car than they had planned. Victoria would receive a stern look from her father due to the lateness of her return, but she willingly suffered the looks. Rory got less sleep than he needed. But he would happily go without sleep if it meant he could spend more time with Victoria.

Their payback for the looks and the lack of sleep came on Friday night, when they could stay in the car for as long as they liked.

They went to the restaurant. Rory told Victoria about his first week of real lab work. Victoria told him about her preparations for the music camp, then updated him on her father's attitude regarding the camp and his attitude toward her staying out late.

Halfway through their meal they decided to go to a movie, so they finished their food and left in a hurry in order to make show time. During the movie, Rory placed his arm around Victoria and she leaned over, placing her head on his shoulder. He felt the warmth of her body and smelled the scent of her hair, a scent he knew from no other source. Sometimes, when he wasn't near Victoria, something would trigger the memory of the scent and he would enjoy the illusion of being close to her. Sitting in the movie with her head resting against him, he drew in the scent and acknowledged the real pleasure of Victoria by his side.

His arm had gone to sleep partway through the movie, but he didn't want to adjust his position and lose contact with Victoria. As they left the theater, he felt the cold zing of hot needles, pricking his cut-off nerves and calling them back to duty. Every little movement of his arm caused a wave of buzzing stings that constricted his elbow, making him want to keep it still.

Outside, as dusk began, they walked along the mall past the stores they passed every evening. Tonight they didn't go in. They were just killing time.

"Do you want to drive out to River Park?" Rory asked. He wanted to go somewhere to be alone. Somewhere that wasn't around the corner from her house where they stopped every night. Tonight he was eager for some privacy.

"Sounds good," she said. They turned and walked back down the mall toward Rory's car.

Rory pulled into a spot at the far end of the River Park parking lot. The sun had set, but a hot, solid flame glowed above the mountains to the west. Orange to red to purple.

"Do you want to walk along the river?" He turned toward Victoria, placed his right arm on the back of the seat, and lifted his knee up onto the boot of the stick shift.

"I don't think so. You know the mosquitoes would eat us alive out there. You brought me here because you knew I wouldn't want to get out of the car."

Rory smiled without embarrassment.

Victoria smiled back and said, "I wouldn't want to get out of the car even if there were no mosquitoes. Besides, I know we planned on staying out late, but I can't. My parents plan to take my brother and sister to a concert in Helena tomorrow. I don't want to put them in a bad mood by coming home late, and them punish me by making me go with them. If we give up some time tonight, we don't risk losing all day tomorrow. Is that okay?"

Rory, a little disappointed, agreed by nodding.

"I still want you to get me all hot and bothered though. If you do, I'll try to get you hot and bothered too." Victoria leaned forward and moved her hand up the inside of Rory's thigh. She kept leaning forward until she could kiss him, and then she pushed him back so she lay on top of him, in the best possible position she could across bucket seats and a stick shift.

———

Rory arrived at the Beach home early the next day to pick up Victoria. They had no plan or agenda, but they didn't care as long as they had the day to themselves.

Rory sat out in the car, waiting, until he saw Victoria waving for him to come into the house. She let him in and told him to take off his shoes, which produced an inquisitive look on Rory's face. He obeyed. She took his hand and said, "We're alone."

She smiled at him and waited, letting him think about their situation. When she saw it register, she pulled him by the hand through the kitchen, down the hall and into her bedroom.

They slid into each other's arms and began their soft kisses. The heat and the movement of their bodies caused their mouths and tongues to move more urgently. Their hands began to roam, first against each other's backs, then gradually around to their sides, and then against each other's chests. Rory's hand pressed and massaged Victoria's breast. When he moved his hand under her shirt, she pulled away from him. Rory stood wide-eyed thinking she was ending their fun before it had begun; then he watched her as she backed away and stopped near the head of her bed. She looked intently into his eyes. Rory waited, willing to let her direct him to whatever they would do next. His face flushed and he felt his ears heat up and begin to pulse. He could feel the pressure of blood flowing in his veins.

Victoria reached up to the top button of her shirt and slipped it out of the hole. She continued down to the next; and when all of the buttons had been released she took off her shirt, uncovering her breasts. She stood, wanting him to look at her. Rory stared and fought the urge to approach her. He stood his ground to allow her to guide their course of action. Soon Victoria moved her hand to the button of her jeans. She released it, slid the zipper down a short distance, turned her back to Rory and slipped the jeans off her hips, down past her knees and finally to the floor where she stepped out of them. He watched her, seeing her soft white skin and soft curved hips. He expected to see panties but she wore none.

She twisted sideways toward the bed. Rory looked at her naked hip and the curve of her buttocks; he looked up the soft line of her stomach and saw the profile of her breast, the curve defining its weight, the hardened nipple slightly above its equator. Again she paused to let Rory look at her body, indicating she wanted him to. Next she lifted the bedcovers and slipped between them. She looked at Rory and said, "Come on."

Rory wore an unbuttoned plaid shirt, which he slipped off easily. Then he stripped off the gray athletic T-shirt he wore underneath. Calmly he reached down, loosened his belt, released the button, lowered the zipper then removed his jeans and boxer shorts in one motion. He lifted his feet one at a time and flipped off his socks. As he moved to the bed he saw Victoria's eyes fixed on his naked body. Her hand reached out and wrapped around his back as he settled himself to rest on his elbow beside her. She kissed him as he bent over her and began to caress her breast. He resisted moving his hand away from her breast for as long as he could, but the sensations occurring within his groin made him want to explore her more intimate flesh. His hand slid down the softness of her stomach where he felt the rise of her pelvic area. He moved his hand to her thigh then down to the inside of her leg. He felt the soft, hot skin.

Rory pushed off of his elbow and lifted himself over Victoria's leg, setting himself on his knees between her thighs. He bent over her, placing his hands on either side of her head. He felt weightless resting on his wrists as he saw that her desire reflected his own. He pushed back, then leaned down to the floor and fumbled with his jeans. When he returned upright, he held a condom out for her to see. She didn't indicate that they should stop, so Rory opened the wrapper and rolled the latex over his erection while Victoria watched. He bent down over her and again placed his hands beside her head while looking into her eyes.

Victoria reached out and placed her hands on Rory's hips, pulling them down, guiding him, so that he entered her completely and then she held him firmly against her.

Their eyes remained connected, deep inside each other's desire. Their eyes said this is what they wanted, this is what they were willing to give to each other, from this time forward.

Victoria relaxed her body and reduced the pressure she used to hold his hips locked against her. They began the rhythm of their first intercourse. Rory released inside of her, feeling pleasure greater than any other he had experienced. He couldn't believe the intensity of this pleasure could be heightened to such a level.

Victoria didn't know if she had experienced everything this shared intimacy had to offer. But she knew she had wanted what they had done, and she knew from the pleasures she had experienced under Rory's touch that she wanted to do this again.

They stayed beside each other, happy with what they had done together. They maintained contact with each other, enjoying the feel of each other's skin. Their sexual urge idled as they looked and touched to maintain the intimacy of being naked together in open daylight. They wanted their first time to last for a long time. When it seemed like they had stopped their sexual activity, and one or the other would move as if to leave the bed, the other would pull them together again, renewing the physical contact, the kisses, the touching and the caressing.

After a time they stopped moving. They lay still beside each other, both knowing they were now different, both knowing they had entered a new stage of life.

Rory raised himself up on his elbow and looked down on Victoria's face as she lay on the pillow. Her hair was wrapped under her head so it all lay to the side away from Rory. It looked as if the wind had blown it out of their way.

"Thank you; that was nice," he said.

Victoria smiled up at him.

He lay back down on her, feeling the skin of her breasts against his chest. He kissed her deeply and began to feel a new stirring. He finished kissing her and pulled away, separating their bodies to stop the new urge. He thought, Is this stirring okay? I don't want to get greedy.

He wanted to experience the pleasure again. Right now. But maybe she didn't, and he didn't want her thinking he was oversexed and oblivious to everything else during sexual moments.

He kissed her again, trying not to make too much skin to skin contact. When he broke the kiss, he looked her in the eyes and said, "It means a lot to me that you and I did this together."

"Me too. You're the one I want to do this with."

———

Nothing they could do would improve their day. Still, with no plan, they decided to go for a drive. No specific destination was mentioned, but Rory found himself driving the roads he took to go to work. He suggested he take her to see the laboratory where he would spend his time while she went off to music camp.

They drove along the two-lane highway and together looked out over the grassy hills. Rory enjoyed his drive to work each day, but having Victoria along to share it with made it even more enjoyable. He liked the look of the country, country he knew. Low hills, broken by river valleys and roads. He had seen so many of them on his journeys to push cows, but on those occasions he drove on mundane roads past ordinary hills, normal trees, and regular rivers. On this trip, he enjoyed the hills, trees, rivers and roads of his life.

He turned onto the road leading down the side of the coulee to the lab. The river crashed down on the rocks behind the white structure sitting in the shade of the hill. The carved-off wall on the other side of the water was split between shadow and light. The grass growing on its brow still reflected a shiny green; from its middle down to the random spray of water, the color was a flat dark gray with light-colored bedrock stripes looking like layers of unpolished jewels. Only the very tops of the cottonwoods remained in the sunlight on their side of the river. The gap leading into the trees was barely visible.

Rory parked in front of the garage doors and pointed out some of the areas of the building. He explained that the mine had been at the far side of the compound by the waterfall, but it had played out over twenty years earlier. They could see a large square of concrete against the hill by the side of the falls: the sealed entrance to the mine that started Copper-Glen. He told her how he wished they could go inside the building so he could show her the lab and all the instruments. She could see his excitement at having her here at the place that excited him so much.

"The tanks," he said, "are in the trees. Let's go for a walk."

She looked at the stand of cottonwoods and saw the path leading into them for the first time.

When they entered the trees and turned the first corner, Rory stopped and turned toward Victoria. He pulled her close to him and put his arms around her, closing them tight. He held her and felt her holding him firmly. Her warmth and the smell of her hair caused him to close his eyes so he could shut out everything except the joy of being with her. He stood holding her for a long time, adjusting the pressure of his hold on her, trying to bring her closer to his body. He felt like he needed to pull her right inside the cavity of his chest.

Chapter 23

As a group they stood, speaking short, clipped sentences, trying to sound casual and often letting their attention wander. The short time left before Victoria's plane would depart moved with the speed of an old dog being put out in the rain. Rory met Victoria's mother for the first time ever, and, for the first time as Victoria's boyfriend, met Mr. Beach.

Due to their concerns over Victoria's current attitude toward music, her parents were happy to see her going back to the music camp. But the small degree of anger they harbored toward Rory did dampen their happiness a little. They weren't sure how they should treat him, since his influence might turn their daughter away from pursuing a career in music. And hadn't he himself turned away from his band activities only a year before? They blamed him for Victoria's change in behavior, which compounded the anger. She stayed out late and recently had begun to argue with them. They didn't object to Rory personally or to her having a boyfriend, they objected to her unexpected conduct now that she had one.

Rory had no mixed emotions; his mood could go no lower. Every aspect of this meeting held the potential for bad results. Rory tried to avoid meeting anyone's parents; he equated meeting his girlfriend's parents to social and emotional torture. On top of that, this was goodbye. He wouldn't see or touch Victoria for six weeks, and he had to share their last moments together with her whole family. But his misery was not yet complete; Werner Brock waited for Victoria in San Diego. This turbulent fact stirred the emotional calm Rory sought. He remembered Gary's comment about Werner being after his girl, and agonized over the afternoons Werner would spend with Victoria.

Six weeks of being without her while Werner saw her every day gave Rory a strong and lasting feeling of despair, even though she hadn't left yet. The not-too-much older man, who appeared to take a stronger than normal interest in Victoria, would attempt to impress her for six long weeks. How to survive, knowing that circumstance?

His memory of their intimacy bolstered his spirits; a soothing hum resonated throughout his body when he remembered the feel and scent of her. The mere thought of knowing they had been lovers satisfied him to a point where he felt he could live through any ordeal, good or bad. Since their first time, they had wanted the experience again but were both too shy to make overtures. The perfect opportunity for privacy hadn't presented itself again, so neither had initiated any sexual contact.

Until last night. They knew Victoria would leave the next day. They knew they needed to create their own opportunity.

So they went out for a drive and found a quiet place to park, then partially removed their clothing in the back seat of the car. Due to a lack of space, they experimented with a few different positions and had difficulty accomplishing what they intended to do. But nothing would defeat their sexual hunger. The sitting position allowed them to overcome their environment's limitations and achieve the desired contact. They made love face to face, seeing the meaning of their act while feeling the physical comfort of the exchange they made.

In the airport, they wanted to look at each other, to see the eyes they had gazed into during their lovemaking, and to acknowledge what now existed between them. But they feared her parents would know what their glances meant if they maintained eye contact for too long.

Victoria's younger sister and brother teased Rory about being Victoria's boyfriend. The lover's skin color changed with each surge of embarrassment, and they kept their distance from each other. All he wanted to settle his nerves was to hold Victoria in his arms until she boarded the plane. He knew he wanted to kiss her goodbye, but with Mr. Beach watching, he feared he would chicken out and only say the words. The Beaches stared at him like birds of prey watch their hunting grounds. Would he cower like a rodent and not make a move that might attract the birds' attention?

Mr. Beach had greeted Rory in a friendly manner and shook his hand when he first arrived. Since then, he had stood back from the rest of the family and acted as guardian father. Rory realized his presence altered the way the family would say goodbye to one another as much as they altered the way he and Victoria would say goodbye.

Mrs. Beach tried to start a conversation with Rory. While they talked, the younger brother interrupted and asked if Rory would kiss Victoria like he did when they sat in his car, then hid behind his mother and giggled. Rory ignored the question and continued his discussion about his summer job. Victoria smiled at her pesky little brother while laughing inside at Rory's change in flesh tone during the little boy's giggles.

The claustrophobic stress of the situation increased every second and he decided it would be nice to get away. An early exit seemed in order, even though it meant leaving Victoria.

They had discussed how they would communicate over the duration of the camp and didn't need to remind themselves of their plan. Rory caught Victoria's eye and gave her a brief nod to indicate his departure. He turned to Mr. Beach and said, "Well, I should leave so you can all say goodbye to each other. It was nice to meet you Mrs. Beach, Mr. Beach." He then looked down at the sister and brother, reaching out pretending to pinch the young boy and said, "I suppose I'll see you two scalawags again sometime." The young brother hid behind his mother again.

Rory then turned to look at Victoria, who stood frozen with her arms by her side, waiting to see how Rory would approach her. He stepped to her and stopped to look at the face he knew he would truly miss over the next too many weeks. He smiled, then slowly passed the back of his hand down her cheek; then he touched her hair, cupping the side of her head softly. He moved closer, put his arms around her and lowered his head to kiss her. He held the kiss, broke it momentarily to look in her eyes, then kissed her briefly once more. He stepped back and still looking in her eyes said, "I'll see you in six weeks."

"See ya," she said back in a cracked voice. She swallowed to relieve her constricted throat.

Rory turned and nodded again to her parents, who both stood solemnly still. His nod conveyed the same respectful meaning cowboys intended when they touched their hat brims. He spied the young brother peeking out from behind his mother and wearing a satisfied smile on his face. Rory wanted to wink but he controlled the instinct. Without another word, he turned and left the gate area. As he walked away, he believed everyone he passed could see the heart inside his chest trying to beat its way out through his ribcage.

The family goodbyes had a clumsiness about them, which Victoria attributed to her parents not knowing how to react to Rory kissing her. She couldn't wait to get on the plane.

After takeoff, her chest emptied and became a void. She would be away from Rory for a long time. Even with the schedule she would keep during the camp, she knew she would have plenty of time to miss him. In an attempt to get her mind off the vacant feeling, she tried to generate the excitement she'd felt the previous years when she returned to the camp. The fun of catching up with the other girls, the idea of discovering the new facilities at her home for the next six weeks, and the thrill of enjoying some of the luxuries the five-star resort offered its guests. She would miss Rory, no doubt, but she didn't intend to pine away in her room. She wanted to make the most of her last camp, both musically and recreationally. She worried that while she had fun, Rory would only have his work to keep him busy during the summer. He would do chemistry at work and he would complete his chemistry project in his spare time, so for him, summer looked like chemistry as usual.

The void came back when he entered her mind. How could they endure this longing for each other? Her only comfort came from knowing she shared this large, lonely void with Rory.

———

The first morning of camp always involved the formation of the orchestra without instruments. They met in a large rehearsal hall and took their positions with all the members of their section. In this manner, the camp director delivered the opening welcomes and announcements while the section members could easily find each other. Leaving the instruments behind allowed the students to renew acquaintances and socialize without the instruments getting in the way.

Victoria, and the two girls she had enjoyed the most during previous camps, stood talking while waiting for the speaker to start. The girl none of them could stand wouldn't be returning this year, so they had some laughs at her expense. Two younger girls they had never seen before hovered nearby. Earlier, they had asked if they had found the oboe section, so Victoria and her friends concluded they were frosh. The three veterans sized them up from the corners of their eyes while pretending to totally ignore them.

"Oh my God! Do you remember those three boys who acted like dorks on the beach every day in Florida? Don't look now, but the sax player turned hunk," one of the other girls said, causing Victoria and the third girl to turn immediately.

"Boy, I'll say," said the other girl.

"Quite an improvement," Victoria responded, "but still only a minor hunk."

"Same old Victoria, hard to impress."

"So Victoria, are you looking forward to rekindling the flame with Werner?"

Victoria looked at her friend and sighed. She knew a ribbing about the special attention she received from Werner the previous year would come eventually.

Mitch Davies

"There was no flame. There wasn't even the least bit of heat. We just talked."

"He stared at you like a sex-starved maniac and managed to get you alone in his rehearsal room. We could barely touch the door handle after you two had been in there for a while."

"Oh boy, here we go. I see you're picking up right where you left off."

"Looks like Werner is too. He's coming over."

Werner walked with deliberate strides in their direction. He'd gone a long time without a haircut and had not had access to an iron, but he smiled eagerly as he approached. "Victoria," he said, "I hope you had a nice trip into San Diego. When an opportunity presents itself, I would like to get together with you. I would like to tell you about my trip, as it went since I left your home, and ask you some questions."

"Sure. I'd like to know how you made out."

"Good." He turned to Victoria's two companions. "And you ladies, are you ready to play your best music?"

The other girls nodded with vacant stares. Their imaginations churned.

"Good." Werner turned to the young girls standing attentively nearby. "Two new oboists join us this year. I presume you young ladies are the very ones?"

The girls stepped closer and indicated they were the very ones.

"Good. We are going to spend a lot of time together, starting this afternoon. I will see you all then." Werner gave a little bow and moved away.

Victoria's friends turned to her with their mouths open, shutting out the two new girls again and not quite able to formulate their questions. Finally one of the girls asked, "What did he mean, 'since he left your home'?"

262

Victoria smiled and raised her eyebrows before saying, "Werner came to Great Falls a few weeks ago for a visit. Then he drove down here."

"He visited you, at home?"

"Yep, he stayed about a week. My father thinks he's the greatest thing since sheet music."

"Oh, Victoria, you started rekindling the flame early!"

"Rekindle? I'd say she's been dumping combustible material all over this fire."

The girls' laughter caused Victoria to turn red. The new girls looked at each other with questioning looks and raised eyebrows.

"There are no flames. He taught in Washington this summer and had time to kill before camp so he came for a visit. Besides, while he visited I introduced him to my boyfriend, so he knows I'm already involved."

"Oooh. You've got a boyfriend. That must twist Werner's shorts big time."

Victoria realized the teasing couldn't be avoided so she decided to let their imaginations run at their own pace.

"You bet, it twisted them big time."

———

Randolph walked very fast. Rory noticed whenever they went somewhere together, he had to increase his strides to keep up. From his lab station back near the fish tanks, Rory looked up and saw Randolph approaching at a sprinter's pace. His security badge swung wildly in time with his steps; his hand held a report Rory recognized as one he had given to Randolph earlier. He looked around his station to see if anything was out of place, and felt warmth radiate inside his lab coat. Randolph loomed over him when he looked back up.

"Rory, there's a bit of an urgent situation at one of the mines," he said, holding up the report. "These measurements you made for Ravens-Butte this morning registered too high. I need you to do them over. Can you do them right away?"

"Ah, yeah. Did I do something wrong?"

"I doubt it. Do the measurements over again, then bring them to me. I'll explain when you bring them in." Randolph turned and sped away, the bottom of his lab coat billowing as he returned to where he had come from.

Rory looked in the logbook to determine the location of the samples in question, retrieved them, then set up to do the measurements again. When he finished, he took his new recordings into Randolph.

"Why did you say the measurements were too high?" Rory asked.

"Sit down. We've been sampling the Ravens-Butte water for about ten weeks now, so I expected lower measurements. Here, let's see." Randolph took the new set of measurements and began comparing them to the ones Rory made earlier. "They're the same. Too high. Here's the problem. Rory, we can't release the water back into the river until we neutralize the contaminates. This particular tank is due for release back into the river next week, but unless we get the levels down the water stays where it's at. So: We need the tank for the next batch of contaminated water from the mine, therefore this batch needs to release on schedule. If we can't release it, there's no place for the new contaminated water. If there's no place for the new contaminated water, then we shut down the mine and wait. Shutdowns cost the company money, and that's not good.

"Whenever this situation comes up, we calculate a new neutralization schedule and use some additional, very costly, chemicals. We've got four days starting tomorrow to get this straightened out, and we need to test with the fish for three days. The key here is to get the calculation right the first time."

"Okay. What do you want me to do?"

Randolph instructed Rory to set up a lab with three samples of the tank water from the Raven-Butte mine. He wanted two setups on magnetic agitators and one setup for heat. Randolph would prepare a set of calculations for neutralizers, then get them checked off by one of the chemists.

Forty minutes later Randolph had his instructions back from the chemists. He sent Rory to requisition the chemicals and then had him apply the three new formulas. Rory logged the start time and would take measurements every hour for the rest of the day while plotting the changing levels of the contaminates. The heat-based test required Rory to heat the water so it could retain more of the neutralizing chemical. When it cooled he would take measurements. He would repeat these steps, adding additional chemicals each time, until he got the contaminate level low enough to test with the fish.

The heating method would achieve the required results sooner, but they wanted to avoid the additional expense of heating the tank water. If one of the agitating tests proved they could receive the same results without heating, then they would neutralize the tank with the less expensive method.

At the end of the day, Randolph stopped by Rory's lab. "Rory, can you get here early in the morning to take the last set of measurements?" Randolph asked.

"Sure, I guess."

"Great. These guys take this type of event very seriously. It costs thousands of dollars to shut down a mine and it takes thousands to start it up again. When a shutdown happens it's not a local problem; the president of the company gets notified and there's hell to pay in the labs. See you in the morning."

Randolph left Rory to mind the three tests. Rory intended to make another set of measurements before he left. While he waited, he looked through the instructions Randolph had received from the chemist and found the calculations used to derive the solution.

The informal format of the calculations confused him slightly, but soon he could follow and understand the procession the chemist made to arrive at the values prescribed for the tests.

He went back to the first page of calculations to go over them again and confirm his understanding of what he read. He congratulated himself for having the basic knowledge to see what the chemists were trying to accomplish.

That night at home, while working on the battery project he still intended to complete for the Mortenson Scholarship, he kept going over the chemist's calculation in his mind. He knew he should concentrate on his project. But he also knew he couldn't do his best work if he wasn't committed to what he was doing. So he packed up the project early and went to bed, where he thought of nothing but the Raven-Butte mine.

Rory left for work in the dark the next morning. As he drove, the sun rose and bored into his eyes. It made him concentrate his vision hard on the road, but his mind wandered. What would the results of the tests show about the tanks?

Randolph intercepted him as he walked into the lab. "Rory, can you come here for a minute?"

Rory went into Randolph's office and sat down.

"As you know there are four tanks at the Raven-Butte mine. Last night it occurred to me that we might have measured the wrong samples, so I came in this morning to check the measurements of the other tanks. Based on the dates and the measurements, we've probably confused tanks two and three."

"Hmm. So there's no problem?"

"Probably not. But we've still got to make sure. It looks like you mixed up the samples—and I wanted to talk to you about the importance of logging them properly."

"Oh. I don't think I mixed them up." Rory said. Randolph sat back in his chair. Rory continued, "I guess it's possible. But I've been really careful to keep them in order when I log them." Rory said in an apologetic tone. His mind raced back to the day before when he received the samples. Had he done anything differently? A queasy feeling infiltrated his abdomen. If he made a mistake by mixing up the samples, then he wasted a lot of people's time.

"Do you still have the control samples?" Randolph asked.

"Yes. They're in the locker."

"Let's go check them out."

Randolph led and Rory raced along beside him. They sped to the lockers where they stored the control samples from each site. Randolph had Rory point out the storage locations he had written in the logbook, then had Rory wait at the entrance to the locker while he went inside. When he came out he said to Rory, "Well, they're labeled correctly and located where the log says. I'll get someone to take samples and do a new set of measurements. You can go on back to your lab and finish your tests just in case we need the results."

Rory returned to his lab with his head down, hoping not to run into any of the other workers. He sat on his lab stool unable to move. The agitators in the flasks spun away and he knew he had to make measurements, but his gloomy mood wouldn't allow him to move. How did he mix up the samples and what did it mean if he did? It took a few long minutes, but his blue funk finally lifted enough to let him get to work on his measurements. If he made a mistake, then he made a mistake. Pay the price and move on.

When he finished his measurements he took the results to Randolph, not knowing if he was delivering the rope they would hang him with.

"Ah Rory, we may still need those, but maybe not. The new measurements of the samples matched the two sets you made yesterday. Which means the samples you tested came from the bottles as marked at the site. They probably got mixed up there, so you didn't do it."

Rory sighed and felt relief percolate through his body. "Man, do you know how good that makes me feel? Why do you say we may not need these results?"

"If they mislabeled the samples at the site, then the tanks are probably on schedule and we'll release on time. Hang on to your results, though. "

For the rest of the day Rory worked with a smile on his face. He had gone from feeling as if he had betrayed the company, betrayed himself, betrayed Mr. Duggin and betrayed the science of chemistry, to feeling like a person doing his work the proper way.

During their evening phone call he told Victoria about the incident and how, for the first part of the day, he had felt like everyone was avoiding him for making a mistake. Feeling he had been assigned work beyond his capability impaired his view of his work and his life's goal. To find out such a thing at the beginning of his chosen career, would destroy his image of his future. Now, he knew he could handle the work.

"You must have felt relieved when you found out they mislabeled the samples at the mine. Is somebody going to get in trouble over it?" Victoria asked.

"I don't know. I'm just glad I did my job right."

"Rory Coleman always does the job right. At least that's been my experience."

Rory blushed. "Thanks. Plus, now I can concentrate on my project for the scholarship.

"What was your day like?"

"Not bad. These girls I'm hanging out with drive me crazy, though. This year all they want to talk about is boys. They flirt with the guys so they can talk about the flirting. It's not like they want to do anything with those guys. Then they tease me for not flirting, because I have a boyfriend. Then they're always asking me about you because they want to know what it's like to have a boyfriend.

"Tomorrow is going to be a long day of them constantly needling me. It's beach day, no practice and no rehearsal. They're going to tease these guys, then yak about it non-stop."

"You probably love it. Beach day, huh? Pretty tough camp they run. I'll check in with you tomorrow to see how much flirting you did."

They said goodbye. She had been at camp for over a week and hadn't mentioned Werner Brock once. Did she omit mentioning him because she hadn't seen him much, or because she didn't want him to know how much time she spent with him?

Chapter 24

"What do you think of the new girls?" Werner asked Victoria as they sat in the practice room where the oboe section met each afternoon.

"I guess they play pretty good. I can barely hear Julie; she sits kind of far away but she sounds a little weak in the lungs."

"Yes, I think you're right. I will give her some breathing exercises. Perhaps that will help."

Silence followed. Victoria had noticed when she and Werner talked, silences like this one had become quite common. The previous year, they had been able to talk about numerous subjects and the dialogue flowed very naturally. This year, their conversations seemed stunted due to her reading more meaning into Werner's neutral questions than really existed, followed by her short, non-committal answers. This awkwardness made it easy for her to stay away from the room; but she felt a twinge of guilt knowing Werner waited for her in the room each day, and so she began to visit him.

From the beginning of the camp, she noticed that he watched her very closely. In the practice room, he treated her like the only student worth teaching. In the full band rehearsals, when he played along, he sat beside her; when he was only listening, he sat behind her. It annoyed her to some degree. She didn't feel smothered by him, he was just there.

Mercifully, the teasing from the other girls had stopped after two weeks. The special attention they gave her had turned into minor jealousy. They felt they didn't get their share of Werner's teaching time, and therefore, didn't get an opportunity to improve. As a result, Victoria felt her friends talked with her less often, and that Werner ignored them because of her. Her noon hours of hanging out with the girls became a little cold, so she found herself inclined to leave them at the beach while she visited with Werner.

"Have you talked at all with your father about the prospect of going to school in Berlin?" This was the first time he had mentioned the conservatory to Victoria since the camp started.

"We talked a bit after you left. But then we kind of dropped it. He still thinks it's a good idea, but I want to check out a few other things before I get too serious about it."

"Well, I hope you give the matter very serious consideration. I would love to see you living and playing in my own city. It's beautiful there despite the surroundings. I could show you so many things."

"It does sound good."

"It's wonderful." He sat still for a moment appearing to contemplate life in Berlin. When he returned from his brief daydream, he focused on Victoria again. "I told your father, when I visited your home, that you are the type of musician the conservatory is looking for. I passed this opinion on to the people at the conservatory. I am very confident you would receive an appointment, if you displayed an interest. They said if you are serious, you should write them a letter so they will send you some additional information."

"Thanks, it's nice of you to say those things."

"I'll give you the address so that you can write. Be sure and tell your father. My old professor suggested the letter recently. I couldn't tell your father this when I visited."

She didn't answer; she didn't want to tell him she was in no hurry to inform her father about the effect this letter could have.

"The others will come soon. Thank you for coming early. I enjoy spending time with you. I would like to do more than just spend time here talking, though. You know, like go for walks, or go to a restaurant at night."

Victoria smiled. An awkward silence followed.

———

For a week after the incorrect labeling incident, Rory had kept in the back of his mind the problem of neutralizing the water more quickly. The calculations he had seen showed him the basic makeup of the chemicals being neutralized and the chemical structure of the neutralizing agent. He kept thinking about alternative methods for mixing the chemicals, methods to accomplish the neutralization in less time and to avoid the costly shutdowns.

When he saw how many times faster they could achieve the neutralization by heating the water before adding the chemicals, he started to mull over the problem from that viewpoint. But how could they heat the large amount of water in the tank so they could use the quicker method? Currently, if they had to heat the water they circulated it through a series of heaters. The water stayed hot while passing through the heaters, but lost most of the heat when it returned to the cold water in the tank. This method required circulating the water through the heaters for a long time to get the temperature high enough. And that took time.

Rory wondered what would happen if they injected the neutralizing chemicals into the water while it still circulated through the heaters. He began to make some of his own calculations. He started by asking Randolph about the heating procedures at the mines. Randolph provided little information and didn't seem at all interested in Rory's thoughts regarding the problem. Rory wanted to know the flow rate of the pumps and how long the water remained at its highest temperature before it returned to the tank. His approach required the heated water to become super saturated with the neutralizing chemical and to stay hot long enough for the contaminates and neutralizers to bond. If the water cooled before the bonding, the neutralizers would turn back into their own compound. Without information regarding water temperature, and the duration the temperature lasted, Rory's calculations could go nowhere. But he didn't want to give up on solving the problem.

Because of Randolph's lack of interest, Rory decided to look at the problem from an entirely different direction; he began to consider a theory that might do the trick.

He spent another week on his theory until he felt he had a pretty good concept of how his process would work. He realized the fine-tuning of the chemistry would require a chemist from the plant, and he hoped that if they decided to work on his theory, they would teach him the chemistry they would use.

Randolph's cold reception during his previous approach on the subject made Rory consider going directly to one of the chemists to present his solution, but he didn't want to overstep his supervisor.

When he finally sat down with Randolph to talk about the problem again, he had all his thoughts in order. First, he explained his approach. Instead of taking a solid and agitating it to dissolve it into a liquid, why not heat the solid into a hot gas and cool it down to a liquid? It would take less time to heat the neutralizing chemicals into a gas than it would take to heat the entire tank of water and once you have the hot gas under pressure, you could release it into the tank of water. The key to preventing the gas from turning back into a solid during the mixing process was to mix the chemicals at a high temperature.

To heat a portion of the water, Rory's plan called for drawing water from the tank into a thin tube and passing it through a heating element. After the water was hot, the gas would be injected into the tube and the super-heated gas would bring the temperature of the water up a few more degrees, to the point where the chemicals would bond. Then the mixture would circulate through an additional coil of tubing and cool gradually. The length of the tubing would provide the amount of time needed to let the molecules in the neutralizing chemicals bond with the contaminates.

Randolph listened to Rory's theory in relative silence, only asking a couple of simple questions. When Rory finished, Randolph nodded and said to leave it with him so he could run the idea by one of the chemists. Rory wondered why Randolph had a neutral attitude toward the plan.

A few days later Randolph called him into his office.

"Rory, they think we're onto something here with this super-heated gas approach. They want to see a little more detail so they want us to put something in writing. Do you think you could write up a hypothesis on this plan?"

"They liked my idea? Wow, that's great. Yeah, sure, I could put something together," Rory said with a slight hesitation in his voice. The words 'we're onto something' dampened his excitement. "Did they say what kind of detail they wanted? Because I can't provide a really detailed chemical analysis."

"That's okay. Write it up like you explained it to me. Add whatever you can with regard to the chemistry. I'll take a look at it before I forward it to the chemists. They're the ones to do the detailed chemistry anyway. They don't expect lab techs to perform the science for them. I'm amazed the eggheads even listened to the idea with an open mind."

"Why's that?" Rory asked.

"Sometimes they expect us to think and sometimes they expect us to do only what they tell us to do. Whatever is convenient for *them*." Randolph said.

Rory frowned. "Hmm. I'll put something together for them."

"Can you do it by Friday, so I can read it over the weekend?"

"I think so."

When Friday came around Rory delivered the outline to Randolph's office, but Randolph wasn't in so Rory left his report on the desk. He didn't see Randolph the entire day. When he went by the office on his way out for the weekend, the outline remained on the desk.

When Rory called Victoria that evening, he explained the whole concept of his solution. She listened intently and often asked questions regarding the development of his theory. Rory answered in detail, happy to have a curious listener.

"So, that's what happened to me this week. What's going on in the world of music, sun and sand?" he asked, then added, "That sounds like one of those old beach movies."

"If this is a beach movie, I'm getting a little tired of it. Thank god there are only two weeks to go. It's been a really long camp this year."

"Don't say two weeks, it still sounds so long. What makes this camp seem longer?"

"I don't know. I guess the other girls aren't as much fun. They're kind of cold now."

"Cold?"

"They think Werner treats me special, so their noses are out of joint."

"Does he?"

"Yeah, but I think it's because he visited with my family. He knows me more than the others, so he's more comfortable talking to me."

"Do you talk to him a lot?"

"I don't know. What's a lot? It's not much fun being with the girls so I do spend a few noon hours talking with him. But that's getting kind of weird, too."

"Weird? What's weird about it?"

"I don't know, it just feels weird. After he mentioned the conservatory, I've felt he's only trying to convince me to go to Germany next year and trying to find out what my father thinks about the whole Germany deal. When he gets talking about the conservatory, I either tune out or try to change subjects."

"How do you feel about the Germany thing? Is it something you're still considering?" Rory dreaded her answer to these questions.

"It's like they're pushing it too hard. Werner and my father bother me about it all the time. I told my father to stop bugging me when I talked to him yesterday. Boy, did he get mad! My mother called me back later to ask me what I said to him, and at first she was mad, too."

"Hopefully they'll figure out, sooner rather than later, that they can't force you to do something you don't want to do."

Rory then remembered something else he wanted to tell her. "Hey, I got something for you to look at. When I got home from the mine today I found a package of school stuff waiting for me. The Mortenson Board sent me information on the four schools on their approved list and two of them have nationally-ranked music programs. If you decide you want to stay in music and don't want to go to Germany, then maybe you could go to one of those two schools and we could go together."

"You get information about selecting your school and you look at the music programs? You should be looking at their chemistry programs, goof ball!"

"Gee, do you think they would make the Mortenson approval list if they had mediocre chemistry programs? They're all nationally ranked, that's a given."

"Oh yeah, right. My brain popped into the null set for a minute. But, us going to the same school sounds interesting."

"I thought so. The package also had information about the interview next week. I sent them the final write-up of my rechargeable battery project, but they didn't mention it in the letter. Who knows, maybe after next week I won't need to pick one of the four schools."

———

Harry brought over the pot of coffee and filled the cups again. Across from Rory, Mr. Duggin finished a piece of coconut cream pie. The dessert had thick firm custard, topped with a mound of real whipped cream, and sprinkled with toasted coconut. When he ordered the pie, he decided to go all the way and make his dessert a dairy-fat extravaganza by asking for a scoop of ice cream on the side.

Mr. Duggin's summer work repairing hiking trails for the state parks department left him tanned and weathered looking. All summer long he had alternated between living in a state camp for two weeks and living in the city for one. He didn't mind the camp food, except the dairy products were limited to milk, butter, and cheese.

Upon his return home the previous Friday, Mr. Duggin had found a letter from the Mortenson Board asking him to contact them regarding Rory's status. He called the Board member and connected with his secretary, and they set up an appointment for the discussion at a later date. Immediately after setting the appointment, he had called Rory to let him know about the contact and to arrange a meeting after his phone appointment with the Board member.

Rory had picked at his own food throughout the meal. He was always ready to eat, but today he lost his appetite waiting to hear what had been discussed between Mr. Duggin and the Board. When they met in the parking lot and Rory asked how it had gone, Mr. Duggin had only said, "Good. We'll talk after we eat."

When Mr. Duggin finally consumed the last crumb of the pie, Rory asked, "So, what did they say? Am I in big trouble?"

"No, but I'm going to let them fill you in on most of the things they told me. I want to give you a little pep talk before you go to your interview, okay?"

Rory nodded and Mr. Duggin provided him with some instruction about how to act during an interview. He told Rory to think about the questions they asked before he answered them, and if he wasn't sure about a question, to ask for clarification. Too many people don't understand the questions, then end up rambling on, hoping what they say somehow forms an answer. He told Rory that to ask a good clarification question shows the interviewer you're interested in the discussion.

"But don't ask questions for the sake of looking interested. If a question doesn't come naturally, don't make one up," he coached.

He made one final point for Rory to remember; "The Board already knows about your aptitude toward chemistry, so there's no need to demonstrate your knowledge of the subject. The interview isn't about chemistry, it's about character. They want to meet the young man to whom they're willing to grant an awful lot of money. They want to know about Rory Coleman when he's not in the lab. Your goal, when you get into the interview, is to make sure and be yourself. You're a good kid, Rory. People can tell that as soon as they meet you. You have nothing to hide. You'll do okay."

"Thanks." Rory blushed slightly. "What did the guy say when you talked to him?"

"In general, he wanted to confirm the procedures you used while doing your experiments. He didn't ask me why you didn't complete your second project, he only wanted to know how you did what you reported. He asked about your regular schoolwork in chemistry, and said he could tell from your report card that you handled the other subjects without any problem. I think if your interview goes well, you won't have anything to worry about."

Rory felt relieved. He thanked Mr. Duggin repeatedly for taking the time to talk with him.

A few days later, Rory arranged to leave work early to attend his interview. Randolph wasn't enthusiastic about letting him off early. When Rory explained his interview was for the Mortenson Scholarship, the comment appeared to go over Randolph's head.

On the day of the interview, Rory reminded Randolph of his early departure and Randolph only shrugged.

Carmen Porter had been a member of the Mortenson Board for the past six years, but had only performed the interview step once before. The candidate on that occasion had been a shy individual. He didn't talk much, but he did answer all of her questions reasonably, and therefore had retained his status going into his senior year. It had been an uneventful interview.

The circumstances for Rory's interview had nothing in common with her previous experience. First, there existed the letter from Mr. Keltch, in which he rescinded his earlier letter of recommendation. Second, that letter had prompted the Board to conduct a preliminary interview with Rory before making him the designate. They felt they needed to talk with him directly, something they hadn't done in the early evaluations. The notes in the file indicated a serious commitment to chemistry. In their opinion, this commitment had caused him to drop his music class, not some character flaw as Mr. Keltch had suggested.

Third, no designate had ever before submitted an incomplete project. Yet Rory had, and was still reporting the results of the incomplete work. Finally, Rory had submitted a second report upon completion of the project. This had been unexpected, since the Board never asked him to complete the project. In his first report, he had indicated his intention to finish the work, but he hadn't indicated he would submit his findings on completion. The arrival of the completed report surprised everyone.

When Rory entered the meeting room, he saw she was reading his file; he hesitated for an instant before sitting, until she nodded an invitation. The chair felt hard and uncomfortable, making him shift his weight a number of times during the initial portion of the meeting. They discussed a few unimportant topics. Carmen asked about the size of his school and what it was like living near the mountains. He asked about living in a big city like her hometown of Chicago.

The casual talk moved Rory along from the short two- or three-word answers, to longer descriptive passages, in response to her questions. Then, once she had him a little more relaxed and conversational, she flowed into the interview by asking him some unusual, thought-provoking questions.

"A lot of what we do in chemistry is problem solving, Rory. A chemist looks at situations and tries to figure out how to improve or fix them. Sometimes it involves looking at accepted truths, and trying to figure out why these things we accept as truths are never questioned. For example, why do you think they make manhole covers round?" Carmen asked this question and then paid particular attention to Rory's expression and posture. She also noted the time it took before he spoke.

Rory furled his brow, then raised his eyebrows. Next he tilted his head a little to the right, frowned, and shifted his weight onto his right elbow, which rested on the arm of the chair. His hand rose to cover his mouth.

"Hmmm. Why do they make manhole covers round?" He repeated the question to buy a little time, then shifted his weight to his left elbow and in the process moved more onto his left haunch. "Well, I can think of two reasons. One, because they're heavy and it would be easier to move them by rolling them. Two, for safety; The lip the manhole cover sits in is smaller in circumference than the cover, so the cover could never fall down into the hole; whereas a square or rectangular cover could slip through on a diagonal. Oh, and three—but this one's pretty weak—it's easier to clean the ledge the cover sits in. On a square hole you would have to clean the corners."

"Anything else?"

"Well, I guess you use less material to make a circle with the same size opening as a square, so they would cost less."

"Okay," she said while making notes. "Scientists do great things. But they can also do some pretty terrible things as well. I would like to know what you would do if you had the capability of making a nerve gas that could kill hundreds of people, and your country asked you to make it, would you do it?"

Rory sat completely upright while remaining perfectly still. Although he looked straight at Carmen, he wasn't seeing her. *How do they want me to answer this question? Are they trying to figure out if I'm some kind of a nut case?* After a few seconds he said, "Man, these are like Miss America questions. I guess it would depend on the situation. During a war, I might do it, but if a lot of people would get killed, maybe I wouldn't. Hmm, I don't know. I think it's the kind of thing you decide based on what's going on at the time."

Carmen made some additional notes, and then went on for another thirty minutes with similar types of questions. Rory found them exhausting. They made him think about situations he never had to think about before, and some of them he hoped he would never experience in real life. Carmen closed the notebook she had been writing in and pushed it to one side. Relief washed Rory's mind, refreshing him; until she grabbed another folder, opened it, and began organizing its contents into a number of piles. *What now?* he thought.

"The formal interview is over now," she said in response to the betrayed look on Rory's face, "but I would like to talk to you about your project work."

"Okay," Rory said, feeling a little apprehension but also a little confidence.

"Your last project unfolded a little differently than most projects the Board reviews. We had no discussion among ourselves regarding your project being submitted incomplete and then resubmitted when completed; therefore I can't give you an indication of the Board's decision on your project. But since I'm probably the only one who will talk to you face to face, I would like to make a few comments to you directly.

"It impressed me that you carried on to complete your work, and I'll bet the rest of the Board was equally impressed." She paused and watched Rory relax slightly. "As you know, many of the greatest scientific accomplishments resulted from accidents, or afterthoughts, or persistence. So, when we received your first report indicating you hadn't completed your project, we had to decide if we wanted our designate to do things according to our timetable, or to work the problem in the manner it deserved. I should tell you we haven't come to a consensus on that point, and there are members of the Board who are arguing rather heatedly on both sides of the question.

"As far as your first report goes, it shows you performed your work believing you were going in the right direction. Your work in the chemical analysis is quite advanced."

Rory smiled at this. "For some reason I really get balancing equations. I see what's needed and balance them."

"Like I said, it shows. Any scientist would start over again when they reached the point you reached, and speaking for myself, I would vote to renew your status as the designate based on the work you did even though you didn't complete the project.

"When I read your follow-up report, I could see beyond any doubt I would have been correct in doing so. When the Board does meet to determine your status, I will present this opinion. As I said before, I didn't discuss this with any of the others and I don't know how they will vote on the subject of incomplete projects, so my favorable view doesn't guarantee you will retain your status as the designate.

"Now, I need to get your curriculum plan for next year. Did you bring it with you?"

Rory gave her the document and Carmen took a minute to review the first page.

"Chemical changes at high temperatures in glass. Sounds interesting. What brought this subject to your attention?"

Rory shrugged and said, "I noticed there's a lot of different kinds of glass out there these days. Glass with different uses and different characteristics. You know, like why is some glass considered unbreakable? Why is some glass used for laboratory work and some not? Then there's glass for artwork like pottery glazing and glass blowing. I found it interesting enough that I want to check it out."

"It does sound interesting. I'll look forward to seeing your report. Well, if you have any questions I'll gladly answer them, if I can. If not, then you'll hear from us soon."

Rory asked a few questions regarding the procedures for picking a school, then left the room feeling the interview had gone well. He felt he had at least one Board member on his side, and in another ten days he would know if he had others.

Chapter 25

This is going to be some week, Rory thought with good cause. Being the last week of summer meant it was his last week of work. His car had made it through with only one glitch and even then he had been lucky. It overheated at the top of the hill leading down into the coulee at work and then rolled to a stop at the far end of the parking lot where it sat and cooled off for the whole day.

And this week, he needed to talk to Randolph about whether or not the chemists planned to proceed with the super-heated gas method of neutralizing the contaminated water. Rory had decided to ask him for an update so he would know their decision before his last week ended.

The final decision of the Mortenson Board also loomed over the week ahead. He felt good about his chances of retaining the scholarship. When he had talked to Mr. Duggin about the good things that went on in his interview, Mr. Duggin had a similar impression. If Carmen Porter's reaction to his work indicated how the rest of the Board would react, then things did look positive.

But, to top the week off, Victoria was due to return home from her camp on Saturday. He couldn't wait to see her even though it meant sharing her with her family. Five more days until he could hold her again; five more days until he could smell her hair, the scent of which had been coming back to him more often over the past few days. He hoped nothing had happened over the long separation to cause her to leave him the way Alyse had left him.

Mondays usually started out a little busier than the other days because he had the weekend samples from the mines to work on, so his first chance to check in with Randolph didn't come until mid-afternoon. When he arrived at his office, he found Randolph reading over the weekend measurements from the various tanks. From this report, Randolph would highlight the tanks requiring additional testing in one color, the ones where the contaminate level indicated readiness to test with fish in another, the ones ready for release back into the river system he left uncolored. Randolph would summarize these tank assignments, then give the list to Rory so Rory could plan his setups for the rest of the week.

Rory approached him in his usual way, standing at the door and waiting to be noticed. Early on he discovered that when he opened the conversation, Randolph usually became grumpy and answered no to any request.

"Rory, what can I do for you?" Randolph's tone indicated a self-inflicted grumpy mood.

Backing away seemed like the right thing to do but he had resolved to find out about his heated gas theory. "I wanted to know if you've had a chance to talk to the chemists again about my idea. It's my last week; if they have any questions or want me to do any more work on it, then this is the last chance."

"No, I haven't talked to them about it. It's in their hands and I'm sure they can do the necessary work from this point on, so I wouldn't worry about it."

"I'm not worried about it, I'd just like to know if they're going to do it, that's all."

"Why, do you expect a reward or some kind of acknowledgement?" Randolph said sarcastically.

"No, not really. It's like it would be nice to know if I had a good idea or not."

"Well, I'll let you know if I hear anything," he said, closing the topic. "I'm going to need to sit with you on Friday afternoon to go over your work in progress and also to do your final review. Make sure you don't get into anything too detailed in the late morning. I'll get this summary out to you as soon as I can."

Randolph returned to his reports and Rory left.

Friday morning Rory set up the last of the fish tanks with a sense of satisfaction regarding the work he had performed over the summer. He felt accomplished with the way he had learned his job and he knew he had become quite skilled at his work. When he looked up from the last fish tank he saw one of the chemists looking over his shoulder.

"How did you like working in the lab here?" the chemist asked.

"A lot. I liked it a lot."

"Good. You did the measurements and tests of the water, right? It's a good thing we didn't experience a shutdown this summer; you're lucky you missed one of those."

"So I hear. We almost had one, though."

"Thank god we didn't. From what I hear it's not likely to happen again either. One of the other chemists said they've come up with a new procedure to fix the slowpoke tanks by using some kind of gas injection. Said Randolph came up with the idea."

Rory froze when he heard this. He could feel his heart rate quicken. Suddenly his knees wanted to bend. Without realizing it, he had sat down on the bench. "Randolph?" he said.

"That's what they told me." The chemist placed his hand on Rory's shoulder, bent down to look at his eyes, and asked, "What's the matter?"

"Nothing. That's good, no more shutdowns," Rory said hesitantly.

"Yes, it is." The chemist looked concerned. But seeing Rory's color returning, he shrugged it off and invited him to come back and see everybody sometime, then left him alone.

When Rory's color did come back, it came back strong. He could feel his ears and cheeks burn hot. He went to get his lunch early and decided to go out to the last tank in the woods to eat alone.

After he had eaten and cooled off, he returned to wait for his afternoon session with Randolph. When Randolph arrived at the lab station Rory couldn't look him in the eye; his heart thumped inside his chest again. They reviewed the setups in each of the lab areas. Rory spoke few words and could only glare at Randolph's feet during his brief explanations. When Randolph had assessed the stage of each test, they left the area and went to Randolph's office for Rory's exit interview.

Randolph hurried through the exit interview and skipped responding to a number of the sections on the exit report form. It took about fifteen minutes and when they finished, Randolph gave Rory the okay to take off early.

"Thanks. I think I'll take you up on your offer," Rory said flatly. "But before I go, did you ever find out if the chemists intend to use my heated gas idea in the tanks?"

Randolph looked at Rory as if he had overstayed his welcome. "No, I didn't."

This time Rory maintained a gaze into Randolph's eyes; then he gave him a half smile, nodded and left.

On a small scale, Rory was glad about what he had learned from the chemist. His idea was good enough to be put to use. Respectable people with knowledge recognized the value of his thinking and would benefit from his thoughts. That made him proud. On a larger scale, he felt disgusted with Randolph for getting away with taking credit for his idea. Randolph wouldn't perform any additional work on the theory because the chemists would take over; therefore he wouldn't have an opportunity to demonstrate that the solution was beyond his capabilities. It sickened Rory to think people like Randolph existed, people willing to take credit deserved by others.

During the drive home, Rory traversed peaks of anger for not letting Randolph know he was a thief. Then he dropped into valleys of hurt for being used by a cheat. He rode a ridge of hate for the person who had stolen his idea and would benefit from something he couldn't do on his own. Finally, he leveled ripples of disquiet to cruise on a plateau of inner calm. He realized he had won; he knew he had created a productive idea.

When he walked into his kitchen an envelope sat on the table. Alone, he stood looking down at the return address printed in the upper corner and he knew the letter was for him. He picked it up; and from its thinness he guessed it contained a single sheet of paper. The piece of paper that could ruin his week or make him happy for life. He held it out at arms length, the edges pressed between the fingertips of both hands. He took a deep breath, nodded to himself—confirming his resolve to accept whatever news the envelope held—and opened it.

His eyes scanned quickly; he saw the word 'pleased' and felt some relief; he saw the words 'retained your status' and yelled, erasing the day's long effort to lay another thick layer of stress over the week's mound of tension.

"Yes, yes, yes!" he bellowed, while throwing phantom punches and twisting his body, left right left.

"What the hell's up with you?" Pat yelled from the living room, causing Rory to stop his celebration.

He didn't respond to his brother. Instead he straightened out the letter and read it more slowly to make sure he comprehended the meaning of all of the words. The Board found his work commendable, and they found the project outlined for the beginning of the coming year to be an indication of his intent to continue working at a high level. He smiled when he read this. He couldn't wait to call Victoria.

Victoria treated the last day of camp as a formality. Get through this day and the final concert and the camp would end. It had been a long six weeks. She wanted to go home to Rory.

Her father was another story. As the camp moved on, she enjoyed herself less each day. When she called home to talk with her family, she tried not to hide the truth from them. So she had told her father that the camp was a dud.

Her father had met these comments with silence, then blamed her ill feelings toward the camp, and the fact that she didn't want to be there on Rory. She wanted to tell him her friendships with the other girls had lost their strength, the resort wasn't as good as the resorts of previous years, and she had found the music selections to be boring. But, he didn't ask her why the camp disappointed her; he let the silence hang between them. And as it hung, she admitted to herself that her father was correct; she wanted to be with Rory.

Musically, she had still performed well throughout the entire camp. During the final morning rehearsal she played flawlessly. Werner had sat beside her, listening, and had commented about her play; but she didn't need anyone else's input, she knew how well she had played.

In the afternoon, she attended a special luncheon for the students attending their final camp. She sat with the other two girls who had been at every camp with her and they all sincerely admitted they would miss each other the next summer. On this sad occasion, most of the students realized they wouldn't see each other again. Victoria allowed herself a few tears and acknowledged the tremendous experience she had gained from the camps. It had all been worthwhile; but with this part of her life over, she wanted to go home.

The camp officials extended the luncheon so the students could spend extra time talking and exchanging addresses. As a result, the afternoon tutorials had been cancelled. The last music of the camp would be the concert performance in the evening. Victoria hadn't planned on staying at the luncheon very long, since Werner had asked her to stop by the rehearsal room for a final visit. She left early to meet with him.

She found him in the room tidying up his sheet music. Her habit had been to walk across the room and sit in the chair where she played and then they would talk, Werner behind his desk, Victoria behind her stand. On this last day, Werner crossed the space between them and sat in the chair next to her.

"I hope this is not our final day together, Victoria," he began their conversation. "I am not going to say goodbye; I am going to say I will see you again. Hopefully in Berlin. Have you any further thoughts about attending the conservatory?"

"Not really. It's still a little early."

"No, no, no it's not too early. I hope that you will write a letter to my old professor to let him know you are interested.

The earlier you let him know, the earlier he can start planning on the makeup of the student group."

"It's too early for me," Victoria spoke in a measured voice, "I am getting a little bit tired of the way you and my father continuously push the conservatory at me. I am not certain I want to go there. If I should become certain about going there, I will take the steps necessary to get admitted. If I am too late and get turned down, then I will accept the consequences. Now you know where I stand on the conservatory, so please stop trying to convince me that it's the best choice for me."

Werner sat quietly as Victoria turned away from him and stared at the floor.

"Victoria, I have a personal interest in you attending the conservatory. I will be among the staff as an instructor at the conservatory when I finish my studies. The reason that I want, so much, for you to attend the conservatory, is so that we can be together."

Victoria looked at him nervously, then turned her head back to stare at the floor. But this time she closed her eyes.

"Victoria, I told you last year that I had developed special feelings for you. I still have them, but only stronger. I want us to be together; I want you to come and live in Berlin so that we can explore a relationship. The conservatory will allow that to happen. So, please consider me while you think about your future."

The previous year when Werner had started a similar conversation, Victoria had been flattered that an older man would want to develop a relationship with her. It had been confusing, but she had allowed the flattery to induce pleasant thoughts and daydreams about establishing Werner as her companion. For a few days it felt comfortable, but eventually it faded and she admitted she could not, in any way, conceive of a romantic relationship with Werner.

She had hoped she had been wrong about her perception of his special feelings toward her; but when he arrived at her home to visit, she had seen something extra in the way he treated her. When the camp started and the other girls teased her, she had denied that anything special existed. But she knew they had touched the truth.

"I'm flattered you feel that way Werner, but..." She stopped to take a breath. She floated somewhere above her chair. "I don't think a relationship between us can happen. You know I have a boyfriend I'm in love with. I want to be with Rory more than anything else in the world."

It was the first time she had defined her feelings for Rory as love. It had crossed her mind before. But now she realized she had passed the intangible boundary and fallen in love. When she said the word out loud to Werner, she confirmed it. Now she had a sense of urgency to tell Rory. He should have been the first person to hear her profess the love she felt for him.

"I know you feel strongly about this boy. I am sure this is the first time you have felt this way about someone and I know how wonderful the first time is. But first loves very seldom last forever." Werner spoke in a very calm voice, not the earnest voice of a man trying to convince someone to choose him over a rival. "I was in love with a girl at age sixteen and she was also in love with me. She was a musician. We discovered a common passion for music and we decided to make it our life together. We shared so many things with each other, our plans, our music, our ideas of what a perfect life should be—and our bodies. All new things, all very exciting.

"By the time we entered university, we realized that we had matured differently. We weren't really headed in the same direction and we weren't really in love. We had come together at the time in life when you must take on challenges without the assistance of your parents. It was new and we waded into this newness together, mistaking the thrill of becoming independent with the thrill of love.

"Everything was new and we shared all these wonderful, memorable things with each other. With the exuberance of youth it is only natural to think that you and your first love have discovered a perfect state of being, and that it will last for the rest of your lives.

"I think you and Rory are discovering the wonder of new experiences, ones that you previously believed you could not reach and this wonder you experience together is being confused with love."

Victoria brooded over his words. He could be right, in the majority of cases; but he didn't know about what she shared with Rory. He didn't know in what way they were together. He didn't know what it meant to them to have each other.

"I understand how you feel, Victoria, and I have told you what I think you are experiencing. I have different feelings for you than those I had for my first love. I will not try to describe them, nor will I try to influence you away from your feelings for your friend. But I must tell you that my feelings compel me to wait for you.

"I am five years older than you, and that may seem like a lot of years at this time in life. But as time goes on, it will amount to no real difference at all. You will see.

"Because I want us to be together again, I cannot say goodbye to you."

Werner leaned forward in his chair and watched her as she continued to stare at the floor. A few seconds later, she looked up at him but she couldn't speak. He leaned forward to kiss her but when he tilted his head to touch her lips with his, she turned away from him and allowed him to kiss her cheek. He slowly drew away from her to sit upright in his chair. She looked out beyond the music stand in front of her and said, "Goodbye, Werner."

During the evening concert, he again sat beside her and played along with her, sharing her music. She concentrated on how she played and became immersed in the music, blocking his presence completely out of her performance. She matched the perfection she had felt during the morning rehearsal and she knew she had moved up to a new level of her art.

When the concert ended, she broke down her oboe and put it in its case. She had a smile on her face when she turned and saw Werner standing, watching her. She continued to smile but said nothing. She hugged the other girls and said goodbye, then moved swiftly out of the hall and back to her room where her things sat packed and ready to go. Now, she could only wait to catch the shuttle to the airport, then wait until her flight took off, then wait until the plane landed in Great Falls. Then she would wait no longer.

Rory called later than usual because of the concert. The sound of her voice made him happy and he told her so. She said his voice sounded so good she wanted him to do all of the talking. He told her how Randolph stole the credit for his idea but added he was over it. He told about how he had screamed and hooted when he read the letter from the Board and how the time, from then until now, had passed so slowly because he wanted to talk to her so badly. Then he told her how this was the best night of the summer, so far, because it was their last night away from each other.

"I can almost taste you, Vicster. I want to touch you everywhere. I don't think I will be able to let you go once I've held you."

"Me too, Rory. I've been so controlled for the past six weeks, but I'm going crazy right now. Crazy because I only have a few hours left to wait."

Chapter 26

Rory arrived at the gate first. When the Beaches arrived, they approached him and Mrs. Beach greeted him politely. Mr. Beach smiled but said nothing. As they waited, Rory made faces at Victoria's little brother and pretended to grab and capture him. Her parents exchanged quiet words periodically, but no conversation developed between them.

As the plane pulled up to the gate, Rory dropped behind the Beaches so they would greet Victoria first. He wanted that pleasure for himself but knew he had to concede it to her family.

Victoria was behind an older woman as she stepped through the plane's door and onto the Jetway. She had intended to get past the woman while still on the plane, but the woman had blocked her by jumping into the aisle and then struggling to retrieve a large bag she could barely reach in the overhead compartment. When she finally had the bag in hand she turned to leave, and as she made her way to the door the bag snagged on every seat.

As Victoria moved to pass the lady in the Jetway, the lady swayed in front of her, causing her to halt. When she tried to move around her on the other side, the lady swayed back and the large bag cut Victoria off. The older woman fidgeted with her purse and bag, switching hands then hoisting them up her arm to hook their straps in the crook of her elbow, all the while snaking her way uphill toward the light at the end of the long tunnel.

As they got closer to the door, Victoria looked over the woman's head and could see her mother's smile amidst the faces in the crowd. Her brother and sister stood in front of her mother; her expressionless father stood behind. She searched deeper into the crowd until she spotted Rory, who raised his eyebrows and jerked his head back as if surprised by her presence.

The older woman opened a slight gap to one side at the doorway and Victoria shot through. She had a clear run to her parents where she stopped and smiled. Then, still holding her purse and carry-on bag, she leaned forward to kiss her mother and father. She spoke greetings as she slid past them, walking backwards. They turned to follow her, asking questions she couldn't quite comprehend. When she felt she had moved far enough to be where Rory stood, she stopped and turned to him. A brief stillness took place as their eyes connected and said a silent hello, then she placed her bags on the floor and stepped into Rory's arms. They held each other tight; their mouths, beside each other's ears, spoke in low voices, words meant only for each other. They pulled back, then kissed each other firmly, holding the kiss but controlling their desire to kiss more deeply. Victoria broke the kiss out of respect for her parents, then placed her head beside Rory's and again spoke private words to him. She separated the embrace but continued to stand in front of him, smiling, then she grabbed his hand and turned to continue greeting her parents.

Rory saw her father's eyes scan down and stop on their clutching hands; then the eyes scanned back up and locked onto his.

The walk to the parking lot was chilled and icy. Victoria tried to keep conversation going by talking about things that had happened at camp, and her mother participated on a limited basis. Rory stayed busy teasing the younger brother.

They had agreed the night before that Victoria would ride home with her parents and Rory would go his own way. They had to see each other briefly at the airport but they had decided that to ensure they could get together that evening, they should split up at the airport and give her parents priority during the first hours of her return. Rory didn't care to spend time at the Beach house making lame conversation, so he yielded to the family again.

As the family turned down the aisle leading to their car, Victoria let them walk ahead while she stayed with Rory.

"You look so good, Victoria. I'm glad you're back."

"You too. I can't wait to be alone with you."

"Call me when you're ready to go."

"As soon as."

They leaned forward and kissed each other without embracing, then Victoria turned to go with her parents. Rory left without looking in the direction she headed, not wanting to intercept her father's eyes again.

At the Beach house, the family reunited with its returning member. Victoria gave gifts to her brother and sister, then answered a flood of light and free questions from her mother and strictly business questions from her father. Over the course of a few hours, consisting of a lot of storytelling by Victoria and a lot of information gathering by her parents, the family relaxed with each other and things got back to normal. Victoria had mentioned her plan to see Rory after their dinner together and had heard no opposition to the idea from either of her parents.

For their meal that evening, Mrs. Beach fixed one of Victoria's favorites and proudly stated Victoria needed a home-cooked meal after six weeks of hotel food. Victoria didn't have the heart to tell her that although she felt the camp had been a disappointment, this camp, by a good measure, had the best food she had ever eaten. Unlike the Florida camp, this camp realized an ocean lay nearby; they served a wide variety of seafood, something she couldn't get with the same freshness and quality at home.

When the home-cooked meal neared completion, Victoria volunteered her brother and sister to join her to do the dishes so she could renew with them on her own. The three talked and laughed through the domestic work while the younger Beaches teased her endlessly about kissing Rory. They hadn't been able to pester her after they saw them kiss when she departed, so when they saw the second round of kissing during her return, their pent-up giggles needed to escape.

When they finished wiping down the countertops, they joined their parents in the living room. Mr. Beach, feeling better for having eaten and for having his daughter back under his wing, smiled at her for the first time since she returned.

"Why don't you stay home with your parents this evening, Victoria? I would really like that," Mr. Beach said sweetly.

"I can't, Daddy. I told Rory I'd go out with him tonight."

Mr. Beach resorted to his sad, let-down smile. "Can't you tell him you'll see him tomorrow? We haven't seen you for six weeks either, you know."

"I know, but I want to see him."

"Well, I don't think you should. It's your first night back; spend it with your family."

"I'm going to go see Rory, Dad. I better go get ready."

If he had not said another word, she would have gone out feeling a little guilty—but otherwise considering things normal between herself and her father. But Mr. Beach asked her a question. "When were you going to tell me about the letter you are supposed to write to the conservatory?"

"The letter?" she responded, not quite grasping the topic. Then when she realized what his knowledge of the letter meant, she felt tingles run up her neck. "How do you know about a letter to the conservatory?"

"I got a call from Werner. He told me about—"

"I can't believe you two." She cut him off angrily. "Do either of you think I should have any say in my own future? Berlin sounds like a really good opportunity. But did either of you two ask me if I actually want to go? No, I don't remember being asked. But I do remember telling you I was still considering all of my options. Did either of you ask me what other options I had in mind? No, you didn't. You both assumed going to Berlin was the obvious choice, and when you didn't hear me flat-out disagree, you assumed I did agree. I don't appreciate you and Werner going behind my back to plan my future. I can't tell you to stop it, but I can tell you I intend to ignore any advice you give me from now on."

Victoria's obvious anger left her parents wondering what to say as she left the room. Mrs. Beach could see the discomfort on Mr. Beach's face as it twisted with the pain created by his sudden heartburn. They heard Victoria dial the phone. After a short pause, she said, "I'll be ready in fifteen minutes."

When she jumped into Rory's car she was happy to be with him; he could tell this by the smile in her eyes. But the ensuing silence concerned him. They had met and briefly touched each other at the airport, but he still feared that something had changed. He wanted to talk with her, but first he wanted to touch her and confirm that she still desired intimacy with him. The things she said at the airport indicated she did, but he would harbor doubts until it happened.

"How was your first afternoon back home?"

"Same as before. My brother and sister went wild. They turned red themselves when they told me they saw us kiss. I kept telling them I was going to go kiss you some more and that I would make you kiss them the next time they saw you. They laughed themselves silly. It was funny." She sat quietly with a smile on her face.

Then the smile disappeared. "I don't even want to think about how it went with my dad right now."

They drove out to the field that they had visited the night before she left for camp. They started kissing, slowly; but six weeks of thinking about each other's flesh made them eager for the touch. Rory slid his hand under Victoria's shirt and cupped her breast through her bra. She reached over and released his buckle and slid down his zipper. She ran her finger across his stomach just above the band of his boxer shorts; his abdominal muscles flinched involuntarily under her touch. Her hand worked its way inside the shorts, down his hip to the top of his thigh then back up over his hip and stopping on his stomach, making the muscles flinch again. She repeated the move. Each time her hand appeared ready to stop on his stomach, he feared the return of the flinch; then when it did stop, the pleasure came on stronger and more uncontrolled than previously.

She stopped her hand movement and he floated somewhere soothing. She enjoyed seeing him relaxed, closing his eyes and releasing control of himself for their mutual enjoyment. She spoke his name, and when she did he returned to her. "I hope you brought something."

"I did," he said, and they moved into the back seat where they removed their clothing and refreshed their memory of the pleasure each willingly gave to the other. When they had fully accepted the other's offerings, they leaned back against the door of the car, holding each other, enjoying the sensations of touching their flesh, realizing the touch surpassed what they had remembered. Victoria pulled up to look at Rory's face, making sure to leave her breasts touching warmly on his chest.

"I love you, Rory. I've been wanting to tell you that."

"I love you too, Victoria. I guess I have for a while."

———

Senior year had been a blur so far. With one week to go before the Christmas break, Rory kept busy melting different compounds together with glass. At the same time, he studied for his midterm exams, and tried to spend every other minute at his disposal with Victoria. Her busy schedule also defaulted every free minute to Rory. They had become inseparable except when their academic activities forced them apart.

Also during this time, Victoria had discovered a higher level of appreciation for mathematics. She had always achieved high marks in her math courses but had only done the work outlined for the class. When one of her teachers mentioned other math theories related to the ones that they studied, she asked for more information. This information led to an extensive horizontal study of the course material. She found the study so interesting that she registered for an additional math class for the final semester.

As a result of her new interest in math, she wasn't as willing to spend any extra time practicing her oboe. Her play had slipped a small degree, which she accepted. But as a result, her relationship with Mr. Keltch and with her father skidded downhill with plenty of friction.

She hadn't told either of them that she had decided not to major in music when she went to college. She knew how her decision would affect the teacher she respected; she didn't know how her change of heart would affect the father she loved.

Her recent decision had come to her when she decided to take the extra math class, and realized she wanted to take math when she went on to university. She kept her decision to herself and had yet to even tell Rory. Her father deserved to be the first person she would tell; after all, he had spent most of her lifetime investing in her musical career.

Rory had been trying to figure out her intentions for school the next year, so that he could make his own decision on which school to attend. If she decided to stay in music, and chose one of the two schools with good music programs on the Mortenson list, he would pick the school she preferred and enroll with her.

They discussed the topic often, and during those discussions she covertly tried to get information about the math programs at the four schools. She wanted to determine if a suitable program existed at any of these schools, so they could still attend together. She did this while trying not to tip her hand regarding her decision, even though she wanted desperately to let Rory know.

The constant pressure her father continued to exert on her to attend the conservatory in Berlin had been reduced only by an imperceptible amount, despite her request that he respect her right to make her own decision. The fact that he favored this choice so much would make it harder on him when he discovered her intentions. Thinking to provide her with another option, he stated that a good program stateside would also be acceptable. After her attendance at the music camp this past summer, and with her continued involvement in the band at school, it never entered his mind that she would not pursue a career in music. When he learned this news, he would be devastated.

"After Christmas," she kept telling herself. "I don't want to ruin everybody's holidays, so I'll tell them all after Christmas."

———

Up until two days before Christmas the temperature stayed well above freezing and there was no snow, only a wind blowing with force. Then a blizzard hit the town with even higher winds, plenty of cold hard snow that stung when it hit flesh, and temperatures in the low teens.

Rory's car had run in the cold weather on previous occasions, but in those cases there had been a gradual buildup of the chill. This sudden change was not to the car's liking, and it decided not to go out in the storm. Rory had already decided nothing could prevent him from going out into the frigid tempest, so when his vehicle let him know he was going alone, he chastised it with a coarse set of phrases that made him feel better but left him with a long walk to the bus stop. After a shivering wait, during which his ribs felt like they would crack from the tremors the cold subjected them to, he climbed onto the bus and went to the back seat by the heater. It warmed his fingers but his toes were still numb when he got off the bus a short walk from Harry's restaurant. From there he phoned

Victoria to let her know the car wouldn't start; he asked her if she could meet him at the restaurant instead.

While he waited, he made an effort to find the bottom of the bottomless cup of coffee and talked with the idle Harry, who complained about the lack of customers, especially through the lunch hour just ended.

Harry had become the assistant manager of the restaurant, although the manager hadn't actually given him the title. He had worked long hours almost every day since he graduated from high school the year before, and as time went by, he kept being given more and more responsibilities at the eatery.

A cold gust plowed its way in through the warm, moist restaurant air and when they looked up at the door, they saw Victoria enter, stamping her feet and performing a little gallop to shake off the cold. She looked far too frozen for someone who had just walked in from her car.

Once seated in the booth, she continued to wear her warm parka and mittens. She wrapped her arms around her torso while rocking to try to warm herself. Her chin stopped quivering long enough to say, "Tea."

"Will that be hot tea or iced tea?" Harry asked.

Victoria jerked to face him and stilled her shivering body, to deliver a look that would melt the frost and stop the wind on any stretch of tundra in the frozen north. She said nothing, but her order had been clarified.

"What happened to you, did you walk or something?" Rory asked with a concerned look.

Victoria tried to answer but her chattering teeth barred the way for words, so she could only nod.

"Why did you walk? Did the car break down?"

She shook her head in response, but seeing Rory's confused look, she stuttered out, "Da-ad wouldn't... giv-ve me the... car."

Once she had some time to warm up and drink some of the tea, she filled Rory in on her walk to the restaurant. Her father wouldn't allow her to take the car because she had never driven on roads this icy and dangerous. She provided him with a number of assurances but he suggested her safest course of action was to stay home. She got mad at him when he wouldn't listen to her reasoning; so she didn't bother asking him to drive her, she just got dressed and left.

"I mean, it's not a long walk, but if I'd known I would get this cold, I might have asked for a ride," she said, as a final shiver worked her over one last time. Her nose still glowed red and her earlobes burned with tingles.

"I guess we won't bother going to the mall then, since we would have to walk."

"You got that right."

"Well that's a shame then, I was going to buy your Christmas present."

"Well, then you should still go. I'll wait here."

Harry joined them off and on between the duties he performed. During his absences they would discuss their school situation, Rory digging to find out which way she leaned, and Victoria trying to find out more about the four schools they had to choose from.

"Why don't you give me the recruitment information you received so I can take a look at it?"

"Sure, there are two with music programs. Does this mean you're not going to go to Germany?"

"No, it means I need something to compare with and I'd like to see all four of them, if that's okay."

"Well, I wanted to go over a couple of them with Mr. Duggin."

Victoria nodded. She had wondered if he had seen a guidance counselor about selecting a school, but it made more sense if he looked things over with the chemistry teacher.

"Have you looked at what type of courses they offer at these schools?" she asked.

"I've looked through them but I can't really figure them out. The course catalogues provide some description about the courses, but I don't know which ones I'm expected to take. And, Mr. Duggin is the only person I can ask to fill me in. You know, it's not like my parents went to college and can give me the benefit of their experience. When Pat signed up at the community college, he didn't have many choices. They just printed him out a schedule. So he wasn't any help either. Have you looked at a course catalogue before?"

"Last year. My mom and I looked at one from Washington and I kind of got the idea of how they worked."

"Maybe you can help me after I check with Mr. Duggin. I'll keep the one from Barrow-Mount—they don't have a music program—but I'll give you the other three."

"Is that the one you're leaning toward?"

Rory hesitated a moment before answering. "Not really. It looks good and they have a good reputation. Plus, on a day like today, California sounds like a good option."

"I'd like to look at it with you. To help you figure it out, if I can."

The afternoon, though slow, went by pleasantly as they had a chance to talk about everything that was critical to their lives at the moment. They joked about the serious and embellished the importance of the insignificant as the storm froze the city to a halt.

Harry decided that with the dinner hour long over with, the temperature continuing to drop and the wind beginning to toss loose objects around in the street, they weren't likely to see too many more customers. He told the cook to wrap up and head for home, and he offered Rory and Victoria a ride. Rory got dressed to go out in the dark and start Harry's car to warm it up for the drive home.

Victoria hurriedly kissed Rory goodbye standing outside of Harry's car in front of her house, then leaned into the wind to walk to the door. It opened and Rory could see her father's arm holding it so Victoria could slip inside. Her father started right in with his questions. Both he and her mother had not heard her leave the house and had been worried about her all day. When they heard she had walked out in the storm, they both began to question her logic.

"You want us to let you start making your own decisions, and you go and do something stupid like walking in weather like this. How do you expect us to allow you to take more control of your future?" her father yelled.

"I'm seventeen; I've already taken control. You weren't willing to help me, so I solved my problem myself, and I made it."

"Putting yourself at risk out in a freezing storm is not solving a problem, it's switching to a new one." Mr. Beach turned purple with anger.

"Well then, I solved that one too," she yelled in answer, and then charged to her room.

Mr. Beach stood seething at his daughter's tone. He didn't realize how hard he was breathing and something inside him told him to find a chair.

Chapter 27

The festive season hadn't lived up to its name, and Victoria was happy to be back at school. Mr. Beach had lost all of his color when she announced that she intended to major in mathematics when she went away to school, and that she had applied for a number of academic scholarships to help pay her way. It had been the most unpleasant event she had ever lived through. Her father didn't get angry and start to yell or raise a fuss; he only sat in his chair, defeated.

"Victoria, Victoria, Victoria," he said, holding his forehead in his hand, "what have you done, what are you doing? Do all of the things we've accomplished mean nothing to you? You've thrown them all away."

"We've talked about this before, Daddy. I told you my plans for my future may differ from yours."

"Yes, I know you said those things, but I never expected this. I didn't think you would give up music completely. This is…" He sat, shaking his head, staring down at the arm of his chair.

Everything they had worked for had accomplished nothing. These terrible thoughts etched deep dark lines across his face.

Two days later she asked to spend New Year's Eve with Rory. Her parents looked at each other and then her father said, "Why ask us? You're the one making all of the decisions now."

Rory had been elated when she told him she wasn't going to Germany, and they set themselves to the task of choosing a school they could attend together. He had wanted to go to Barrow-Mount in California, but either of the two schools with ranked music programs would do as long as they went together. When she revealed she had given up music in favor of math, she created the strong possibility of going to California, since Barrow-Mount's math program had an excellent reputation.

Victoria applied to all four schools and scheduled her university entrance exams. They would be bound for California if Barrow-Mount accepted her.

The final stage of Rory's last project for the Mortenson Scholarship neared completion. This project had been the most enjoyable work to date. He still couldn't believe his favorable turn of events. The work gave him a sense of accomplishment, Victoria had the marks to get accepted at Barrow-Mount, and he would attend his first choice of schools with her.

He acknowledged that while he himself felt extremely happy about the situation, Mr. Beach must feel severely disappointed. Losing all chances of achieving the future he had envisioned for Victoria must hurt him a great deal, and he hoped Mr. Beach didn't blame him. He could accept that he and Mr. Beach had no relationship. Neither had really tried to establish one. He didn't feel comfortable attempting to create a relationship he didn't want. After almost a year of dating Victoria, he had exchanged words with her father on only two occasions. Odd but not unreasonable, since at this point he still hadn't introduced Victoria to his parents either.

One morning, she had asked about going to his house to meet them and he said he didn't see the point. His comment caused Victoria to stop eating her breakfast muffin as they sat in the training room below the school stage.

"Rory, I think it's important for me to meet your parents and for them to meet me. We're going away to live together. I think they would want to know who you're going away with." Then she turned pale. "Your parents do know you have a girlfriend, don't they? You've told them about me, right?"

"Yes, they know about you and who you are," Rory responded. "To be quite honest—and you would need to know my parents so you don't take this the wrong way—they've never asked a single question about you. They just accept that you are my girlfriend and that's that."

"I guess if I did know your parents, I might understand. But I don't," she said sarcastically.

"If you want to meet them, fine, but it will be weird. I've told you about my parents. It will be an unreal situation."

"So you don't think I should meet them before we go?"

"I don't think it makes any difference if you do."

"Why?"

"How did my meeting your parents change anything? Did it make any of our lives better or worse?"

"You didn't have to meet them to change things. Me having a boyfriend did that."

"Exactly. The two times I did meet them didn't change a thing. If you meet my parents, nothing's going to change either."

"So that's it, you're not going to take me to meet them?"

"I know it's not normal, but my parents aren't normal."

"So?"

Rory shrugged. "Okay. Let's go after school."

Dirty snow with black ice edges remained piled in the shade of the house, barn, and storage shed. Rory drove in an arch toward the house, then backed up beside the shed into his usual parking spot. Ice snapped under Victoria's foot when she stepped out of the car. She looked around and saw the clutter that spotted the yard.

Inside the house she stood alone in the kitchen, waiting for Rory to return from his mother's room. She could hear Rory speaking in a low, muffled voice. When he came back to the kitchen, he told her his mother wasn't feeling very well and that maybe she would come out later. They went back outside and walked toward the barn.

Victoria felt relief out in the fresh air. Inside she had felt stuffed into a small place where she took the space meant for others.

When they entered the barn, they heard a rhythmic grinding noise. They turned into his father's work area where Mr. Coleman shaped a horseshoe with a rasp. He spotted the shapes moving into his doorway and stopped.

"Hi," he said.

"Hey, Dad. I want you to meet Victoria."

Mr. Coleman tossed the rasp clattering onto the bench and peeled off his gloves. He rubbed his hands together to make sure they were clean then approached his son and the girl he had brought home.

"Victoria. I didn't know she had such a pretty name, Rory." He reached out and shook Victoria's hand. "I'm Toby Coleman. What brings you two out here?"

"Nothing, just stopping by," Rory said.

"Well, I don't know anything about entertaining company, but I do know you're probably better off not doing it in a barn. Let's go in for some coffee or a soda or something."

They turned and started toward the door and as they left the room, Rory's father reached to turn out the light and knocked over the pitchfork leaning next to the switch. Rory and Victoria turned when they heard it crash on the floor.

"Oops!" Mr. Coleman said as he restored it to an upright position. Then he began a nervous narration that lasted the entire time they walked back to the house. "I was out here peckering around with some stuff. That shoe's a perfectly good shoe; it just needed a gouge smoothed out of it. I don't know how the gouge got there but I wasn't ready to turn that shoe over to being a game piece so I thought I'd better get to it and maybe salvage it, 'cause I think it will fit on my horse. Victoria, you should come out some time and ride my horse, he's real gentle and likes people and I wouldn't worry about his shoes. Just 'cause I was fixing that one to put on him doesn't mean the ones he's got are any problem. He can still run and buck a little. That is, come on out and ride if you like riding horses. Rory never told me if you ride, I only thought if you wanted to you could. Rory used to ride a lot but not any more. I don't remember the last time Rory rode a horse but it must have been last summer when we were working some cows. So what will it be, coffee?" He kicked off his rubber boots, taking his socks off about halfway with them. He padded across to the stove, stepping on the dangling flaps of sock as they folded under his feet. He shifted the kettle, already filled with water, to the front burner as he turned on the flame.

"Victoria likes tea, Dad. Do we have any tea?" Rory asked.

"Hell, that's a good question." Mr. Coleman stared at the cupboards, wondering where to start looking. "I don't think I've ever seen tea bags in this house."

"Coffee would be fine, Mr. Coleman," Victoria said, not wanting to cause a fuss.

"Coffee it is then," he said, relieved the problem was solved. "We have plenty of that. And please, Victoria, call me Toby."

The kettle boiled and Mr. Coleman poured water into the cups in which he had spooned instant coffee. He placed a mug in front of each of them, then placed a can of evaporated milk in the center of the table. The small triangles cut in the top of the can had browning clots of thick liquid clogging them. Rory wiped one of the holes with his thumb then wiped the gunk on his jeans before he poured the milk into his mug. He placed the can in front of Victoria, who had watched him with her eyebrows hooded over her eyes and an inquisitive frown. She looked at him. He raised his eyebrows and pointed at the milk with his head, indicating she was better off adding it than not.

She did, and then Mr. Coleman took the can and poured some of the milk into his mug.

"It's hot, so you better wait a minute or two," he warned.

Rory listened while his father and Victoria chatted about useless subjects. When the coffee had cooled for a few minutes, Victoria took a taste, then turned to Rory with genuine surprise and declared this coffee the best she had ever tasted.

"You've got to be kidding!" Rory exclaimed.

"No, this coffee is better than any of the stuff you tried to get me to choke down."

Rory threw his head back and laughed. His father looked back and forth at the two of them, not knowing why they were smiling it up over something simple like coffee.

Mr. Coleman smiled because everyone else did. Then he turned to Victoria. "Mr. Rory here is going away to school next year; what do you plan on doing when he's gone?"

She looked at him with a cautious smile on her face, then at Rory, hoping for a sign to help her formulate an answer. Rory stared back blankly.

"I'm going with him," Victoria told Mr. Coleman. "We decided to go to the same school."

"Are you a scientist, too? I should have known Rory would meet a scientist like himself."

"No, I'm going to major in math."

"Math…you're going to do math? That's like sleeping on rocks." Mr. Coleman shook his head as he spoke. "Where are you two going to go? Rory won't tell us where he's going to live next year."

"Dad, we don't know yet," Rory answered. "I told you I haven't decided on the school. We're waiting to hear back on Victoria's applications. It's not as if I won't tell you, it's that there's nothing to tell."

When the door to Mrs. Coleman's room opened, both Rory and Mr. Coleman turned their heads immediately. Victoria's head followed as she reacted to their new focus of attention. Mrs. Coleman emerged wearing sweat pants and a long wool sweater with a tie around the waist. One side of the woolen belt hung lower than the other, and as if the belt wasn't enough, she also had her arms crossed holding the garment shut. Her hair looked tidy but not brushed.

"Hi Mom, you feeling better?" Rory asked while standing up from his mother's chair. Mrs. Coleman shrugged in answer.

"I'd like you to meet Victoria," Rory said.

She greeted Victoria and sat down in her chair.

Mr. Coleman shifted in his seat then took a sip from his mug, looking over the rim at his wife. "Well, I'd better get back out to the barn or I'll never get finished." He stood and went to the sink, where he dumped the remains of his coffee and left the mug. He told Victoria he enjoyed meeting her, then slipped on his boots and disappeared.

Rory took the chair his father had vacated and they talked for a few minutes about school and a few other minor subjects.

Knowing his mother wasn't one to socialize for long, and recognizing she wasn't feeling very well, Rory suggested it was time for them to leave. His mother said goodbye and left the kitchen before either of them had made any preparations to go.

Victoria looked over at Rory, feeling confused about what to do next.

"Let's go," he said, "There's nothing else to do here."

Driving back downtown, Victoria asked, "Is your mom okay?"

"No." Rory's tone did not invite further questioning.

"Your Dad's really nice. I'm glad I met him."

"Yeah, he's all right. You notice he didn't ask any prying questions. When you said we were going away together, he could have asked a lot of stuff. But he didn't. Do you know why? It's because he doesn't want to learn something he may have to take a stand on. You know, like if we planned to live together, would he have to object? Hell, he didn't even ask you for your last name."

"Hmm. You will tell them where you're going to go to school once you know, won't you?"

"Oh yeah. I think they have a right to know."

After what she had seen, she wasn't so sure.

After a month that they spent avoiding issues that could cause a larger rift to develop between them, a truce took form between Victoria and her father. Mr. Beach began to ask her about the school she had chosen, what the cost would be, how she had arranged for scholarship funding, what her dormitory arrangements were, and when she planned on leaving. Victoria appreciated his interest and believed he had begun to accept her decision. She remembered Rory saying she was lucky her parents paid attention to the things she did. When she mentioned she and Rory had picked the same school, her father blanched but said nothing.

Barrow-Mount University had accepted Victoria, so Rory contacted them indicating he would attend as the Mortenson scholar. He had only to submit his final project and get the final approval of the Board but Barrow-Mount reserved him a spot.

At the end of March the Board confirmed Rory would receive the scholarship funds.

Everything fell into place for them. They would complete their final year of high school, enjoy the summer, and then head off to a life of new experiences and new responsibilities. They continued to work hard at their schoolwork and would surely end the year with perfect marks, except for the lower grade Victoria expected to receive from Mr. Keltch.

He had used his old technique and ambushed her with a counselor's appointment when he heard from her father that she intended to drop out of music after high school. As a senior, she had expected an appointment; but Mr. Keltch's presence in the counselor's office surprised her. At first he approached the discussion in a calm manner and regarded her choice to major in math with respect.

When he finally started to probe for the reasons she had abandoned what they had all been working so hard for, he began to change moods and to berate her for her decision. Twice the counselor asked him to control himself, once when he raised his voice and accused her of changing who she was, and again when he implied she had chosen the wrong people for her friends. He reminded her that for years she had trusted the advice of her father and himself while eagerly pursuing the career path they had planned for her, and then asked her what both men had done to lose her trust. She didn't answer him. She only glared at him. So he told her they had done nothing; they had lost her trust because she had placed it with the wrong person, and adopted a set of views that didn't reflect her best interests.

Then she spoke. "Mr. Keltch, we've been through this argument before, and I've been through it with my father as well. I've given both of you my answers to your concerns, and those answers remain unchanged. If you can't add anything new to your arguments, then we don't need to do this again. Why can't you accept that what I've chosen for myself doesn't meet with your approval, and leave it alone?"

A visibly agitated Mr. Keltch stood and took a step toward Victoria.

"Mr. Keltch?" the counselor said, stopping the music teacher.

"I don't know why I bothered," Mr. Keltch began. "I've been preparing you for four years. I've given everything I've got to students like you, the students with ability, so they can go on to become successful. I don't get anything for the time I invest in you except the recognition from other student's parents, other music teachers and other musical institutions. Recognition that I deserve for developing great musical talent. Recognition that I can take a raw talent and mold it into a refined artist.

"I created the greatest opportunity for you by getting you to dig deep within yourself to cultivate your extraordinary talent, talent you wouldn't have discovered without me pushing you to your limits.

"Now I don't get to see the results of my work, because you don't realize what I've done for you. Thank you, Victoria; thank you for wasting my time."

"Mr. Keltch, that is completely inappropriate," the counselor said, while standing to address the other teacher. "I think you should leave."

Victoria sat in disbelief at the attack he made against her and her right to determine her own future.

Chapter 28

"I was just a statistic for that prick. You were going to be his poster child. But he shouldn't pull off stunts like that," Rory said to Victoria when she told him about Mr. Keltch's verbal attack.

"I know. I've been waiting for him to blow for weeks. He's been nice as pie in class, although he does tend to ignore me."

"Three more months and we won't have to worry about him anymore."

They stood sharing a frozen cola in the parking lot of a convenience store before Rory was to drop Victoria off at home.

At home, she decided not to practice the oboe and instead tended to her math homework until dinnertime.

The three Beach children, after going about their regular dinner preparations, sat together at the kitchen table eating. Things had changed, and the dinner conversation had lost its humor. The younger brother and sister didn't want Victoria to go away to school, and continually came up with reasons for her to stay and live with the family forever. They didn't understand how she could want something that required her to leave, and she couldn't find the words to explain her mixed feelings about not living with them any longer.

They stopped teasing her about Rory and when she mentioned him, they would look away from her and their smiles would disappear. They no longer joked and played with Rory when he came to pick up Victoria, and she began to think they blamed him for taking her away.

She kept telling herself that the dour mood she had created in the Beach house couldn't be avoided, and she would be leaving for school the next year anyway.

She returned to her room to do more math homework after they ate. Her parents arrived home and she could hear them preparing for their late meal. While her mother warmed up their food, her father greeted the children. Later in the evening, Victoria took a break from her studies and went into the living room to sit with her father.

"Mr. Keltch called me down to the counselor's office today," she said.

"Oh, he did? Good. I asked him to have a talk with you."

"You did? Why?" Victoria said, staring at her father suspiciously.

Mr. Beach rubbed his cheek and lips with the tips of his fingers, thinking of how he would answer. "I haven't given up, Victoria. I called him last week to see if he had found a way to convince you to change your mind." He saw her sit taller and squint at him. "Now hold on, and hear me out before you start yelling at me again."

"But that's not right."

"Hold on, please." He tilted his head and held up both hands with their palms outward. Victoria relaxed upon seeing his pleading expression. "When he told me he hadn't talked to you about it, it surprised me. He didn't seem too upset about it. I told him how upset I am, but I wanted to give you some time to think about your decision. I told him I hoped you would change your mind, and that soon I would approach you to let you know that it isn't too late. You see, you could still get a music scholarship to a good school and if you decide you want to go to Germany, we could call Werner to see if you still had options there."

He saw Victoria prepare to speak.

"Now, I asked you to hold on until I finish. I knew if I brought up the subject, I'd risk making you mad again, so I tried another way to find out if you had any second thoughts. I hoped Mr. Keltch had some ideas about your frame of mind; but when I found out he hadn't talked to you at all, I asked him if he would. I wanted to find out how you currently felt about your choice, to determine how we could get you to change your mind."

"That's it." Victoria could no longer remain silent. She jumped out of her seat, jabbing her finger in the direction of her father. "I've had enough of you trying to get me to do what you want me to do. I don't want to play the oboe any more. I lost my interest a long time ago. Do you know why? Because you wouldn't let me play it and practice it and enjoy it the way I wanted to. It always had to be the way you 'knew was best for me.'

"I'm sick of it. I realize I used to get a lot of enjoyment from what I could do playing music, but the enjoyment has faded. I get my enjoyment from something else now, and it's as strong and maybe stronger than anything I got from the oboe. Let me enjoy it. Let me follow my own plan. I'm tired of following your plan."

Mr. Beach sat in shock, watching this display of anger from his daughter. When she stopped her admonishments, he saw he had lost her.

"Victoria, wait. You don't know how much it means to me that you should have a successful career and for you to play in a famous orchestra. Taking the stage with the New York or the Philadelphia would be a dream come true for me. I've wanted that all my life and it's yours if you want it; you could make it come true.

"You can't throw it all away for a boy. He made you think you wouldn't be happy with the career you had planned and could certainly achieve. He made you think the opposite of everything we've taught you. I can't sit back and let you believe what we've done is wrong because he's clouded your thinking.

"Victoria, I want you to reconsider your choices and drop this idea about math. I want you to come to your senses and get back to music, as everyone knows you should. I can't support your decision to go to school and take math."

None of their previous arguments had made her father this mad, but Victoria's anger matched his in intensity. Anger that he continued to force his will on her, anger that he had enlisted Mr. Keltch to aid in his manipulation—and rage that he accused Rory of confusing her into making an errant decision.

"I don't expect you to support my decision. I expect you to understand that I made it. You and your assistant meddlers are the only ones making the assumption that I'm not capable of making the right choice for me. You don't know how much relief I feel, now that I'm going to do what I want to do and that I don't need your support."

Victoria walked past her father and past her mother, who had listened to their argument from the doorway. She went to her room and picked up her books and placed them in her backpack. She walked out onto the porch carrying her pack, jacket and shoes, where she stopped momentarily to put on her garments. She walked at a brisk pace to Harry's restaurant and stopped to catch her breath in the foyer before calling Rory.

He met her, and they sat and talked over coffee spiked with evaporated milk. When they left, they drove out to the private spot they had been enjoying since the night before Victoria left for music camp. Tonight, with the sun down and the wind blowing colder than normal, they sat and stared out at the sky. Rory had his arm around her, not to console her in her now quiet mood but to support her and share her stand. He knew she felt bad about the difficult turn her relationship with her father had taken, and he knew she wished she could make it better. Even more deeply rooted in his mind, he respected her for making her own choice and he respected her right to make it.

They sat for an unmeasured time in silence. She inhaled deeply, holding in the air then slowly releasing it. He would stay all night if she wanted, but eventually she said it was time to go.

Parked in front of Victoria's house, they sat quietly as Victoria delayed her return to the house. She worried that her father had waited up for her and that they would start the whole fight over again. Rory saw her brother and sister peering at them from the window. The wind increased in strength, bellowing out a low howl as it ran through the trees and between the houses. It had cooled and inside the car, fog blanketed the windows.

Victoria leaned over to Rory and put her face close to his. She thanked him for meeting her and said she'd better get inside. She placed her lips softly over his mouth, but he pulled back quickly, frightening her. Her heart pounded as she looked wide-eyed at Rory, who was trying to look around her. When she turned to see what attracted his look, she jumped again. Her sister's tiny fist beat the window beside her head in a frantic attempt to get her attention.

The younger girl grabbed at her hair with her free hand trying to control it as it whipped in the wind. She had a look of torment on her face as tears washed sideways from her eyes. She stood bent over, shivering, trying to communicate with Victoria. In the doorway of the house, Victoria could see her little brother shivering and wiping his eyes as he held the door open, waiting for his sisters to come inside.

Victoria opened the door and kneeled on the sidewalk in front of her sister. "What is it? What's wrong?"

"It's Daddy. They took him and Mom to the hospital."

Victoria pulled her sister close to her as despair and concern for her parents amplified the pounding in her chest. She lifted her head and looked off over the treetops, focusing somewhere in the distance, then briefly closed her eyes and tightened them shut. Rory leaned over the passenger seat trying to figure out what had happened, and saw her tranquilly holding her sister in the turmoil of the wind and the situation. She seemed unwilling to move, then suddenly turned to Rory.

"Come on, Rory, let's go inside," she said, then stood and guided her sister toward the open door of the house.

"What happened before the ambulance came?" she asked her sister once they were inside and she had her brother and sister calmed down.

"Daddy was sitting in his chair and he started to look sick. Then he started to look scared, so mom moved him onto the sofa to lay down. When she went to the kitchen to use the phone, she looked scared too." Her little sister began crying again as she remembered the scene.

"When did this happen? How long ago did they leave?" Victoria asked.

"I don't know. A long time ago." Her sister cried harder.

She sat on the sofa and held them both tight. She knew she had to get up and go to the hospital, but she needed to hold her family for a moment before she could move. She wished she could stay and hold them all night, afraid to go and find out what had struck down her father.

Rory watched without speaking as they shared the pain they felt for their father and shared the comfort that came from being a family.

Victoria reached a point where she knew she had to move. Her brother and sister wanted to go with her, but she told them it was too late—though they could stay up until she phoned them. She asked Rory if he would stay with them and he agreed, feeling some relief at not having to see her mother.

"Do you want to take my car?" he offered.

"No, I'll take our car. Mom will eventually need it. I'll call you when I know what's going on. If I can leave, would you come and pick me up?"

"Yes."

"When you do, can you bring the kids? They will want to see Dad. And if they can't see him, they will want to see Mom."

"I will."

At the hospital, the nurse at the reception desk took Victoria back into the unit. Her mother sat inside a cubicle made private by a faded orange-checkered curtain suspended from a rail mounted to the ceiling. When her mother saw her, she stood and walked toward her to prevent Victoria from seeing her father. She tried to move past, but her mother grabbed her around the waist, pulling her close. They cried together and each sob increased her fear for her father.

"What's wrong with Daddy? Is he okay?"

"No. You can see him in a minute, but he doesn't look good," her mother responded between sobs. "I don't want you to be too scared when you see him. Tubes are sticking out of him in different directions and wires run everywhere. He's been sleeping since we got here so don't expect him to look at you or talk. You can talk to him but they don't know if he can hear you. They say he's stable and they plan on moving him to intensive care. He's had a heart attack."

Victoria closed her eyes and let all the air out of her lungs. They walked back to the curtained cubicle.

Mr. Beach lay peacefully on stiff white sheets. Across his legs lay a thin blue linen blanket. Tape covered most of his face, and bandages supported a plastic tube inserted in his nose. His exposed chest had large patches of hair removed from areas where small white cloth patches stuck to his skin. A wire led from each of the patches to a cart laden with small blue machines with a collection of dials and meters on their faces. Another tube was stuck in his wrist and his arm had a wide black band wrapped around it with thicker tubes connected to a machine with red numbers on the front. A low and regular beep came from the cart. Mr. Beach rested with his head turned away from Victoria.

She felt her chin tighten, then quiver, causing her lower lip to tremble. Silent sobs jerked her chest and shoulders. Shocked, she stood and watched her father, wishing for him to get better; she wouldn't let herself think of the circumstances that had put her father in a hospital bed.

The third tug on her arm brought her back to her mother, who stood, with worry on her face, looking directly into her eyes.

"They want to check him again. It will take a few minutes and then he'll need to rest. When they're done we'll go to the cafeteria."

They stood back while the nurses took Mr. Beach's vital signs and checked the drip rate on the suspended bottles. He rolled his head straight and opened his eyes for a few seconds. He didn't look around and he didn't acknowledge seeing anyone; as he closed his eyes again, he rolled his head back to the side.

When they sat at the table in the cafeteria, the first thing Mrs. Beach asked Victoria was, "You drink coffee now?"

"No, not really." Then Victoria asked, "Do you want to go home for a while? I can stay here with Dad."

"No, I'm okay. How are your brother and sister?"

"Pretty upset. I better call them. I asked Rory to stay with them."

"Oh." Her mother said, then remained silent for a moment. "You should go home and stay with them. They'll need you. I'm okay here, and I'll call you and let you know how he's doing. There's not much we can do here anyway."

She gave her mother the keys to the car and said she had arranged for Rory to bring the kids so they could at least see her for a few minutes. When the kids arrived, they got out of the car and stood on the sidewalk holding onto their mother while they cried. Victoria stood with her arm around Rory; his crossed her back and his hand gripped her shoulder. She watched her mother explain to her brother and sister in a soft voice how the doctors were working to make their father better. Mrs. Beach kissed them both, then stood and hugged Victoria.

"I'll call you when I hear anything," she said, and watched her family climb into Rory's car.

Shortly after one in the morning, they convinced Victoria's brother and sister to go to bed, and not long afterward the youngsters slept deeply.

Rory held Victoria as they sat on the sofa. She rested lying across his lap with her head on his chest. He could detect the slight scent that he enjoyed so much. He looked down at her sleeping face, feeling proud that she felt enough comfort and trust in him to fall asleep in his arms. A while later, Victoria stirred and sat up. She looked at him, slightly disoriented, and said she would be fine and suggested that he go.

Later, she lay still and sleepless in her bed. She saw the sad look her father gave her when she hadn't practiced her music. The times when she had disappointed him, and the times when he had disappointed her, competed for her conscience. Finally she fell asleep, comforted in knowing she and her father would get over this rough spot and make their relationship even stronger.

A few hours later when the sun began to rise, the harsh metallic ring of the phone caused her to sit upright in her bed. The second ring caused her to throw the covers off and run to the kitchen where she picked up the phone before it rang a third time. Silence except for background noise. Then she heard her mother clear her throat but still no words.

"Mom? Mom, is that you?" No answer; but now she heard crying. "Mom? Mom, what's happened?"

―――――

Great Falls enjoyed one of its rare windless days. The row of trees that grew along the side of the gravesites stood almost full of fresh new leaves. Clouds passed overhead but the sun warmed the mourners throughout the majority of the service.

A small group of friends, neighbors, and music students stood watching the family as they tossed handfuls of earth over the casket sitting on a web of belts that would lower it into the grave. Rory, dressed in dark dress pants, a dark shirt, and a black denim jacket he had just purchased, stood at the edge of the group. He had been relieved when Victoria told him he shouldn't stand with the family. The service ended and everyone gave their condolences. When Rory approached Mrs. Beach and Victoria, he spoke to Mrs. Beach, telling her how sorry he felt for their loss. She thanked him but made no other comment. He looked at Victoria and nodded, shutting down his desire to talk with her.

He hadn't seen her since the night Mr. Beach went to the hospital. They had talked on the phone, but he could tell Victoria's need for family meant she wasn't ready to see him yet. He wanted her alone, though, even if for only a few minutes.

The Beaches invited everyone over for a light lunch after the service. When he arrived, he watched as Victoria kept busy seeing to the arrangement of food and beverages while trying to chat with each of the mourners. Rory grabbed a plate and some punch, then stood against the wall by the kitchen doorway so Victoria couldn't miss him. When everything and everyone had been tended to, Victoria poured herself some punch, then came to him.

"Hi," she said with cheer in her voice, cheer he hadn't heard for the past few days. "How have you been doing?"

"Don't worry about me; are you okay?"

She smiled a tight smile and nodded, "Yeah, I guess."

"How's your mom and the kids? They seem okay."

"They're good, they're doing okay."

"Good."

"Rory," she said, looking into his eyes so he could see her intent, "Can we get together later?"

"Yes."

"Good. I'll call you when things are over with here. I need to get out for a while."

It seemed like forever had come and gone twice before the phone rang and Victoria asked him to pick her up. When she came out to the car, she said she wanted to be alone with him, so he took her back to his house. His father and the horse were off to some ranch, Pat worked at the gas station and his mother read in her room. They went out to the barn.

Rory took a blanket off the old cot his father sometimes slept on, and spread it on top of the haystack at the back of the barn. They climbed up and lay beside each other on the blanket. After some gentle kissing, Victoria rolled on top of him and began unbuttoning his shirt. "I missed you so much. I kept thinking about holding on to you, touching your skin and having you inside of me."

Rory's hands searched under her shirt until they found her bare breasts. He held them firmly to confirm the touch of her. He reached down and released the snap on her jeans. They removed their clothes and pressed their naked skin together while kissing and exploring with their hands.

Victoria reached into the pocket of Rory's discarded jeans and searched for the condom she knew she would find. They fell into a slow, stroking rhythm, alternating between looking into each other's eyes and closing them, feeling the pleasure flowing through their bodies. Pleasure reaching out to tingle and soothe, erasing the sadness and need they had felt over the days of loss.

Chapter 29

With the combined help of Mr. Duggin and Victoria, Rory established a list of courses to take as a freshman at Barrow-Mount. With his list completed he directed his attention to Victoria's first-year's courses. His attempts to discuss the subject usually met with reasons to delay making any selections.

Since her father's death a few weeks earlier, Rory noticed she had changed slightly. Her mood overall seemed good, but sometimes she drifted away from the immediate situation and seemed uninterested in what went on around her. When she laughed it seemed polite rather than genuine.

He also noticed that she never seemed to think about the future. If she did, she wasn't willing to discuss it. He, on the other hand, wanted to get high school over with and get on with the next stage of life. Moving to another city with Victoria couldn't come quickly enough to suit him, and he continually attempted to engage her in topics related to plans for their next school year. When she showed less excitement about the subject than he did, he would let it go, believing she continued to experience problems dealing with the loss of her father. She never talked much about how she felt, not to Rory and not to her mother.

Only when they embraced and made love did he feel the relaxed Victoria of the past. Then, she met him eye to eye, she initiated acts of love and acted confidently in their exchange of bodily pleasures.

Rory's concerns for her peaked as he watched the calendar advance and she still avoided making any plans for school. He asked her again about making her course selections, reminding her that the earlier she sent them in, the more likely she would receive her first choices. She told him she understood, but still made no effort to make her selections.

Another week went by before Rory touched on the subject again; and when she told him she still didn't want to sit down and choose her classes, he decided to press her. Something he should have done earlier, but the discomfort he felt at the thought of applying pressure had prevented him from doing so.

"You don't seem too eager to get moving on school next year. Is something going on?" he asked, hearing his voice waver.

Victoria thought about the question, then answered, "Yeah, kind of. I've been reconsidering whether or not I should stay with music, rather than math."

Rory pursed his lips and looked away from her. "There's no music program at Barrow-Mount. We'll need to change schools."

"I know Barow-Mount is your first choice," she said, "and it may be too late to change. I don't want you to change schools, so if I do decide to stick with music, I'll probably go to Germany. There's still an opportunity there."

Rory's chest cavity collapsed into an empty pit of lost dreams.

"Germany... oh man," he said slowly, in a breathy voice of despair.

She saw how much her words affected him and she tried to explain. "I haven't decided yet, in fact I can't decide. The night before he died, my father asked me to reconsider my choice. I'm treating it like his last wish. If he had lived, he might have convinced me to reconsider, so I'm giving him the benefit of the doubt and doing what he asked.

"I'm reconsidering, Rory. I'm worried that if I went to Barrow-Mount, I might not get the most out of it. I don't want to take math and be with you while my father's last wish hangs over us."

"So you'd rather pursue music, something you already decided to give up, across an ocean without me," Rory said.

"That's not it. If I decide on music, it's because I want to be a musician after all, and because it's the best thing for me right now." Then she said reflectively, "Maybe I'll go to Germany and find out music wasn't right and I'll come back for math; but Rory, I haven't decided."

"So when were you going to let me know?" he asked in an understanding tone.

"Soon. I waited because if I decided to stick with math, there would be nothing to tell. You wouldn't have to be upset."

"When do you think you will know?"

"I don't know; it's a tough decision." Victoria held her hands palm upward.

———

Waiting wore at the core of Rory's being. He waited for high school to end so then he could wait for summer to end while the whole time he would wait for Victoria to end the suspense.

The unrelenting slow creep of final exams constantly reminded him that the end of high school life approached and she had yet to indicate her leanings for the new life they would begin. Rory didn't bring up the subject again. He had seen how constant prodding had backfired on her father. If she asked for his advice, he would give it. But she hadn't asked.

He discussed the matter with Harry one evening at the restaurant while waiting for Victoria to meet him.

"So what will you do if she changes her mind and goes to Germany?" Harry asked.

"Nothing. I'm still going to go to Barrow-Mount. What else would I do? It just won't be the way I wanted it."

"And she hasn't said nothing since you first talked to her about it?"

"Nothing."

He had talked to Gary about the problem as well, one day sitting on the concrete stairs looking out over the parking lot.

"So that's why Keltch sucked up to her again. He must know she's thinking about staying in music."

"What, he's sucking up to her? Shit, if she's told him then he's trying to brainwash her into going."

"Who knows but something good might come out of this. You'll be free to bang all the chicks in California."

"Shut up, Gary."

Rory didn't discuss Victoria's revisitation of her schooling options with any of the adults he knew. He didn't think they could provide any meaningful input, so he shared his agonizing wait with no one—other than Gary and Harry. When he and Victoria spent time together, they went on as if nothing significant percolated in the background. They studied together, met for muffins and juice, went to movies and stayed out late on weekends. During those times he wondered whether she would make his life a happy, fascinating pleasure or a dreary, depressing drudge.

The excitement of being with the one he loved, and doing the things he wanted to do, was dampened because he held back on the many things he wanted to say that could sway her decision. His love for her made him want her with him under any circumstances with just one exception: he wanted her with him, only if she wanted it, too.

He feared the worst; he feared he would lose her completely. He had heard that when faced with fear, you must act. You had to either attack the fear head-on, or go on with your life as if what you feared didn't exist. Unfortunately he could attack nothing; and going on normally was impossible.

Victoria saw how he looked at her with a constant question in his expression. She knew waiting for her decision created difficulty for him, but she could only deal with the guilt she felt by acknowledging that she too existed in a difficult time. She wanted her own life of limbo to end. She over-analyzed every argument of her decision and she over-analyzed every action she took to make her decision easier. Why did she tell Mr. Keltch about reconsidering her plans? It had nothing to do with him. She had no girlfriends she could talk with, and in the past she had always talked to him about decisions related to music. Maybe he was the person to help her understand why her father's wishes pulled her back.

Why did she even feel she had to honor her father's wishes? She had explained her feelings to him over and over. He had been aware of her exploration of other interests for a long time, and every reason she had given him to explain why she wanted to drop music held true today. Still, when she announced her choice to pursue math, hadn't she also evaluated the damage she'd done to the bridges leading back to music, in case of an emergency return?

These questions tumbled endlessly in her mind and she knew her answer had to be based on her own interest. No matter what she decided, Rory would go to Barrow-Mount and complete his degree in chemistry. She had no need to worry about his future. Her decision had to come from what she felt would be best for her own future, not anyone else's.

The flipping and flopping of over-analysis left her in a state of crazed exhaustion. On more than one occasion she had made up her mind to stick with math, but then another final review confirmed she wasn't ready to make a final choice. Another spin, another twirl, another lap.

———

Rory had never entered the Beach house when he called for Victoria if one of her parents was home. Victoria had asked him to come up and knock on the door, but he would always sit out in the car and wait for her to discover him. Her father had been the main reason he preferred to stay in the car, and her father's death hadn't changed Rory's preference. He didn't want Mrs. Beach to think that in the absence of the father, he had become brave enough to come to the door.

The radio played while he waited. Even though he wasn't listening to the music, he didn't hear the sound of Victoria's approach; he jumped when she opened the door.

"Oof, you scared me."

"Why didn't you come in?"

"I don't know," Rory said in a sullen voice.

Final exams had ended. During the last week of school they enjoyed evenings in which they could freely do whatever they pleased. Classes consisted of blow-off activities like extra reading, trivia contests, movies and house league sports. A full week of killing time allowed them to treat each night like a weekend night.

The daylight hours had taken on their natural extension and the sun warmed them into the late evening. The constant wind weakened to an enjoyable breeze.

Rory and Victoria sat on their favorite circular bench under a caged sapling, planted in a hole with an iron grate wrapped around its thin trunk. From their bench, they had a full view of the Main Street Mall and its population of busy students wandering up and down the sidewalks in and out of the shops. The two held orange drinks they had purchased at one of the outdoor food stands, but neither drank with any interest.

They sat in a quiet contemplative mood, neither wishing to initiate the conversation they didn't want. Until:

"I've decided, Rory," Victoria said, as she placed her drink on the bench beside her.

Rory stared at a joint between two of the bricks that made up the surface of the mall. He nodded to the bricks, then turned to Victoria with a tentative smile on his lips.

"And?"

"I have to go to Germany."

His tentative smile curled a little higher at the corners, becoming ironic. His stomach fell through the trap door he had been expecting to open. His heart raced, then quickened even more when he saw Victoria turn pale, tears rolling down her face. His vision blurred, as tears welled on the edges of his own eyes then cascaded off his cheeks. He looked down to see them soaking into the bricks.

It took a minute for his breathing to return to normal. When he felt his voice would deliver sound, he said, "You *have* to go? Victoria, you don't *have* to do anything. You mean you *want* to go."

She ignored his accusatory tone.

"I think my father died because of me. I think if I hadn't been so mad at him and so definite about my decision, he wouldn't have been so upset and he wouldn't have died." She sobbed as she spoke. When she controlled her sobbing, she sat straight and looked at Rory, now willing to accept his accusations.

"That's all wrong, Victoria. You couldn't know your father had health problems. Sudden heart attacks happen without warning. You can't blame yourself for that."

"I do."

"It wasn't your decision that caused it. And even if it was, that's no reason to feel you should change your plans."

"Rory, he wanted me to go to Germany. He wanted it so much it killed him when I said I wouldn't. How can I now go on and do something that upset my father so much that it killed him?" She bent her head and sobbed again deeply. She wished he would put his arm around her; but he stayed in his position, staring at her.

"Victoria, I know it hurts to think about what your father wanted, but it's going to hurt more when you realize someday that you didn't allow yourself to have what you wanted. You can't sacrifice yourself for somebody else's dream."

"It's my dream now, Rory. My father's wants and the wants of my music teachers used to be my driving force. I realize that cost me a normal life. You told me about being myself and doing things for myself, and I opened my eyes. I saw what I wanted and I made a decision to do it.

"But when my father died, I had to rethink everything. When I did, I made another decision, one as much in my own best interests as the first one. You haven't had to think much about what you want to do because you've always known. You haven't had people dragging you into things you didn't really enjoy but in the end, maybe you did. I've had to stop being led into my future, and start directing it instead. Music is what I've always been—maybe what I should be—and my father's death is pointing that out. I'm going to Germany for me. You don't know what it's like to be turned around like this. I'm the one that changed."

"Maybe for a little while," he paused, "but now you've changed back."

Victoria felt a bite from Rory's words. "No, that's not true."

"Victoria, you're going to do what they wanted you to do. When Mr. Keltch hears this, do you think he's going to think he won? You bet he is. The sad part is you don't realize that you lost."

"I'm going to Germany because I want to."

Rory could see her willingness to accept her loss. Pressing her would only lead to her resenting him.

"When will you leave?"

"Same time you plan on leaving. I don't want to stay around here without you," she said sadly, looking down.

Rory slid across the bench and lifted her chin so he could look into her dark eyes. He kissed her softly, then put his arm around her. They leaned back on the bench together. Victoria buried her face in his chest and cried while holding tight to a handful of his shirt. Rory's chin rested on the top of her head. His indrawn breath carried her scent into his lungs and he said, "This is going to be awful."

Chapter 30

It hadn't rained for weeks during the unusually hot month of July. The air provided no cooling effect, because it didn't move. The river flowed in the valley beyond the dam, still moving with intensity through the pastures where the cattle grazed in winter. Where the river deepened, the banks of the fertile soil dropped off as if cut with a jagged blade. The rancher fenced along the edge to keep the animals from going too close to the river, where the earth could cave in under them. Then the river widened, becoming shallow as it curved around a hill, exposing the rock bottom of the bed's outer edge.

Rory stood in the middle of the gray area of river-washed stones, piling rocks. He wore old basketball sneakers and cutoff jeans, wet from his recent dip in the cooling river. The rock pile started as a game to see who could build the highest tower; but then they joined forces, and instead of stacking them one on top of the other, they created a foundation and began to build a cone of stones. Victoria scoured the rock bed looking for the flattest and most interesting rocks, bringing the ones she could carry back to the pile.

She dropped her latest load and stepped over to Rory, who stood with his back to her. From behind she put her arms around his waist and rested her chin on his shoulder. Her damp shirt cooled his back. They stood swaying silently, enjoying the comforting rhythm.

"Whose idea was this anyway?" Rory asked.

"You said you could pile them higher than I could."

They had left the city early in the morning and driven to the dam. They chose a picnic site on the grass above the river rocks near a cluster of cottonwood trees.

They hiked down the river for a while, then came back and had their picnic in the shade of the trees while the sun reached its apex to the south. The early hour of their departure, the drive in the warm car, the tricky hike along the river bank, and the food that tasted so good when eaten outdoors, made them tired and drowsy; so they napped after lunch. Rory slept snug up against Victoria's back with his arm loosely draped over her side. When they awakened, they went to the shallow part of the river to swim, and as they walked back across the rocks, Rory challenged her to build the rock towers.

The cone they collaborated on stood chest high on Rory with another stone or two to go. Victoria went to search for a proper capstone. Within a few minutes, she called for Rory to help her carry a large flat rock she believed worthy of the honor.

They hauled the rock to their cairn and Rory adjusted some of the top stones to level them. Then they heaved the large flat rock onto the top.

"It needs one more," he said.

"You find one and I'll find one, then we'll see which one looks better."

They went off in different directions looking for the perfect finishing stone. Rory returned with a pyramid-shaped fragment. Its crooked angle made it point in an odd direction. Victoria returned with an almost round stone lighter in color than any of the others; when Rory saw it perched on top of the cone, he conceded her choice was the obvious winner.

A surge in the heat, along with their exertion building the rock pile, made another swim mandatory.

When they had cooled off, they sat facing each other as they straddled an old barkless log anchored to the riverbank by its deadened roots.

"I think I'm going to leave next week," Rory said, "Will that give you enough time to make your flight arrangements?"

Since she had told him of her decision to go to school in Germany, he had not talked of their separation. He thought about it, though; he thought about it a lot. Many times he had become angry and wanted to confront her regarding her decision, so that he could convince her to go to school with him instead; but then he would be trying to get her to do what he wanted her to do. That was her father's game, and Mr. Keltch's game. Rory's game had never gotten started. Now he assumed it never would. He felt he had lost Victoria. He had his own future and would do his best to make it a good one. But he knew it would never be as good as a future with Victoria.

Now he was setting the time for her to go. She had given him that responsibility, and he had to make the time to separate reasonable. It would probably be the last thing they would do together.

Victoria took her time answering him but finally she said, "Yeah, I'm sure I can get it done."

"Let me know which day works out best for you."

"Okay." She paused, then said, "I hate this."

Since school had ended they saw each other every day. They tried to act normal. But how could normal be possible between them now? When she touched him, anguish rippled through his body; and each ripple reminded him that the touch would soon go away forever. She could see the anguish and the want in his eyes. She could also see his determination not to interfere with her choice. She wanted to be with him every minute of the time they had left, even though they were tortured by the reminder of what their plans had been.

"Next summer we can come back and see if the rock pile is still standing," Victoria commented, wanting the talk to be about reuniting rather than parting.

"You don't know if you're coming back next summer. And I'm not coming back for any other reason than you."

"You won't come back to visit your family?"

"Maybe a short one. What else would I do here? I couldn't stay here all summer. It's weird now that there's nothing here for me anymore." His slightly bitter tone concerned her.

"How will I know if you're here or not?" she asked.

"We'll stay in touch. When you know your address, send it to your mother. I'll do the same and hopefully your mother will pass them on." Rory sighed. "Man, we're both going away from home, we don't know our new addresses, and I don't have a clue how to phone Germany. Boy, am I looking forward to this."

They half-heartedly scraped at the powdery wood of the fallen tree.

"I'm going to miss you, Victoria. I already do."

She couldn't look up at his face because she knew she would cry. Her head nodded agreement while she held a vacant stare focusing on the wood. She could hear the soft rippling noises of the river as it passed nearby.

"I'm so sorry, Rory. I know I'm causing us to part. I know it won't be easy for either of us."

"Yeah." His voice flat. "Come on, it's time to head back."

Neither spoke much on the drive home.

———

Victoria cried for the first hour of the early morning flight to New York. She already felt the void of not being with Rory, and she knew the feeling would intensify. A new peal of pain rang through her each time she acknowledged that she didn't know when she would see him again. Christmas had been ruled out when her mother said she wanted to visit her in Germany over the holidays. She felt it best to spend their first Christmas without Mr. Beach away from the memories their home would conjure up. So maybe in the summer Victoria would see Rory. She had to fulfill a few summer commitments at the conservatory, but it wasn't clear how much of the summer those commitments would consume.

On the flight across the Atlantic, she slept. When she was awake, she kept her mind off of Rory by thinking about the new things she would experience in Berlin.

She changed planes in Frankfurt, amazing herself at how easily she had handled going through customs. In a country where she didn't speak the language, doing something she had never done before, she made herself proud at how calmly she accomplished the process and the change of planes.

The shorter flight to Berlin triggered the return of the void. She was arriving at the place where she would live without having Rory nearby. As the plane went into its final approach, she wished the flight would go on longer and that she wasn't on the verge of arriving at the beginning of her new life—a life she knew would be stimulating but lonely. When she felt the plane bump down onto the runway, she felt a slight loss of breath. A thin chilling layer of sweat accumulated at her hairline and collar.

She stood when the seat belt light went off and she saw the aisle quickly plugged with travelers. She didn't mind if they took their time. But soon they started to flow and everyone moved swiftly out of the plane. The next thing she knew, she was walking down the Jetway at a pace she wished was slower. *Why are these people in such a hurry?* she asked herself.

At the end of the Jetway, she kept her eyes down as she moved from the flexible walkway into the rigid building. She took a few steps, then lifted her eyes to scan the crowd. In seconds she spotted the waving hand of Werner Brock.

———

The interstates marked a bold blue line on the road maps Rory had used to plan his route to California. He knew the many long straight sections of road would get him to his destination more quickly, but he felt they would be boring. Besides, he wasn't really in a hurry; he intended to get there early to look around the campus and get his bearings. If it took an extra day or two, who cared? He had looked at other routes, and had settled on one with a number of points of interest and easy access to car mechanics if his tired old vehicle needed a major overhaul along the way.

The exact time and place when he would next meet Victoria remained unknown. If he only knew when that might be, then he could bear the pain. He hoped time and school would help him get over the disappointment of moving on alone, and he knew the vacancy he had in his life would never be filled unless she returned.

He left Great Falls early in the morning. Since he was headed west, the sun wouldn't be in his eyes until afternoon, but he would fight the wind all day. Rory Coleman hit the highway. He picked one with plenty of curves, some steep mountain grades, numerous beautiful vistas, deep valleys, probable detours, a few resting places—and bumps that could jar any young man's soul.

Other Novels by Mitch Davies

The Inn of Fallen Leaves

Finalist 2015 Best Indie Book Awards – Contemporary Fiction

Journey to feudal Japan and the banishment of the samurai class. In a quiet inn on the Nakasendo highway, disillusioned samurai, Itashima Chobei is confronted by Akiyama, a samurai on a mysterious errand. Akiyama's actions turned the serene mountain Inn of Fallen Leaves into a state of chaos.

Also at the inn is a beautiful woman, Miyo. While she is attached to one, she is coveted by the other. Both men are driven by the respect for her love. When Miyo abruptly disappears, Chobei must pursue Akiyama across the beautiful yet brutal Japan of the 1860s. Both samurai face an ultimate question: is there still a place for loyalty to a clan, or are the lives of individuals more important?

Information regarding books by Mitch Davies is available at:
www.pensmithbooks.com

Stolen Breeze

Finalist 2015 Best Indie Book Awards – Action and Adventure
All Ben Beck wants is to start over with a new opportunity so he decides to throw himself in the middle of the Pacific Ocean with a confusing group of strangers.

No level of smooth sailing could prepare him for being attacked or being at the wrong end of a pointed gun. From the idyllic life of charter sailing and Polynesian island hopping, to a life and death struggle on a tilting yacht deck at night, Ben can't help but wonder if the other members of his crew are friends or enemies.

He doesn't find out until he wakes up with a throbbing headache after sneaking into a mooring at night and has a meeting with the law.
Will the crew, the sea, or a stretch in jail shred Ben's canvas? Find out. Catch a Stolen Breeze!

Undertow of Loyalty

The Problem

Neil Henberlin somehow became a spy. He'd agreed to help Canada's Security Intelligence Service (CSIS) trap a foreign government in the process of stealing his company's new super computer technology. His part was safe and simple — pretend to be seduced by a Chinese double agent and make it look like he was passing secrets. The real spies would take care of the rest.

The Complication

He couldn't tell his wife of his new found adventures as a spy. So, how was Leyna supposed to know the affair with the beautiful Chinese girl wasn't real? After all, she'd seen it with her own eyes when she followed them to a downtown apartment. What else could she think? How could the man she loved treat her so badly?

The Confusion

Henberlin returns to work after a romantic weekend with his wife to discover that a double murder has taken place in his downtown apartment. On top of that, his fellow employees greet him as if they'd seen a ghost. The murders, the spying, the jealousy, and the police investigation toss the pieces of his life spiraling toward chaos.

Keep reading to find out how to get more information about books from Mitch Davies.

On Twitter at @mddaviesagain

On Facebook at
https://www.facebook.com/Mitch-Davies-204759449534161/

Join the mailing list at:
www.pensmithbooks.com